the COLLECTOR

the COLLECTOR

CAMERON CRUISE

MIRA®

ISBN-13: 978-0-7783-2408-9
ISBN-10: 0-7783-2408-7

THE COLLECTOR

www.MIRABooks.com

Printed in U.S.A.

To my muse, Leila, and my anchor, Andrew.

Prologue

Your name is Dog.

You don't find the name cruel, only ironic. When the kids first begin calling you Dog, you think of them as acolytes, unable or unworthy to say your name outright. They say it backward.

Dog.

God.

It's been that way all your life. Few are worthy.

You remember all the names you were taught as a novice: Ra, Brahma, Zeus, Quetzalcoatl, Odin. You close your eyes and whisper your own name, adding it to the list. Your skin feels on fire with your brilliance. In some corner of your mind, you understand that the sensation is really pain. This time, he beat you with his belt.

You give a secret smile. The pain brings with it the power of knowledge: you're the one in control now, pulling the strings.

Bloodletting, you were taught, is an important ritual, one that has endured through the ages. Druids would kill a man by slicing open his midsection to divine the future from the convulsion of limbs and the pattern of blood. India's Thuggee cult, followers of Kali, Hindu goddess of death, mutilated their strangled victims by stabbing the eyes and ripping out the intestines. Centuries ago, Aztec priests reached into the chest cavity to pull out the still-beating heart, the life force flowing from the altar, nectar for the gods.

You, too, require your sacrifice.

At this late hour, it isn't difficult to get by security, if that's what they call the dozing guard with his chair propped against the chain-link fence. You pass roped-off mosaic tiles and ancient stones and statuary that look like so many Tinker Toys, broken pieces bravely pieced together like something precious. Each day, lines of tourists worship here with their cameras and their guides, but you covet something very different.

Walking down the limestone path, you pass two coeds speaking in hushed tones in what sounds like German. You will yourself invisible, just another student no one will remember come morning. The girl with shining blond hair slips a glance your way with a smile, giving the greeting, *"Grüezi."* Swiss, then. You can't help it. You smile back.

The full moon shines down on the ruins like stage lighting. You know the exact moment the play begins because you follow the main characters here. You don't miss even a second. You know he will take her somewhere safe, somewhere deserted. There is no one but you to stand as audience.

She follows willingly for the moment, but you expect her to put up a fight.

From the shadows, you watch them argue. She makes a slashing gesture with her hand, letting him know her answer. *No. Absolutely not!* That's when he makes his move.

He grabs her by the hair, shoving her forward. He strikes her, over and over. She bleeds from her mouth and nose, but she is a strong woman; she doesn't falter. She swipes her clawed fingers across his face, at the same time kicking wildly. Only, by now he has the rope around her neck.

He pulls her down to the ground. Sadly, you are reminded of cattle being branded rather than a religious ceremony. You had hoped for better.

You have extraordinary hearing and take in the music of her death as her breath begins to gurgle deep in her throat. You can't see her face—he is hunched over her, blocking her from view—but her legs and arms flail in drumbeats on the ground.

You know his vision is merely to kill her and take his prize.

He is quick—too quick. Her death doesn't do her justice. You want to scream in frustration. *Not like this!* you plead silently, knowing that she deserves a much grander homage to her life and work.

When she finally stops moving, he releases his grip on the rope and falls back on the ground beside her, winded as if he's fought some great battle. But soon enough, he rises to his knees. He searches frantically through the pockets of the windbreaker she's wearing, finding his treasure. You wonder how he convinced her to bring it here. He cradles the stone against his chest in relief.

After he leaves, you approach in complete silence. Standing over her, you see the rope he used to strangle her, still around her neck. Sloppy.

Her skin reminds you of the moonlight reflecting off the ancient marble surrounding you. You kneel down, stroking the blood from her bottom lip with your thumb. There's not enough light to give her much color. The blood looks like a dark stain on her white skin. You suck the blood off your thumb. It tastes like an old penny.

You know what you want, picturing her blue, blue eyes. But you also need to be careful.

Suddenly, you hear a wheezing breath. You watch her chest rise as she chokes in a lungful of air. Her eyes open. The fingers of her right hand spasm to life. That's when you move in like a spider racing across its web.

You grab the rope by both ends. There's no time to act on any of your grand plans; the idiot before you made sure of that. Standing over her, you know the exact moment she recognizes you. The knowledge of her fate is there in her startled gaze.

As she struggles, you hum to yourself a childhood favorite.

There was an old woman who swallowed a fly.
I don't know why she swallowed a fly.
Perhaps she'll die....

You smile, knowing that, in the end, they all die.

1

Trisha Tran, soon to be Trisha Chance, tried not to be annoyed. She glanced nervously at the digital clock built into the dashboard.

She was going to kill her mother. Stuck in Tommy's sweltering Honda Civic—the air-conditioning was out again—she waited for the light to change at the intersection. She had her windows down, and cast an anxious look at the homeless man standing on the corner just a few feet away. He was jabbing his finger in the air, debating some invisible adversary, his sunburned face twisted in the heat of the one-sided argument.

She turned away just as the guy caught her staring. She could feel her heart begin to race. *Great, just great.*

It didn't matter that here in the paradise of Orange County the homeless were a daily sight. Just about anything had Trish jumping out of her skin today. Gawd, she hadn't seen Aunt Mimi since the last death day celebration.

The light changed and Trisha roared the Honda into the intersection, earning a glare from the diminutive woman seated in the passenger seat. Her mother reached for the radio and dialed in yet another Vietnamese station. Trisha allowed herself a long sigh. What a waste of time.

Trisha didn't have a lot of time to waste. She was graduating summa cum laude from Chapman University and had a wedding to plan. The last thing she needed was to indulge one of her mother's silly superstitions. But here she was, negotiating the traffic jungle of Little Saigon to see a fortune-teller.

The worst of it—her fear that Aunt Mimi might say something bad. Then she and Tommy would really be hosed. It had practically killed her parents when Trisha had introduced her blond-haired, green-eyed fiancé. She hadn't even let on that she was dating a white guy until Tommy proposed. She didn't think her parents could handle any more bad news.

Suddenly, the car next to her swerved across two lanes of traffic. Trisha slammed on the brakes, just missing the guy's bumper. The idiot came to a complete stop in the turning lane. She tried to shut out the obvious—the whole Asians-are-bad-drivers thing. But the man behind the wheel proved to be some old Jewish guy wearing a yarmulke. Beside her, her mom chanted a soft prayer.

Trisha wondered if it wasn't some sort of a sign. *Turn back!* Like maybe it wouldn't be such a great idea to sit for a reading with Aunt Mimi.

She gave herself a mental scolding. *Stop being so melodramatic!* She concentrated on the road ahead. Trisha knew the wide boulevard lined with industrial parks and strip malls was a far cry from what a tourist would expect exiting the 22 Freeway and its promise of "Little Saigon." She remembered the first time she'd brought Tommy here. She could tell he'd been disappointed. Tommy was from San Francisco, where Chinatown was a thrill ride of colorful storefronts and throngs of tourists.

Here in Westminster, California, Little Saigon was low-lying and spread out, dotted with auto body shops and trailer parks. Only strategically placed storefronts displayed some of the architectural details once found in old Saigon: tiled and curved roofs, the old French colonial charm, doors positioned according to the principles of feng shui. Trisha had read somewhere that one of the malls designed to be a tourist attraction was going to be razed to make room for track homes.

She reached over and turned down the music blasting from the radio—she swore her mother was going deaf—earning another disapproving look from Má.

Tommy, Trisha's fiancé—just about everyone called them TNT—was always telling her she needed to be more patient with her parents. He didn't see how going to a fortune-teller to pick a date for their wedding should be such a big deal. He didn't understand the Vietnamese way, that fortune-tellers and astrologers had insane amounts of influence. God forbid a man born in the year of the Tiger marry someone born in the year of the horse.

That's what had Trisha worried, of course. That her mom would use Aunt Mimi in some power play to stop Trisha from marrying Tommy. Depending on what Auntie said, her mom could sputter on about doom and gloom and bad luck, maybe even take to her bed. The next thing you know, Trisha's marriage dishonored the spirit of her ancestors. Then everyone would get on board with Má. She could be pretty cagey that way, her mother. Definitely manipulative.

Trisha bit her lip and wondered if it wasn't too late to turn back. But they had already passed the Asian Garden Mall with its Happy Buddha statue extending welcoming arms to shoppers ready to drop some cash. The two-story building housed some of the largest jewelry stores in Southern California. Her father said there were big bucks behind a project to expand the mall, an attempt, her cousin claimed, to turn Little Saigon into a sort of Bermuda triangle for tourists, Disneyland and Knott's Berry Farm being only a few miles away.

Her cousin, of course, saw any such attempts as "cultural imperialism." At family gatherings she would rant about the evils of being "othered" and what she called fundamental questions of "commodification" and "objectification" of their culture— whatever that meant.

Trisha didn't worry about stuff like that. It wasn't her mission in life to change the world for the Vietnamese immigrants who had made their home here in California. Right now, all she wanted was to get her mother off her back.

She clutched the steering wheel, telling herself everything would turn out okay. Heck, if she could get her father to accept Tommy, anything else should be a piece of cake—even a visit to Aunt Mimi.

She turned into the familiar housing track, focusing on just that. She was in touch with her Vietnamese side, sure, but she wasn't obsessed with it. Whatever happened today, she knew in her heart that she and Tommy were meant to be.

The track homes lining the street didn't look like much. Most were modest single-family dwellings. Only, in the crazy real estate market that was SoCal, these houses could be worth close to half a million dollars.

Aunt Mimi's house didn't stand out in any particular way, just a single-story ranch-style in cream stucco with a composite roof. You had to step inside to see just how lucrative the fortune-telling business could be. Mimi had clients all around the world. Trisha had once overheard Má say that Auntie could charge several thousand dollars for a reading.

Mimi wasn't really her aunt. She was part of their sprawling extended family, some second cousin of her father's. But she was probably the most powerful member of the Tran family. Trisha had tried to explain to Tommy how it worked. In Little Saigon, a fortune-teller wasn't like those psychic hotlines advertised on cable television. There wasn't a neon sign of a palm flashing outside Auntie's door. Mimi was well known and highly respected, a high-class clairvoyant. Unlike a lot of astrologers and fortune-tellers in the area, her influence stretched beyond the immigrant community. Mimi often bragged about her prestigious clientele, many of whom were Westerners.

Trisha pictured Auntie in her head. Mimi favored St. John suits and gold jewelry. Lots of it. Trisha remembered one family gathering during Tet, the Vietnamese festival for the New Year. Tet was the most important celebration of the year and took weeks of preparation. For the Vietnamese diaspora in Little Saigon, Tet marked the arrival of spring and the day every man, woman and child grew one year older. At just such a gathering, Trisha had admired a heavy emerald cuff on Mimi's wrist. Má had told Trisha the bracelet clocked in at close to $10K.

Trisha wondered about that sometimes. If it was really okay to make that kind of money off people's fears and dreams... Not that she'd ever say anything bad about Aunt Mimi. No way.

She pulled up in front of the house and took a deep breath. But her heart kept hammering in her chest. She tried to channel some of Tommy's faith. *It's going to be okay, Trish....*

She helped Má out of the Honda, then hurried ahead to open the wrought-iron gate. Her mother wasn't getting around so well these days. Arthritis, the doctor said.

Opening the gate, Trisha noticed with surprise the heavy iron bars over the windows of Aunt Mimi's house. She frowned. *Those are new.*

The courtyard smelled of jasmine. The lush tropical growth covered the fence, practically hiding the white stucco house from the street. White ginger as high as Má was tall bloomed across the entry like a fragrant screen. Trish wondered if the plants were an attempt to shield clients from nosy neighbors.

She held her mother's arm as they climbed the two short steps to the front entrance, pretending with a nod of her head to listen to her mother's stream of advice on how to act and what to say. Má used Trisha's Vietnamese name, Tuyen, which meant "angel." All Vietnamese names meant something.

Tommy had started calling her that lately, after he'd overheard her parents use it. Trisha was her middle name, her Anglo name. Tommy said it made him feel special to call her Tuyen, and he did make it sound romantic with his American accent. But then Tommy could make just about anything sound sexy.

She smiled. Sometimes he just called her Angel.

She helped her mother sit down on the wooden bench set against the wall of the brick entry. She rang the doorbell and was a little surprised to find a thumb-size camera lens staring out at her from beside the door. She didn't remember Aunt Mimi having some mega security system—not that it didn't make sense. Mimi lived alone and she had tons of expensive stuff to protect inside.

Trisha sat down next to Má on the wood bench in the entry, hoping they wouldn't have to wait long. The place was all decked out for visitors. A lion, believed to be an incarnation of the Hindu god Vishnu, as well as a symbol of the power of the king, dribbled water from a toothy grin. Baskets and planters overflowed with florescent pink impatiens and fuchsias. It was a pleasant place for Mimi's desperate clientele to wait. Trisha figured Mimi was really part seer, part therapist. People were willing to pay for advice on just about anything.

Trish reminded herself she had come for Má's sake. Some of Trisha's earliest memories were of her mother lighting the joss sticks that smelled of sandalwood, and setting out a bowl of sweet rice alongside fried melon seeds and sugarcoated strips of coconut dyed pink, yellow and green. The meal was meant for the departed spirits of her ancestors. Somehow, in her mother's mind, ancestor worship didn't conflict with Catholicism.

Like many Vietnamese, her mother's life revolved around *thay boi*, oracles hired to divine wedding dates, burial schedules, store openings and just about anything else. Every autumn Má bought moon cakes; every New Year she tended to Bà's grave in preparation for Tet.

Trisha frowned. Hadn't she challenged her parents' beliefs enough with her decision to marry Tommy in the first place? She didn't want them to think that she was giving up who she was just because she was marrying a Caucasian.

Only, when her mother launched into what was sure to be another long-winded lecture, Trisha glanced at her watch. *Gawd. How long is this going to take?* She excused herself and stood to knock on the door.

To her surprise, when she banged the door knocker, the door drifted open, unlocked.

Which was pretty weird. Why the camera and the bars over the windows if Mimi was going to leave a door open? Trisha looked back at her mother, who rose slowly to her feet. Suddenly, Má pushed Trisha aside and rushed through the door, calling out Mimi's Vietnamese name.

Má's barging in didn't surprise Trisha one bit. Her mother and Mimi were pretty tight. Mimi came to the house for tea all the time. Usually, she gave Má pretty good advice. There was only this one time she had Má in tears. Má never said what Mimi had told her, but two weeks later, Bà, Trisha's grandmother, passed away. Weird.

Since she could remember, Trisha had studiously avoided the woman she called "Auntie." Mimi used Tarot cards, and some of her readings could be eerily accurate. Like the thing with Bà, and the time Mimi warned the family to beware of the "friendly snake." A couple of weeks later, they found out her father's business partner was embezzling a bunch of money. There were a ton of stories like that about Mimi. Really, it gave Trisha the willies to think that someone could see her future.

She felt a cold, hard ball in her stomach as she stepped inside the foyer, her high-heeled mules making a staccato sound on the marble tile. The house seemed strangely quiet.

It bothered her, this growing fear. She wanted to shut out her mother's voice inside her head. *What if Tommy isn't the right one, Tuyen?* Or more likely, what if Mimi told the family he wasn't? Could Trisha really elope as she'd threatened?

She frowned, finding herself face-to-face with the most gawd-awful painting. The enormous oil took up half the wall in the living room and showed a squat, grinning demon sitting happily on a heavenly throne. Mimi had told her the story behind the image. It came from a Buddhist text, about a demon who fed off the anger of others. A heavy red mist oozed from his scaled body, forming a bloodred aura.

Aunt Mimi collected all sorts of demon paraphernalia. She'd told Trisha her little demons protected her. Walking past the canvas, Trish glanced nervously away from the bug-eyed figure in the painting, thinking, *Right...*

Aunt Mimi had a really posh setup. Furniture made of exotic tropical hardwoods stood on beautiful Oriental silk rugs. A huge mirror hung over the fireplace, with an intricately carved Chinese frame depicting a phoenix. At the other end of the room stood a beautiful lacquered screen inlaid with mother-of-pearl and seashells. Four mythical creatures had been painted onto the individual panels: a dragon, a turtle, a unicorn and a phoenix. The four often came together to form a superpower of prosperity, luck, love and strength.

Trisha followed her mother into the den, admiring the juxtaposition of modern, white leather sofas bracketing the traditional rosewood table. A black vase at the center held several wicked-looking leather shadow puppets from Bali. The figures were believed to have great spiritual power. They were "brought to life" during special ceremonies performed by a puppet master. Supposedly, the puppets portrayed good and evil, but this collection steered heavily toward the dark side. But then Trisha figured that, if you already knew the future, you could probably sleep pretty well in a house full of demons.

Her mother walked past an altar cabinet holding an impressive stone Buddha. There was a small china plate piled with oranges as an offering. Incense burned alongside, giving off a hint of sandalwood. An enormous plasma screen dominated the wall on the opposite side of the room.

But along with the incense, Trisha smelled something else—something not so pleasant. She wrinkled her nose, following Má into the kitchen.

Really, it was freaky quiet. Trish lived in an apartment off campus, with four other girls. Someone was always up making noise at just about any hour of the day or night. For a minute she thought maybe Mimi wasn't home, and she could skip the whole ordeal.

Only, that was another thing that didn't make sense. They had an appointment, and Mimi was nothing if not professional. And the door swinging open like that—no way Mimi would have left her house unlocked if she was out.

Inside the kitchen, Trisha watched her mother open the door to the garage to show that—yes, indeed—Mimi's white Beemer was still in residence. Again, Trisha smelled something strange mingled in with the sandalwood. It reminded her of Brillo pads. Or the heavy iron skillet they kept on the stove back at the apartment. She looked around to see if maybe Mimi had left something out, some meat that might have gone bad. But the kitchen looked pristine.

Her mother closed the door, for the first time appearing alarmed.

"Maybe we should wait outside?" Trish ventured, hoping that they could just forget the whole thing and leave.

No such luck. Her mother called out again for Mimi in Vietnamese. Trisha could tell her mom thought something was wrong. And maybe it was. She knew Mimi kept a fortune in jewels here at the house.

Leaving the kitchen, Trisha remembered another reason why the quiet house struck her as odd. Mimi had a bird. A small parrot called a conure. She kept it in her office. Every time Trisha had come to visit, that screeching bird had driven her half-crazy. It was like some sort of freakish guard bird, going off every time Mimi let anyone in the house.

From down the hall, Trisha heard her mother scream.

"Má!"

She raced toward her mother's screams for help. She found her back in the den, standing in front of the altar cabinet, her mouth gaping as she faced the Buddha.

Trisha saw the bird immediately. Or what was left of it.

She hadn't noticed it there before. It was a small bird. A sun conure, she remembered. The coloring blended in with the oranges, almost disappearing there on the plate with the offerings. The dead bird had been placed before Buddha, a sacrifice.

The head was missing.

Her mother covered her mouth with both hands as if to hold in her screams. Trisha backed out of the room, her eyes still on the Buddha and its strange offering. Her back hit the doorjamb. She let out a small mewling sound.

Má turned to look at her. The expression on her mother's face, how she stood so still, reminded Trisha of a deer catching scent of something.

Má whispered Mimi's name under her breath before calling it out louder and louder. She pushed Trisha aside and ran back into the hall.

They found Mimi on the floor of the room she used as an office. She wore one of her beautiful white St. John suits. Where her aunt had been stabbed, the blood blossomed like some crazy Rorschach test over the white knit.

Her eyes were empty, bloody sockets. And there was something stuffed in her mouth.

It was the bird's head.

This time, Trisha screamed right along with her mother.

2

No one ever gets used to death.

It could stab you through the heart or spray your guts across the wall with a bullet. It could slam into you on the sidewalk and knock you right out of your shoes.

Quick. Clean.

Or it could be a dark business. Strange and wicked. Bent.

Detective Stephen "Seven" Bushard watched his partner walk around the victim's body. The woman lay dead on a canvas of her own blood, her arms and legs posed as if captured midrun. The white suit seemed almost like an accent, as if maybe there'd been some attempt at a pattern. White carpet, red blood—white suit, red blood. A pebble dropped on a quiet pond.

Seven's partner, Erika Cabral, knelt alongside the victim to examine her face.

"The parrot's head in the mouth is a nice touch," she said.

"Looks like Polly got more than just a cracker."

Erika rolled her eyes at him, never big on his jokes. Seven's partner was dressed in a simple corduroy jacket and jeans, her thick chestnut hair pulled back in a messy topknot. On anyone else, the outfit wouldn't turn heads. But the fit of the jeans, the slight peek of cleavage… If she wasn't such a ball buster, his Latina partner could lead half the force by the nose.

"You ask me," she said, "someone didn't like what the vic had to say."

"Could be," he admitted.

"Ever heard the expression, don't kill the messenger?" Erika asked.

Tran was a well-known psychic, a woman paid to see the future.

The crime scene tech, Roland Le, had already taken video of the scene and had moved on to stills. He snapped photographs in a carefully choreographed dance they knew all too well. Seven had seen it a hundred times, death. But he'd never get used to this.

Whoever killed Mimi Tran was a grade-A whack job.

The victim had been sixty-one, information delivered by the officer who had first arrived on the scene and secured the premises. He'd interviewed the two women, relatives of Tran, who'd been unlucky enough to step into this nightmare. The medical examiner would set the time of death, but Seven could take a stab at it just by the smell in the room. Another blazing day in sunny California and the place reeked of death.

Mimi Tran liked the color white: white carpet, white leather couch, white lacquered Italian office furniture. The color choice made a stunning contrast to the blood.

He knelt down to examine the near-black splatters on the carpet. Teardrop shapes led toward the door, then, abruptly—almost as if she'd been spun like a top—the trail turned in on itself, bread crumbs leading back to where the victim had fallen. Mimi Tran looked to be about five feet nine inches tall, approximately 160 pounds, no easy pickings. And still, someone had tossed her around like a rag doll.

There'd been no signs of a forced entry. The vic had an elaborate security system that had been disarmed. Both facts indicated the victim knew her killer.

Seven stared at the blood on the walls and the white sofa. However it had gone down, Mimi Tran had put up a fight.

The body now lay on the floor, bloody sockets where her eyes should have been and a bird's head shoved inside her mouth. The blood where she had been stabbed flowered across the white wool of her suit like some flashy pattern by those designers his sister-in-law loved so much. Chanel or Gucci. Tran still wore some impressive jewelry—diamond studs the size of fat peas, gold bangles shining from her wrists, a dragon pendant with fiery rubies for eyes—taking robbery off the list of motives.

On the wall, there appeared strange markings, like maybe someone had dipped a finger in Mimi Tran's blood and started to paint some weird wallpaper design, then changed his mind. There were exactly fifteen marks, each no bigger than a man's palm. To Seven, they looked like Egyptian hieroglyphs. Or maybe one of those cave paintings you see in museums. The tech on the scene had already tested the stuff and made a preliminary determination. It was blood.

"My best guess?" Roland said. "He used a feather from the bird. You know, like a paintbrush."

Erika came to stand next to Seven. Still staring at the body, she asked, "You okay?"

She said it like it was nothing, just a little chitchat between friends. But he knew what she meant.

Of course she'd ask.

He shook it off. "Just tired of this shit."

They didn't often get cases like this. Gang shootings, traffic accidents, domestic disputes gone bad—the everyday stuff, sure. But this was different, like some sort of ritual killing.

"I want a couple of close-ups of the markings on the wall," Seven told the tech.

"Tell me something I don't know." Just the same, Roland knelt down to take the stills.

They'd dusted for fingerprints and interviewed the relatives. They'd confiscated Tran's laptop and PDA. Every nook and cranny of the scene had been documented. Pretty soon, the coroner's office would remove the body for autopsy.

And then they'd have to figure out what the hell it all meant.

Seven stepped closer to one of the bloody symbols painted on the wall. He frowned, staring at the marks, trying to make them out. Two horizontal lines curved around a small circle…an eye? Made sense, given the condition of the body. Taking out a pen and notepad from inside his jacket pocket, he made an attempt to copy the image.

He tried to figure out what it might mean. Someone was

watching—all-knowing and all-seeing—lording his omnipotence over the now blinded victim?

"Roland? These make any sense to you?" Seven asked, pointing out the bloody images on the wall.

The tech shook his head. "It's not Vietnamese, if that's what you're asking." He looked over at the body. "Neither is that."

But Seven might argue with him there. No one was immune to this kind of violence.

"The niece said she had an appointment to pick a lucky day for her wedding," Seven said, moving on to the next symbol, a shaky copy of the first.

"Not my gig," Roland said. "Fortune-tellers, that's more old school. When Wendy and I got married, we went to the Buddhist temple to pick a date."

"Old school or not," Erika said, "business wasn't hurting. Did you get a load of that Beemer in the garage?" She gave a wistful sigh. "A 735i. My dream car."

"Never too late to marry for money," Seven kidded.

"Yeah. Because I meet so many rich guys on the job." Erika flashed her best smile, the kind that could sell toothpaste.

Erika was all of five feet, two inches tall, maybe 105 pounds soaking wet. But she carried herself with the confidence of a woman who wore a badge and could regularly put men in their place on the firing range. She had the classic good looks of many Hispanic women. Her clothes didn't flaunt her curves, but you could see she was proud of her figure just the same.

She turned back to the victim's desk and slid back the top page from the desk calendar using the eraser end of a pencil. "It's like my *mami* always told me, Seven. A woman needs a man like a bull needs tits."

"Right. And I'm sure she said it just like that, too."

Seven had met Erika's mother, an elegant woman born in Cuba who looked as if she might still wear a veil to church on Sundays. But he had to admit, Erika's mom wasn't exactly the poster child for happily-ever-after. Just last year, Milagro had moved on to husband number three.

Getting his attention, Erika motioned Seven over to the desk. Three wooden statues stood on the desk lined in a row like good soldiers. They were old, maybe even museum quality. They had monstrous heads, and their bodies appeared to be covered with hair, looking like some sort of incarnation of Bigfoot.

"What do you think these little guys are?" she asked. "Some kind of idols?"

"It's definitely not your everyday table decoration."

She glanced back at the body. "Could be a ritual killing."

"That, or the killer was one sick fuck."

That was the problem, of course. If they'd come in and found some poor vic with her throat cut and her diamonds gone, the job would get chalked up to a home invasion gone bad. Asian communities were ripe for the picking when it came to burglary. A deep-seated distrust of banks usually meant a lot of cash stuffed under the mattress.

But this was different. Already, a crowd had gathered outside, neighbors whispering about the bizarre circumstances surrounding Mimi Tran's death. Nor would the colorful nature of the victim's trade help to keep things low-key. Soon enough, reporters would be buzzing around the story like flies on shit.

And then the speculation would begin: was this a one-time deal or just the beginning?

There'd already been a leak. While the cop who'd arrived on the scene had done a decent enough job, one of the witnesses, the victim's niece—a coed from Chapman University—had kept her trusty cell phone in hand. Her fiancé was just outside, champing at the bit to see her. Seven understood the beginnings of a small memorial had already been erected for Mimi Tran, complete with incense sticks, bowls of rice and fruit, and a framed photograph of the victim covered with flowers.

"Let's go with the obvious first. Mimi Tran is a psychic," Seven said, thinking out loud.

"The kind that likes St. John suits," Erika said, naming the designer of her outfit. "And a few other things. Patek Phillipe watch, Daniel Yurman necklace, Shelly Segal shoes. Not cheap."

He gave her a look. "Aren't you the little fashionista."

She shrugged, sending him a flirty glance as she batted her eyelashes. "I'm a girl, aren't I?"

The family was Vietnamese, but swore that nothing at the crime scene had anything to do with custom or religion. No one had ever threatened Mimi Tran as far as they knew. She was well liked and respected in the community.

"Too bad we're not just up the road," he said to his half-Cuban partner.

"Santeria?" Erika asked, naming a religion comparable to Voodoo that flourished in Cuba. She again rolled her eyes at him. "Because I'm such an expert on the stuff?"

In Westminster, their turf included the largest population of Vietnamese living outside of the motherland, with a hodgepodge of Cambodian and Korean immigrants mixed in. But just up First Avenue would be Santa Ana, an area dominated by Hispanics. Seven could definitely see Santeria, or something like it, mixed up in this.

Still, whatever had happened in this room, he imagined no one was an expert.

Seven stepped around the blood splatters, coming closer to the body. He was careful not to disturb any evidence. She'd been stabbed in the back, chest and abdomen, a trinity of vital organs: heart, lungs and stomach.

Only, something about the blood didn't strike him as right. He remembered when he'd first entered the room. Blood and the smell of it appeared to be everywhere. But now that he looked closer, there didn't seem to be enough of the stuff. Almost as if someone had strategically spread out splotches of red to make it look like there was more.

These houses were built on slab, usually with a layer of linoleum under the carpet, which was Berber—not a lot of absorbency. Any liquid from the body would spread out through the fibers of the rug.

Mimi Tran was no small woman. *If she'd bled out, here on the carpet...*

He was thinking about the blood on the rug, examining the

crime scene, putting the pieces together when suddenly, it all changed in his head. Just like that, he was staring at a different body, experiencing a different crime.

He closed his eyes against the memory, trying to block it out. Before he knew what he was doing, he backed away from the corpse, almost tripping.

Shit.

He forced his eyes open, telling himself to be *here,* in the present. He held perfectly still as the room came back into focus. He took a couple of deep breaths, trying to calm down. All he needed was to screw up by trampling on evidence.

He took a few more steps away. *Best to let the crime scene guys finish up*. He told himself he was just giving Roland a little space, ignoring the fact that Erika had no such qualms.

He didn't want to admit that it could be something else. That suddenly murder had become personal.

With her sixth sense, Erika was instantly there beside him.

"I'm fine," he said, a bit more gruffly than he'd meant to. "Really," he added, softening his tone.

She was just worried about him. But that was the problem. He didn't want her concern, didn't want anyone to connect the dots and figure out that a homicide detective didn't have the stomach for the job anymore, couldn't come in close and stare at those bloody holes where her eyes should have been, dissecting the situation like a professional.

So he kept to the markings on the wall, focusing there.

The killer had been in a hurry. Maybe even caught in the act by the relatives who found the body. At first, Seven had thought it was some sort of calligraphy, the kind you see on storefronts or painted on shop windows. But up close, it didn't look so much like writing. Despite his question to the tech, he was pretty familiar with the different calligraphy in the area.

He put in a call to the security system guys. He had some passing knowledge about the system in the victim's house, his brother having installed something similar. Ricky liked to brag about all the bells and whistles.

From what Seven could see, Tran's system was heavy-duty, just like Ricky's. Nothing you would expect in this neighborhood.

"It was disabled," Erika said, coming up from behind. "Maybe by the perp."

"Or the victim," he said.

"Whoever did it," she answered, "they knew the code."

"Which probably means the victim let them inside. Someone she knew?"

"A client maybe?" Erika asked.

"A client? So whoever she'd let in would be here for a reading?" He looked at his partner. "Guess she didn't see it coming?"

"Funny," Erika said. "Really, Seven, you should take it on the road."

Just then, his cell phone went off. It was a special ring, one he had set up just recently. He could feel his guts twist at the familiar tone, a neutral arpeggio.

Erika looked up. She recognized the ring and knew what it meant. "I can take care of things here," she said.

He wanted to ignore the call. He didn't want his life to interfere with his work. He wanted to escape, run away from his own drama and disappear into the facts of the Tran murder.

He didn't want to see that other dead body in his head.

"Don't be stupid," Erika said, reading him. "Go."

He fumbled with the cell phone, but didn't take the call. Erika shook her head, walking away, making it clear she was washing her hands of him.

The ringing stopped. But he knew she would call again.

Turning for the door, homicide detective Seven Bushard went to deal with his own ghosts.

3

Seven sat in his car, staring at the LCD screen on his cell phone. Three missed calls, all from the same number.

Beth was nothing if not persistent.

He slid back against the headrest of the Jeep Cherokee, the unkind thought ringing with guilt. After eight months of this crap, he knew the drill: Beth couldn't handle the giant slice of reality being shoved down her throat. Not alone.

And he was Ricky's brother. Nick, his nephew, depended on him. Beth was family. End of story.

This time, when the phone rang, Seven picked up.

"I'm fifteen minutes away, Beth," he said, starting the Jeep.

He drove past the crowd gathered around the Tran place and headed out of the housing track. Beth had recently been diagnosed with panic disorder. Seven shouldn't have let it go to the forth call.

Only, he couldn't help wondering if maybe Erika was right about his relationship with his sister-in-law.

If you just let Beth get through the damn panic attacks by herself—without stepping in and making it all better…

Erika thought Beth needed to learn to stand up for herself. What the hell had she called it? Some psychobabble about him being an enabler?

"It's just guilt, Seven. Pure and simple," he could almost hear Erika saying in his head.

Getting off the freeway ten minutes later, he was still wondering how much longer he could keep dropping the ball into Erika's lap. The chief had told Seven to take more time. *As long as you need...* But Seven needed to get back to normal, and that meant work.

He was lucky to have Erika covering for him, that was for damn sure. There'd been a lot of carping about how fast she'd come up the ranks to detective. Some finger-pointing about the fact that she was a Hispanic woman, as if somehow she'd hit the job lottery being a double minority. But all that mattered to Seven was that she was a good cop—the best damn partner he was likely to have.

Unfortunately, he'd messed up there, too. After a night of tequila shooters, he'd gotten a little too familiar with that gorgeous body. It was a testament to their partnership that they'd made it through the morning—and months—after.

Going south on Bolsa Chica, he headed toward Huntington Harbor. His brother lived in a posh neighborhood where half the homes were on the water. He'd heard about this list on one of the news shows. Huntington Beach was number eight in the country when it came to homes selling over a million dollars.

Ricky had made a killing on the place, buying it when the market had taken a dip. A million-dollar teardown. Now the place was worth well over five million. Not that it mattered. Ricky had it all leveraged. Beth would probably lose everything.

Seven tried not to imagine her reaction when she discovered that the one thing she'd relied on from Ricky—money—was gone.

Well, they'd manage. Seven had some money put away. By summer, Beth and Nick could move into the rental property Seven had bought with his dad some years back. He did the mental math, moving the pieces of their lives around like chessmen. Imagine, the family fuck-up in charge, while Ricky, the "good son," the plastic surgeon, did time. It was freaking biblical.

The whole thing sounded too damn much like a soap opera. Ricky having an affair with his male nurse at his plastic surgery practice. The affair going sour—Scott wanting Ricky to leave Beth.

Ricky offered money, undying love. It wasn't enough. Scott wanted it all. The fights grew more abusive. Scott started making threats, tailing Beth. He knew where Nick went to school, that sort of thing.

It was made to look like a car accident. Only Ricky had done a pretty lousy job of covering his tracks. It was clear from the blood evidence that Scott had been dead before the crash. There had been a curious *L*-shaped blood spatter on the window. Apparently, Scott's blood had splashed against it long before the car came to an abrupt stop. Momentum kept the blood slipping across the glass.

When faced with the evidence, Ricky confessed. He'd put a full two hours on tape with homicide in Laguna, where the "accident" took place, before asking for counsel.

Seven remembered it almost as if the whole thing happened yesterday. Erika had called bright and early.

Sit down, honey. This is going to be bad....

You knew it was something when tough-as-nails Erika tossed around words like *honey*.

The cherry on top? Laurin, Seven's ex-wife, also got in touch...right after Ricky hit the six o'clock news. Here he was in the middle of hell, and his ex-wife calls to tell him, *Jesus, Seven, I'm so sorry.... Is there anything I can do?* And by the way, she's expecting twins with her new husband. Twins, for God's sake. Seven took the news like two shots straight to the head.

He was happy for Laurin, sure. But he couldn't help feeling a little sorry for himself. Like he'd been left behind because Laurin, bless her heart, had moved on. She was leading this totally normal life with a real family...while he fought to keep the pieces of his from slipping through his fingers like sand.

Seven punched up the music, The Beatles belting out the end of "Hey Jude." He reminded himself this wasn't about him. It was about the people he loved. Nick and Beth.

When he turned up Ricky's street, he saw Beth was waiting for him out on the driveway. She was wearing a baby-blue sweater set and ankle-length pants. She had on ballet slippers and her shoulder-length blond mane was held back by a black hair band. She hugged her arms across her chest as if trying to hold everything inside.

They'd made a pair, she and Ricky. Both blond and blue-eyed, they looked like god and goddess. If the brothers stood next to each other, no one could imagine they were related. Just under six feet, with brown hair and hazel eyes, Seven was everyman to his brother's golden boy.

Out on the cul-de-sac, Nick played basketball. Looking just like his father, the kid put everything into his hook shot.

Seven slowed down, just watching what, for all intents and purposes, was the perfect picture of domestic bliss. Ricky had installed the hoop on the curb last year. Just eight months ago, Seven had been working up a sweat with his brother on the drive, giving as good as he got.

As soon as he pulled up and stepped out of the Jeep, Beth came up to him, throwing herself into his arms.

"I'm sorry," she said. "I know I shouldn't call when you're at work. But I just couldn't deal anymore."

He could smell the alcohol on her breath—not that he blamed her. Beth had been self-medicating with alcohol for a while now. Seven watched his nephew over her shoulder. Nick just kept bouncing the ball, pretending Seven wasn't standing just a few feet away, trying to hold his mom together as she fell apart.

That's how Nick was getting through the crisis. Pretending. *Abracadabra. Nothing's wrong. I don't feel a thing.*

Seven felt a rare surge of anger. He wished Beth could be stronger for Nick's sake. The kid was hurting, too.

But it didn't help to start throwing around blame. That's why he wanted to get back to work. Investigations like the Tran case took a dispassionate observer. He could crawl inside this cool place he'd carved out in his head, where nothing but the evidence mattered.

He wouldn't have to think about Ricky and the shit he'd dumped on the family. Wouldn't feel his guts getting ripped out every time he saw his ten-year-old nephew and thought about what the future held.

"I was making this pact with God," Beth said, still clutching him. "If everything turned out okay, I promised I'd be stronger."

"Don't worry about it," Seven said, putting his arm around her and steering her back toward the house. "You got some coffee?"

She nodded, wiping her tears. Inside, Ricky had one of those espresso bars. The man loved his coffee.

"Hey, Nick," Seven called out to his nephew. "You okay?"

"I'm okay," he answered, sending up a three-point attempt that went wide.

Seven followed Beth inside, knowing it was a lie. The fact was none of them were okay. On the television crime shows, it was all about the victim's family—their loss, their quest for justice. But Seven, the homicide detective, had seen the other side, how one unforgivable act could affect a family.

His brother had killed a man. And it wasn't just Ricky who was paying for it.

Erika stared at the woman's mouth. Mimi Tran had thin lips and a bad overbite, as well as a penchant for dark lipstick. Erika would have suggested a lighter shade.

She walked slowly around the body, getting to that place in her head where all other considerations melted away and she focused right here, right now.

There were three basic methods of determining time of death. Rigor mortis usually set in three hours afterward, beginning in the facial muscles, then slowly spreading to the extremities. Approximately thirty-six hours later, the process reversed itself and the body became supple again. To Erika's trained eye, Mimi Tran appeared stiff as a board.

As well as assessing rigor, the medical examiner would take a temperature reading. A number of factors, including Tran's size and the hot room, would determine a possible time of death, but the process was far from exact.

Then there was lividity, during which red blood cells eventually leak into the body from the capillaries, making a permanent color change on the skin where the blood settles like sediment in a muddy pond. With her pen, Erika pulled back the collar of Tran's St. John suit to expose the skin where one shoulder blade pressed against the carpet. The skin was a deep wine-red, showing the body hadn't been moved since the heart stopped.

With her latex-gloved hand, Erika pulled out a magnifying glass from inside her jacket pocket. She knelt down. The bird's head stuffed inside the victim's mouth…it was elemental, almost primitive. Definitely something religious or sacred.

Erika was all too familiar with these sorts of rituals. She'd grown up in Santa Ana, the daughter of a Cuban immigrant married to an American of Mexican descent. Her mother was an educated woman, but still, Santeria had been part and parcel of her upbringing.

Even for a seasoned homicide detective, the sight of those bloody, empty eye sockets might prove too much. But Erika didn't pull away from the grotesque image. That wasn't her style. She fell into it, trying to see where it could lead her.

Like any good investigator, Erika had a healthy dose of intuition. With time, she'd come to realize hers was sharper than most. Seven called her ability "uncanny." Her mother had a different name for it. *El don de la doble vista.* Only, Erika wasn't buying that sixth sense crap. Her job required a sharp eye and tedious hours gathering evidence. That's what got convictions in the courtroom. If good instincts and a little imagination helped, well, hell. Why not?

She cocked her head in thought. The victim was a psychic. A successful one, judging from the posh surroundings and the high-end jewelry.

So, this was about power. But what kind? Money? Prestige? Warring factions in the occult world here in Little Saigon?

Or was this about something more sinister? Had Mimi Tran been searching for a darker power?

Erika frowned. She had experience with the damage that sort of struggle could cause. The need for miracles. The lies behind the desire to control.

She turned her focus to the victim's hands. Defensive marks. Mimi Tran had put up a fight. But the missing eyes…it seemed almost a cliché. The idea that, as a psychic, Mimi Tran had "the sight."

"So what's the connection to the bird's head?" Erika asked herself.

Taking out a penlight, she pointed the beam into the victim's mouth. With the magnifying glass in her other latex-gloved hand, she peered closer.

Something there? Inside the bird's beak?

"Hey, Roland?" She motioned over the tech.

She had him take a couple of close-up shots. She pulled out an evidence bag and a pair of tweezers from her jacket pocket. With the penlight held between her teeth, she knelt carefully over the body.

She remembered a game she used to play with her brother as a kid. Operation. The goal was to use tweezers to remove tiny plastic game pieces from a body without touching the sides. Her brother and mother always messed up, but not Erika.

Slowly, she pried loose the object from inside the tiny bird's beak. In the beam of the flashlight, the thing glowed a rich sapphire-blue.

It looked like a glass bead. Or maybe more like a crude gem?

"Holy shit," the tech said, snapping more pictures. "What is that?"

Erika carefully placed the bead in the plastic evidence bag. "Your guess is as good as mine."

She put away the penlight and held the plastic bag up to the ceiling light. Suddenly, the glass bead turned a bloodred color.

Erika glanced upward. The lights in this room were fluorescent...

Shielding the bead with her body, she again reached for the penlight. As soon as the incandescent light struck the bead, the color of the gem changed back to a dark blue.

And something else. Something inside the bead flashed white. The gem appeared to catch the light, like one of those star sapphires. Only, in this case, a single white stripe appeared, making the thing look like a cat's eye.

"Weird," the tech said, snapping a few more pictures for good measure.

Erika glanced back at the blinded body of Mimi Tran.

She told Roland, "Looks like it's an eye for an eye."

4

David Owen Gospel II felt the woman stir beside him on the bed. The fact that she was still asleep irritated him just a little bit. But he held back any reprimand. It was still early.

He reached and stroked the black sleek hair, admiring her lovely naked back. He considered himself a collector, and this woman was one of his finest pieces.

Her name was Velvet. He was certain that wasn't her real name. Most likely, it was the translation of her Vietnamese name. In Vietnam, many first names had special meanings, like Kim for gold, or Tam for heart.

David thought the name suited her. Her skin, her dark, liquid eyes and waist-length hair, all of it felt rich and smooth.

He always gave her jewelry. He liked that best about Velvet. She was high-class, never grasping for his money. Jewelry seemed so much more civilized an exchange. And he knew she found him attractive; many women did, liking that air of power that could only come with age and experience. And David kept himself fit. Velvet had often complimented him about his gray eyes and silver hair. She didn't have a problem with the age gap—almost forty years—between them.

As soon as she felt his touch, she turned and kissed him, gracing him with that lovely perfect smile as she caressed his face. But Velvet knew her business. Quickly, she slipped out from beneath the silk sheets. Donning a robe he'd bought her, an artistry of lace from a particularly fabulous lingerie shop in Paris, she hurried off to the kitchen.

Over a breakfast of jackfruit Danish and Vietnamese drip coffee, he read the paper. His beautiful Velvet sat across from him in the condo's jasmine-scented courtyard, reading some tome on corporate taxes. Velvet was finishing her law degree at Whittier. He looked forward to hiring her on as in-house counsel for Gospel Enterprises, a privately owned development company that made more than the gross national product of most small countries.

It wouldn't be easy to lure her in—she'd have many lucrative job offers. David anticipated that Sam Vi, Velvet's thug of a cousin, would be his chief rival. David smiled against his coffee cup. He knew work at Gospel Enterprises would appeal to Velvet's imagination. What could she really do for Sam other than keep his ass out of jail?

Of course, she'd have to get over the whole sleeping-with-the-boss issue. That's one of the things he found tantalizing about Velvet. She had scruples.

Today, she would find a beautiful pair of ruby earrings waiting for her on the bedside table—he'd bought them just last week. They were antiques, presumably worn by Marie Antoinette herself, although he wasn't naive enough to pay a premium for something so improbable. But Velvet would like the story.

He reached for the newspaper, thinking of what Velvet would look like wearing the earrings and nothing else. Suddenly, the image of her naked and reaching for him vanished.

David sat up, staring at the newspaper on the table. The smile faded from his face as he read the headline: Vietnamese Fortune-Teller Murdered in Ritual Killing.

There was a photograph of Mimi. A publicity shot by the looks of it, taken some years ago. He felt his body go numb.

"What's the matter, David?"

Velvet didn't have a hint of an accent. Though her parents had immigrated, she'd been born in Orange Country and was American through and through. She looked at him anxiously. Her eyes dropped to the newspaper.

"Oh, my God!" Her law book fell to the floor as she stood. "Oh, my God. I have to call Sam."

David closed his eyes, hearing Velvet's bare feet on the kitchen tile as she raced for the phone inside. His whole life wasn't just crashing down around him, he told himself. It wasn't.

He didn't wait for Velvet to get off the phone. He wasn't going to fight Sam for her attention, not now. Back in the bedroom, he dressed quickly. Within a few minutes, he was driving like a demon, weaving through traffic on the 55 Freeway to reach the empty carpool lane. He was alone in the vehicle, but didn't worry about being pulled over in the black Aston Martin he drove at breakneck speed. David Gospel paid for posh dinners at fund-raisers for important candidates to local and state office. He didn't pay for anything as mundane as a speeding ticket.

When he arrived home, he found his wife waiting in the front room. Meredith rose to her feet from the sofa, a mousy woman who looked as if she were trying to make herself disappear, she was so thin. On the glass coffee table, she had the morning paper opened to Mimi Tran's photograph.

"It's not what you think," she said in that whisper of a voice.

Over the years, David had come to realize it was her voice he hated most—more than her Bible-thumping or her thinning brown hair, or even that stick figure she preserved like some prima ballerina. Her voice grated in its softness. It seemed to say, *Don't pay attention, I'm not here, I won't disturb.*

"David?"

He ignored her, instead heading for the stairs. The house had been designed around its fabulous view of the main channel and a sweeping staircase with its railing made entirely of Lalique crystal. But the beauty was lost to him now as he headed for his office, his wife at his heels.

"Listen to me, David. You're wrong! You've been wrong all along! Please, David—"

He shut the office door in her face. His wife made some feeble attempt at a knock, but even in anger she couldn't manage the strength for a decent pounding. Him, he would have used both hands. Knock the fucking door down!

There'd been a time when Meredith could give as good as she

got. But that all changed after she found God. These days, his wife was nothing more than a dried-up Puritan of a woman. A fanatic.

He grabbed the remote control off his desk and gunned it at the mirrored wall across the office, punching in the code. Immediately, a section slid open, revealing a hidden room behind the glass.

Gospel Enterprises had many businesses under its corporate umbrella, including a security company specializing in safe rooms or "panic rooms," a place sealed off from the rest of the house where clients could wait out a home invasion until the police or on-site security arrived on the scene to save the day.

David's room had a very special purpose. The place was more like a giant walk-in vault. Inside, he could control temperature and humidity. Hell, he could house the fucking *Mona Lisa* here if he had to, probably under better conditions than the Louvre and its conga line of tourists.

Inside the vault room, he punched in yet another code, this time using a keypad on the wall just above the built-in wooden cabinetry, one of five such keypads in the room. A velvet-lined drawer slid open, the kind often used to house expensive jewelry. David's held a much different collection.

He stared down at the clay tablet written in a script adapted from cuneiform, one of the oldest written representations. This particular tablet dated back to the seventh century B.C., but the story from ancient Sumeria was far older. The Epic of Gilgamesh was, in fact, the oldest written story on Earth.

There was a heated debate in archaeological and linguistic circles concerning whether the epic was composed of eleven or twelve clay tablets. Many translations didn't include the twelfth tablet, considered by some to be an independent story, or perhaps more of a "sequel." But David knew better. He was staring at a missing thirteenth tablet, one he had purchased for his collection through the efforts of people like the now very dead Mimi Tran.

A necklace lay to the right of the tablet. It was a beautiful piece, the unstrung beads placed in a half circle around a central crystal, jewelry purported to have belonged to the goddess Athena herself. In this light, the gems appeared a deep blue. But he knew how easily the crystals could change to a bloodred.

The central stone, the Eye, looked more like a milky, raw diamond the size of a peach pit. In the low light, it had a lovely blue sheen. Like flaws, bits of metal floated, trapped inside. Several strands of wire had been wrapped around the crystal, creating a pendant that could hang from a necklace. It stared up at him, clouded and unseeing.

He felt himself shaking. There was little in this world that David feared. Normally, it was matters beyond the physical realm that held his imagination. But his son—Owen's capacity to completely fuck up—could grab David by the throat and bring him to his knees.

Leaving the drawer open, he stepped out of the vault. He dropped onto the leather couch of his office and stared at the mirrored opening, the remote still in his hand. Inside that vault waited some of the greatest treasures the world of the occult had to offer. Precious pieces he'd carefully brought together, willing to meet the price of the greediest tomb raider.

David was not a young man. It had taken forty-two of his sixty-plus years to gather his collection. The tablet, of course, was the centerpiece, a map that had led him to the Eye of Athena. In Mimi's hands, he'd seen that dead crystal glimmer to life. And there were other treasures mentioned in the thirteenth tablet, gifts that, according to legend, had been given to Gilgamesh by the wild man Enkidu, magical objects Mimi Tran, with Sam Vi's connections in the illegal trade of artifacts, had vowed to help David find.

But now Mimi was dead.

"Fucking Owen," he said, cursing his son.

The problem, of course, was that this had all happened before. Another woman, a psychic, just like Mimi. Seven years ago, the police had come to David's door with a search warrant. They'd turned the place upside down, looking for their evidence, finding nothing. David had made damn sure of it....

Owen had been eighteen years old—old enough, David had hoped, to cover his tracks. But no. He had found Owen sitting next to the spa in back of their Newport home, acting for all the world as if nothing was wrong.

Only, the kid had been licking blood off his fingers.

Instinctively, David knew the blood wasn't Owen's. Unfortunately, there'd been a hell of a lot of it. The asshole had tracked it through the house…his car had been filthy with it. The cleanup had been a bitch.

Luckily, David had discovered his idiot of a son before the cops could get their hands on him.

Seven years ago, David had thought he was in the clear, siccing his bulldog lawyers on the city, threatening to sue whoever had the balls to point the finger his way. Shit, he'd brought down more than one career in that battle.

And now the nightmare was starting all over again? No way. No fucking way.

There came another tap at the door, the sound so meek he would have missed it if the room hadn't been perfectly quiet. With a sigh, he punched in the code to shut the mirrored door to the vault.

"Come the fuck in, Meredith."

Like a good servant, she opened the door and let herself in, leading with her offering: a tray holding a martini glass and shaker. Jesus, the woman had timing.

She gave him a nervous smile. "I thought you might like a drink."

"Really." His wife didn't drink, but she was good at peddling the stuff. Especially at times like this. She was the family's anesthesiologist, dispensing her drugs to numb away the world.

She moved soundlessly to put the tray down on the glass coffee table before the leather sofa where he sat. She poured the martini from the shaker into the glass and sat down, leaving plenty of space between them.

"You're wrong about Owen." She smoothed the skirt of her dress over her knees and folded her manicured hands neatly on her lap. In another life, Meredith had sported designers like Prada. These days, her simple print dresses looked more like something she'd picked up at Wal-Mart.

"Owen has made mistakes," she continued, "but we're his parents, David. We need to forgive and forget. He's different now, a changed man since his missionary work."

She didn't dare look at him as she spoke. Instead, she stared ahead, giving him a view of her profile. His wife had a perfect nose, courtesy of a plastic surgeon. Again, another life...the one they'd lived before Owen.

David knew all parents wanted to believe the best of their child. He himself had fallen into that trap. He'd given Owen every advantage, right? What more could he have done?

But then comes the day when a parent realizes the truth. Their world falls apart, and the truth hits them square between the eyes.

For David, a master collector, that day had come long ago. The day he'd finally realized that his son, his perfect and beautiful little boy, had started a collection of his own.

Owen had been ten years old. It still turned David's stomach, a thought of those bloody bits and pieces he had found buried in the tin box out in the rose garden. When he'd confronted Owen, the kid had just stared up at him with those strange, unblinking eyes.

Even after that, David made excuses. He told himself it was just some silly mistake, those bloody pieces. He had tried to share a few stories, and the boy had become confused. David and Meredith discussed the situation with Owen's psychiatrist, someone they could trust to keep a secret. The doctor had concurred. His son wasn't dangerous. Just misguided.

Dr. Friedman explained that David's temper didn't help. But there David might disagree. Beating the crap out of Owen may not have helped his son's condition, but is sure as hell made David feel better.

For a while, it seemed as if things were going to be okay. Until the day Owen turned eighteen and the cops showed up at their door asking about Michelle Larson.

"Where is he?" David asked now, not touching the drink.

Meredith kept staring straight ahead. "I don't know."

"Hiding. Like a coward."

Her head snapped around. She gave him a venomous look. Only for Owen did she ever dare put up a fight. "Owen is working. You should know—he does work for you, doesn't he?"

"I don't keep track of every *employee,* Meredith."

Of course he'd called the Newport Beach offices. It was the first thing he'd done on the drive home. According to his assistant, Owen was conveniently out. An art opening for some friend down in Laguna.

David remembered throwing the cell against the dashboard, losing it. He could still see that image of Mimi in his head, her photo in the paper bringing back thoughts of Michelle and her death.

When they'd first started taking Owen to Dr. Friedman, he'd explained how Owen had somehow gotten it all mixed up in his head, the collection thing. Because of the stories David had shared with his son. Apparently, the world of the occult did not make for good bedtime conversation.

Owen had been too young to understand where his dad was coming from. In his sessions, he kept talking about the Moon Fairy. When Dr. Friedman asked David what that meant, he'd feigned ignorance. But he knew.

The Moon Fairy was one of several bedtime stories that David had shared with his son. Like Gilgamesh, the Moon Fairy was about a man's quest for immortality. In the tale, a magician offers to make an elixir for the king that will make him immortal. For his potion to work, the magician would need 999 of the youngest and most beautiful children of the kingdom. The magician assures the king of the elixir's success if the king also includes his own daughter. But the girl's mother, the Moon Fairy, saves her by turning the girl into a rabbit and taking her to the moon.

David didn't have a clue what the big deal was, but he'd kept quiet, knowing that Dr. Friedman would probably start blaming him again for all the kid's problems. Like it was some kind of child abuse to tell Owen a story?

David knew he'd made mistakes, sure. Losing his temper and punishing Owen. And maybe he had kept the kid a little on edge with his tales about the occult, sometimes using his knowledge as leverage to put Owen in his place. How was that any different than the stories parents told about the Bogeyman? But Dr. Friedman explained how that, too, had messed with Owen's psyche. Funny thing, how it was always the parents' fault.

That's when David realized Dr. Friedman was just like everyone else, completely full of shit. Back then, they hadn't made the connection between Owen's eyes and any psychological condition. Still, David had his own theories about his son's twisted behavior and how to handle it.

Up until this morning, he'd thought he'd done just that. Neutralized the threat. David clenched his jaw. How could Rocket have let him down?

"Don't you want the drink?" Meredith asked.

For a moment, he'd actually forgotten she was there. He took a long, hard look at her, the mother of his child.

He tried to remember who she'd been all those years ago. A feisty and elegant woman educated at Smith College back East, she was the consummate diva, the only child of Judge Martin Wescott, a man who held more than a little influence in this town.

David had never loved Meredith, true, but he'd respected her. Back then, he'd believed she was a great choice as a life partner, someone who could reign supreme among the pseudo society of Orange County, the famed OC.

Well, he couldn't have been more wrong. And God, did he hate her for it.

He picked up the martini and ceremoniously placed it in front of his teetotaler wife. "You drink it," he said, leaning forward menacingly. "You're going to need it, darling."

It was all he had to say. Almost a silent *boo!* Meredith jumped to her sensible Cole Haan loafers and slid the martini glass back onto the tray. She sloshed vodka over the sides of the glass the whole way to the door.

"My wife," he said, almost laughing out loud. How many other things had she fucked up in his life?

He closed his eyes, suddenly exhausted to the core. He needed to regroup, call Rocket, his right-hand man, and get him back on the job with Owen. David didn't have the luxury to sit here and feel sorry for himself.

He stood and punched the code into the remote once again. He walked back inside the vault as the door whooshed open. Maybe he'd always known Owen wasn't cured. That it was all an act, Owen showing up from his travels abroad all repentant and asking for another chance.

With a sigh, David braced himself over the opened drawer, staring at the tablet and necklace housed there with such loving care, realizing that he'd need to start over now that Mimi was dead. Which meant calling Sam.

"Shit."

He was about to close the drawer, lock up tight and take Meredith up on that martini, when something caught his eye. The pattern of the beads circling the Eye, the central crystal…he hadn't realized it before.

He looked closer now, his heart stopping, just stopping.

There, at the back of the necklace. Was a bead missing?

He looked closer, counting quickly. He knew exactly how many beads should be circling the Eye: twelve. Only, no matter how many times he counted, he came up one short.

Shit. Shit!

He couldn't catch his breath. He thought of Mimi Tran's last prediction. All that crap about the danger of invisible things or something like that. He hadn't paid the least attention, focused only on that slight glimmer of life she could bring to the Eye when she held it.

Like a blind man, he patted the black velvet liner, as if indeed the missing bead had somehow become invisible. It had to still be there, safe and waiting.

The floor seemed to drop out from under him. His knees hit the carpet as he grabbed for the open drawer to stop himself from careening face-first to the ground. His chest felt tight and hard and heavy, like cement. He thought he might be having a heart attack.

That which is invisible is always the most dangerous.

Those had been Mimi's last words to him, he was almost certain of it. Like all of her prophecies, it was cryptic, something that would require careful interpretation.

That's what he'd paid Mimi to do. See the future. Help him in his quest to find that precious path to immortality.

Only, Mimi was dead now and a precious piece of the Eye was missing. Soon enough, the police would come a-knocking, a deadly distraction when he needed all his concentration.

The fact was, David Gospel didn't fear anything as mundane as the police arriving with a search warrant.

If only....

5

The precinct in Westminster wasn't much. After the clock tower and its Tudor splendor—a tribute to the city's English namesake—the landscape degraded into utilitarian government offices. Seven and Erika worked for the Crimes Against Persons unit.

With a population just under ninety thousand—nearly forty percent Asian—the city averaged two murders a year. Seven and Erika were the only homicide-robbery detectives. Given the city's budget, they didn't have the luxury of limiting their caseload to murders like Mimi Tran's. Homicide-robbery shared space with family protection and the gang enforcement unit, the idea being that, during major investigations, everyone came together to work as a team.

Which didn't usually include the mayor. Unless, of course, the case landed on the front page, with the potential of being there for a nice, long stay.

Currently, the post of mayor was held by a woman with the unfortunate name of Ruth Condum-Cox—Dr. Ruth (with a nice long roll of the *R*, just like the sex therapist and talk-show personality), but only when she wasn't around to hear that quaint little sobriquet.

Seven had often thought that if your name was Condum, you should probably have the presence of mind to steer clear of a man named Cox. But not Dr. Ruth. She'd taken it to the next level and hyphenated.

But then what did he know? Memorable name like that? It might just work on a campaign poster.

Ruth Condum-Cox had a face that said she should lay off the plastic surgery. Hard to tell her real age, but she was simulating her late fifties pretty well. She'd made her money in real estate and favored power suits. She'd run on a tough-on-crime platform, giving her more than a few friends on the force, including the chief of police. Chief Flagler now hovered over Seven, acting like the Tran case was one hot potato he wanted served on someone else's plate.

"The last thing we need is to let a case like this put Westminster on the map," Condum-Cox said, jabbing her finger at the newspaper. "Look what Scott Petersen did to Modesto, for Christ's sake. Not to mention Michael Jackson and that fiasco. Jesus, the overtime alone will kill us."

Seven looked over at Erika. Day two into the Tran investigation and they were already getting heat from the brass to wrap things up?

"Mimi Tran had no gang affiliations that we know of."

This scintillating piece of good cheer was provided by Detective Harold Pham, a new face to the family protection unit. Pham was half American, half Vietnamese, and liked playing Johnny on the spot. Given the audience, he wasn't likely to miss his shot.

Condum-Cox jumped on it. "We need to follow up on just that sort of thing. What else do we have?"

Seven looked at the chief, wondering how long he was going to let the game of Let's Play Detective roll along. Since when did the mayor's office lead an investigation?

"No weapon, no motive…nada," Erika said, flipping through the file. "The autopsy is scheduled for later today."

Condum-Cox frowned—or at least she made an attempt. Not much got past the Botox. "Autopsy? But I thought the cause of death was obvious. She was stabbed, right?"

"Multiple times. But we still need the medical examiner to confirm she bled out," the chief said.

Condum-Cox nodded. Suddenly, she stiffened. She turned a wide-eyed stare on Seven, as if just realizing something.

"Detective Bushard, your brother was recently convicted of murder."

It wasn't a question.

Seven felt himself flush. "He pled guilty to second degree, yes, your honor."

Seven could see the gears turning in the mayor's head. A lead detective with a colorful background like Seven's wouldn't help her cause, not if she wanted to keep the networks off their backs.

The look she gave the chief was priceless.

"Detective Bushard and Detective Cabral are our most seasoned investigators. They have a top-notch record," the chief said, coming late to Seven's defense.

Not to mention they were the only two detectives in homicide for the city of Westminster—with a caseload that made Seven more than once wish he could clone himself.

Of course, none of that mattered at the moment. The long hours he'd put in; the tremendous responsibility he'd shackled on like a ball and chain, costing him his marriage. Hell, what was personal happiness compared to bad publicity for the city? He could almost hear fifteen years on the force being flushed down the crapper.

"Chief, I hate to interrupt, but—" Erika tapped her watch "—Detective Bushard and I have an interview with a vital witness for the Tran murder." She glanced anxiously at Seven. "No promises, but this could be the break we need."

Suddenly, all worries of a *60 Minutes* segment vanished from the mayor's porcelain face. "Well, goodness gracious." Condum-Cox attempted a smile. "Proceed, of course."

Seven grabbed his jacket, following Erika's lead. "This might take a while."

"Not a problem," the mayor said. She waved them off, turning to the chief and the crestfallen Pham, who would be staying behind.

Outside, the sun felt warm on Seven's face. "So," he asked Erika, knowing full well she'd just bailed his ass. "What's our hot date?"

She pulled on her Christian Dior sunglasses. They weren't even fakes. She said spending money on shit like that made her *feel* rich.

"Starbucks." Looking more like a starlet than a homicide detective, she headed for the car, a tan Crown Victoria. "I don't know about you, but I could use a latte."

* * *

Erika ordered a vanilla latte—nonfat, decaf, sugar-free.

"What's the point?" Seven asked, grabbing his double espresso from the barista.

"A girl's gotta watch her figure."

"Right," he said, holding the door open so that they could sit outside. "What are you, a size two?"

"Puhleeze!" She sat down at one of the cement benches. "Size four. That size two shit is for anorexic models with boob jobs." She leaned forward, showing a hint of cleavage exposed by her button-down shirt beneath her jacket.

She cocked a single brow and lowered her voice to theatrical huskiness. "These babies are real."

"No kidding?" He held back a smile, trying not to give her the satisfaction of cracking up.

She winked. "I figured you'd know the difference, cowboy."

This time he did laugh. Ricky had been a plastic surgeon in Newport Beach before the AMA suspended his license. He'd had stories. The fact was, a boob job here was about as ubiquitous as a Lexus or a Mercedes on the 405 Freeway.

Seven took a sip of his espresso. "What's going to happen when there's no secret-weapon witness that we conveniently had to interview? Urgently? The chief is going to chew your ass."

She rolled her eyes. "Give the man some credit. The chief knows what's up. Dr. Rrrruth—" she rolled the German *R* "—may pull the strings, but that doesn't mean the chief has to like it."

Seven shook a finger at her. "You know, for someone who rocketed up the ranks by strategic ass-kissing, you sure don't know what's good for your career."

"The key is *strategic*. I'm no Pham." She wrapped her hands around the latte. "The sad fact is, he'd actually be a good cop if he wasn't so busy climbing over bodies to score points."

Seven took a minute, focused on the espresso, waiting for the levity to dissipate. Eventually, he told her, "I wish you hadn't put it on the line like that with the mayor."

Again, she gave a roll of her eyes. Erika had an arsenal of facial expressions, like a sexy raised brow or a killer smile. "But I did, so let's forget it, okay? Now, help me come up with something the chief *will* like."

He'd been thinking about the case all night, unable to get that image of Mimi Tran out of his head. He and Erika had been going over their notes from the witness interviews, the mother and daughter who had found the body, as well as neighbors. That's when, like some celebrity evading her paparazzi, the mayor had made her entrance, the chief in tow.

"It's a blank slate right now," Seven said.

"Yeah?"

Erika grabbed a notebook from her purse, one of those mailbag types that could carry the kitchen sink if she needed. He'd seen smaller suitcases.

"Blank slate," she said, slapping down a pen on the notebook for good measure. "At your service."

He shook his head and picked up the pen. That was the problem with him and Erika: their curious meeting of the minds. They were a good fit.

He gave her a hard stare. "I wasn't kidding. I don't want you going down with the ship, okay?"

Which was exactly what would happen. He wasn't fooling anyone. Since Ricky hit the six o'clock news, Seven's own life had gone upside down. And he wasn't near getting his act together. Now, murder and the mayor had landed on his doorstep for good measure.

"I said forget it. Now here—" she placed a dot at the center of the page and wrote "Tran" over it like a label "—is our murder victim."

She drew several lines radiating outward and labeled the first one "occupation—psychic."

"We start with Mimi Tran's client list." She drew several more lines radiating from there, each presumably representing possible clients and suspects. "We have her laptop and her PDA."

"There was also a desk calendar back at the crime scene."

"Exactomundo." Erika tapped the page. "So we find out who saw her last and why."

Going back to the center, she drew another line. In capital letters, she wrote "BLACK ARTS."

"The bird?" he asked.

"It wasn't exactly a scene from a Disney movie, now was it?"

"Oh, I don't know. You ever see *Snow White?*" He gave an exaggerated shiver. "That queen."

He drew his own line and wrote "Fucking Bizarre."

She smiled. "That, too."

"Maybe we look for someone who thinks Mimi Tran shouldn't be dispensing doom and gloom."

"She gives some really bad mojo to a client. They begin to think they can erase the prophecy by getting rid of Tran."

"As good a motive as any," he said.

Erika drew another line and put a big question mark at the end. "The bead inside the bird's beak. It was weird. When I held it up to different light sources, incandescent or fluorescent, it changed color. Like somebody turned on a switch, blue to red. No blurry transition, like those mood rings in the seventies. And then there was this sharp white line down the center, making it look like a cat's eye."

"Remember the symbols on the wall?" Over her question mark he wrote "All-seeing Eye."

Erika cocked her head. "Could be."

Hurriedly, he drew another line radiating out from the question mark, now in the mode. "And those wooden idols on the desk, they looked old. Museum quality. Maybe the bead is some sort of artifact?" He wrote the word as he said it, in capital letters.

"Something looted from an archeological site? Maybe sold by dealers on the black market?"

"Like the Getty."

Just recently, the J. Paul Getty Museum in Los Angeles had hit the headlines. And not in a good way. There'd been quite a brouhaha concerning the Italian government's claim that the Getty's newest collection of masterpieces had been looted from ancient ruins and laundered—just like drug money. Most controversial were pieces like the *Morgantina Apollo*. The black market made it almost impossible to ascertain the history of these important pieces because, by necessity, the laundering process destroyed evidence about the origins of the artifact.

Museums like the Getty were credited with stimulating the illegal trade in antiquities. In an unprecedented move, the Italian government had filed criminal charges against one of the curators, claiming collusion with the dealers who'd sold the museum the collection.

Seven reached for his notebook and flipped to the hand-drawn symbols he'd copied from the crime-scene walls. He turned the notebook for Erika to look at.

"So there's eyes painted on the wall, and the bead has a cat's eye thing going."

"And the victim is missing her eyes. Maybe it's not so complicated," he said. "Putting it in her mouth like that. Drawing the image with blood on the wall. Could be a warning of some kind. She was in on this looting deal and double-crossed someone?"

"Maybe." Erika took a sip of her latte, looking out toward the street. "Ever heard of the evil eye?"

He finished his coffee and tossed the cup into a nearby trash can, making the rim shot. "The evil eye? Come on. I thought you said you didn't believe in that stuff?"

She shrugged. "But I grew up with *that* stuff. From the day I was born, I didn't go out in public without my *azabache*," she said, holding up her wrist. She wore a gold bracelet from which hung a piece of jet.

Seven knew she wore the bracelet out of nostalgia. It had been a gift from her mother. Erika explained about how *el mal de ojo*, or the evil eye, was usually transmitted inadvertently by someone who was envious or jealous. The story would go that a mother would take her new baby into town and a childless woman would say something like, "Oh, what a pretty baby." Next thing you know, the kid has a fever or is vomiting. An *azabache*, or piece of jet, protected its wearer from the evil eye.

"Look," Erika said, dead serious, "lots of cultures believe in this stuff. But the fact is, in this case the only person who needs to believe is the perp."

He shook his head. "I think I'll go with what's behind door number two." Seven drew another line on the paper radiating out from the central dot.

He wrote *Greed* and underlined the word twice.

"So it's just some sort of camouflage, the bird and the bead?" She looked at the diagram, the lines radiating out from the center, letting it sink in.

She smiled and tapped the word. "Greed. I like it."

He glanced at his watch. "You think it's safe to go back to the station? Take a look at what's on the victim's PDA?"

She stood, grabbing the notebook and her purse. "Are you kidding? Dr. Ruth is long gone. It's lunchtime. Prime fund-raising hours. By the way, how did it go yesterday with Beth and Nick?"

He shrugged, knowing she would eventually get to that. "How does it always go? She took a Xanax and I took Nick to Taco Bell. I stayed a couple of hours, put them both to bed."

Out in the parking lot, he opened the door to the Crown Vic and got in. He kept waiting for the lecture, knowing it was there on the tip of her tongue. But Erika just started the car.

He looked over at her profile. He could see she was trying hard not to say anything. She made no move to back out of the parking space, just let the engine run.

"I can feel the disapproval beaming back at me from across the car, Obi-Wan," he said.

She pressed her lips together, as if maybe she'd hold back. But then she let out this sigh and turned to him. "I'm sorry, but it's been over eight months. How long are you going to sacrifice yourself on the altar of Ricky's sins?"

"God, you Catholics. The drama." He stared out the window, having nothing new to add to the debate.

But Erika was a bulldog. "First, your French-Canadian self is just as Catholic as me—practicing or not—so don't be throwing my religion in my face. Look, I know you have Nick to think about. But here's the thing. So does Beth. That boy should be *her* primary concern."

Her tone said it all. As long as he was holding Beth's hand through the crisis, she wouldn't step up.

Erika gripped the steering wheel, her jaw set. She looked to be bracing herself.

"Okay," she said, plunging in. "I'm going to say it. It's a mistake but here goes. Beth wants in your pants and she's not stopping until she has you, ring on the finger and all." His partner turned to look at him. "Face it, Seven. She wants to replace one brother with the other."

"Give me a break," he said, completely disgusted by the idea. "Her life is falling apart. Hooking up with me is about the last thing she needs right now."

Erika shook her head. "You don't know women, Seven."

"Oh, so because my marriage goes south—a marriage that I was way, *way* too young to take on—I'm a total loser when it comes to women?"

"And don't we sound a tad defensive? What's the matter, partner?" she asked. "Are you worried that because you fucked up once you don't deserve to be happy? Is that what your life is about for the next twenty years, while Ricky does time? Stick around and fix your brother's mess?"

Before he could respond—and dammit, he wanted to—Erika's cell interrupted. She picked up with a frown.

After a minute, she glanced over to Seven with a look of surprise. He braced himself. It took a lot to surprise Erika.

"You are not going to believe this." She slapped the phone shut and put the car into Reverse. She pulled out of the parking space. "That was Pham. We've got a live one."

Again, that radar between partners. "A witness?"

Erika peeled out. "In the flesh."

6

Most days, Paul Rocket had a kick-ass job. He'd wake up to Pink Floyd's *The Wall* pulsing on the Bose sound system and do a set of push-ups right there on the cabin floor. Afterward, he'd head into the galley and blend up a protein drink. He liked Ultra Megaman. That shit put on muscle like nobody's business.

Rocket wasn't into steroids. He'd seen too many guys go nuts on the stuff. Why the hell take the risk when he could get the same results with diet and exercise? Hell, he'd read just about every book printed on nutrition. Not to mention the stuff on the Internet.

Oh, yeah, Rocket was living the life. He'd watch the sunrise on the deck of his fifty-five-foot schooner, dialed in to CNN on his laptop while powering down his drink. The sun sparkling on the water in Newport Harbor—now that was something. Imagine, Paul Rocket—ex-Special Forces, ex-mercenary—enjoying this slice of paradise. Afterward, he'd hit the gym. He had a membership at Gold's. All courtesy of Mr. David.

Mr. David was a great man. Travel, money…hell, anything Rocket ever wanted, he just had to ask.

Like he said, most days, Paul Rocket had a kick-ass job.

Today wasn't one of those days.

He stepped into the art gallery and looked around at the bizarre shit hanging on the walls. The black-and-white photographs showed a bunch of naked bodies twined together so that you couldn't tell where one started and the other ended. Looked like a bunch of dudes, too. People actually paid money for this crap?

As he crossed the open room, men and women scurried out of his way like so many rats. At six foot four and 265 pounds, Rocket was used to that. His father had been a huge Samoan asshole who'd left his mom when Rocket was only five and his younger brother still in diapers. But at least he'd passed on his gene pool. Rocket had a tattoo of a cobra on the back of his shaved head but he preferred Armani suits and Bruno Magli shoes. People didn't expect that, a man like Rocket dressing with class.

He looked around at all the rich boys and girls. This was the OC. To these folks, Rocket was an alien life form.

The thing was, today Rocket wasn't the muscle. He was the babysitter.

He saw Owen leaning over some babe in the corner of the room. This one was skinny and blond and could barely stand despite the noon hour. Shit, was that dress made of red rubber? And there was Owen, getting an eyeful.

Rocket couldn't figure the kid out. He looked so *normal,* charming even. But Rocket knew better.

He could tell the exact moment Owen knew he was coming up behind him. The kid had radar for that sort of thing. Rocket wondered sometimes if he had superhearing or something because of his eyes. Sometimes nature did things like that—took a little in one area and made up for it in another.

Rocket had been in Special Forces before he'd fucked up in Nicaragua and gotten his ass kicked out of the military. He'd been working for Mr. David ever since. Important people like Mr. David needed security, and Rocket was the best. Only—despite all his training—the kid had gotten the jump on him a time or two.

He'd mentioned it to Mr. David once. How quietly the kid could move. Mr. David had only laughed, saying that Owen was just like his creepy mother.

Mr. David didn't care much for his wife. It was the only thing Rocket couldn't respect about the man.

For Rocket, family was key. His mom lived with his baby brother, Anthony. Anthony was a cop and had a great wife and two daughters. Mom loved looking after those girls. They lived in Cincinnati, and Rocket always made a point to fly out and visit whenever he could.

He sent money, too, Mr. David making it possible for him to help out. Those girls, they were going to college. Rita, the oldest, she could probably go to Stanford or some shit like that. The kid had brains.

That's why Rocket could understand what Mr. David was doing, protecting his son. A man had to take care of his own, right?

When Owen had first started acting weird, Mr. David pulled Rocket off security and asked him to start watching the kid full-time. Rocket was a little ashamed that he hadn't always gotten the job done the way Mr. David meant. Sometimes the best Rocket could do was make sure the kid didn't get his ass thrown into one of those foreign jails.

But those seven years roaming the globe… Mr. David had been happy with the kid's progress. And Owen did seem different since they returned from his "missionary work" abroad, especially around Mr. David. But that only made Rocket suspicious. He wondered if it was all an act.

If maybe he should warn Mr. David.

But then things had quieted down. Mr. David had Owen working in the family real estate offices—if you called what the kid did work. And Rocket had his schooner docked in Newport Harbor.

He just hoped this didn't turn out like that time in Nicaragua.

Owen smiled now, his eyes zeroing in on Rocket through the yellow lenses of his sunglasses.

Owen was tall, with blue eyes. Handsome, even. And he dressed like a million bucks. Every once in a while, he even gave Rocket a little fashion advice.

But there was something in that face. It had to do with his eyes. The boy didn't blink. Some weakness in some muscle…he wore sunglasses all the time because his eyes could get damaged from outside dust and debris. He had to constantly put in drops to keep his eyes lubricated.

But it always struck Rocket as a little creepy how he could just stare and stare at you. Like now.

Sometimes, he'd get this expression on his face. Rocket had seen that look before. In Nicaragua, he'd worked with mercenaries, soldiers willing to work for just about anybody if the money was good. There'd been this one guy, the kind that liked the blood and gore a little too much.

Rocket knew some of the things the kid had done. Mr. David had filled him in when he'd first asked him to look after Owen, not wanting Rocket to go into this thing blind. They'd had the kid seeing a psychiatrist and taking pills. But Mr. David told Rocket he was the extra peace of mind. So Rocket stayed at the kid's side while they'd toured around the world, working for different religious organizations.

His opinion? You could stuff that kid in a fucking monastery for the next ten years and Owen would still come out all wrong.

But then, maybe Mr. David knew what he was doing. The boss was smart. Hadn't he graduated from some big-name school? Mr. David had made Gospel Enterprises what it was today, taking the family company to the next level. He knew what he was up against with Owen. And people could change, right?

"Rocket, my man," Owen said. "I didn't think art was your thing."

"Mr. David needs you back home."

Whenever he talked to Owen, he never called Mr. David "your father" or "your dad." It was always "Mr. David." Rocket made a point of it.

"Really? How incredibly boring." He turned back to the blonde in the wild dress. Really, the only thing holding that girl up was tight rubber and the wall. "Sorry, darling. Looks like I have business to tend to."

"Come *on*, Owen." She played with his tie, using it like a leash to pull him closer. "I thought we could have some fun together."

Rocket had an idea of what Owen thought was fun. He didn't know what kind of shit the girl was into, but she should be happy if Owen gave it a pass.

"Next time, sweets," he said, giving her a light peck on the lips.

Owen sauntered ahead, leaving Rocket to follow. Rocket didn't mind. Actually, he preferred never turning his back on him.

Owen stopped in front of one of the photographs near the gallery entrance. It took Rocket a minute before he realized the woman in the photo was the girl still holding up the wall, the one in the rubber dress.

Only, in the photo, she wasn't wearing clothes. She was wrapped in cellophane.

In the photograph, she held one end under her foot as the plastic twined around one of her thighs and up her torso, just like a snake on a branch. She was holding the other end over her face, with her tongue pressed against the cellophane as if she were licking it.

Rocket turned away. He'd seen a man killed in just such a way, suffocated with a plastic bag over his head.

"What do you think?" Owen asked, staring up at the photograph. When Rocket didn't respond, he laughed. "Not to your liking?"

Owen reached out and traced a finger over the girl's mouth, where her lips pressed against the plastic wrap. "I bought it for my office. Spent a bloody fortune on it."

Standing behind Owen, Rocket looked at the photograph again and shook his head.

What a piece of shit.

It's just like he'd thought this morning when Mr. David called: this was going to be one hell of a day.

7

Pham had the witness set up in the interview room. He was practically falling over himself in his rush to hand her on to Seven and Erika. Not a good sign.

It didn't take long to figure out why.

Gia Moon was movie-star beautiful. Seven had always had this thing for Jennifer Connelly, and it was almost as if the actress had walked into the precinct to pay a visit—swear to God, the woman could be her twin. Long swan neck, black shiny hair, skin to die for, as Erika would say. And those blue, blue eyes. Definitely Oscar-worthy.

Yup, Gia Moon was something. She was also a couple of fries short of a Happy Meal. At least that was Seven's take on things after listening to her story.

They hadn't bothered videotaping the session once Pham filled them in on the witness's special talent, just Erika taking her statement.

"So let me get this straight," Erika continued. "You didn't know Mimi Tran?"

"That is correct."

She spoke using this precise diction. He could see she was irritated, as if she'd already gotten wind that they weren't buying what she was selling. Still, he couldn't help staring. There was something mesmerizing about her face and its near-perfect symmetry.

She was dressed simply in jeans and a T-shirt. No makeup—didn't need it, in his opinion. But there was paint on her hands, like maybe she'd been fixing up the den and dropped the paint-brush in her hurry to run on over to the precinct and tell her story.

"When I read the article in the paper," she said, "I realized I had to contact the police."

Erika took a moment. Seven recognized that carefully controlled expression on his partner's face. Erika didn't like people wasting her time.

"Because you had a dream?" she prompted.

"I *thought* it was a dream, Detective. But after I read the article in the paper, I knew it was more than that."

"You're talking about a premonition?"

"Yes."

"But you called it—" Erika pretended to check her notes "—a vision?"

Gia Moon didn't answer right away, but he could see the tension in her shoulders. She wasn't enjoying the attention. In fact, she looked ready to bolt...which was unexpected. Usually the crazies who showed up with important "evidence" after a story like Tran's hit the paper couldn't wait to have their say.

"You can call it whatever you wish, Detective," she said.

Erika didn't even glance up from her notes. "Actually, I'm using your words, Ms. Moon. In your *vision,* you saw Mimi Tran being murdered in her home?"

"No. It wasn't clear like that. It never is. It's like a dream, subject to interpretation. I saw a woman in danger. I saw blood—or at least the color red."

She seemed to be making an effort to remember—or perhaps edit her words now that she knew she would be held accountable. She glanced down at her fingers.

There, under her nails, the color of the paint. Red.

"When I read the story in the paper," Gia Moon continued, "certain things from my dream suddenly fell into place, making me think it was Mimi Tran's murder I saw."

"You have these often?" Erika asked. "These...visions?"

Moon frowned. "I don't see why that would matter, but yes. I often have visions of this sort."

He liked that schoolteacher tone. Not many people took on Erika. Seven had to admit it was a bit of a turn-on. Really, it was a shame about the batty part.

"But this is the first time you've contacted the police?" Erika pressed.

Seven caught a slight hesitation before Gia answered, "Correct."

"Why is that, Ms. Moon?" he asked, seeing an opening.

She turned to look at him. Her smile—shit, he felt it right down to his toes. But he kept his eyes steady, knowing that was one of his talents. Intense interest…the kind that got people to open up.

"I think that would be obvious, Detective," she said, still with that devastating smile. Like it was a joke between them. "The police don't exactly *invite* my kind of input."

"In your dream, Ms. Tran was killed by a demon?" Erika's tone said it all. *And why would we?*

"As I explained, that doesn't mean she was literally killed by a demon. It could be a representation, a symbol for the killer. He could have a tattoo or it could be a piece of jewelry he wore."

"Really?" Erika said. "How very mysterious…and vague."

Seven almost cringed before he pulled up a chair and sat down, giving it a shot. "Can you describe the demon?"

Gia Moon closed her eyes, as if getting a bead on the thing with her "inner eye." He almost smiled, but stopped himself.

"Scales," she whispered. "Red mist. Black, protruding eyes." She opened her eyes and stared at Seven. "Very large teeth."

Seven glanced at Erika. Gia Moon had just given a fair description of the painting in the entry to Tran's house.

Which didn't necessarily mean shit. Scales, big teeth, protruding eyes—sounded like your basic demon, right? The newspapers had mentioned the victim was Vietnamese and a fortune-teller. It could be a common enough image given the culture.

On the other hand, the description of the painting might indicate that Gia Moon knew the victim…that she'd been inside her house.

"Go on," he said.

"She felt fear. All-consuming fear," she said. "She was terrified. At the same time, there is something familiar about this demon. I think she had encountered him before—but never the violence. The attack confused her. She hadn't expected the attack. That's why she invited him inside."

"She invited the demon inside?"

There had been no signs of a forced entry—information that Seven knew hadn't been printed in the papers.

"She fought him." Now Gia wrung her hands, almost as if washing them in the air. "There's blood coming from her hands."

The victim *had* had defensive marks. But anybody who watched *CSI* regularly could come up with that much.

"He was…so hungry." Now her eyes looked unfocused, as if she were again slipping into some scene only she could see. "He fed off her fear. There was a lot of blood, but he wanted more. He liked it when she tried to run away. But then she died. Too quickly. He didn't like that."

It was almost as if she was speaking in a trance. Jesus, he thought, if this was an act, she was good.

Suddenly, she focused back on Seven, waking up. She took a deep breath and stood. She shouldered her purse.

"I felt compelled to come here and tell you about my vision. For what it's worth, of course."

"Hold on." Seven stood, as well, taking her arm to try and stop her from leaving.

Only, the instant they touched, static electricity—coming hard and fast and unexpectedly—shocked the two of them apart. They stood there, staring at each other.

Moon was petite, maybe five foot three. Seven was just under six feet. She had to look up to meet his gaze.

But those eyes, they could zing right through a man.

"I'm sorry," she whispered.

The way she said it, she was apologizing for something very different than that silly shock between them.

"A woman is dead, Ms. Moon," he said, trying to keep his voice steady. "We take any information that you may provide very seriously."

"All right."

He watched as she sat down again. He could see she was just as shaken as he. She took a moment to steady herself.

He sat down beside her, but Gia Moon turned to Erika, addressing her. "You'll want a test, of course. Something that lets you know I have information never leaked to the press."

Erika glanced at Seven. *Is this chick for real?*

"There were eyes everywhere," Gia Moon said. "And there was something in her mouth." She spoke as if tired of jumping through hoops. She was searching for the quickest way to cross the finish line. "Something very old—very powerful. And small. Blue. No, red. Perhaps made of glass. I would start there."

Seven felt the blood freeze inside his veins. *Holy shit.*

"Seven, why don't you start the videotape?" Erika asked.

"I'm on it."

His partner leaned forward, now completely focused. "What do you mean, start there?"

"With the object. This blue or red piece," she elaborated, with another tired gesture. "It's—" she seemed to struggle for the right words. "It's very old. Museums. Private collections. It might be a gem of some sort. Whatever it is, it's missing. Someone is looking for it. He wants it back."

Nothing she'd just told them had been reported to the press. Even if she'd managed somehow to speak to the two witnesses who had found the body, neither of them knew about the blue bead.

"Go on," Seven said.

Gia Moon again stood, the motion part of her story rather than an attempt to leave. "She invited him inside. She punched in the alarm code, disarming the security system."

Gia acted out the gesture, stabbing her finger in the air as if punching in the numbers herself. Seven noticed that her hand was at the same level as Tran's actual keypad.

"It was a horrible death. But she didn't die the way you think." It was almost as if she were reading some script in her head. She opened her eyes. "And he isn't near done."

"You're talking about another victim?" Seven asked, standing as well.

She nodded. "The demon. He'll kill again. And if my dream is correct," she said, speaking as if it were nothing to her, what she was saying, "I'm next."

Mimi Tran wasn't worthy. Her death lacked finesse.

You prefer to remember another time. Another woman. A better experience.

Puerto Rico.

You smile. You never forget your first time.

You're in San Juan, the night of the festival. At midnight, everyone will walk backward into the ocean, dreaming of love.

You make a wish. There is nothing wistful about your dreams.

The palm trees on the beach are permanently bent from the sea breeze. At that moment, the sky above doesn't threaten, as it has all day. As the music pumps the bikini-clad crowd into a frenzy, you watch families, children, lovers, on the beach, all preparing for their ritual baptism.

You feel their energy pulse with the beat of the conga drums from the salsa band. They walk around as if the party never stops. You, on the other hand, know exactly when this party will end. You're in control.

Security is tight. There are armed police in Kevlar vests everywhere. Some convention of elected officials is in town, your only bit of bad luck. But you don't care. You have the power of life and death. You're not afraid. You're God.

Tonight's festival is a pagan ritual. Every man, woman and child will walk backward into the ocean and throw themselves into the sea, cleansed of their sins. Only, you know that it's you who will do the cleansing. You look forward to it.

Palm tree trunks glow with artificial light on the manicured grounds. A band performs on a floating stage set up in the shallows of the private beach. Three women dressed in white sway their hips in a motion as old as time.

The crowd doesn't need encouragement. Grandmas dance on

the shore with toddlers, husbands stare adoringly into the eyes of their wives as they salsa knee-deep in the ocean. On the floating stage, men and women wearing cowboy hats follow along in a dance with the natives—a contingent from Texas.

You stare at the ramparts of an ancient fortress dating back to when this was an important military post, its shores decorated with cannons, the walls built to keep out the English Armada. The fortress is lit up tonight. Lightning flashes in the distance.

The women at the Bacardi booth keep the rum flowing. Every other man or woman carries a plastic cup, laughing and drinking. The cups are stamped with the Barcardi emblem: a bat. Here, the bat is a symbol of good luck.

As midnight approaches, the pulse of the party revs up. Couples once dancing poolside become part of the mass migration to the beach. Suddenly, the crowd converges. You stand body to body with strangers, getting drunk on their alcoholic stupor, but your eyes follow only *her*. You were at dinner when she and her boyfriend fought. You've learned women take all sorts of shit from men, but now, she's alone.

One of the singers in the band explains the ritual for the tourists. People grab hands and begin wading backward into the warm water.

You come to stand alongside the woman. Like everyone else, she wears a barely there bikini. You've been waiting all night for this moment.

She takes your hand and smiles. She's blond with blue eyes. You hear her slur her words as she tells you how amazing this all is. Like New Year's, she says. You hear a touch of the South in her voice. Texas, then.

Beach balls are tossed into the ocean by hotel staff as the crowd counts backward. Ten, nine, eight… The girl squeezes your hand. She tells you her name is Mary.

Like the Virgin, you think, squeezing back.

At the count of five, you take Mary's hand to your mouth and kiss the back of her fingers. She has beautiful hands, soft and slim. Mary giggles. You can see she likes her Barcardi.

The crowd is thick now. You stand practically on top of each other, trying to make room for all. You throw yourselves backward into the ocean. The tradition requires you do it twelve times, giving more than enough opportunity.

Mary never comes back up.

No one notices as she fights, kicking her legs. Her struggle blends with the ritual dunking. You're tall for your age. And very strong. The crowd is throwing balls and dancing in the water. Fireworks light up the sky and the sound of the band covers her fight for air. Slowly, you feel the life slip away as her body grows limp. You submerge alongside her and bring her fingers to your mouth once again. You taste blood with the saltwater.

You lift her into your arms like a lover. You lower her one more time in the water, sending her adrift.

You slip out of the sea and across the sand, exhilarated.

Back by the pool, a giant TV screen shows the NBA finals. Tourists take photographs of loved ones, cataloging the moment.

You don't need a camera. You will never forget this night.

Kids slide into the pool, screaming. Spanish and English mingle in the warm, muggy night. Off in the distance, the skies now threaten a downpour, while the pool bar glows neon blue. Striped towels are handed out freely; no need for a card key tonight.

The sand poolside feels warm between your toes. You look out toward shore, where people still dance in the water. There are hammocks between a few of the palm trees, as well as striped cabana chairs. You slip into one. Again, you reach into the pocket for your souvenir. Dark clouds drifting in the night sky begin to blur the stars.

You marvel at how well it went. You were careful to slip in at the last second and take Mary's hand in yours. No one will remember you standing with her. It was dark. That helps.

You head back to the hotel entrance. At the pool bar, an armada of bartenders flip bottles to the rhythm of a song you don't recognize. They dance and concoct their magic potions for the women smoking and swaying to the music on the submerged concrete seats. You notice a tattoo on the small of the back of one lady, but don't linger. You're not greedy.

You slip inside the hotel, passing the emergency personnel scrambling by. They will try to revive Mary. They will not succeed.

They will find the tip of one of her pinkies missing where you bit it off. Not what you want for your treasure, but it will do.

Your heart is racing as you make your way to the hotel gardens. A television shows a newscaster reporting that the festival on the beaches is going well. He reassures viewers that security is tight. It's safe, folks. Come on down and enjoy.

You enter the gardens. No one is around. Everyone is back at the pool and beach.

You listen to the frogs. They're famous here, making a soft, *coo-kee* noise. It sounds like there's hundreds just here. You open your mouth and take out the tip of Mary's pinkie.

Now you know why they call this the island of enchantment. It's beautiful and surreal, listening to the frogs sing.

You look down at the finger piece settled in the middle of your palm. It's small, only to the first joint, but you did like her hands and there wasn't a lot of time.

You're in paradise and now you have a part of Mary. All your wishes tonight have come true....

You open your eyes, returning to time present.

Mimi Tran wasn't nearly so nice. But she had a purpose.

The eyes, her life source, are yours now.

That's the way it has to be from now on. You kill with reason. It's kill or be killed. You are God and you serve a higher purpose.

And you already know who is next.

8

Gia Moon stared at the six-by-four-foot canvas. She'd come home from the police station and headed straight for her studio, dropping her purse on the concrete floor at the entrance.

She'd started work on the painting at one o'clock that morning. That's when she'd woken from her dream.

She hadn't woken gently, slowly easing to the surface of wakefulness. That's not how it happened, these visions. She'd sat up abruptly, gasping for breath, horrified by the images still burning so brightly inside her head. Her daughter had uncharacteristically slept in her own bed that night, a godsend.

In her bathroom, Gia had splashed water on her face. Grabbing a robe for warmth, she'd headed for her studio in the garage.

This is what she did; it was who she was. The woman who painted nightmares.

Her mother had warned her once. *You're so strong. Be careful. Dark spirits are always attracted to the strong.*

"No kidding, Mom," she said, staring at the painting of the demon who had killed Mimi Tran.

That morning, she'd taken only a short break from painting for coffee—it wasn't her day to drive carpool, another lucky break. She'd had more than enough time for her vision to become almost fully realized on the canvas before she'd read the article in the paper, making the connection.

Gia reached into the back pocket of her jeans and pulled out the detective's card. When she'd gone to the precinct, she'd wanted to blurt out her story and leave. Mission accomplished.

She propped the card up on the easel.

They hadn't believed her. She'd expected that.

She took a long breath and stared down at her hands. They were shaking. She balled her fingers into fists.

I'm next.

It had been a bold declaration, one she hadn't planned on making. But she had a temper, and she'd let herself get pushed.

Not good, Gia.

Sometimes, she could understand what had driven her mother all those years. People wanted proof, something tangible. They wanted the world to make *sense.* Things needed to add up, like a mathematical formula. Forget about dreams and visions and the kooks who claimed to have them.

Erika Cabral was one of those skeptics. The kind of person who thought Gia only wanted to scam the desperate out of their money.

The interview had been surprisingly nerve-racking. Gia didn't like the spotlight. She required anonymity. To the outside world, she was an artist, a painter whose pieces some claimed showed a glimpse into another world. But it was all below the radar. Those few souls who managed to find her never asked for more than peace of mind. In exchange for connecting with lost loved ones, they kept her secrets.

Now, that might not be possible.

"Wow. That is one ugly mother."

Hearing her daughter, Gia turned toward the door. She had no idea how long she'd been standing there. She had a habit of "losing time" when it came to her paintings. Past three o'clock, she told herself, if Stella was home from school.

Her daughter walked into the garage studio, popping her gum, a vile habit she well knew her mother despised. Gia figured that was the point. Stella dropped her backpack in the middle of the floor. Gia didn't comment on that, either.

The girl came to stand next to her and immediately fell into the painting.

That's what Gia called it: falling in. It happened all the time with Stella. Gia watched as her daughter's eyes grew unfocused. That was the problem with Stella's gift. She was too sensitive, didn't have strong enough defenses. She hadn't learned how to guard herself—and, in complete denial of her gifts, she wouldn't allow Gia to teach her.

Stella took a step back, away from the painting. In complete silence, she reached out and slipped her hand in her mom's.

Gia pulled her little girl into her arms. At twelve years old, Stella was still under five feet, small for her age. Gia kissed the top of her head. Stella had Gia's black hair and blue eyes. But the curls—those riotous curls brushing the tops of her shoulders were all her daughter's.

"Okay," Stella said, pushing back to once again look at the painting. "I already hate it. What is it?"

"I don't know, baby. A demon of some sort."

"It killed somebody, didn't it?"

"I'm still trying to figure that out," Gia said. "Maybe lots of somebodies."

Gia didn't bother to try to hide things from Stella. She'd learned a long time ago the futility of that—nor did Stella appreciate her efforts at protecting her. Gia chose instead to try and explain what her daughter saw. But even then, she fell short. Half the time it was Stella who told Gia the meaning behind her art, such was her daughter's talent.

The painting didn't show Mimi Tran's lifeless body. Gia rarely painted death, choosing instead to objectify such things.

Mimi's symbol was the red eye. It faced the beast, ready to do battle. But the monster proved too powerful. Part of the eye melted down the side of the canvas, the heavy red paint flowing like a river of blood off the edge.

Gia used her paintings to make sense of the images that came to her in dreams. Sometimes it worked, other times she just had macabre works of art to show for her efforts.

"They didn't believe you, did they?"

"The police? No, darling," she said. "They didn't."

She didn't ask Stella how she knew about the police. Gia

hadn't told her about her trip to the precinct or the conversation she'd had with the detectives there. Her daughter preferred to pretend her ability was a fluke, or a figment of their imagination. She did the ostrich thing, getting angry whenever her mother pointed out the obvious.

I don't want to be a freak like you! That's what she'd screamed the first time her abilities came shining through.

There'd been a time when Gia, too, had said those very words to her own mother.

Stella gave a sigh that sounded much too old for her years. "I don't know why you even try."

"Because I was supposed to."

"Your guides," Stella said, in the voice of a supreme skeptic.

In the world of psychic phenomena, often times guides from the other side would help a medium make contact. They served almost as an umbilical line to the dead spirits trying to communicate. While many had names, Gia's own guides chose to remain anonymous.

She bit her lip and stared at the simple business card propped on the easel. Detective Seven Bushard. City of Westminster. Homicide.

She remembered the electric shock of his touch.

She'd felt his sadness like a blow to her chest, making it difficult to breathe. She'd seen his story like a movie in her head. His brother and the man he'd killed. The vision had been dark and murky and without a lot of details, but grisly nonetheless.

From the moment the detective had walked in to that interview, he'd been watching her with an almost hungry stare. Gia knew what it meant to have people want something from her.

You say you had a dream?

That was the other detective. The woman, Erika Cabral. Gia recognized that tone. *The freak...the nut job.* It only made her smile, because she could clearly see an entity standing next to Erika, shedding a protective white light.

Gia never argued with a disbeliever. Sometimes she wondered if that's not what she wanted. *Don't believe me. I did my duty. My conscience is clear. If you don't make use of my knowledge, that's not my concern.*

Only, she couldn't really say that now. Mimi Tran was different. This time, Gia wasn't the uninvolved observer.

She might very well be responsible for that woman's death.

She looked back at the card, remembering Seven Bushard's words on parting.

"Call if you have another…dream," he'd told her.

"The man. Is he going to hurt you, Mommy?"

The question came from nowhere, as they often did. Gia always forgot how connected she was to her child.

She'd been thinking about the detective when her daughter asked the question. Stephen Bushard wasn't who she feared.

She answered, "No, sweetie." She kissed her daughter again, giving them both the pabulum. "I'll be fine. We both will."

9

The county coroner's office was located in Santa Ana, a city that touted itself as the financial and political center for Orange County. It was over seventy-five percent Hispanic, originating with a Spanish land grant—seventy acres of which had been purchased from the Yorba family by William H. Spurgeon. Driving up the road from Westminster, Seven was always amazed how quickly the signs changed from Pho 54 to Taqueria.

Seven had grown up in nearby Huntington Beach, graduating from Marina High School. Go Vikings! With Little Saigon so close, the school's Asian population was double that of the state average.

Even back then, there was this idea that Asian students were ruining the public school system, making it too hard for your red, white and blue American to succeed. How could Patty or Jake compete against someone who lived in the library, for God's sake, tanking up on Top Ramen and green tea for another all-nighter of studying?

Whenever he heard someone spouting that crap, Seven always asked if maybe Asians were inherently more intelligent? No? So it's all about good old-fashioned hard work? Well, there you go.

People made choices. They sacrificed. So quit bitching and just compete, right? God knows Ricky, his brother, hadn't been the hit of the party scene. That had been Seven's job in life.

Back in high school, Seven managed to get into enough hot water that his mom had threatened military school. It was a kind of periodic thing, like Easter or Christmas. *Military school, Seven. I will do it!* Once, she'd even taken him to tour a couple of places. Seven smiled at the memory, because the tactic had actually worked. Suddenly, he was passing all his classes.

But Ricky…it was the sweat of his brow that got him a full-ride scholarship to the college of his choice.

Still, Seven had to admit, the county coroner, Alice Wang, was the poster child for the Asians-are-hard-to-beat argument.

Alice was in her early fifties. She wore glasses and styled her hair in a sensible pageboy—Alice wasn't spending a ton of time in front of the mirror. She had places to go, people to cut open.

Alice had a gift. Best damn medical examiner he'd ever worked with.

Mimi Tran lay on a metal table with paper draped strategically over her lower body—an attempt at dignity sabotaged by the fact that half her insides were on display and a tag hung from her big toe like a Christmas present.

Your average Joe didn't know that it was the smells you remembered most from your first autopsy: body odors and the scent of half-digested food. Seven figured Alice and her crew must be used to it. Him, he was breathing through his mouth.

Alice Wang stood over the body of Mimi Tran. With the scalpel, she'd made a Y incision, from shoulder to shoulder and down to the lower abdomen. She'd already removed the breastplate using the circular saw waiting with other instruments next to the body, exposing the internal organs, which had all been weighed. The quickest way to know if there was something wrong was through weight.

Now she was in the process of ladling the stomach contents into a plastic container, like soup. She used tweezers to examine the particulate matter.

Apparently, Mimi Tran had had a light lunch before dying.

"Jellyfish," Alice said, holding up a rubbery string with the tweezers.

"Not the sort of thing you keep in the fridge from the local deli?" Seven asked.

"I'm guessing not this time," Alice said, pulling up a small, brown lump with her magic tweezers. "Escargot."

"Jellyfish *and* snails?" Erika made a face. "Tell me you're kidding."

"This from a woman who has no doubt tickled her palate with the likes of calves' brains and cow tongue?" Alice asked, making Seven wonder how many stomach contents from the local taqueria Alice had examined.

"Calves' brains." Erika stuck out her tongue in disgust. "*Mi abuelita* made me eat them. But now tongue isn't half-bad when it's prepared right."

"Well, the Vietnamese love their French food," Alice said. "You'd be surprised how many Vietnamese view the hundred-year French occupation with fondness. Go to any expensive Little Saigon restaurant or club and you're going to hear French music or see pictures of the Eiffel Tower and the Arc de Triomphe hanging on the walls. Ever been to La Veranda?"

Seven had heard of the place. It had the reputation of being one of the best restaurants in Little Saigon. "Haven't had the pleasure."

"Marble pillars, sparkling fountains…looks like a plantation right out of the colonial past. They serve escargot and frog legs right alongside pickled *daikon, nuoc mam* and rice paper. But I think what the victim ate was less traditionally prepared, a more innovative kind of fusion."

"Who knew you were such a foodie, Alice?"

"Everette and I have been members of the same gourmet club for years."

Seven tried to imagine. Maybe if you studied enough stomach contents, food became a hobby.

"Three hours after eating, ninety-five percent of your stomach contents will end up in the small intestine," Alice continued. "The process stops at the time of death. Given what I'm seeing here—" she nodded toward the plastic container "—I'd say a power lunch at some chi-chi restaurant just before she died. I'd look for something high-end. That was a real nice St. John she had on."

"Ah, come on, Alice," Erika said. "We know you have a closetful of those. Isn't Everette an anesthesiologist?"

"With three kids to put through college," Alice reminded her. Then, looking thoughtful, she added, "The victim was a psychic?"

"Well-known, from what people in the area say," Seven stated.

Alice nodded. "Not that it's relevant to the cause of death, but I found some unique cell damage in the prefrontal cortex of her brain."

"You want to dumb that down for my partner, Alice?" Erika said, managing to keep a straight face.

"The prefrontal cortex, that's the area just behind your forehead. It has the ability to control activity in other parts of the brain. Think of it as a kind of volume-control switch. When I examined the victim's brain, I saw significant atrophy in the prefrontal cortex. The tissue samples I looked at under the microscope showed axonal damage."

"English, Alice," Erika reminded her. "English."

"Cell damage, necrosis. The victim's brain had an old injury."

Seven frowned. "Not that I believe in this stuff, but are you saying she was damaged goods? That she couldn't have psychic ability because her brain was messed up?"

Alice shook her head. "Quite the opposite. I'm saying our victim might have thought she was psychic *because* of the damage to her brain. There are studies that show religious beliefs reside in the temporal lobes, the part of the brain near your ears. When a temporal lobe is stimulated, the person can experience a presence associated with God or a spirit, depending on their personal beliefs. Some researchers in the area claim that humans are programmed for spiritual experiences."

"But in our victim, you said it was the prefrontal cortex that was damaged, not the temporal lobe," Erika said, confused.

"Exactly," Alice declared, as if she'd just made her point. "The part that controls activity in the temporal lobe was damaged. It's a leap, but I wonder, what if the injury in your victim's brain caused the temporal lobe to become excited, giving her what she thought were psychic experiences?" When Erika and Seven stood in confused silence, Alice added, "There's a condition called temporal lobe epilepsy. The seizures stimulate the temporal lobe."

"The part that experiences religion?" Seven asked.

"Correct. During a seizure, the patient experiences smells and sees things that aren't there—they hallucinate. She was a psychic, right? I wonder if the damage to her brain caused the temporal lobes to become excited, just like those of an epileptic. Your victim could very well believe she was having a psychic occurrence, when in fact she was having seizures."

Erika looked at Seven. Neither knew what to make of the new information.

"But again, I digress," Alice said. "You'll be more interested in the cause of death."

"That seems pretty obvious," Erika said.

Alice smiled. Not something you saw every day, the coroner smiling.

"So you would think—the cause of death, exsanguinations. But that's where it gets interesting."

Alice leaned over the body, motioning the detectives closer. Like any good M.E., Alice didn't have any problem with the dead.

She lifted the torso. "Here, she was stabbed from behind. Probably while she was running away, given the angle." She let the corpse settle back on the table, and glanced up. "We know from the defensive wounds on her hands that she tried to fight off her attacker. And the eyes, they were removed cleanly, using something very sharp. Have you found the murder weapon?"

"Not yet."

"It's a seven-inch blade. Very sharp. I'm thinking one of those Japanese chef's knives."

"Weapon of opportunity?" Seven asked. "We'll check the kitchen to see if anything is missing."

"I prefer the Santoku myself," Alice said. "Those things are a dream for mincing and dicing."

Again, Seven held off a shudder, trying not to think about the coroner preparing food items. He glanced back at the Y incision, imagining Alice with a chef's knife instead of her scalpel.

"And here—" she pointed to the next wound, at the victim's

side "—here the knife didn't penetrate as deeply. She managed to get away. But this one?" She pointed to the heart. "That would have been fatal."

"Would have?" Erika asked. "She looks pretty dead to me, Alice."

"Not the point. She didn't die from her wounds."

Erika glanced at Seven, both remembering the words of the psychic, Gia Moon. *She didn't die the way you think.*

Again, Alice flashed that elusive smile. "Along with the damage to the brain, your victim had a heart condition. Probably undiagnosed. Happens a lot with women. She had a ninety percent occlusion to the left coronary artery, the main pump to the heart," Alice explained. "For someone like that, if the heart starts beating faster, the blood flow is insufficient to feed the muscle. Basically, her heart stopped before she could bleed out."

Alice looked up at both detectives. "She had a heart attack. Given the circumstances, I'd say something scared your victim to death."

In the parking lot, Erika was carrying on like a hamster in distress.

"It's bullshit, Seven, and you know it. 'She didn't die the way you think,'" she said, repeating Gia Moon's prediction. "If she didn't do it, Gia Moon knows who did—and not because she had some woo-woo vision, like she wants us to believe. You ask me? She's looking awfully good for the murder."

"You don't think you're jumping the gun just a little here, Erika? What do we really have on this psychic?"

Erika crossed her arms and gave him that look—right between the eyes.

"Of course." She slapped her palm to her forehead as if to say, *What was I thinking?* "She's just a *really* good guesser. Why didn't I think of that?"

"I'm not saying you're wrong—"

"And that name, Gia Moon. Come on! Sounds like a freaking *X-Files* episode."

"I admit the name is a little too cute."

"Cute? Did you know Gaia is one of several names used for the Earth Goddess?"

"Okay, sure. But—"

"Gia Moon. Earth—moon. She freaking made it up."

"So I have a cousin who her changed her name to Comedy, for God's sake. Jesus, Erika. She's a psychic. Maybe that's what they do. Become Madam Zelda or Sunshine. *She* came down to the station. Why would she do that if she's involved?" he asked. "She wants to get caught?"

"Wouldn't be the first time. Maybe she needs the attention? Or suffers from a guilty conscience? Only she tries to cover up with her hocus-pocus crap."

"Hocus-pocus crap?" He grabbed his partner's wrist, showing the gold bracelet with its jet stone. "Sounds kind of harsh coming from a woman who carries an ass-your-watch-it."

"*Azabache,*" she corrected, talking about the amulet. "And it was a gift." She twisted her hand away. "It's just a silly superstition. This chick wants us to believe she's in touch with the powers-that-be. That some demon killed Mimi Tran and now she's next."

Erika stepped right up to him. It still surprised him how someone five foot two could look so intimidating. But Erika had it going on, the stance—the stare.

"Are you tell me that you're buying her story?"

"You know how this goes down, Erika. Once you start believing you *know* who the perp is, that's when the righteous work stops. You lead the evidence rather than letting the evidence lead you. So maybe I'm not ready to slap on the cuffs just yet."

He started toward the car, forcing her to do the same.

Truth be told, he didn't know what to make of Gia Moon. At first, sure, he'd chalked her up as another nutcase. It happened all the time at the station. A provocative case such as the Tran murder brought out the crazies like a full moon.

But what his partner said was true. The stone in the bird's mouth, the fact that she knew it changed color, the painting in the foyer. And now, the cause of death. *She didn't die like you think*... It was a little close to the mark.

Walking to the vehicle, he could still see Gia clearly in his head. He had a good memory for things like that, but this was different. He pictured her eyes, so blue in contrast to her sleek black hair. How alluring she looked in just a plain T-shirt and jeans. During the interview, she'd seemed almost resigned to the fact that no one would believe her. She was doing her duty, coming forward like a good psychic citizen...knowing all along she'd be ridiculed. He remembered how badly he'd wanted to tell her she was wrong, that no matter what, he'd give her a fair shot.

He opened the car door and sat down on the hot passenger seat, waiting for Erika to start the engine. He just couldn't imagine Gia involved in the bloodbath he'd seen...and maybe not for the reasons he'd given Erika.

Because Seven had another reaction to Gia Moon. One he hoped his partner hadn't tuned in to with her Latina sixth sense.

He told himself he was vulnerable. Hell, the last few months, he didn't know where his head was at—that night with Erika being a prime example of his lack of judgment.

And that call from his ex, Laurin. The breakup of his marriage hadn't exactly been a high point. Talking to Laurin only reminded him of past mistakes. Big ones.

He hadn't been paying attention, hadn't noticed the changes in Laurin. And maybe that's why she left. He'd made her feel invisible, when another man made her feel loved.

She'd left a note: *I don't love you anymore, Seven.*

Short and sweet.

Maybe that's when he'd felt the big slap across the face. That call from Laurin about her shiny new life. And here he was, stuck in a spot where time stood still, because his brother had changed the rules.

Bad guy—good guy. Seven couldn't tell anymore.

"Look, the case is bizarre enough," he told his partner as they made their way down Bolsa Avenue. "Let's just play this one straight, okay? Cross our t's and dot our i's."

"Oh, sure. Sit around and wait for a suspect to fall into our laps? Or, God forbid, wait for someone else to die." She kept her eyes on the road. "Come on, you haven't thought about it? The whole serial killer scenario?"

Like his partner, he stared straight ahead, watching Little Saigon pass in a wash of color. Red-tiled roofs, Vietnamese signs, painted shop windows in strip malls advertising supermarkets, nail salons and gift stores. A rice rocket—a Honda Civic tricked up with fancy spoiler and audio equipment—cruised past.

A serial killer. Of course he'd thought about it. Everything about the death of Mimi Tran evoked the possibility of a twisted mind.

"I'm betting our little Miss Moon knows more than she's letting on," Erika said. "Like that stuff about checking private collections and museums. She gave me an idea."

"Museums?" He shook his head. "I'm moving around the rabbit ears, Erika, but I'm still not getting any reception."

"Meaning," she said, "we need to do a little research. You in for a drive, partner?"

This, as she flipped on the turn signal and headed for the on-ramp for the 22 Freeway.

He was thinking, *Like I have a choice?*

He said, "Lead on, Drummer."

10

In the opinion of David Gospel, there was nothing worse than an ungrateful child.

You could put your kid in the best schools, read all the right books, make sure he had the very best of anything and everything. And still he turned rotten, like bad fruit.

The best part? It was all Daddy's fault. You hit him, you didn't hit him. Too lenient, too strict. You didn't spend enough time with little Johnny or maybe you were too controlling. Poor Johnny was overscheduled.

You criticize any tiny thing he does—a story he wrote, or a stick-figure drawing—and you're accused of ruining the poor little shit's self-esteem.

Whatever happened to resilience? Sure, David came from money, but his father had made damn sure his kids couldn't touch a dime until they earned their own fortune. And Jesus, the crap the old man said to him? Nothing was ever good enough, right?

That's how you motivate a man. You let him know he needs to do better. Be better. You push.

You didn't get more if you didn't ask for it.

The day Owen was born, David started his grand plan. His boy—his firstborn son—was going to have a leg up on the poor muttons of this world. Sure as hell, he'd be better off than his father. That's the way it was supposed to go. Each generation helped the next achieve greater success. That's how you built a dynasty.

Thousands of dollars in therapy later, they'd told him he'd raised a monster. There were no more therapy sessions, no more pills. Just something spoiled and depraved.

He'd tried everything, even an exorcism, for Christ's sake—Meredith's idea. Owen was sick and Christ would save him.

It had been both repulsive and beautiful, the exorcism, reminding David of the early years when he'd been active in secret societies—the reenactments in particular. When Owen was old enough, eight or nine, David had even taken him along, still maintaining hope for his ambitions for his son. There'd been a moment during the exorcism ceremony with the priest when Owen had turned to look straight at David, as if remembering their special times together.

He could still hear the strange music of his son's screams and the soft chorus of the priest's murmured prayers during the exorcism. He'd watched as Owen pulled out fistfuls of hair and clawed at his eyes until he'd had to be restrained. The boy had panted for breath like a creature giving birth, and when the final crisis came, he'd arched his back at an impossbile anlge to howl at the ceiling. The sight had been exquisite, so lovely, in fact, that for one instant, the doubts had come: That beauty, the perfection of the moment, could it be an act?

David recalled Meredith, with tears streaming down her face, holding Owen afterward, saying her baby had been saved.

And Owen did seem different. Enough that David had eventually bought in to Meredith's "Jesus Saves!" theory.

Just in case, he'd sent Owen away for missionary work. For five years, Owen helped build schoolhouses in Kenya, taught English in the Amazon jungle and traveled up and down the Ganges. He'd gone to places like Darfur, lawless places where people died of hunger in the street or were shot. Why not give the kid a little perspective? Let him see how the other half lives?

Rocket had been his insurance. And now it was Rocket's job to fix whatever he'd fucked up.

David looked at Meredith seated across the room, her skinny elbows digging into the custom-made Mitchell Gold couch. Meredith had picked out each and every item in the house with an interior decorator. That queer had practically cost David his left nut, he'd been so expensive.

Meredith didn't believe in anything ostentatious—not anymore. She'd give every fucking penny he earned away if she could.

But David didn't see any reason to change just because God apparently saved his kid. He wasn't building his kingdom in some make-believe heaven. With interests throughout Orange County, he'd made damn sure his charitable donations worked for him. Like now, with Condum-Cox. His campaign contributions to the current mayor were about to pay off, big time.

And this house… It was one of thirty-two exclusive homes on Bay Island, right down the street from Roy Rogers and Dale Evans's old place. Not to mention what was once the John Wayne estate. David Gospel could afford the best.

He'd never believed that the-meek-shall-inherit-the-earth crap of his wife's. If David believed in a god, it was himself. He had the power.

At first, it was all about the money. Hell, why not? Money was an easy way to keep score. And he'd enjoyed the gauntlet his father had thrown down to his three sons. Be better….

Only, as it turned out, the money thing hadn't been much of a challenge. David's marriage had given him money to play with. Soon enough, he'd moved into politics. Not as a candidate, no way. Who the hell wanted some asshole looking into his tax returns? He was the puppeteer, pulling the strings behind the screen.

The amazing part? That, too, hadn't taken long to conquer. The whole thing turned into just another rubber-chicken dinner, with some blowhard sucking up the oxygen in the room.

That's when David started his collection.

He'd learned pretty early on he had the power to make and break lives. The people who worked for him owed him their livelihood, and they were fucking grateful for it.

So why stop there? Why limit his goals to the here and now?

There was power to be found beyond what the sheep on this earth coveted. He just had to know who to pay to get it.

He'd started by looking into secret sects—Freemasons, Rosicrucians—and for a while, he'd gotten off on the lure of being one of the chosen, an initiate in a secret society. But theirs was not the kind of enlightenment David sought. Fuck universal peace or cosmic consciousness.

He began looking into more obscure sects, surprised at the number of powerful men willing to put on costumes and parade around, reenacting rituals from ancient Babylon and Egypt.

But then David began to realize it was more than the illusion of supernatural powers that he coveted. He needed something more solid, a physical *object* of power.

He started reading about psychic archeology, a branch of anthropology that used the paranormal to uncover ancient sites of archaeological importance. The more he learned about the discipline, the more David started to think, *What about the artifacts themselves?* Certainly, there must be objects of power that had survived through the ages, buried somewhere for him and his considerable resources to find.

Sure, he'd hit a hiccup or two along the way—Owen being his number one pain in the ass. But it wasn't supposed to be easy. Look at the search for the Holy Grail and the Ark of the Covenant. If it was easy, every sorry ass out there would have what he had.

He looked again at his wife. There she sat, her bony butt swallowed by that sofa. She hadn't moved since he'd told her he'd called Rocket, those bug eyes of hers just staring at him.

Watching her now, he thought about all those nature versus nurture arguments. Maybe the only thing wrong with Owen was a case of bad genes.

He heard the doorbell and Maribel, their housekeeper, answering the door. Meredith turned anxiously toward the entrance, twisting her wedding band round and round on her ring finger.

If Owen looked like his mother, it was as if someone had taken a dim bulb and turned up the wattage. Shit, the kid could have been a model, he was that handsome. Tall, with blue eyes and sandy blond hair. David remembered Meredith having eyes like that once. Now her eyes were a flat, dead blue.

Owen had been born with this condition. His eyes just didn't blink. Something about the muscles of the upper lids being weak. The condition had been mild enough that they'd gotten away with cosmetic surgery when Owen was just five. There'd been a few follow-up surgeries, as well.

Owen had to wear sunglasses all the time, even indoors. And he put drops in his eyes. David thought it gave his eyes a special gleam.

Entering the room, Owen tossed his coat on the settee. He flopped onto the cushions and rested the heels of his Esquivel ankle boots on the armrest. Owen had good taste in clothes, leaning toward the more cutting-edge designers. He had the build for it.

"I bought the most amazing piece of art today." He glanced over at Rocket, who stopped near the door. "I don't think Rocket approves. And Mom will have a seizure if she sees it."

He held his finger up to his lips and winked at his father.

David could feel his stomach turn. The kid looked so fucking normal….

He'd had a couple of drinks earlier, thinking to relax a little, maybe simmer down before Rocket hauled Owen in. It hadn't worked.

Slowly, his son's smile faded. Those pretty blue eyes narrowed, giving Owen the look of someone searching for the nearest exit.

"What's going on?" he asked.

David still had the newspaper on the coffee table, turned to the article about Mimi. With just the slightest tilt of his chin, he pointed out the *Register.*

Owen stared at the headline for a minute, looking almost perplexed. David knew the exact moment his son realized where the conversation was headed.

"You can't think—"

"Don't be an ass, Owen. Of course that's what I think! What else, for Christ's sake!"

Owen jumped to his feet. For an instant, he looked as if he

might actually try to run for it. Instead, he began pacing across the room. He raked his fingers through those platinum highlights. "So every time a body shows up around town, you're going to point the finger at me?"

Rocket made himself scarce, not one to linger in these types of situations.

"I think the connection is a little tighter than that, Owen. Mimi Tran was a psychic in my employ. Just like Michelle—"

"Jesus Christ, are you kidding?" Suddenly, Owen was bent over, laughing. "Another one of your psychics, Pops?"

Owen's expression turned feral as he walked over to David. The younger man placed a hand on each side of the armchair, leaning menacingly over his father.

"Do you know how stupid you sound sometimes? *I have magic objects that make me all-powerful, all-knowing.*" His tone was a solid imitation of David's deeper voice. "You can hire a fleet of psychics and you're never going to be God, old man."

"Don't push me," David warned.

Owen narrowed his eyes, making them look almost colorless in the room's dim lighting. "Who really believes that shit, Daddy dearest? Not anyone with half a brain. But you, *you* travel around the world, buying your *collection.*" He leaned closer, saying in a stage whisper, "You know something, Pops? I think even Rocket knows you're a fucking head case."

David smiled up at his son. He could feel those martinis pumping inside him.

He exploded out of the chair, taking Owen with him. He had him on the ground, pinned by the throat, before the kid even knew what hit him.

"You're calling *me* a head case?" he asked in a cool voice. "You killed Michelle. And now Mimi's dead."

Owen flailed his arms and legs, trying to dislodge him. But David had a good twenty pounds of muscle on his pretty-boy son. He tightened his grip.

"What happened with Michelle was different and you know it!" Owen managed to spit out.

"You slit her throat! You drank her blood!"

"It wasn't like that!"

"I know what you are, Owen!"

Before David could do any more damage, Rocket pulled him off. Meredith knelt down beside Owen, propping up her son. David shoved Rocket away, ready to take another shot, but Meredith held up her hand.

"Stop it, David. You're drunk!"

Her voice, her tone. The world seemed to spin. He remembered Michelle's sweet face—and his son sitting at the spa just outside, licking the blood off his hands.

David had always wondered if he'd done the right thing, covering up for Owen. He'd owed Michelle better. But he'd been afraid.

He walked over to his son, now cradled in his mother's arms. *He's a monster...a freak,* a voice inside David's head whispered. He crouched down and looked into his son's eyes, searching for the truth, believing in his heart he would know somehow if Owen was playing him.

Michelle was different....

Incredibly so, David thought. Unlike Mimi Tran, who'd been in her sixties, Michelle had been only twenty-three. Still, she was a powerful clairvoyant. He'd been seeing her for almost a year before things crossed the line from professional to personal.

That day in the backyard, an eighteen-year-old Owen had confessed everything to David. Glassy-eyed and crying, he'd told his father it had all been a terrible mistake, Michelle's death. They'd been having an affair behind David's back. Only, Michelle had suddenly gotten cold feet. She wanted out...and she'd threatened to tell David.

That's when it happened. He'd pushed her up against the counter. He hadn't seen the wineglass there....

There'd been blood everywhere. She'd severed her carotid artery on the broken glass when he'd pushed her against the counter.

One minute, I was kissing her...sort of forcing her, you know? Because I loved her and couldn't think that she wouldn't want me anymore. Then she started making this gurgling sound in her throat. That's when I saw the blood.

David had made a quick decision then and there. Cover up. Make sure that the police wouldn't trace her death back to Owen, putting Gospel Enterprises on the front page. But he always wondered if he'd done the right thing.

He remembered thinking about those macabre trophies he'd unearthed in the backyard when the kid was only twelve. Despite decomposition, David was pretty sure he'd been looking at animal parts...something small and vulnerable that his son felt a compulsion to kill, maybe even torture.

Now, he studied his boy, once again wondering what he should do.

"Okay," he said softly, almost to himself. He stepped back. "Okay."

He raced up the steps to his office. Once inside, he grabbed the remote. He waited for the mirrored door to open a crack before he sidestepped through. He punched in the code, waited impatiently as the drawer slid open.

He counted again, as if it had been a bad dream. But the stone was still missing. There, on the black velvet where a small blue stone should have nestled, there was nothing but empty space.

He began searching frantically. The stone. It had to be here somewhere. It had just rolled out of sight. The action of the drawer opening and shutting could have dislodged the piece from its velvet depression.

He kept looking, feeling into the corners of the velvet lining. Next, he crept along the floor on his hands and knees.

"Shit!" He sat back against the custom-built cabinets, trying to catch his breath.

It has to be here!

Only it wasn't. And he knew it. He felt it in his gut.

He forced himself to focus through the haze of the alcohol. Meredith was right: he was drunk and out of control.

He'd already called his security guy, Jack. He was the best in the business, telling David long ago that he was being too cocky storing his collection in the house with such minimal security. David knew he'd fucked up, but he was also banking on Jack being good enough to find out what the hell had happened. In the meantime, David needed to think.

He stared up at the drawers filled with his treasures. Each and every object was sacred to him. The thought of taking them somewhere else—someplace where they wouldn't be readily available to him—it was almost too painful.

No. He wouldn't move his collection. Not yet. There was no reason to panic. He'd been careless, that's all. This time, he'd listen to Jack, put in all the bells and whistles. Whatever Jack said he needed to keep his collection safe, he'd have it installed: motion sensors, cameras at every angle.

He felt suddenly reassured. Sure, Mimi was dead; that in itself was a disaster. But why take the next step? Why assume a connection to Owen and Mimi just because his kid fucked up with Michelle?

David pulled out his cell phone, punched in the number he knew by heart, a private number given to very few.

"Sam," he said into the phone. "We need to talk."

11

Seven thought they were through the worst of it once they passed the Orange Crush—the sobriquet given to that special spot in Orange County where five highways converged, including three major freeways, the 5, the 22 and the 57. But no, there'd been a SigAlert on the 60, some jackknifed big rig. It took them over an hour and a half to get to Claremont and the five colleges.

Seven was familiar with the Claremont Colleges, a group of universities that both stood alone and pooled resources. Pomona, Scripps, Harvey Mudd, Pitzer and CMC. His brother had been accepted to Claremont McKenna College way back when it had been named Claremont Men's College. Pomona, too, offered him one of their coveted berths.

Seven remembered how it had been in those days. Ricky was five years older than Seven. Watching him in high school was like watching one of those superheroes on television. His brother was bigger than life. He was a scholar and an athlete—captain of the varsity volleyball team and the debate squad. With Dad's curly blond hair and big green eyes, he was a good-looking kid who didn't have time for girls.

And shit, did he have confidence. As far as Ricky was concerned, nothing was out of reach.

Seven looked like his mother: brown hair, hazel eyes, stocky build. He'd ended up just under six feet tall, so if he'd ever had the discipline for a sport, it wouldn't have been volleyball. He didn't have Ricky's height or dexterity.

Seven's father was a retired mechanic; his mother still worked at the senior center in Huntington Beach. He and Ricky had been raised in a modest middle-class home just a few miles inland from the Bolsa Chica Wetlands, a place where kids could still hike and fish and bird watchers hung out in fatigues with binoculars around their necks and telephoto-lens cameras on tripods. At least until they finally paved the place over and covered it with more million-dollar houses…a debate that had been going on for as long as Seven could remember.

But here was Ricky, dreaming big. He'd graduated near the top of his class at Marina High, earned magna cum laude from Occidental College. Next, he'd tackled medical school.

Seven remembered how proud his dad had been—a doctor in the family. No one like Ricky had ever graced the Bushard family tree. He was every parent's dream.

But even that hadn't been enough for Ricky. He'd wanted the best—a house on the water, a trophy wife and a kid in private school. A yacht he never had time to use.

Seven remembered the day he'd looked at his parents with that perfect smile and asked, "Do you know how many plastic surgeons there are in Newport Beach?"

SoCal. The land of the surgically enhanced.

For his part, Seven rode under the radar, having a hell of a good time smoking a little weed and downing Samuel Adams as his brother toiled. He'd graduated from high school…barely. He'd attended Golden West College, the local two-year community college, what his father referred to as UBL, the university behind Levitz, a furniture store on one of the main drags. Hell, if it weren't for Laurin pushing him, Seven wouldn't have gotten even that far.

His parents, who thought for sure he was landing in jail on a DUI, had been proud when he'd graduated from the police academy—or more likely relieved. Their little misfit was growing up, heading into the real world of responsibility as a cop.

But when his marriage broke up, the comparisons came again. *He just isn't Ricky….*

That's what really blew about the situation. It wasn't just his parents Ricky had failed. *Seven* had been proud of his brother. He had looked up to him. Depended on him.

How does that happen? How does someone you know and love and respect just go fucking psycho on you? The good son—the beloved big brother—turned killer?

"You okay?"

He kept staring out the window, watching the bucolic town of Claremont roll on by. Erika and her damn radar.

"Quick. Hand me a piece of paper," he said, pretending to grab his pen. "I think I'm having a traffic-induced vision. That psychic shit could be catching."

"Like the flu," she said wryly.

Yeah, the trip had been a bitch, giving Seven way too much time to sit in quiet contemplation.

When they finally reached the campus of Pitzer College, Erika parked in front of the administration building. After getting directions, they headed straight for the archaeology department.

"Where did you hear about this guy, anyway?" he asked.

"Lois."

Lois Banks was the guru of the precinct. As the watch commander, she knew just about everything about anything. If Lois said Professor Curtis Murphy was the go-to guy, as far as Seven was concerned, the man was golden.

Walking down the hallway, Seven noticed how all these intellectual types had a thing about their office doors. Cute signs and photographs covered most, or cartoon strips like *The Far Side* and *The Boondocks*. To Seven, the hall looked more like a college dorm than an office building. Maybe the professors thought the artwork made them hip, one with the student body.

But Murphy was different. His door remained pristine, bare of anything but his nameplate and office number. Interestingly enough, the look was that much more intimidating. Here was a man who didn't conform—or just maybe didn't give a rat's ass one way or the other.

Erika had said Professor Murphy was expecting them. But the

closed door didn't look too inviting. She knocked. Seven heard what sounded like a muffled curse coming from inside.

After a minute, Erika knocked again, louder this time.

"Come in!"

Erika looked at Seven and shrugged. She opened the door, leading the way inside.

Stepping into Murphy's office was like walking into another world. Forget the clean lines of the door; inside was chaos. There was a long table filled with pottery shards and other objects covered in dirt. *Shit, was that a finger bone?* Shelves crammed with books, some stuffed in sideways, looked ready to blow like popcorn in a Jiffy Pop tray. Glancing at the equipment on the table, Seven couldn't decide if the guy was getting some painting done or about to conduct major surgery.

In the corner behind his desk, Murphy sat bent over an Apple notebook. One thing was certain: Indiana Jones, he was not.

Seven could see by his waistline Murphy liked his chow. Short, with a hairline that was already beginning to say, "See you later," he looked to be in his mid- to late fifties, and very scholarly. Glasses, pipe on the desk, jacket with leather patches on the elbows hanging from the coat rack, the whole shtick. Using only two fingers, the professor kept banging away on the laptop, ignoring the fact that the detectives stood at the ready.

Erika looked over at Seven. He knew what she was thinking. The guy could be on the verge of a moment of sheer brilliance—something on the order of deciphering the Rosetta Stone.

On the other hand...

"Professor Murphy?" Seven did the mandatory flash of the badge. "My name is Detective Bushard. My partner, Detective Cabral, and I are here from the Westminster Police Department. It concerns a homicide."

He could have been talking about a new hairstyle for Malibu Barbie for all the attention the guy gave him.

After another glance at his partner, Seven stepped forward and slapped his badge on the desk with a nice loud whack!

Murphy stopped what he was doing, looking startled. He

stared up at Seven as if seeing him there for the first time. "I'm terribly sorry. I was in the zone."

Looking at the guy, Seven realized he was a good ten years younger than he'd first assumed. The glasses and the receding hairline didn't help, nor did the paunch. Apparently, the professor wasn't the fieldwork type. Still, looks could be deceiving. According to what Erika said on the ride over, the Professor was tops in his field. How that was supposed to help with the Tran murder was still a mystery to Seven.

"No problem." He gave the man a smile. "But we're on a bit of a time crunch. It concerns the death of Mimi Tran—"

"Of course, of course." Murphy pushed himself away from his computer and stood. He held his hand out, suddenly Mr. Amicable, giving both Seven and Erika a hardy shake. "The Vietnamese fortune-teller. I read about the murder in the papers. But how can I help you, Detectives? I understand this is a contemporary death." He gestured over to the pots and bones on the table. "My bodies are usually hundreds, possibly thousands, of years old. Not to mention the fact that my forensic work is a bit shoddy. Not my area, really."

Erika showed him the photograph of the bead. "But this might be?"

The professor's eyes lit up like a Vegas slot machine. He practically ripped it out of Erika's hand. He took his time examining it, at one point fumbling through his desk drawer to retrieve a magnifying glass for a better look.

"Where did you find this?"

It was almost an accusation.

"I'm sorry, Professor," Erika said, "but that's confidential. Part of the ongoing murder investigation." She moved in, working her magic. Not many men, whatever their age or sexual preference, could pass up her smile.

"But judging from your reaction?" She tapped the photograph. "I'd say we came to the right place to ask about this little item."

Murphy looked up from his magnifying glass. "If it's what I

think it is, this would be a formidable find. Do you actually have the artifact?"

She sat down in front of the desk, crossing her legs, getting comfortable. Seven did the same.

"We have the object in the photograph, yes."

"The stone changes color." Murphy remained standing, a sudden urgency in his voice. "Red to blue, blue to red. Nothing gradual. No murky shift into green. Just like, *pow*, it's a different stone."

Seven glanced at Erika. "So you do recognize the piece?"

"Oh, yes." The professor couldn't have looked more pleased. "Well, this is interesting." He shook his head, almost as if he couldn't believe his good fortune. "The sacred object this came from is the stuff of legends." He nodded, almost to himself. "You have, indeed, come to the right place, Detectives. Things that aren't supposed to exist are a bit of a specialty of mine."

"We're all ears," Seven said.

Murphy sat down behind his desk. "Ever heard of Agamemnon's Mask? It was found by Heinrich Schliemann, a renowned archaeologist with a special interest in Homeric Troy. He made several key finds, including Mycenae and Troy," the professor said, not waiting for an answer. "Greece," he added, in case that needed clarification. "He found the mask in 1876."

"I've read about it," Erika said, surprising Seven. "It was supposed to be the burial mask of the great Greek king Agamemnon. Only it turned out to be a fake."

"Not a fake, no…although it is not Agamemnon's burial mask, as Schliemann claimed." Murphy propped his fingertips together, the image of a professor ready to lecture. "Of course, questions have been raised about its authenticity. But most in the field consider it to be a legitimate find, most likely from an older tomb. Circa 1500 B.C. While Schliemann has been accused of profound dishonesty in his archaeological reporting, no one has ever proved that he manufactured a fake or tampered with an authentic find."

Murphy pushed against his desk with his feet, causing his chair to roll across the wood floor to the bookshelf behind him. Despite what looked like complete disorder, he grabbed one volume from the jumble like a magician pulling a rabbit out of a hat.

"Schliemann popularized archaeology, bringing in gobs of money. His critics, of course, suggest at too high a price. Great treasures were spirited away by the aristocracy of foreign powers to display in their gardens and museums. The Greek government is still at odds with Great Britain over the Elgin Marbles, pieces taken from the Acropolis."

He rolled the chair back to his desk and dropped the book in front of Erika and Seven. It was *The Iliad*.

"Homer writes about a rocky place called Pytho. It's the name given Delphi in ancient times. There you can still see the rock where the Sibyl, the prophetess of Gaia, interpreted the rumblings of Mother Earth. Apparently, the area was prone to volcanic activity."

"Gaia?" Erika asked. This with a sharp look to Seven.

Seven nodded, getting a sick feeling in his gut, watching the coincidences piling on thick.

"What exactly is *this?*" She again tapped on the photograph of the bead.

"See the distinctive design inside the stone itself? Like a eye? The artifact in the photograph dates back to the time of Gaia and her Sibyl, and is inseparable from Homer's Mycenae," he said, picking up *The Iliad,* and waving it like a prop. "Mycenae is a city shrouded in myth and legend. It was the center of power during the Archaic period. According to tradition, it was founded by Perseus, the very hero who killed the Gorgon, Medusa. A Cyclops presumably built the city walls. Like most Greek history, the story of Mycenae is a cocktail of fact and fiction."

"Difficult to tell when myth takes over?" Erika suggested.

"Exactly. Homer tells us of Agamemnon, king of Mycenae, hero of the Trojan War. According to myth, Agamemnon insulted the goddess Artemis, sister of Apollo, by killing one of her sacred animals. Not only plague ensued, but a disastrous lack of wind kept his army from setting sail for Troy. He later sacrificed his own daughter, Iphigenia, to appease the goddess, who then allowed him to avenge beautiful Helen's abduction."

"Nice guy," Seven said.

"Don't worry. He got his just desserts. He was killed by his wife, Clytemnestra, in his bath. Revenge for sacrificing their daughter and for taking as his mistress Cassandra, the Trojan princess and prophetess he enslaved. Although some say the curse that followed Agamemnon stemmed back to his father's crimes. Fearing his own brother's bid for the throne," Murphy continued, "he killed his brother's children and served them to the poor man for dinner."

"Jesus, those Greeks," Seven said, earning a kick from Erika under the table.

"One of the reasons the authenticity of Schliemann's find was called into question was the discovery of the Beehive Tomb, what was believed to be Agamemnon and his father's true burial chamber. His death mask would have been found there. The tomb itself is a fantastic piece of artistry. Shaped like a beehive, it was buried under the earth, a style originating from the Mycenae shaft tombs—although there is certainly a heavy influence from the Minoan tombs of Crete. Unfortunately, Agamemnon's true burial chamber was found looted by grave robbers, probably in ancient times. This—" he raised the photograph "—would have been part of that treasure."

"You said it was part of a larger piece?" Erika asked. "Something worth killing for?"

The professor suddenly fell silent, looking uneasy.

"Professor?"

"I can't say for certain—I can only postulate without examining the actual piece."

Erika knew exactly where he was going. "Perhaps that could be arranged. At our offices, of course, under strict supervision."

Murphy seemed to think about it, weighing his options. "Everything I know about this particular artifact was postulated by Professor Estelle Fegaris of Harvard, one of archaeology's more colorful characters. Estelle herself was a bit of a Cassandra."

"Meaning she was a psychic?" Erika asked.

"Goodness, yes. Her family claimed to trace its ancestry back to the original Sibyls of Gaia. She made some amazing finds, bringing tons of attention and money to the program at Harvard…until she revealed her involvement in psychic archaeology."

"Psychic archaeology?" Seven asked.

"It's quite an interesting field, actually. Not as 'out there' as you might expect," Murphy explained. "There's a pretty famous case, the Glastonbury Abbey. Frederick Bligh Bond, an architect, was hired by the Church of England to find the remains of the chapel in the early 1900s. The Church, of course, didn't know that Bond was an occultist. He sought out the services of a friend, an automatic writer—a psychic writing while in an altered state of consciousness. Through his friend, Bond petitioned spirits associated with the Abbey to help him find the chapel ruins. During the excavation, Bond found everything exactly as the spirits had foretold."

"Weird," Seven said.

"Fascinating, actually. In many ways, archaeology is a field that requires intuition. People like Bond and Estelle Fegaris just take it to another level. But it was her connection to Dr. Morgan Tyrell and his research in parapsychology that finally did her in at Harvard."

"Who's Tyrell?" Seven asked.

"Dr. Morgan Tyrell, a maverick in the field of parapsychology. He studies psychic ability and its effect on the brain. Of course, he's since left the university as well, ousted for his controversial methodology…as well as his love for the ladies, some rumored to be students. Very frowned upon by the Trustees."

"Imagine that," Erika said.

"Not that it hurt Morgan. He set up his own institute, privately funded. The Institute for Dynamic Studies of Parapsychology and the Brain in San Diego."

"So how is Estelle Fegaris connected to the artifact?" Seven asked.

"It was basically her life's goal to find the necklace called the Eye of Athena. This bead would have been part of that necklace," Murphy said.

Thinking they might be able to go to the horse's mouth, Seven asked, "How can we get ahold of Fegaris?"

"You can't. She died some years ago, unfortunately. Killed, presumably, by the very underworld figures she dealt with in order to find the lost treasures of the Beehive Tomb. Although no one was ever prosecuted, there was some suspicion surrounding a student. He was subsequently cleared of all wrongdoing and sent home by the Greek authorities."

"So tell us about this necklace," Erika said. "This Eye of Athena?"

"According to Estelle, it was a necklace worn by Athena herself—an amazing object of power that was first used by the Sybil, then later, by the Oracle at Delphi. Somehow, it found its way into Agamemnon's hands."

"What kind of power are we talking about here, Professor?" Erika asked.

He looked at them both as if he was talking to someone slow-witted.

"Why, the power to tell the future, of course."

"We found it in a parrot's beak," Erika said. "The bird was decapitated and stuffed in the victim's mouth. Does that mean something to you?"

Murphy shook his head. "Nothing at all."

The first short answer of the day, Seven thought.

"Thank you for your time, Professor." Erika stood and handed Murphy her card. "One of us will call to talk about the possibility of a physical inspection of the artifact."

"May I keep this?" he asked, holding the photograph of the bead. Erika paused a moment. "Of course."

"I look forward to your call, Detective."

Once outside the office, Erika and Seven walked briskly back to the car. It wasn't until they were both inside, that Erika asked, "What do you think?"

"A dead Vietnamese psychic and now tomb raiders?" He dropped his head back against the headrest. "The whole thing gives me a headache."

Erika put the car into Reverse and backed out of the parking slot. "And here I thought things were just getting interesting."

Back in his office, Professor Murphy flipped open his copy of *The Iliad* and slipped out a folded sheet of paper. He smiled, seeing that his hands actually shook.

"Jesus," he whispered, trying to catch his breath.

The paper was old enough that the edges had yellowed. How many years had it been since he'd even looked at this?

He picked up the phone, dialing the number on the sheet of paper. He had never really thought he'd have an opportunity to call this number.

His pulse revved up the instant he heard the woman's voice on the other end.

"I may have something for you," he said.

12

Terrence McGee stared at the tall blonde standing at his office door. To be precise, she wasn't standing at his door, or even in his office, for that matter. Terrence didn't have an office or a door. He had a cubical. Still, being the head honcho of the ragtag team of ten that made up the National Institute for Strategic Artifacts, NISA, Terrence had a rather nice cubical.

NISA had a distinguished history—something along the lines of Roswell and Area 51. It was an offshoot of the famed STAR-GATE program, the collective name given to a group of intelligence programs initiated when the military perceived a possible "psy-gap" with the Soviet Union. Most of the research involved intelligence gathering through remote viewing, the ability to train psychics to observe or control events from great distances.

A lot of people pooh-poohed STARGATE as one of those paranoid military programs, but Terrence, an intelligence officer with the National Security Agency at the time, had been part of an oversight committee. He'd seen firsthand the results of one remote viewer by the code name 009. The things he'd witnessed still haunted him, making him wonder if there wasn't this whole other dimension. Could psychic powers be something akin to when quantum physics first came on the scene, with its study of subatomic particles? It was there all along, we just didn't know it?

The FBI guys liked to joke that NISA was their *X-Files*, the agency's purpose—to find artifacts of global importance—merely a cover for their true mandate: discover legendary objects

of power that could have possible military significance. Th
NISA officers were buried in a basement of a nondescript fed
eral building in D.C., understaffed and underfunded. Unfortu
nately, in an era of international terrorism, artifacts that might o
might not exist got the short end of the stick when it came to na
tional security issues.

The young lady waiting at the entrance was Carin Barne
Built like a pole-vaulter, Carin stood just over six feet. She'd bee
part of the NISA team for more than a year now. Terrence fig
ured she was in his office maybe twice a week with a new "find.
At the moment, dressed in a black pullover and jeans, she wa
bouncing up and down on her toes in what looked like black ba
let flats, her body language saying it all.

Another find....

Terrence didn't discourage her. Quite the opposite. Enthu
siasm was a gift down here in the rabbit hole.

The problem was it never lasted. Typically, it took a mere te
to fifteen months before a new recruit gave in to total apathy o
transferred out to something that actually mattered. The Hol
Grail, the Spear of Destiny, the Ark of the Covenant—thes
things weren't exactly falling out of the sky. And then there wer
the poor schmoes who got demoted into Terrence's able hands
NISA being a kind of FBI purgatory.

In a way, Terrence himself had been sentenced here. A well
spoken black man with a degree in linguistics, he should hav
gone far within the military hierarchy—if only he'd been will
ing to play the game.

Terrence used to be a vital part of the NSA, the National Se
curity Agency. Like many young black men, he'd entered th
military thinking to pay for his education. He'd grown up i
Oakland, California, and found solace in the local library. He'
tested high enough that the military paid to put him through th
prestigious Monterey Institute. Fluent in five languages, he'
been a rising star.

But as is often the case, the faster you rise, the bigger the tar
get. When he ended up running afoul of a top bureaucrat, he wen

from a corner office with a window to the basement in a nonde-script building. It wasn't a demotion per se. Terrence was top dog at NISA. But unlike his position at the National Security Agency, there was no possibility of promotion. From here, the next step was retirement.

The curious part about his current situation was how much happier he was locked away in his basement cubical. He recalled toasting his aborted career with a bottle of Springbank single malt when his wife had pried him out of his funk with a few choice words. Even now, he smiled, remembering he was married to a saint of a woman who had the impossible gift of looking at the glass as always half-full.

Whenever he pointed out this cliché in her personality, she would only smile and say, "Some people are just born with the happy gene, Terry. Luckily, I gave mine to Kelly."

Their daughter, Kelly. Now a budding assistant professor of math at NYU.

"You never know, Terry," she'd said with a quick kiss. "This could be your dream job. No one to tell you what to do…?"

Which was the point. He'd never been very good at taking or-ders, despite his military background. It's what got him that basement cubicle in the first place.

And now, with more white than black in his closely cropped hair, he was beginning to wonder if he hadn't become a bit complacent.

Unlike Carin. He had to give the woman credit. At eighteen months and still going strong, she was a true holdout to the nor-mal apathy that accompanied a job of searching for things that might not exist.

Right now, her face literally lit up with excitement, her blue eyes shining as she held up a file folder.

"I found something," she said.

Of course you did, Terrence thought.

But he put on his reading glasses and motioned her into his roomy cubical. He held out his hand for the folder.

And for the first time since he'd committed himself to this

basement office—well, cubical—Terrence McGee found himself caught off guard.

He flipped through the pages, reading quickly. "Where did you get this?"

Carin sat down at the chair beside his desk. Immediately, her legs started pumping up and down like pistons. "A source. In California."

Carin was thirty-five, brilliant and unmarried. She had a doctorate in neurobiology from Caltech and was completely dedicated to her work here at NISA.

Her work *and* her younger brother. She had an autistic brother named Markie fifteen years her junior. She'd been caring for him ever since her parents had died in a car accident seven years ago.

"This," she said, tapping the file, "is an extremely reliable source."

Terrence allowed himself a small smile. She was practically hyperventilating.

"The Eye of Athena," she said, with something approaching reverence in her voice.

It had been years since he'd even heard the name. Not since the death of Estelle Fegaris.

Not many people knew of the artifact's existence. Some even said it was a figment of Estelle's imagination. She claimed to be a descendant of the Sybil at Delphi, a title belonging to one of many a prophetess who reportedly received her powers from Gaia, the goddess of the earth and the mother of Cronus and the Titans. The Eye of Athena was a necklace presumably worn by the Sybil and later by the Oracle at Delphi. According to Fegaris, the Eye magnified the powers of the prophetess who wore it, somewhat like a lens magnifies an image. Fegaris spoke of the piece as if it were a family heirloom.

Fegaris had always been a controversial figure in her field, psychic archaeology. She tended to be a little too successful in discovering archaeological finds of great significance. When it became public knowledge that Fegaris herself claimed to have psychic abilities—powers she used in her work—her very credibility came under fire, psychic archaeology not exactly being in the mainstream. And then there was her partnership with Morgan Tyrell, the famed parapsychologist. Eventually, the top names in the field proclaimed her a fraud.

Terrence knew better.

Eventually, Fegaris had been marginalized by her contemporaries, but by then she had her own following. They called themselves Lunites, a reference to the Greek word *feggari,* meaning moon. Carin Barnes had been one of the group's most fervent members.

He knew in his heart the Eye was Carin's raison d'être here at NISA. With the death of Fegaris, she needed their resources. Still, it wasn't as if he could afford to turn down someone with her qualifications, even if she was a closet fanatic. And God bless her, looking over the file, he realized she just might have an honest-to-God lead.

At the back of the file was a fax of a photograph. Not very good quality, he thought, squinting past his reading glasses. He took off the glasses and gave them a dirty look as he placed them on his desk. He hated getting old.

"All right," he said, leaning back in the chair. "What's the story?"

This was what Terrence always asked his people. He liked open-ended questions. In his organization, Carin was a "finder." He wanted the finder to guide the discussion.

Theirs was far from an exact science. In point of fact, it wasn't science at all…even if most of the people who ended up in his basement cubicles had an alphabet of degrees behind their names.

"It's a bead from the necklace," Carin said, pitched forward on her chair. "It has to be the Eye, Terrence. I can feel it in my gut. And here's the punch line. They found it at a murder scene."

Carin's blue eyes met his, her rare smile practically the "ta-da!" before lifting the veil to show her prize.

"The murder victim, Terrence. She was a psychic."

From years of practice, he kept his expression neutral. Just lifted his hands as if to say, *So what?*

"You're kidding," she said, visibly deflated by his lack of reaction.

"From what the file says, Carin, your source hasn't even examined the piece."

"Look at the photograph," she said, jabbing her finger at it. "The distinctive cat's-eye line down the center. The detectives from homicide even said it changed color, just like that." She snapped her fingers. "Blue to red."

"And?" he asked, holding up the page.

"Come *on*," she said.

He could see that Carin didn't like to be challenged. She'd been an acolyte of Fegaris for too many years—one of those trowel-carrying neophytes willing to work for grub and a tent over her head just to be part of the expedition. Still, up until today, he couldn't fault Carin's work. She hadn't made the Eye her focus at NISA. Quite the opposite. Besides, he couldn't deny that one of the reasons he'd wanted her on board in the first place was the well-thought-out presentation she'd made about the existence of the artifact.

Shuffling back to the grainy faxed photograph, Terrance had to admit he could feel a hitch in his pulse.

He handed the file to Carin, meeting her gray-blue eyes. In many ways, she reminded him so much of himself. She was the kind of agent who went with her gut…and wasn't often wrong.

"So what do you propose to do?" he asked.

"I want to go back there. To California. I want to see the stone firsthand."

Terrence tried to imagine what it would be like to let Carin loose on the local authorities, flashing her badge and talking the talk. But then again, why not? She'd worked harder than most. It might be nice to give her a taste of fieldwork before she started growing moss.

Terrence asked, "Are you free for lunch?"

"Of course," she said, doing a poor job of hiding her surprise.

He stood, getting his coat. Time to give Carin an education on the importance of subtlety—not the woman's forte.

He smiled. "I'm okay with any kind of food. Just as long as the place has good coffee. We're going to needs lots of coffee."

13

Seven wasn't much of a drinker, not anymore. He figured he'd done enough partying as a teenager. His liver could use the break. These days, he indulged in the occasional beer. But he'd seen too many cops use alcohol like a tranquilizer, trying to wind down from a job that never let you forget.

Tonight was different.

By the time he and Erika made it back to the station, they had just enough time to arrange for Professor Murphy to examine the artifact the next day. After an hour of comparing notes, Erika had taken one look at Seven and come around the desk to close the file in front of him.

"Whatever is sitting on that desk," she told him, "trust me, it can wait till morning." She handed him his jacket. "Tonight, you're partying with me, cowboy."

The office had cleared out a good hour earlier. Only he and Erika had stayed behind to go over their notes on the Tran case. They were coming up on nine o'clock, and Seven thought Erika had a point. The words were beginning to blur.

They'd ended up at Erika's favorite bar, the House of Brews. It was an upscale sports bar: pool tables, jukebox and big-screen televisions within viewing range of every corner. The fireplace and couch were a homey touch. So were the paintings. Huge canvases of beautiful women staring soulfully at the diners, all done by the artist Noah.

Seven and Erika settled into one of the booths at the back. He passed on his usual beer, going straight to a martini. Kettle One, dirty, two olives.

He said after a while, "You were right."

"About so many things," Erika said, putting down her cosmopolitan. "But what exactly are we talking about?"

Erika had been on a cosmo kick ever since someone had given her the box set of *Sex and the City*. Seven thought it was kind of cute, the frou-frou drink thing. He didn't often see the girlie side of his partner.

"You're right about Beth," he said. "And Nick. I'm not helping them."

Erika stared ahead, as if she was thinking carefully about how to respond. Seven gave it a minute, eating one of the olives.

On the big screen above the bar, the Angels were playing the New York Yankees. They were still called the L.A. Angels of Anaheim—the result of some lame lawsuit. Like they couldn't figure out where the hell they were from? Last time Seven checked, home games were played right up the road in *Anaheim*. Whatever.

The place was packed, almost everyone rooting for the Angels. They were ahead by five runs, but it was still early, only the top of the fourth.

"Wow," she finally said. She shook her head and picked up her cosmo. She pretended to drain the glass.

"Wow?" he asked. "That's it? That's all you got?" He glanced up at the big screen. "Lately, you've practically run your own advice column on me and Beth."

She put down her drink and turned to give Seven her full attention. She was a beautiful woman. He tried to forget that sometimes. Tried to think of her only as his partner, the person who watched his back. But the fact was he remembered every inch of those curves. Even how her hair felt sliding between his fingers.

He hadn't slept with another woman since that night six months ago. Erika was right; he'd been raised Catholic. He knew about penance.

She shook her head. "You're really asking for my advice?"

He made a show of looking around the booth. "You see any-body else sitting here?"

She smiled. Never a good thing, that smile. He braced himself.

"Okay," she said. "Your darling Beth is using you. And here's the sick part—you know it and you're still falling in, toeing the line. Now, I'm of the opinion that a bit of that is okay. The whole leaning on the brother-in-law thing, why not? Hell, in some cultures, when a woman is widowed, the brother-in-law steps in and becomes her husband."

"For God's sake, Erika—"

"Hey," she said, holding up a hand to silence him, "you asked."

He stuffed the last olive in his mouth and chewed.

"You both love Ricky," she said. "So you help each other through the crisis. Except, it's run its course, right? Time to cut the cord…or tie it up tight." She leaned over the table, meeting his gaze. "Which do you want, Seven?"

He sat up straight. "You are way off."

She gave a tired sigh. "That's just denial talking."

He didn't mean to put the glass down with so much force, spilling half the martini. "She's my fucking sister-in-law, okay?"

Erika toasted him with the cosmo. "Excellent choice of words."

He forced himself to just shut up, let the anger drift away. "I'm only going to say this once, so I will be *very* clear. I do *not* want to sleep with Beth."

"Yeah? Well, you didn't plan on getting into my pants, either, now did you, cowboy?"

He raised his martini in a mock toast. "And what a great idea that turned out to be."

She put down the glass and gave him a mischievous smile. "Oh, I don't know. At least we got it out of our systems."

He shook his head, but he couldn't help cracking a smile right back at her. "You are a piece of work, Erika."

"Some might say a masterpiece."

"A cheeky masterpiece."

She made a face. "Who uses words like *cheeky* anymore?"

"Who calls anybody *cowboy?*"

"You're right," she said. "Asshole. So much better. I'll remember that for next time."

He finished the martini, acting as if she was full of shit. But he liked her honesty. And he thought maybe it was time for him to give some of it back.

"Did I ever say I was sorry?" he asked quietly.

She laughed. "Oops. Was I supposed to be the brokenhearted girl over the whole thing?" She rolled her eyes. "It was just sex, okay? And between you and me?" She leaned forward to say in a stage whisper, "You're kind of the girlie one in the partnership."

He smiled. "Maybe you're right. Because, lady, do you have a pair on you."

Suddenly, they both busted up laughing.

She reached over and gave his hand a squeeze. "I'm just saying to be careful with Beth, okay?"

He nodded. "I guess there's a part of me that likes it. Taking care of things. Being the good son. All those years, it was always Ricky." He met her gaze. "Maybe it's my turn, you know?"

Because they were all depending on him. He came from law enforcement. It had been up to him to navigate the system before it swallowed his brother whole. On advice of counsel, Ricky pleaded out. They'd given him fifteen to life. And Seven was there to make sure he'd been treated okay.

Right then, Jeter hit a home run for the Yankees, sending the place into chaos. He could barely hear his cell phone when it went off with that special ring.

"So, cowboy—I mean, *asshole,*" Erika said, nodding to his phone, "what are you going to do?"

He waited, thinking about making a joke, that maybe he liked *asshole* better, after all. But he kept hearing his phone ring, thinking instead that Erika was right, it was more than time for him to let Beth stand on her own two feet.

"Shit," he said under his breath, picking up. Into the cell phone, he said, "I'll be there in fifteen minutes, Beth."

He stood and dropped a twenty on the table, avoiding Erika's eyes. "Drinks are on me, okay?"

She grabbed his hand before he could take off, giving him some final words of advice.

"Denial. It's a powerful emotion." And when he didn't respond, she gave his hand a squeeze and told him, "Take a cab. I'll sober up here."

She watched him leave. It broke her heart to see him like this. Damn Beth. Damn Ricky and the whole Bushard clan.

They'd done a number on Seven, that was for sure. And God knows Erika knew what families could do to a person.

She sipped her drink, thinking about how close they'd come to really talking about that night. The fact was, she'd been more girlie about the whole thing than she ever let on.

Seven was a peach. Dreamy hazel eyes, thick chestnut curls and a smile that could knock you down from ten feet away. And those shoulders—she could still remember the thrill of holding him in her arms, naked. She'd have to be dead not to find him attractive. Then there was the whole my-life-is-in-your-hands thing between partners. Those were powerful emotions.

But what she needed was just that, a partner, not a lover. Not many guys had enough self-confidence to treat her as an equal. They just saw a pair of tits and a nice ass. But not Seven. Shit, he even let her drive.

Besides, she'd never in her life had a decent relationship with a man. She wasn't about to screw up what she had going with Seven. Not for sex.

Suddenly, another drink magically appeared next to the one she'd almost finished. The waitress pointed out the guy sitting at the bar. He was tall, worked out. Nice, thick dark hair. Just her type.

He gave a short wave and flashed a sexy grin.

It happened all the time. Her mother used to say to her, *Chiquita, eres muy sata.*

Hot stuff.

Of course, she hated it. Hated that, no matter where she was or what she was doing, some guy would come on to her.

Hated that maybe she wanted just that.

For an instant, she thought of Seven listening to the ringer on his phone, trying his hardest not to pick up. Giving in.

They weren't so different, she and her partner. They both had baggage they weren't ready to face.

She finished her drink and picked up the other. She walked over to the guy at the bar and sat down.

She thought he had nice eyes.

"The name's Adam," he said, holding out his hand.

Shaking it, she said, "Suzy."

She never gave her real name. She wanted it to be anonymous. She was a homicide detective. She didn't think it was the city's business what she did on her own time. And sometimes guys had weird ideas about screwing a cop.

Like she'd told Seven, it was just sex.

"Hello, Suzy."

He gave her the up and down, letting her know where they were going with this.

"So, Adam. What do you do for a living?" she asked, lifting the drink and giving a playful smile.

Denial, it was a powerful emotion.

14

Net High was a swanky über-club and restaurant owned by Sam Vi. The place had opened just last year, Little Saigon's answer to the growing crowd of OC socialites salivating over "on-the-list" establishments.

Unlike other clubs, the lounge-cum-cyber café wasn't tucked away between a nail salon and a video store in one of the dozens of strip malls canvassing the area. The Net High was a stand-alone building designed to look like a Buddhist temple, a massive concrete structure complete with red plaster pillars and three imposing pagoda-style tile roofs.

In David Gospel's opinion, you shouldn't mix your five-star cuisine with a boba bar and karaoke. The place was overdone: Asia on steroids. Sam even had those ridiculous revolving spotlights, usually reserved for a Hollywood premier, lighting up the night sky like the fucking bat signal in Gotham.

Sam, who owned a string of cyber cafés, considered the Net High his crowning jewel. He even had a back entrance for his celebrity clientele, whoever the hell that could be.

David hiked up the steps with Velvet on his arm. Tonight, she'd pulled back her hair in a classic French twist, looking elegant and refined in a little black Donna Karan dress he'd bought for her. They stepped past an enormous statue of Happy Buddha incongruously set before a trio of bent palms, the trunks lit up like Christmas with fiber-optic lighting.

The club reminded David of Sam—overreaching. The place

didn't know what it wanted to be, so it went for broke: cyber café, restaurant, boba bar and dance club. Hell, they served soursop martinis and bragged of a clear acrylic dance floor over a river of live koi. The Net High was a playpen for some uppity young asshole with too much power and money—Sam to a T.

There were more than twenty cyber cafés in Little Saigon. Forget video arcades or students checking e-mail over a latte. This was the new Wild West. Here, computers allowed high-speed connection to a cyber world where "shooters" chased one another, gun in hand, ready to blow each other's heads off.

There was plenty of muscle and city ordinances to deal with the overload of testosterone. Shit, you practically had to give a urine sample to log on. Still, the regulations didn't stop young men with twitchy thumbs. The main "saloon" of the Net High was exclusively designed for gaming.

As the block of muscle euphemistically called a host led David and Velvet toward the back stairs, David glanced over to see a member of the Black Dragons—a local Vietnamese gang—empty the clip of his keyboard machine gun into his human target on the flat screen. Next to him, a Wally Girl, wearing low-rider jeans and a wifebeater shirt, a tattoo of a butterfly on her shoulder blade, watched while drinking a neon-pink boba tea. Through the drink's fat straw, she sucked up one of the soft tapioca balls that sat at the bottom of the milky tea and chewed on the gelatinous ball in boredom.

That was something else Sam had a piece of here, the gangs. He had started in a gang himself, but it hadn't taken long for the kid to get into the home invasion racket. If they lived, the victims were so traumatized, they seldom contacted the police. By his twenties, Sam moved on to auto theft and extortion. He had a big piece of the local "security" in this town.

Next came drugs and prostitution, working with the Wo Hop To Triad, the equivalent of the Chinese mafia in San Francisco and L.A. David suspected that the Net High was a cover for some serious money laundering.

Only these days, Sam Vi was cleaning up his act, going legit. He needed to shed his black sheep image—he dreamed of making himself a brand-new man. All in the name of love.

Sam Vi had recently announced his engagement to Trudy Hershberg, the newspaper heiress. He'd given her a rare blue diamond for a ring. Reports differed on how many carats, but sure as shit, the thing was worth a damn fortune.

Not that David blamed the kid. Trudy H., as she was known in the tabloids, was sex on a stick. In David's opinion, she was also way out of Sam's league. Tall and willowy, with red hair that might actually be natural, she had a family name that could launch a thousand reality shows à la Paris Hilton, if that's what she wanted.

The thing was, Trudy H. was a celebutante and Sam Vi was a thug. David didn't give him good odds. No way that family was opening the door to the likes of Sam.

Then again, Sam could be Trudy's *F.U.* to Mommy and Daddy. For all David knew, Sam might be producing her movie, or record deal, or maybe supplying her with some nice blow. David didn't give a shit what was in it for Trudy H.

But in Sam's case, it walked and quacked like love. God knows Sam had a good thing going with the triad. And now he was willing to throw it all away for some skinny-assed white chick? David wished him luck.

David knew he was part of Sam's plan to make himself over for Trudy H. Along with several questionable holdings, Sam now had his own construction company. Recently, there'd been a lot of talk about sinking some real money into Little Saigon, the four-block radius at its heart being part of an ambitious growth project courtesy of the town's "pro-development" mayor, Ruth Condum-Cox. If Gospel Enterprises bowed out of the project in favor of a local entrepreneur, that being Sam Vi, David could come in through the back door as a subcontractor. It could be a win-win for everyone.

Only now he had the Mimi Tran case to deal with. Ruth was a personal friend and a past business partner, but even David's leverage had limits. If he needed his hard-won collateral with the mayor to save his ass on the Tran situtation, then Sam and his dreams of becoming Little Saigon's construction baron be damned. David had already arranged a lunch meeting with Ruth, a preemptive strike before the shit hit the fan on the Tran case.

It was Mimi Tran who had brought David to Sam Vi. At first, David had had real hopes that Sam could deliver on some impressive promises. Sam bragged about connections to the illegal antiquities trade back home, something to do with the successive Chinese dynasties that ruled Vietnam, and relics hidden there. David bit, hook, line and sinker. The Eye of Athena wasn't the only artifact mentioned in the thirteenth tablet. Not by a long shot. David had long ago traced his next step to Vietnam and the community here in Little Saigon.

Unfortunately, David had seen squat from Sam. And now with Mimi dead, he was beginning to wonder if he ever would. The fact was, the only useful thing that little shit had ever done for David was introduce him to Velvet.

David and Velvet were led to a corner booth in the Karaoke Kingdom, one of two private upstairs rooms—the other being a very hush-hush VIP lounge over the Lotus Blossom, Sam's French-Vietnamese fusion restaurant. The Karaoke Kingdom was off-limits to regular patrons, tucked away from the ruckus of online gaming and DJs mixing hip-hop.

The room was a sophisticated blend of Chinese and French colonial decor. Red paper shades covered chandeliers for decadent lighting. Rich upholstered furnishings circled tiny glass tables about the size of a Frisbee. Woven floor coverings and acoustical tiles further dampened the noise level. There was an impressive collection of contemporary Vietnamese art on the walls representing a dreamlike world of women painted in soft lines, the images almost poetic.

On a small stage at the back, Sam Vi was singing Sinatra's "My Way" in a raucous, off-key voice. There was nothing subtle or poetic about the punk. He was dressed in an Ozwald Boateng suit, à la Jaime Fox in his Oscar moment. At almost six feet,

Sam actually pulled off the damn outfit, looking fit for the pages of *GQ* with his slicked-back hair. You could probably peel a papaya on that jaw.

Wailing into the mike, Sam was surrounded by three Asian beauties in barely there black dresses and superhigh heels—Trudy H. nowhere in sight. The three girls practically wet their panties as they accompanied Sam on the karaoke machine like backup singers.

Velvet placed her perfectly manicured hand on David's, trying to settle him down.

Jesus H. Christ.

David knew making him wait was just as much a game for Sam as the boys playing Counter-Strike downstairs on their computer monitors. Forcing David to sit here and listen to that crap blaring from the speakers, Sam was letting David know who called the shots.

David ordered drinks from a waitress dressed in a traditional *ao dai,* a long, four-paneled dress with tight sleeves and a high collar worn over flowing trousers. Velvet had told him the colors had special significance: white for the very young, pastels for the unmarried, richer colors for older women. At the Net High, black was the *couleur de rigueur.* The waitress wore a gauzy upper layer over lemon-yellow, with black trousers beneath.

David watched the waitress leave with their drink orders, his fingers drumming on the tabletop. Velvet picked up his hand and kissed his knuckles, giving him a smile. Tonight, she wore only diamond stud earrings and a jade ring he'd given her. As far as he knew, she'd never taken that ring off. Sitting there in the soft light, she looked just as ethereal as the women in the paintings.

After mangling another Sinatra song, Sam threw down the mike and jumped off the stage. He put his arms around two of his three honeys and walked back to David's corner booth, acting as if he'd just noticed him waiting there.

"David, my man, what can I do for you?"

The women cleared out like trained dogs given a hand signal. Sam squeezed into the booth next to Velvet, putting his arm around her bare shoulders.

David knew Velvet and Sam were distantly related, cousins of some sort, but it was hard to imagine any connection between the two. Velvet was elegant and educated. Like her name, she reminded David of something lush and sophisticated, the complete opposite of a snake like Sam.

Sam glanced at David's drink. "Let me guess," he said. "Grey Goose martini. Shaken, not stirred," he said in a fake English accent. He snapped his fingers. "Ready for a real drink?"

Immediately, another waitress in traditional garb showed up carrying a tray and two glasses, along with a bowl of shiny eggs an exotic turquoise blue, and a can of sweetened condensed milk. There was also a bottle of Perrier. At tableside, she opened one of the eggs and emptied the yolk into a glass. Next she added condensed milk and Perrier. She mixed the ingredients with ice.

"*Sua hot ga,*" Sam said, holding out the glass for David.

"No thanks," he answered, bypassing it to reach for his martini.

Sam laughed, then practically chugged down half the egg drink. The waitress whisked away the second glass, leaving them alone in the room with Velvet. The only music playing on the speakers was a traditional Vietnamese strummed guitar.

"You know why I'm here," David finally said.

Sam sat back, his arms resting on the cushions of the sofa. The look he gave David…talk about your inscrutable Asian! The punk just waited, appearing cool as you please as he stared down his aquiline nose.

"A shame really, Mimi's death. We have a saying in Vietnam." He leaned toward David. "Better one drop of blood than a full pond of water. She will be missed by the Tran family."

"Well, she's sure as hell going to be missed by me," David said, losing his grip on his temper. "Listen to me. Someone broke into my vault. They stole a bead from the Eye."

A hint of a smile crossed Sam's face, the change in expression so slight, David almost missed it.

Suddenly, it came to him, the real possibility that Sam or one of his minions was in on it. Manipulating David. Fucking with him.

"You don't look very surprised, Sam." Even as he spoke, the

pieces fell into place for David. "But maybe there's a reason for that? Maybe you know who took the bead?" Maybe the punk *was* involved.

David leaned forward meanacingly. "For all your so-called big connections, you've delivered shit. Were you getting a little desperate, Sam? Did you think you could rob me and sell back my own collection? Is that it?"

Sam sipped at the egg drink. He licked his bottom lip. "If only I was your problem."

David reached across the table and grabbed Sam's hand before he could take another sip.

Three hired muscles suddenly appeared, ready to wrestle David from the booth and throw him to the ground. Sam raised his hand to stop them.

"David, my friend," he said with a perfectly bleached smile. "Don't lose faith so quickly."

Sam picked up a strand of Velvet's hair and twirled it around his index finger. He pulled her toward him and kissed her ear. Velvet kept her eyes on David, silently pleading with him.

"Mimi was unique," Sam said smoothly. "She had the true gift. You told me yourself how, in her hands, the Eye glowed to life."

Glowed to life, David thought, remembering those feeble moments of hope when the metal trapped inside the milky blue crystal glimmered, giving the central stone of the Eye a pulse like a heartbeat. Yes, in Mimi's hands, the Eye did gather some sort of light, but it was ever so slight. And now he was beginning to think it was just a parlor trick. Despite all his experience, had he been taken in?

That which is invisible is always the most dangerous.

Maybe Mimi was trying to warn him, trying to tell him in her own way that Sam was full of shit. That he had nothing.

"She'll be difficult to replace," Sam continued, "but luckily for you, I found someone else." And when David turned to glare at him, Sam said, "Take heart, David. I'll show you your treasures soon enough."

That small assurance…

David could feel his heart thumping inside his chest, almost as if it were trying to force out his doubts. He was falling face-first, right into that tiny glimmer of hope. And in Sam's eyes, he could see that the little shit knew it.

Returning the punk's smile, David thought to himself that when this was over, when he truly had what he needed from Sam, the cops were going to have to use tweezers to pick up the pieces of this little prick.

Sam dropped the lock of Velvet's hair, his gaze still on David, baiting him. "You don't have to trust me, David. Our little Velvet found her for me. Didn't you, cousin?"

David turned to her in surprise. She couldn't even look at him.

"When I heard about Mimi," she whispered, staring at her drink on the table, "I thought you might need help."

David tried not to choke on his disgust. Velvet was supposed to have his best interests in mind. Jesus, he deserved her loyalty—he paid for it, didn't he? But here she was, calling Sam first? Letting David walk into this setup?

But then he remembered what Sam had said earlier: better a drop of blood than a pond of water. In Vietnam, family came first. Even distant relatives had a stranglehold.

He waited until Velvet looked up to meet his gaze. He could see real fear in her eyes; fear of him or Sam, it was difficult to say.

"As for the necklace—" Sam slid out from the booth and stood; he straightened his suit with a practiced hand. "There you have a big problem, my friend."

He leaned over the glass table, getting into David's face. "A little bird told me the police have the missing bead from your necklace." He came close enough to whisper in David's ear, "Guess where they found it? In Mimi's mouth. But maybe you knew that already?"

David felt the seat fall out from under him. The room started to spin.

Sam pulled away, taking a good look at David's reaction. "Now, is there something you forgot to tell me? Maybe *you* went to see Mimi. Things weren't happening fast enough. You lost your temper...."

David recoiled in horror. "I didn't kill Mimi, and you fucking know it. I needed her!"

He patted David on the shoulder. "Try to stay out of jail, will you, David? You won't be much use to me there."

David closed his eyes. He couldn't catch his breath. *Oh, shit. Shit!*

Sam gave Velvet a peck on the cheek. He said, "Take him home, Velvet. Make him forget a little, will you?"

15

Beth jabbed an accusing finger at the documents on the kitchen table. "Look at that…that pile of *shit!*" She took a long drink from the wineglass. Judging from the heaviness around the vowels, it was far from her first.

Seven picked up the moving papers. Scott's family was looking for their blood money, having filed an unlawful death suit. Seven made a mental note to call Ricky's lawyer tomorrow.

"It's okay, Beth. I got it."

She shook her head. The dark circles beneath her eyes and deep grooves around her mouth said it all: she was a woman defeated.

Beth Allen Bushard had grown up in Newport Beach, the daughter of an orthodontist and a real estate agent. She had perfect blond hair and a year-round tan courtesy of the local tanning salon. She worked out with a trainer. She considered her Senior Presentation, for the National Charity League—the debutant ball—one of the biggest moments in her life, right after her marriage and the birth of her son.

Seven still remembered the wedding—a Princess Di-type gown and five hundred of Beth and Ricky's closest friends. Seven, the best man, had used a microphone to introduce the wedding party of no less than thirty as the bridesmaids and ushers stepped into the grand ballroom of Newport Beach's most exclusive Yacht Club.

Seven and Laurin had eloped straight out of high school. They'd had one of those quickie Vegas weddings with Elvis presiding. At the time, they'd thought it was a hoot. Of course, the marriage lasted about as long as the wedding.

Beth was a communications major from USC and considered her sorority sisters family…family that scattered like rats on a sinking ship once it became clear that her husband had killed a man.

She was a good wife and mother. And she was falling apart.

"You shouldn't have to do any of this." She punched her fist into her thigh. "I shouldn't have to do this." She punched her thigh again, harder this time.

Seven grabbed her hand before she could keep hitting herself.

"Hey," he said. "It's going to be okay."

She shook her head. He'd been saying the same thing for months and she'd stopped believing him.

She looked up, her eyes swimming. "Nothing is ever going to be okay again and we both know it."

She reached for him. It was getting to be a regular thing, holding his brother's wife and comforting her. At first, it had just been a reflex. He'd needed the holding as much as she did. But now, it started to feel strange, the relationship shifting in a way he hadn't meant.

He looked into Beth's brown eyes, at her mascara, uncharacteristically smeared. She felt so frail in his arms, almost ethereal.

He remembered Erika's warning. *Time to cut the cord…or tie it up tight*.

He thought about it, dealing with the possibility that Beth was looking for more than he could give her.

Only, instead, something unexpected occurred.

Right then, it wasn't Beth's face he saw, but another's.

Shining black hair juxtaposed against a porcelain complexion. Vibrant blue eyes. Freckles. Gia.

He shut his eyes, closing off the image.

"You hate this," Beth said, seeing his reaction.

He stepped away, shaken by what had just happened. He thought about that spark of static electricity when they'd touched. *Something there…*

He focused back on Beth, feeling suddenly too sober. "We'll get through this, Beth. As a family."

She bit her lip, looking embarrassed by her sudden show of emotions. She nodded. "Okay."

He helped her upstairs to her bed. Watched as she reached for the bottle of medication at her bedside.

"That was an empty bottle of wine on the kitchen counter, Beth," he said, letting his concern sound in his voice.

She took out a pill and swallowed it back with a glass of water. "I'm okay," she said, giving a wan smile. "It may not seem like it sometimes, but I know my responsibilities. I'm...careful," she said, replacing the bottle on the nightstand. "I just need sleep." She kicked off her flats and slipped under the covers still wearing her slacks and sweater set. "You'll check on Nick for me?"

"Always," Seven said.

Outside the bedroom, he closed the door behind him. He'd known a wrongful death lawsuit was inevitable. What Beth hadn't figured out was what little difference the lawsuit would make to her and Nick. Ricky had left behind a financial disaster.

Seven turned for the stairs, wondering how to break the news to the already fragile Beth, when he saw his nephew waiting for him at the foot of the steps.

"Is Mom okay?"

Nick was the spitting image of his father. Curly blond hair, green eyes. One day, he'd be taller than his uncle. But right now, he looked really small. And scared.

Seven nodded, coming down the stairs to put his arm around his nephew. "She's going to be fine. It's just tough, you know? For all of us. How about I cook us some dinner?"

"I'm not hungry."

"Come on. Whatever you want, buddy."

His nephew looked up at him. In those eyes, Seven could see all the pain the kid had buried inside.

Jesus, Ricky.

"You know what I wish sometimes, Uncle Seven?" Nick said. "I wish it had been him. Dad, I mean," he said in a broken whisper. "I wish that Scott had been the whack job and that he had killed Dad, not the other way around."

The horror of that admission was right there on the little guy's face.

Seven took Nick by both shoulders. He crouched down, coming eye level to his nephew. He said in a strong, sure voice, what he called his cop voice, "Hey, I think that sometimes, too, okay? And who can blame us? That doesn't make us bad people—that just makes us angry and hurt. Human nature, buddy. And I'll tell you something else. I think if your dad had told someone how mad and scared he was, about Scott, I mean, instead of keeping it all inside—if he'd showed half the courage you just did by talking to me—maybe Scott wouldn't be dead. You get me?"

For the first time since that horrible day, tears filled Nick's eyes. He threw himself into Seven's arms and just started bawling.

Seven held him tight, knowing the release had been long overdue. Happy to see it.

"It's okay," he told Nick over and over. "It's okay."

When he could finally talk, Nick whispered in Seven's ear, catching his breath between each halting word, "Why couldn't you be my dad?"

"Hey, I'm not turning down the job." Seven pushed the boy's limp body away just enough so that Nick could see his face as he spoke. "Your dad's going to be in prison for a long time. And I think maybe, just maybe, by the time he gets out, he could be a different man. Someone we can trust again. And if we're strong enough, if we work really hard at it, we might even be able to forgive him. But in the meantime, anything you want, Nick," he said, trying not to choke on the words. "Anything."

His nephew nodded, taking a deep breath.

"We just take it one day at a time, okay?" Seven brushed the hair from the kid's face, then hugged him again. "God, I love you, Nick. And I'm sorry your dad was a selfish shit and did this to us. But it doesn't have to defeat us, okay?"

For the longest time, Seven stood holding his nephew. If he could help Nick, be there beside his nephew as he navigated the years ahead—now that was a job worth being put on this earth to do.

"Now. Men need food to be strong," he said in a mock caveman voice. He threw his arm around his nephew's shoulders and headed for the kitchen. "And I'm starving," he said, lying through his teeth.

"Pancakes?" Nick asked hopefully.

"You got it."

He gave Nick a high-five. Stepping into the kitchen, he prayed Beth had some kind of cookbook. How the hell did you make pancakes, anyway?

"You pay attention and learn, grasshopper," he told Nick. "Your uncle makes one mean pancake."

"My uncle doesn't know how to cook," Nick countered.

Seven smiled, suddenly feeling okay. "So find me a cookbook, will ya?"

16

The history of Vietnam began four thousand years ago, when a dragon prince married a fairy princess.

Together, the two conceived one hundred children, a number much too large even for the immortals. And so they agreed to split their brood. The fairy princess, Au Co, moved to the mountains with half her children, while the dragon prince, Lac Long Quan, took to the lowlands with the rest. To this day, the Vietnamese considered the dragon to be the luckiest of all creatures. They are the "Children of the Dragon."

Velvet sat at the vanity in the master bath of her condo, staring at her reflection in the mirror. The Dior makeup she loved so well lay lined up before her, gleaming from its individual gold cases. She watched the woman in the mirror, telling herself she was one of them, the Children of the Dragon. A woman of luck.

She reached for a cotton pad and soaked it with makeup remover. With a few swipes, she divided her face in half in the mirror. One side showed a woman in full makeup, reminiscent of a geisha, a woman born to please men like David Gospel. But the other side, the clean-faced woman—bare of mascara and lipstick—this was the law student who used only her intellect to improve her position in life.

She stared at herself in the mirror, confused by the two sides reflected there.

After leaving the Net High, David had taken her back to her condo. Their sex had been hard and fast, edging on violent. He'd been angry, believing that she'd betrayed him...and Velvet had never shied away from a good fight.

Afterward, she'd walked him to the door in a silk robe embroidered with dragons. There, she had kissed him tenderly...and before he could pull away, letting her know that he was unforgiving, she had spoken those forbidden words.

"I love you, David."

And then she'd shut the door.

Velvet reached for more cotton and finished removing her makeup. She considered herself part of a new generation of Vietnamese. She wore Versace and listened to indie rock. She drove a Mercedes. She attended law school and studied *Vogue* like a textbook. Her name was on the list of the most exclusive L.A. nightclubs.

And still there was a part of her that was rooted here in Little Saigon. Even with her shaky Vietnamese, she got by in the coffee shops talking about what it was like to grow up Vietnamese in a place where Vietnam evoked images of rice paddies, sweltering heat and an unending war. Like her people, she struggled to make a new life—a new *identity*—for herself. And yet she'd never been able to shed the traditions of the past.

Part of Velvet's tradition included Sam Vi.

Sam was a gangster, through and through. Within the community, he was more myth than man. But Velvet had known Sam before any of the darkness had taken hold. He'd driven her to her first dance in his brother's sleek Vega. He'd been her first kiss, an experiment that was more about teaching her the ropes than anything sexual. To Velvet, Sam was *dong-bao*. Born of the same womb.

But that had changed with the gangs. She remembered trying to talk to him once, telling him he was going down a bad path. But Sam, he'd just given her a smirk and said something like, "Keep studying, Velvet. Someday, you're going to be somebody."

She'd seen it in his eyes then. Sam Vi was going to be somebody, too. And he'd do it in his own way.

No, she didn't admire Sam anymore—she didn't even respect

him. But in her heart, he was like her brother. And she cared for him very much.

Velvet's mother died when she was fourteen. Sam had been her rock during that time, mourning right along with her. Unlike Velvet, Sam had been born in Vietnam. He'd lost his father in the war. He knew what it was like to grow up on your own, without someone to guide you.

At her mother's funeral, she remembered him taking both her hands in his and telling her she would never have to worry about anything. That he'd take care of her. Velvet had two older brothers, but they'd never been close. Her father was a quiet man. With the death of Velvet's mother, he seemed to shut down, a turtle slipping back inside its shell. Without her mother, Velvet felt isolated in her grief.

But there was Sam telling her she wasn't alone. She remembered how happy that promise had made her.

Sam had paid for college. He would have done the same for law school if she'd needed it. He'd told her she had a job waiting when she passed the bar…as Sam's private counsel. She should think about commercial law, he'd told her, now that he was an important businessman…while Velvet wondered if she shouldn't, for Sam's sake, specialize in something of a more criminal nature.

She hated the fiasco that had been the last months. Hated that it all centered around Sam's relationship with Trudy H. That Sam could be so gullible.…

But then, even though he was powerful and successful, she'd never considered Sam the brightest bulb.

But maybe that was the point. Trudy H. was another rung up the ladder.

It was something endemic to the community, this need to push forward. Almost as if they were saying it was all right that they'd left Vietnam, as long as it was for something better.

For Sam, the pinnacle was David Gospel. He'd studied the man, his family, his rise to success with Gospel Enterprises. Sam wanted to make himself in David's image, Vietnamese version.

As for Velvet, she told herself it was love and not money that had brought her to this point.

Mimi had first contacted Sam about David. David had become a regular client by then, and Mimi had seen an opportunity. More than anything in this world, David Gospel wanted more magic baubles to complete his collection. It made him vulnerable to the likes of Sam.

And here was Mimi, in Sam's debt. She told Velvet that the cards had counseled her on her course of action. Together these two men could form a strong alliance. But Velvet always wondered if that wasn't just an excuse. The meaning of the cards was often influenced by the context in which they were read.

She thought of her own situation—how much she, too, owed Sam.

So Sam had sought out Velvet, calling in yet another marker. "I need your help, Vee," he'd told her. He always called her that, thinking it was cute how the nickname corresponded with his own name, Sam Vi.

He'd given her instructions: become David's confidante. "You don't have to sleep with him," Sam had said. "He's just some old geezer, anyway. Keep him company. Make him like you. You're a smart girl, Vee. And very beautiful. You'll know what I need."

To be his spy. If David should ever become suspicious or unhappy about the progress of their "project" together, Sam would expect a call. That had never happened, of course, making Velvet's job easier. But she dreaded her meetings with Sam. She hadn't wanted to betray David. And tonight, she'd done just that.

Maybe that's why she'd started sleeping with him. Her own interpretation of the Confucius ideal of *chun-tzu*—the noble individual. A sacrifice was needed. And David was far from an old geezer. He was, in fact, a generous lover, handsome and charming. He'd shown Velvet a world she'd only dreamed of. He had stories and experience; he'd met famous and interesting people like Donald Trump and the Dalai Lama.

And he had a sense of humor. That had been the most surprising part. The arrogance and the polish she'd expected. But not the laughter.

She told herself he didn't care for her—he couldn't possibly. But it didn't matter to Velvet. She'd fallen in love just the same.

But then came that push-me/pull-you of her obligations to Sam. He was family. Part and parcel of her traditions. In her closet, alongside her Versace suit, hung several traditional *ao dai*. She made offerings of food and lit joss sticks at the altar she kept for her deceased mother. She celebrated Tet with Sam and other relatives, the day that every Vietnamese turns a year older.

On the vanity, she reached for a Dior lipstick a bright crimson-red. Staring at her reflection, she drew a big *X* over her face on the mirror.

She didn't know how to say no to Sam. Just like her Vietnamese pedigree, he was part of who she was.

But she would learn. That much she promised herself. It would break her heart, but very soon, Velvet would say no to David and Sam both.

It was after he'd put his nephew to bed that it suddenly hit Stephen. That gut feeling nagging him all day…he finally understood.

He saw the whole thing like a movie in his head: Gia Moon standing to mimic Mimi Tran punching in the code and disabling the security system. At the time, he'd thought it was strange, how she'd held her hand at the exact level of the actual keypad built into the wall.

Fifteen minutes later, he was back at the office. He pulled up the interview with Gia Moon on his computer screen. These days, everything was digitized, the images downloaded onto a secure server. He watched the footage from the interview with Gia Moon on the LCD screen. She stood to punch numbers into an invisible keypad. Once, twice…six times, she jabbed her finger forward.

Seven glanced down at the file folder next to the computer. Typed on a sheet of paper on the top was the code to Mimi Tran's security system. It had six digits.

His pulse took a hit, the martini having worn off hours ago. It was almost midnight. Luckily, he knew Rob's cell number by heart.

Rob Maxwell worked for the Forensic Services Unit. Best damn computer guy on the face of the planet. The only thing that stopped Rob from taking over the world from the likes of Bill Gates was this one flaw: he was a bit of an asshole. Actually, he was a prick with the personality of a caveman.

So Rob Maxwell was basically kept chained to his dungeon office at FSU, not that he seemed to mind one bit. Seven actually thought the guy was a hoot, as long as you didn't take him too seriously.

But the really great thing about Rob Maxwell when you were working on a case was the added plus that he needed very little sleep. Midnight was just the beginning of his hours online in the virtual world of elves, giants and warrior knights.

Now both men sat at Rob's computer at FSU, where they'd agreed to meet. Rob was your typical aging punker, complete with skintight pants and deconstructed shirt held together with about twenty safety pins. His hair was dyed jet-black, and had been cut within an inch of its life, except for the bangs, which hung in a "devil lock" to his chin. He carried a beat-up copy of *A Clockwork Orange* to work every day, reading it like a Bible over his vegan lunch. In Rob's twisted way, he thought it was the height of irony that he worked for the police department.

Tapping hard and fast on the keys, he complained to Seven that the job he needed done with the interview tape was a piece of cake.

"Jesus man, once, just once, I wish you yahoos upstairs could come up with something—you know—*real*. Something that might actually challenge me."

"But then," Seven responded, "Oh Big Giant Brain, how could my lowly intellect ever presume to conceive such a query?"

Rob seemed to like that one. "Amen, brother."

Rob had a photograph of the crime scene up on the screen. With a bit of envy, Seven noticed Rob's computer was a thirty-two-inch flat screen. The image showed the wall at the crime scene with the security keypad built in. Rob shrank the image to fit half the screen, then brought up the image of Gia Moon frozen in place, finger extended, ready to punch in her numbers.

"You know, I practically had the Grand Vizier on his fucking knees, ready to hand over the Sword of Eternity when you called," Rob said, shaking his head but still typing.

"Like I said, I owe you," Seven replied, his eyes on the screen.

"And then some. Okay, so we plug in our magic software that calculates the best fit between the two images." He changed his voice, slowing it down to make sure that his minion could understand the Big Giant Brain. "And abracadabra."

As he spoke, the right side of the screen, the image showing the keypad at Mimi Tran's house, merged with the image of Gia Moon in the interview room. Rob played around with the two until everything lined up just right. Gia Moon now stood directly in front of the keypad, as if ready to start punching in the code.

"And here we go," Rob said, hitting the Enter key.

Immediately, Gia began tapping in her numbers. Rob had changed the background of the interview-room footage to include the keypad on the wall of the Tran house.

Seven watched carefully. "Run it again," he said.

Rob did.

"Can you zoom in?" Seven asked.

He snorted. "Stupid question. Hey, you want to see her do it naked? I can even give her a Pamela Anderson boob job."

"Focus in on her hand and the keyboard," Seven said. "I want to see what numbers she punches in. Slow it down."

This time, Seven could clearly see the code that Gia punched into the keypad. He wrote it down, then compared the numbers to the actual code in the file.

Rob looked over. "Did you get what you wanted?"

Seven stared down at the two separate sheets of paper.

0-6-1-7-6-0.

It was the same number.

"She knew the victim's security code," Seven said softly, almost to himself.

Rob nodded. "Bitching. Guess she did it."

Seven braced himself, still looking at the numbers in disbelief. He remembered Erika's warning. *If she didn't do it, Gia Moon knows who did.*

Answering Rob, Seven echoed Erika's words now. "That, or she's a hell of a good guesser."

17

Erika stared at the side of the bed where the sheets lay crumpled. She had a pounding headache and her eyelids felt as if they were made of sandpaper. She glared at the bedside clock.

Three-oh-six in the morning and she was wide-awake.

It was the usual drill. She'd send away whatever Tom, Dick or, in this case, Adam, she'd pounded back a few too many with, fall asleep—or more like pass out—and wake up just a few hours later.

She gave the clock another dirty look. Three-oh-six freaking a.m.

She threw her arm over her eyes, sinking back into the pillow. She had some pills for the headache, but she wasn't much for taking anything. Not her sort of poison.

Her poison came on two legs, usually with dark eyes and an overload of testosterone. Always over six feet tall. She could afford to be picky.

She thought about poor Seven apologizing for their one-night stand. He didn't have a clue.

She sat up in bed. After a minute, she got up and walked into the kitchen to grab a glass of water.

She knew Seven took the blame, thinking it had been all his weakness, their sleeping together. He was a nice guy, Seven. It would never occur to him that maybe *he* was the one being used.

The thing with men started when she'd lost her virginity her sophomore year in high school. She knew it was all tied up with some shit about looking for a father figure. She'd even talked to a therapist once—not that it helped. Like she didn't know she had abandonment issues? Who wanted to talk over all that daddy-didn't-love-me crap with a stranger taking notes?

She stood over the sink, the empty glass in her hand. That night with Seven she'd reached a new low. He'd been going through so much because of his brother and she'd taken advantage.

Not that it excused anything, but she never would have crossed that line if her father hadn't come back from the dead.

The thing was, Alfonso Cabral had never been dead. It was Milagro, Erika's mother, who'd had him declared legally dead after a seven-year absence. The truth turned out to be much harsher than her prick-of-a-father croaking. Alfonso abandoned them, leaving Erika, her brother, Miguel, and her mother to fend for themselves.

The worst of it? He hadn't disappeared because he'd been wanted by the cops. He wasn't ditching creditors, or his bookie. He'd gotten sick of them. He'd wanted out.

So he'd moved to Costa Rica, where he'd started a brand-new life. A life that included Consuelo, his new wife, and their two baby boys, Jose and little Alfonso Jr.

Last year, he'd moved the whole kit and caboodle back here to Santa Ana. He said he wanted back into Erika's life. A man needed his family.

What bullshit....

She turned on the faucet and filled the glass. Alcohol always dehydrated her. She didn't want to wake up in the morning nauseated, with her head feeling like it was splitting open.

Still holding the glass, she turned it in her hand, not taking even a sip.

Now, Erika and her brother were expected to watch their father raise his two youngest? They were supposed to sit around while Alfonso gave his two baby boys all the love and attention that had been missing from their lives?

The twisted thing about the whole mess was Erika's reaction when she'd found out that dear old dad was still very much alive. She'd blamed her mother.

Milagro had lied to her kids. Using some perverse reasoning, she had convinced herself she was sparing her children by keeping them from the truth. She'd told herself they were better off thinking Alfonso was dead than knowing they'd been abandoned.

But Erika had a different theory. That it was *mami* who didn't want to face the truth. She didn't want to have to answer those ugly little questions that came along with the truth, either.

Her husband had left her and her two children high and dry—and Milagro had been part and parcel of that decision.

There was a little voice inside Erika's head that whispered her mother could have prevented the failure of her marriage. If she'd been prettier, less passive, more... Erika didn't know what.

She hated that little voice.

In the kitchen, she sat down and stared at the still-full glass of water. She fought the desire to call Seven. For a time, after the thing with his brother, he'd done that a few times. Called her up and they'd talked. But he'd stopped after they slept together.

She missed those middle-of-the-night talks.

She drank the water quickly, downing it in one long gulp. She slammed the empty glass on the table. She knew it wouldn't do any good to wake up Seven with some lurid confession. *Hey kiddo, you know that night we slept together? It's kind of a bad habit with me...one I really plan to kick once I can face myself.*

Instead, she brought her laptop into the kitchen and turned it on. Dead fortune-tellers, strange artifacts...the case was going to be one giant headache.

Or a ton of work she could disappear into.

Erika smiled, pulling the laptop closer.

She hadn't liked Gia Moon—liked even less that the psychic had been dead-on about key details in the case.

Erika grabbed a Diet Coke out of the refrigerator, figuring she needed the hit of caffeine. Back at the computer, she opened a file and started transcribing her notes from the interview with the professor about the glass bead. She'd never admit it out loud, but all that supernatural stuff scared the crap out of her.

Earlier, Seven had asked her about Santeria. Well, she had more than a passing acquaintance with the practice.

She'd been eight years old. Her mother and she had gone with a friend to the home of an acquaintance. Erika had been given something to eat, a tart made with coconut and chocolate.

Only she and her mother had eaten the pastry.

They'd both become very ill. Her mother recovered after a day, but Erika had only grown worse, breaking out in a strange rash. The pediatrician had given her pills and creams, but nothing seemed to help. In desperation, her mother had taken her to a *santera*, a priestess, a white witch.

The ceremony that had followed was something Erika would never forget. Her mother had dressed her all in white. Like an angel, she'd told Erika. She'd been taken inside a room that was completely white. And there had been a strange smell, too. Incense maybe. The *santera* had also dressed in white. She remembered the woman chanting and praying over her.

According to her mother, the rash had disappeared then and there. Like a miracle. The only thing Erika remembered was the woman taking her hand and looking into her eyes. Speaking Spanish, she'd told Erika she belonged to her now, that Erika would always be protected. She called herself Erika's guardian angel.

That had been almost twenty years ago. Her mother hadn't stopped spending money on the *espiritistas* and *santeros* ever since. To this day, Milagro, whose name literally meant "miracle," believed the priestess had saved Erika from whatever had poisoned her. Erika wasn't so sure. But she found the memory unsettling…particularly her mother's dedication to those bloodsuckers during the years that followed.

"Maybe that's what I need," Erika told herself, pulling out her notes from the interview with Professor Murphy. "*Una limpieza.*" Rid herself of those bad vibes.

But she wasn't much for the pity-party scene. She focused instead on trying to decipher her shorthand.

After a while, she sat back and picked up the Diet Coke. "What the hell is a Greek artifact doing in the mouth of a Vietnamese fortune-teller?" she asked out loud.

Murphy had been a real character. Still, he seemed to know

his stuff. She flipped the page in her notebook, coming across the name Estelle Figaro circled on the page.

Erika frowned, taking another sip of Diet Coke. The professor had said something about the woman being a bit of a Cassandra.

To jump-start her brain, Erika logged on to the Internet and clicked over to Google. She typed in "Cassandra," skimming through a short blurb.

Cassandra makes an appearance in many plays and stories where she is depicted as a prophetess...

Erika returned to her notes, circling words like *oracle* and *sibyl* and *psychic archaeology.* The professor had said that Figaris, as the name appeared the second time she'd written it in her notebook, had worked with a guy named Morgan Tyrell. Something to do with Harvard and research on parapsychology?

She Googled the name Morgan Tyrell.

The first entry that came up: Institute for Dynamic Studies of Parapsychology and the Brain.

"Okay, so Figaris or Figaro, or whatever," she said, summarizing her notes out loud, "believed she had psychic ability and now she's dead. Another dead psychic connected to the bead."

So maybe the key was finding out more about "Madam F" and how she'd died? For all Erika knew, she'd been found with a bird stuffed in her mouth, too.

"All right, Estelle," she said. "Let's see if we can find you somewhere in cyberspace."

On Google, she typed in "archaeology" and "Estelle Figaris."

Google came up with: *Do you mean Estelle Fegaris?*

"Good old Google," she said, hitting the search prompt.

18

You watch the security people fiddling with their wires and cameras. No one notices you. You have a talent for that...the ability to make yourself invisible.

The lowly cows actually believe they are ignoring you. They don't understand that you can get inside their heads. It's you pulling the strings, not them.

You watch as they set up the video feed with lots of motion sensors. It makes you tingle inside to watch how he protects his collection. These are his children. Inside this room he hides his mojo.

You remember his stories like lullabies. Freya, the Norse goddess of love and magic, fornicating with her hideous dwarfs for the prize of the Necklace of Brisings. Prisoners buried alive as sacrifice for consulting the Sibylline Books. He showed you oracle bones. But when you saw the bronze Etruscan liver marked into sections representing the gods in the heavens, you were lost.

The ancient Etruscans—the Rasna—an advanced society that preceded the Roman Empire and brought the practice of haruspicy to life. They have a mysterious language, unrelated to any other tongue—unique, just like you. But more importantly, they are experts at the art of divination.

Haruspicy is their method: the reading of entrails to tell the future. Such diviners were consulted throughout history. Emperor Claudius created a college of haruspices. Pope Innocent agreed to their services as long as their rites were kept secret. You've seen a copy of the *Libri Tagetici*, a collection of writings dedicated to the childlike being who brought haruspicy to the world.

In ancient times, the haruspex would inspect the entrails of ritually slaughtered animals in order to interpret the divine will. In preparation, the diviner must have the proper attitude of respect for the gods. He must be sober and wear clean, festive clothes. He should fast for at least twelve hours before the ritual…three days is best.

That's where you made your mistake with Michelle. You weren't ready. The vestments, the fast, it was all off.

You were too hasty in your desire for blood, the slaughter—a broken glass across her throat—too impulsive. You didn't follow a plan. Your lust made you unworthy of Michelle, flawed and distracted. Her blood on your hands mesmerized. The police came long before you were ready. A neighbor calling 911.

You hadn't wanted to wash your hands. It was all you had left of the moment. Blood, her life source. But he forced you—he made you clean your car and burn your clothes. He destroyed your memories, taking everything. He steals.

Only he is allowed a collection? Fuck him.

He destroys yours—you destroy his.

It took you a long time to get over the loss. In hindsight, you realize how paltry your early collection was, how unworthy of you. Entrails of birds and cats. A child's game.

You collect things of much greater worth now.

Mimi was easy. You don't like that. You think there should be more…more blood, more emotion, more…everything.

You like it when she fights. Good versus bad.

Mimi is evil—and a fraud, which you believe worse. She didn't understand that only you have the power to manipulate thought. Like Michelle, she *pretended*.

But you know the truth. The power he seeks, it's not his. It's yours alone.

Now you watch his stupid sheep, knowing that there's nothing these menials can do to stop you. He should, of course, take the collection away to a safe place. Not that it would matter. You will hunt him down. You'll take what you want, when you want it. You have that power.

But you know he'll never let his treasures out of this house. Leave his children? Hide them for safety's sake? His hubris will not allow it.

In a way, you understand. You could never part with your own collection. It stays here, close by.

In your pocket, you have the latest addition. A feather, tipped with dried blood. You fondle it lovingly.

The bead in the beak, the beak in the mouth. You smile at the image.

In the book *Dracula,* Dr. Seward's zoophagous sanatorium patient, Renfield, feeds flies to spiders, and spiders to sparrows. When he is refused a cat, he eats the birds, trying to absorb their life force.

There was an old lady who swallowed a fly…perhaps she'll die.

Yes, she dies. So will the next one. And the one after her. You will kill his endless supply of whores and frauds.

You stroke the feather in your pocket. You have her name now. Very soon, you'll have another treasure.

You look up at the camera and smile. You are invisible. And your eyes are everywhere.

Gia sat up in bed. She grabbed her throat, unable to breath. She felt as if she were drowning, choking on something.

Blood! Blood everywhere! In your mouth…down your throat. It's filling your lungs.

Beside her, Stella groaned softly and turned over on the king-size bed. Gia forced herself to calm down. When she could, she slipped out of bed and stumbled into the bathroom. She splashed cold water on her face and looked up into the mirror.

There was blood dripping from her eyes.

Horrified, she pushed away from the sink, scrubbing her face with her hands as if trying to wipe off the blood. Her back hit the wall, the towel rack digging into her spine.

"It's just a dream, Gia," she said, her eyes shut tight. "Just a dream, just a dream."

Taking a deep breath, she forced herself to look up into the mirror again, trying to focus. This time, her eyes were clear.

"Just a dream," she whispered.

A bad one.

Back in the bedroom, she glanced at the bedside table. The clock read 3:06 in the morning.

She watched her daughter sleep, her chest rising and falling in a gentle rhythm. Gia tried to match her breathing to Stella's, waiting until her heart rate reached normal.

The images were stronger this time. More distinct.

He's closer.

She grabbed a sweatshirt off the rocking chair in the bedroom and headed for her studio.

Two hours later, she put down the paintbrush and stretched her back, trying to ease a cramp. She felt like one of those women at the Salem witch trials. Their accusers would press the life out of them by placing a board on top of them and adding one stone at a time. She could feel the weight of her dreams crushing her.

Guilty or innocent? she asked herself.

She looked up at the painting, where she'd been able to flesh out some detail from the shadows, wondering what it all meant.

"Bird entrails," she whispered, trying not to judge what she painted.

She could still feel that tightness in her chest, the breath being choked from her. She'd experienced that once, many years ago. And that's what scared her most. She felt now, as she did then, on the brink of death.

The first dream, she'd been in the killer's childhood. Puerto Rico...not what she'd expected. It didn't fit the pattern—which didn't necessarily mean anything.

She sighed, examining the enormous canvas. That was entirely the problem—how not to let her own thoughts and fears manipulate her vision. The spirit coming through could very well be only the messenger, guiding her to the real killer. She couldn't let her own dark past influence the message.

She reached out to touch the canvas, where she'd painted what looked like a stylized eye. This image she knew only too well. The Evil Eye.

She'd learned a lot about objects of power like this. Some thought the eye came from ancient times, representing the blue eyes of Athena. If someone wished you harm, the curse would merely bounce back to them, the amulet keeping the wearer safe like a force field. Gia had just such a bracelet hidden away. A gift from her mother.

She stared up at the jumble of images on the canvas. She didn't know how long she sat there, falling into those images, but her hand began to tingle. She glanced down.

In her hand, she held a blood-tipped feather.

She dropped the feather with a gasp, jumping to her feet.

But when she looked down, she saw it wasn't a feather at all that she had dropped. On the wooden floor lay her paintbrush, red paint splattered across the shop-blasted concrete.

She slumped back into her chair. *Great.*

This spirit liked to play games.

After she cleaned up, she looked at the clock. Almost six in the morning. Pretty soon she'd have to wake Stella and get her ready for school.

Gia stood before the painting, looking at the one dark corner she had yet to give definition to. She'd never felt so drained.

She was playing a dangerous game. If she was wrong, how much could a mistake cost the people she loved? Already, too many had died.

A few minutes later, she slipped into bed next to Stella, hugging her. Gia thought about the woman detective, the flash of sadness she'd received when she'd touched Erika Cabral's hand.

Her father had abandoned her.

Gia held Stella closer, wondering what lingering questions her daughter might have about her own missing father. Dreading the day she would have to tell her the truth.

Even now, Gia questioned whether she was doing the right thing, taking them both into the eye of the storm. Was she fooling herself, believing that she could protect Stella?

Well, there was no stopping it now. The spirit was locked in to Gia and her energy. Even if she tried, she couldn't pull away.

It was almost as if she were courting him. She was part of his game. Part of his collection.

There was nothing she could do now but try and keep one step ahead.

19

Thomas Crane focused on the woman pictured on his computer's screen saver. She was smiling, her hair pulled back off her face in a ponytail that made her look like a girl in her teens. She wore shorts and a T-shirt and carried a trowel in her hand. The dig was just outside Mycenae; two marble columns stood in the background.

The photograph had always been his favorite. Sometimes, when he stared at the screen saver long enough, he could feel himself slipping away, surprised to discover that an hour or more had passed.

Like today. He'd spent the morning checking out The Lunite Web site. There'd been a lot of activity lately, people posting on the board about the death of a fortune-teller in California.

All sorts of information showed up on The Lunite Web site. Thomas knew most of it was crap: a new conspiracy theory or a sighting of the Eye. Once, there'd even been a rumor about Spielberg making a movie about the life of Estelle Fegaris, a sort of Indiana Jane thing. The board had lit up like Christmas for weeks. Turned out the whole thing was bullshit.

But this fortune-teller in California. Now that sounded like something interesting.

Thomas Crane smiled. He hadn't felt this good in years. Twelve, to be exact. Right around the time his sorry-ass pregnant girlfriend—a woman he'd asked to marry him—had left him.

No, that wasn't right. She hadn't left him. That made it sound as if he'd done something wrong.

She'd *abandoned* him. She'd *stolen* his kid. She'd sneaked out in the middle of the night, making him look like a fucking idiot to his friends and relatives because he couldn't hold a family together.

She'd left him in Greece. The day she'd found out about her mother's murder, he'd dropped down on one knee and asked her to marry him, knowing that she was carrying his child. She'd smiled and said yes.

Two days later, the cops picked him up and she'd disappeared forever.

Only, by then Thomas had already called home with the news. He'd told William, his big brother, all about his wife-to-be and the baby. William, who had the perfect wife and family.

Every day, Thomas thought about it. Abandoned. Humiliated. Cuckolded.

And his reputation? Gone. Destroyed. The best work he could get these days was on the level of a shovel bum for a couple of lame archaeological digs in New Jersey. Thomas Crane, a man who had once thought to take a position at Harvard.

When she'd come to him and told him she was pregnant, he hadn't exactly been excited. He'd been screwing around with the boss's daughter. But afterward, he started thinking maybe it wasn't such a bad thing that he'd knocked her up. He'd need support to get away with this thing he'd done. Who better than the daughter of the woman he'd killed?

Two days later, when the cops came to get him, he found out that his fiancée—the woman who was carrying his child—was the very person who had handed him over to the authorities.

But then, you couldn't count on people being grateful. He'd learned that lesson the hard way.

Those first few months afterward, all he could think about was getting her back.

After a couple years, he just wanted her dead.

She was the sword hanging over his head, the one person who could show up someday and point the finger, just like she'd done in Greece. The reason he couldn't get back his career, always worried that she'd show up and nail his ass with her accusations.

You killed her! He could almost hear her shouting her accusation in his head.

Fucking bitch.

There'd been a time when he'd been right there in the thick of things. He'd been Estelle's protégé. He'd held the Eye in his hands. How many people could say that?

But it had all gone to shit. The Eye was gone. So was the money.

And it was her fault. She could have saved him. Instead, she'd bailed, leaving him nothing.

He moved the mouse, erasing her face. He checked the board for any new postings. He sifted through the dross of "maybes" and "what-ifs" and "I heards," trying to find *something*. When that didn't pan out, he started searching the Web for information on the dead fortune-teller.

And then he smelled that peculiar scent: like burned sulfur.

That was always the warning. He'd smell the odor of something burning. Next his hands would begin to shake. He tried to stand, reach the couch to sit down, but he didn't make it. Instead, he fell to the carpet, flopping like fish with a seizure.

When it was over, he couldn't remember what had happened. It was like that a lot. Like losing time. When he sat up, he looked up at the computer screen and saw her face.

And then it all came back to him.

"You destroyed me, Gina," he whispered to the photograph.

He took a deep breath and squeezed his hands into fists to keep them from shaking. The doctors couldn't figure out what the hell was wrong with him. They tried pushing some stupid pills on him. Antiseizure medication. But he knew better. These attacks were all her doing. The witch had put a hex on him. And there was only one way to stop her.

Blood must be spilled—a sacrifice made. The rules hadn't changed since the dawn of time.

He rose to his feet and stumbled back to the couch, collapsing onto the cushions. Reflected in the mirror above the hearth was a tall, thin man with a receding hairline and graying blond hair. His cheeks were sunken and he hadn't shaved.

He was aging fast, half the man he used to be. Slipping away into nothingness. He wouldn't make the grand discoveries he'd planned all his life. There wouldn't be a Chair named after him at a major university. His name wouldn't be published in the textbooks.

Not unless he found the Eye.

And for that reason alone, he needed to find her. He would force her to take him to the Eye.

And then he would kill her.

And he would get away with it.

Just like before.

20

Erika paced up and down the squad room, waving her hands in the air. She did that a lot—used her hands to talk. She said it was because *she* was Latina. She informed Seven that, despite his very French-Canadian grandfather, *he* couldn't have a drop of French blood or he, too, would use his hands.

Only now she was holding a cup of coffee, and Seven kept wondering when that damn latte would fly right out of her grip and across his desk, propelled by one of those animated hand gestures. The woman was pumped.

"So I started reading up on this Fegaris chick. Remember the professor, Murphy? All that stuff about psychic archaeology and how Fegaris was this colorful figure in the field? Well, let me tell you, the woman is practically the cult goddess of archaeology."

Seven tried to imagine the female version of Murphy, the professor they'd gone to see about the glass bead they'd found in the parrot's mouth. But the picture came out all wrong, the woman appearing bald and wearing glasses like Murphy, carrying a substantial spare tire.

"Twelve years after her murder, Fegaris has this Web site, like she's a legend and everything about her had to be memorialized. They call themselves The Lunites, followers of Fegaris. You see, the Greek word *feggari* means moon. Luna? Moon? Get it?"

"No," he deadpanned. "Because I didn't get past kindergarten."

"It turns out," she continued, completely ignoring him, "it wasn't just her psychic abilities that turned Fegaris into the black sheep of archaeology. She didn't exactly run a tight ship on her digs."

"Okay, that one you can explain."

She was way ahead of him. "Fegaris helped finance her digs by training amateurs and letting them in on the fun. The practice goes back to the nineteenth century, a pay-to-play sort of thing. Only, colleagues argue these amateurs end up messing up digs with their lack of experience. Fegaris had them in droves after Harvard dumped her. She was searching for the Eye of Athena, 'a treasure beyond all worth,' according to the Web site."

"Wait a minute. They called it that? A treasure beyond all worth?"

"Yup." Erika flashed a smile. "Just like Harrison Ford in *The Temple of Doom*. Presumably, the necklace has this power to help the wearer see the future. The Eye became Fegaris's raison d'être. After she lost her position at Harvard, she became completely obsessed. The Eye is like the Holy Grail to this woman."

Seven grabbed the coffee from her hand after another precarious gesture. "How many of these things have you had?"

Erika shot him a look that said she didn't appreciate the interruption. "Trust me, I need the caffeine. So, just like the professor laid out for us a couple of days ago, Fegaris learns the Eye is part of this looted tomb. Apparently, tomb raiders cleaned the place out back in ancient times. It's called Agamemnon's tomb—even though his dad, Atreus, is supposed to have been buried there with him, so it's also called the Treasury of Atreus, which is kind of confusing. I mean, is it a treasury or a tomb?"

"Atreus, that's the guy who cooked his brother's kids for supper?"

"Bingo. Seven, you *need* to see at least a photo of this place, this Beehive Tomb. It's like the freaking pyramids, it's *that* impressive."

Without the latte in her hand, she was free to really express herself, her arms waving all over the place.

"It's like walking inside a giant beehive," she said, "all made of huge, chiseled stone. Each piece fits together perfectly. Nobody knows how they did it back then, because some of the stones they used weigh, like, *tons*. It's a mystery, just like the pyramids. So is the missing treasure they buried. It must have rivaled the stuff they found with the Pharaohs."

But then the lightbulb flashed on over his head. "Wait a minute. Didn't the professor say Estelle Fegaris was killed by looters?"

Erika nodded. "Yeah, but the tomb was looted in ancient times. The people who supposedly killed Fegaris—the case is still open—were modern-day gangsters working the black market in antiquities. And it gets even weirder. Fegaris apparently *predicted* her death. Left a bunch of psychic-type clues, pointing the finger to one of her students. Of course, they couldn't make it stick, so the Greek authorities let the guy go."

"And you're thinking, another dead psychic…how can this be a coincidence?"

Her expression turned serious, her animation suddenly reined in. "It's no coincidence."

But he wasn't so sure. "Come on. This was what? Ten or twelve years ago?"

"Why does that matter?" she demanded. "The very definition of a serial killer includes a cooling off period. Think about it, Seven. Remember that bind-torture-and-kill guy in Kansas, the BTK murderer? The guy waited longer than twelve years before sending the police more letters. He missed the attention."

"Okay, sure," Seven said. "But if this bead we found is worth so much, why leave it behind at the scene of the crime?"

She rolled her eyes, as if he was being dense. "It's only *one* piece of the necklace. Someone has the rest, right? Besides, why should it make sense? We're dealing with some sick fuck."

"Or," he said, "someone trying to make it look like that."

Erika raised a brow and sat down across from him. He could see from the expression in her eyes that she was putting it together, using her partner radar.

"Give," she said, when he hesitated.

He wasn't so sure he was ready to show his hand. He hadn't said anything about the night before with Rob from FSU, how the two of them had gone over the footage from the interview with Gia Moon, discovering that she knew Mimi Tran's security code.

I guess she did it. That had been Rob's take on things: guilty. Seven didn't think Erika would disagree.

And still he had trouble going there. He could see that image of Gia Moon, her blue, blue eyes staring up at him, wide and guileless. She didn't strike him as a woman who had anything to hide.

And then there was the bite of that static charge when they'd touched.

So he made a decision. The security code. He'd go straight to the horse's mouth. Then, after he had a better grasp of the information, he'd tell Erika. Let her weigh in.

"Seven?" Erika prompted.

He said, "Here's the thing. While you were expanding your consciousness, reading up on archaeology and the Holy Grail, some of us were doing *real* police work. I went over Tran's PDA."

That was something else he'd done early this morning. Checked Mimi Tran's handheld personal digital assistant device they'd found in her office.

He slipped the printout across the desk to Erika, trying to rationalize his actions. He wasn't exactly lying to his partner, he was just dealing with one lead at a time. The PDA was something more tangible.

He tapped the date of the murder. "Remember what Alice said about Mimi Tran having had a light lunch before she died?" he asked, referring to their meeting with the coroner.

Any PDA had software that allowed the user to synchronize the device with a desktop computer. The software also allowed the user to print out a hard copy of any data on the PDA, like a personal calendar—which was what Seven showed Erika now, pointing out the fact that Mimi Tran had scheduled a lunch with a "D.G." on the day she died.

They had met at a place called Le Jardin. Seven flipped through the log, pointing out to Erika every time D.G. came up. The initials appeared to be a regular thing. Once a week at Le Jardin.

"So, Erika," he said. "How do you feel about Vietnamese food?"

* * *

Seven confessed he'd never eaten Vietnamese food.

"Weird, huh?" he told Erika as they drove down Brookhurst into Garden Grove. "I grew up a stone's throw away from the largest population of Vietnamese outside of their country and I manage to skip out on one of their biggest contributions—the food. How does that happen?"

He'd eaten Chinese and Thai. Japanese, for sure; sushi was practically a staple of the SoCal diet. He'd even had Korean barbecue. But never Vietnamese.

Erika pretended to think about it. "Let's see. This from a man who considers a burger from In and Out fine dining?"

"Unless you count Lee's Sandwiches," he amended. "I've had plenty of those."

Lee's was the Vietnamese version of a deli chain. You couldn't go three blocks in Little Saigon without running into one. They were as ubiquitous as Starbucks anywhere else. They served a wide array of Euro-Asian style sandwiches, but specialized in *banh mi,* a Vietnamese take on the sub. The sandwiches usually involved a lot of pork served with interesting condiments.

Erika gave a short laugh of disbelief. "If memory serves, you order the turkey club on the ten-inch baguette with a Coke. Not exactly a step into the exotic."

"What do you know. Next time, I might just order myself one of those avocado smoothies. I've always wondered what those things taste like."

He could see she was trying hard not to smile. "*That* I'd like to see. Really I would, cowboy."

He shot her a look as she drove. "You don't think I'll do it?"

But Erika just rolled her eyes and braked in a California-style stop—not stopping at all, just slowing down enough to make sure there was no oncoming traffic before crossing the intersection. A few blocks later, she turned into the parking lot.

Like most restaurants in Little Saigon, Le Jardin was hidden in a strip mall. But once Seven and Erika stepped past the entrance, they left the world of strip malls far behind. Seven wasn't sure if the place was five-star, but it had to be close.

The decor was modern: the confetti design of the carpet, an arched facade painted red accenting the window frames, a blue-and-gold-striped counter. There was a view to the open kitchen and a bucolic painting near the entrance. Pristine linens covered tables bracketed by rattan chairs. Acoustic guitar warred with Vietnamese spoken by lunch guests and bustling waiters in white shirts and black ties. There wasn't a white face in the place.

According to the manager, Mimi and her guest preferred dining in the courtyard.

"She came here a lot," the man said. "With Mr. David. That's his table right there." He pointed to the far side of the courtyard, to a private corner. "He orders the white asparagus and crabmeat soup. That's his favorite."

"And Ms. Tran orders the jellyfish salad?" Seven said.

"*Goi sura tom thit.* Every time."

Seven pulled out his notebook. "You have a last name for David?"

"Of course," the manager said. Only he didn't volunteer the name. Instead, he peered anxiously at Seven. "Look, this is a very good customer. An important man. I don't want to make trouble."

"I thought he and Mimi Tran were just having lunch?" Seven asked in a casual voice.

Again, the manager seemed to think about it. He was in his fifties, definitely old enough to be part of the old guard, someone who had come to this country as a refugee with a healthy distrust of authority figures. Seven wondered if that look of fear and suspicion ever disappeared.

"David Gospel." The manager glanced back at the room teeming with patrons. "If that's all, Detectives?"

"For now, yes. Thank you."

Erika followed Seven outside. They didn't say a word, acting very casual, as if it was an everyday thing for them to have a name like Gospel—a top player in the local economy and politics—come up during a murder investigation.

According to the printout from the victim's PDA, Gospel may very well have been the last person to see her alive.

It wasn't until they reached the car that Erika stopped and looked at Seven.

"D.G. is David Gospel?"

She said it as if maybe she'd imagined the manager saying the name.

"David Gospel," Seven echoed.

He was pretty sure she mouthed the words *holy shit* before she opened the Crown Vic's door and slipped inside.

21

The psychic was back. And she was talking in nursery rhymes.

"There was an old lady who swallowed a fly," she said. "I don't know why she swallowed a fly—perhaps she'll die."

Gia Moon had been waiting in the interview room when Seven and Erika arrived back from Le Jardin. She was dressed in jeans and one of those embroidered cotton tunic tops, looking very much the artist. Her hair fell loose down her back, thick and black, and she kept looping the long bangs behind her ears in a nervous gesture.

On the floor beside her was one of those canvas mailbags, making Seven wonder about women and these huge purses. What the hell did they carry around inside those things, anyway? An earthquake kit? And what were men missing out on with their skimpy wallets?

"There was an old lady who swallowed a spider. That wriggled and wiggled and tickled inside her."

Listening to Gia recite the rhyme, Erika wore a look of total disbelief on her face. Not that it bothered Gia Moon. She just kept on going.

"She swallowed the spider to catch the fly. I don't know why she swallowed the fly—perhaps she'll die."

Seven thought the two women made a fair contrast. Erika, too, wore jeans, the pricey kind they advertise in the magazines to fit every curve...and she didn't mind bragging about it. She'd tucked them into brown suede boots that matched her corduroy blazer.

Seven knew Erika was vain about her figure, and she had cause to be. *Muy caliente* didn't begin to describe the Latina homicide detective with her large brown eyes and flowing curls.

Erika had once told Seven about this magazine article that claimed Latinas were twice as likely to reapply mascara, going for a more dramatic look. He remembered how she'd batted her lashes at him while she'd said it.

In contrast, Gia's hair looked as if she'd stepped right out of the shower and let it dry naturally. Again, her face was bare of makeup. Seven figured that with those sooty black lashes rimming her eyes, anything like mascara would be superfluous.

But while Erika's beauty tended to intimidate, Gia came off as soft and fragile. Seven doubted the image fit. Watching her now, he wondered what else could be part of the act.

Under her short nails, he saw paint again, the same shades of red.

"It goes on," she said, talking about the nursery rhyme.

"No kidding?" Erika said, sitting down, her stoic expression saying it all. *This is such bullshit....*

"The animals get bigger and bigger. It ends with a horse. There was an old lady who swallowed a horse. She's dead—"

"Of course," Erika said, finishing the rhyme for her. "So you think next time we're going to find a horse's head stuffed in the victim's mouth? Did you see that in your dreams, too?"

Gia stared up at her, unblinking. "You don't understand."

"It's a game," Seven said, putting the pieces together.

She turned to focus those brilliant blue eyes on him. "That's right. The bead, I saw it more clearly this time. It's part of a necklace. The killer will keep giving you bits and pieces of it, like bread crumbs."

She reached for her purse on the floor. She pulled out a folded piece of paper. Watching her closely, he could see her take a breath, like someone bracing herself to plunge into dicey waters. She unfolded it and spread it out with shaking hands.

It was a pencil sketch of a crudely made necklace. The piece was intrinsically beautiful. The thing looked like it belonged in a museum.

Seven took the paper, frowning at the sketch. A string of small stones surrounded a central crystal the size of his fist. It seemed to be held together by some sort of wire wrapped around each stone.

She'd done a beautiful job, giving only a few details, allowing for the imagination to fill in the blanks.

Only one section was rendered with exquisite precision, making it seem almost as if it were spotlighted there on the paper. She'd shaded that bead to show even the cat's-eye line down the center.

It looked identical to the one they'd found inside the bird's beak.

"Find out whoever has this," Gia said, "and you'll get closer to the killer."

Erika took the sheet from Seven. Other than the photograph they'd shown Professor Murphy, no one outside of homicide had seen the bead they'd found at the crime scene.

Only here it was, sketched to perfection.

"It hasn't been reported stolen yet," Gia said. "Whoever has the necklace, either they haven't figured out it's missing, or they don't want to reveal they had the necklace in the first place."

"So now you're doing police work?" Erika asked, still holding the drawing. "Wow. You ever thought about being a cop? Really, you're *good*."

Gia Moon leaned across the table and grabbed Erika's arm. She looked into her eyes and said, "His name is Alfonso. He left when you were seven. You had to grow up fast. And yes. He is very sorry."

Erika dropped the sketch as if she'd been burned.

Seven could see the breath leave his partner's chest...and he knew how she felt. He was having trouble sucking in the oxygen himself.

"Sorry," Gia said, sitting back in her chair. "I don't usually do that, but I need you to believe me." She turned to Seven. "The killer. He's hungry again, ready to take his next victim."

"The last time we spoke," Seven said, sitting down beside her, "I believe you said you were next."

She sighed, looking exasperated. "I don't know. Maybe. That's what I thought, but now I'm not so sure. Sometimes it's difficult to interrupt what the spirits show me."

"Meaning," Erika said, still looking shaken, "you were wrong before…so maybe you're wrong now?"

Gia shook her head, her tone emphatic. "It's going to happen, Detective. And soon. The energy in my dream—it's closer, stronger. He's playing a game. I don't know the rules or the timing." She turned to Seven. "Look, I wish I could give you the killer's name, rank and serial number. But I can't."

Erika raised her brows at Seven, warning him not to fall for those pretty blue eyes and that desperate expression. She tipped her head toward the hall, wanting him to join her outside.

To Gia, she said, "You'll excuse us?"

In the hallway, Erika barely waited for Seven to shut the door before she started in.

"Did you see that drawing? Everything's blurry and indistinct, *except* the bead found at the crime scene." She started pacing, shaking her head. "It's too good, Seven."

"It's not like she's the only one who knows what this thing looks like," he argued, saying the obvious. "What about that Web site for The Lunites. There had to be some kind of image there?"

She shook her head. "Nada. Just a lot of speculation about what it could look like."

"And the professor? Murphy certainly seemed to know all about this thing—"

"Bullshit." She came up to him, talking in a rush. "I said it before, Seven. Your psychic did this."

He watched Erika's chest pumping up and down, her breathing hard as she waited for his reaction. *Your psychic*. Already, that connection was spelled out between them, a great divide between partners.

Seven knew he was taking a chance, and still he asked, "What she said in there about your father—"

"That stuff about Alfonso? You're not taking that shit seriously, are you? Like it's some kind of secret? Next, she'll be talking about your brother going to prison for murder, as if it wasn't headline news." Erika put both fists on her hips, spitting mad. "It's a parlor trick, Seven. She's hiding something. She knows who murdered Mimi Tran and she doesn't want to implicate herself." Erika leaned into him, speaking in a harsh whisper. "If this is a game, I'm telling you right now, cowboy, she's the master of ceremonies."

But her expression said something different; she wasn't so comfortable with Gia and her insights.

"So why not keep with it?" he asked. "We pretend we believe her. Get as much information as we can...let her show her hand?"

Erika closed her eyes. He could almost see the steam coming out of her ears.

When she got herself together, she said, "So it's Ouija board detective work from now on?"

"You got something better?" he asked.

He didn't wait for her answer. Instead, he walked into the interview room, shutting the door behind him. He knew Erika. She wasn't coming back inside. That would involve eating too much crow.

Gia Moon stood next to the table, her mailbag now slung over one shoulder, as if she was ready to take her leave. He noticed the drawing still on the table. He folded it and put it away, making sure it would be part of the file.

"Sorry," she said, revisiting her apology.

"Because?" he asked.

She shrugged, her thumb hooked around the strap of her purse. "I'm not usually so...intrusive," she said, referring to her interaction with Erika and her insights about Alfonso.

"Funny thing. You don't look the least bit sorry."

She lifted her chin. "Okay. Maybe I'm not. Sometimes it helps jump-start the process, a sort of show of proof." Suddenly, she gave a sheepish smile. "But I have a feeling it didn't work."

Seven told himself he wasn't about to believe in the supernatural. He actually agreed with Erika; there had to be a gimmick.

But he also knew his job. He was the cool observer. He needed to take in information, not filter it out. Later, he could analyze. But once you shut the door on a source, you had nothing.

"Would you like to get some coffee?" he asked. And when she

hesitated, he said, "Come on. You didn't make the trip down here just to recite some nursery rhyme and show me a sketch. There has to be more to it. And I happen to be a good listener."

Unlike Erika, whom he imagined standing just outside the door in high dudgeon, her stubborn jaw locked in place.

"Your partner left," Gia said.

He tried not to react, as if someone reading his mind was an everyday thing. He just stood there, waiting her out.

"All right," she said. "Coffee."

As she walked past, he thought he heard her say, "If that's what it's going to take."

Erika still hadn't caught her breath. She was jogging—no, sprinting—back to the Crimes Against Persons unit. She hadn't even looked when Seven stepped back inside to finish the interview.

When Gia touched her—when she'd said those things about her dad—Erika felt like someone had just ripped open her head.

She had no idea how that woman had gotten her information on Alfonso. According to all legal documents, Erika's father was dead and buried. Her mother never changed the paperwork.

Moving down the hall, Erika told herself to calm down. That's the way these people operated. Like those magicians in Vegas, they put on a good show and they knew all the tricks. There was no reason for her to freak out like this. What happened back in the interview room wasn't real.

And yes. He is very sorry.

"Shit," she said out loud.

How long had she waited to hear those words from Alfonso? *I'm sorry, Erika. What I did to you and Miguel was wrong....*

"Shit, shit, shit."

Erika told herself to get a grip. How many times had an *espiritista* or a *curandero* taken advantage of her mother in that very way? Whenever Erika called mami, her mother was buying some new herbal treatment or making a payment for advice. People could always take advantage of Milagro because she *be-*

lieved…just like she'd believed Alfonso before the bastard abandoned his family.

Well, that wasn't Erika. She would never be that naive.

Back at the office, she unlocked the drawer to her desk and grabbed her purse. Not for one minute did she believe that Gia Moon had a gift.

The woman was a fraud, pure and simple. And Erika planned to prove it.

Just like Gia Moon, Erika had a couple of tricks up her sleeve.

22

Seven realized he'd been wrong about never trying Vietnamese food. He'd forgotten about the coffee.

He'd read somewhere that Vietnam had surpassed Colombia in producing and exporting the bean. *Ca phé sua nong,* black coffee—a kind of mule kick to the head—was his usual. Always ordered with a croissant. On hot days, he even dabbled in the more exotic—filtered coffee balanced with the sweetness of condensed milk and served over ice.

He liked it best at the very Anglo-sounding Coffee Factory, a place with too much polish to conjure up images of anything other than Starbucks despite the French menu and scenic pictures of Vietnam on the walls. Given Erika's present state of mind, the Coffee Factory might not count as a Vietnamese culinary experience. She'd probably want him to down one of those jellyfish salads before she gave her epicurean thumbs-up.

He and Gia met outside at one of the bistro tables under a tan umbrella. He'd ordered *ca phé phin,* as plain as it gets. She had *ca phé den da,* iced coffee served with black tapioca pearls.

"Does that really count?" he asked. "I mean as coffee. I think I've eaten cheesecake with less fat and sugar."

"It practically is a dessert." Gia smiled at him from across the table, taking a sip through the straw.

She had a nice smile, he thought, with even white teeth. She was, in fact, a beautiful woman—and someone connected to the grisliest murder he'd come across in his career as a detective. It was something he needed reminding of…especially sitting here under an umbrella, sipping a couple of coffees together.

"This place reminds me of my childhood," she said.

"You've been to Vietnam?"

"No. Never there. But the whole French thing. I loved Paris. My mother and I used to travel a lot. I guess I miss it."

"Santa Ana, Little India, the Armenian Quarter, Little Tehran, Little Arabia," he said, listing the melting pot that was Orange County. "All just a short car ride away."

"I know." She stirred her coffee with the straw. "But life gets rather busy. Sometimes just a couple of miles away seem too far."

He realized he'd made the same excuse dozens of times. He wondered when it all started, the hamster-on-the-wheel existence. He had a small house with a mortgage. A new car. He even had an investment property he owned with his father—the same condo he planned to move Beth and Nick into when Beth finally got around to realizing she'd need to sell before debtors started in with the liens.

Just like everyone else, he was working his ass off to salt some money away. God knows he'd taken a hit on the market. That Intel stock.

His ex-wife hadn't asked for a dime—he suspected she hadn't wanted the connection.

No, Laurin didn't need him anymore. But everybody else did. His parents, Nick and Beth…they were all relying on him, hoping he'd keep solid and not melt away like the mirage his brother had turned out to be.

"Everything will work out," Gia said from across the table.

He glanced up, hating that zing she'd just delivered to his gut. "What do you call that, exactly? Mind reading?"

This time, her smile didn't reach her eyes. "Yeah. One of my better tricks."

He smiled back, telling himself to rein it in. "It's just a little…unnerving, you know?"

He reached across the table, intending to give her hand a reassuring squeeze. Letting her know *we're all in this together;* playing good cop to Erika's bad.

Only, when he touched her, he felt that same shock of electricity.

It was more subtle this time. He could almost believe he'd imagined it. But there was Gia, pulling her hand away, reacting.

Without looking at him, she fell back in with her coffee, sipping the java through her straw as if it were the most amazing thing she'd ever tasted.

Okay, he thought, leaning back in the bistro chair. *Okay.*

"Do you have any children?" he asked, returning to his agenda.

That was the reason he'd brought her here, away from Erika and the sterile atmosphere of the precinct. He wanted to draw Gia out, make her trust him. He knew that was something he was good at. In a pinch, he could be charming as hell.

He and his partner knew their individual strengths. People tended to flirt with Erika and open up to him. How did Erika put it? *You have that avuncular thing going.* He'd had to look the damn word up afterwards: avuncular. Relating to or suggesting of an uncle.

"I have a daughter," she answered.

"Really? How old?"

Gia put the coffee aside and held back her smile. "Twelve going on thirty."

They both laughed.

"I know what you mean. My nephew." He shook his head. "Amazing what they think they know at ten."

"Amazing what they *do* know at ten."

Another round of laughter.

He already knew from her statement a lot of personal information, like the fact that there was no Mr. Moon in the picture.

"I have to believe girls are so much worse," he said. "I mean, with boys, you just need to make sure they don't kill themselves trying to see if they can fly using a bedsheet for a parachute. But girls…"

She tapped her head. "It's all in here and very complicated."

She flashed another smile. He could well imagine what Erika would think if she could see them now.

Avuncular, my ass.

"Why haven't you worked with law enforcement before?" he asked.

"Don't take this wrong, but it's difficult enough working with you and Detective Cabral."

"I give you that," he said, nodding. "So why this time?"

She shrugged. "My dream. It was…disturbing."

"That first day, you didn't seem too disturbed."

She frowned. "What makes you say that?"

"You said you were next, but didn't ask for protection," he said, stating the obvious.

"Maybe I believe in myself enough to know I can help you more than you can help me."

Again he nodded, as if he thought the same. "How does that work exactly? You helping us?" Because so far, she'd given them only puzzles.

She looked away. He almost missed it, that wistful expression. At that moment, she reminded him of Ricky, that last time he'd seen his brother. Back then, Seven had still believed it was all some horrible mistake, Scott's murder.

"He has a low energy," she said in a soft, sure voice. "It's been that way since he was young. There have been mood swings. He hears voices in his head. He could be abusing drugs—alcohol, most likely. He'll show impulsive behavior and have memory problems. Poor concentration. He might suffer from anxiety or a physical problem with no obvious cause. There's something wrong with his eyes. That's why he takes them like trophies from his victims. People think the eyes are the windows to the soul, but he sees a life source. And he wants more."

Seven waited, giving her a minute. "Wow," he said. "I don't remember there being any mention in the papers about the condition of Mimi Tran's eyes."

He'd meant it as an accusation. Once again Gia Moon had pinned herself to the crime, showing special knowledge. To him, it was evidence of guilt.

But she didn't take it as a threat. Instead, her own eyes grew unfocused. Her breathing grew shallow.

If this was an act, it was a good one.

"He took Mimi Tran's eyes," she said in a raw whisper. "And it's not the first time. He gets supreme pleasure from inflicting pain, even if it's his own. There are other trophies. A collection. Like a feather dipped in his victim's blood. He used it to paint something. He commits the most unspeakable crimes with a cool head. And the voices in his head—they tell him he's better than the rest of us. They tell him he's God."

Seven could see that it took her a few seconds to focus back on the present, as if she was coming out of some sort of trance. Suddenly, she looked embarrassed.

"I thought you said you painted for a living," he said.

She held up her hand, showing again the red paint under her nails. "An artist through and through."

"Well, that was a pretty impressive profile of a serial killer. For an artist, I mean."

She took a deep breath. "Dark spirits are a specialty of mine."

"You want to elaborate on that?"

"Depossession."

He frowned. "Are we talking exorcism?"

"Despite the fact that Western medicine dismisses possession as a cause of personal distress, many cultures insist that it is a reality. A spirit or entity attaches itself to a human host." And when he looked skeptical, she added, "There *are* cases where an individual doesn't fit any category of mental illness."

"So you call it spirit possession?"

He knew the minute he said the words he'd made a mistake. He could see her shut down, a wall rising between them. But he couldn't stop himself. He'd been thinking about Ricky, how it would be grand to just say some evil spirit got ahold of him.

"Hey, I get it," he said, trying to recoup. "No one believes you. So let's just get beyond the obvious and assume I don't. But I want to understand. Okay?"

She met his gaze. "What I do is dangerous work. I don't like to advertise. But you might as well know that I do seem to draw these sorts of spirits. I am a painter. But the things I paint…it's not always a pretty picture."

He remembered the crime scene he'd walked into at the Tran house. If she'd seen anything like that, he couldn't imagine living in her head.

"You said he's playing a game. Any idea what the rules are?"

She thought about it. "Don't get caught."

Seven gave her a disappointed look. "Is that all I get?"

"Revenge," she said.

"Right." Again, she was speaking in generalities, the kind of thing anybody could come up with.

She gave a tired sigh and pushed the coffee away. "Sorry to disappoint you," she said. "I don't know how to turn it on or shut if off."

"It's all right," he said. "I was pushing. Now how about you? Do you think you might need protection?"

"No."

"Wow. That was kind of fast. So fast that a guy might think you hadn't really put enough thought into your answer."

She held up her chin, looking like a woman who hadn't asked for help in a very long while. "I don't need help. Not yet."

She said it with such authority. For a fraction of a second, Seven wondered if she could actually be the real deal….

"So how does this gift of yours work?"

"I can't help you with your brother," she said.

She delivered the words like a shot from across the table. He had to catch his breath because the salvo was so completely out of context from their conversation.

And yet, that's *exactly* who he'd been thinking about. His brother. Seven had still been mulling over the possibility that Ricky could be one of these possessed people. What if rather than slamming him into jail, they could just sic a priest on him and shove out the evil? It made a tidy little explanation for what had happened…how one day, his brother had been this totally normal guy, and the next, he'd killed a man.

She sighed. "Sorry."

"You do a lot of apologizing."

"Not normally, no."

"Look, I can imagine what a giant pain all this is. Always having to explain yourself. But I was wondering about…your methods. Let's say I came to you as a client. I had some…depossession work to do. How do we start?"

"Depossession usually involves a spirit that fails to move on. I have guides. They help me talk to the spirits. I try to convince them it's time to leave."

"Spirit guides?"

She smiled. "I know how this must sound to you, Detective."

"Call me Seven, please. And actually, I get it. I mean, I watched *The Sixth Sense*. You see dead people."

But the joke fell flat. Sitting across the bistro table, she looked exactly like a woman who wanted to grab her car keys and that ridiculous mailbag she called a purse and just take off.

"Hey. I'm here, aren't I?" he asked softly.

"Yes." She sat back. She placed her hands flat on the table. "Yes, you are."

"I may not believe, but I want to understand. Especially if it takes some whack job off the streets. You get me?"

In response, she closed her eyes. She took a deep breath, keeping her hands spread out on the table. He'd taken a yoga class once with Erika. The way she was breathing, it's what they called a cleansing breath.

"The killer," she said, "he comes to me in dreams because it's a fluid state. Easy for spirits to cross over. As I told you, I tend to attract the darker spirits. An inherited trait, I'm afraid. From my mother's side. So far, it's been very juvenile, this spirit. As if maybe that of a child. Or childhood memories, I'm not sure which."

"No *kid* had anything to do with what I saw at the murder scene."

She opened her eyes. "The demon is different from the possessed. I have no idea how old the possessed person could be. I don't even know if it's a man or a woman."

Seven gave her another smile. He couldn't help it. The whole conversation was so out there. "It must be hell on sleep."

"You have no idea."

There were indeed dark circles under her eyes. He held back the urge to reach out and brush his thumb there. Instead, he held on to his coffee cup, the desire to touch her so strong it actually made him jumpy.

"You should talk to him," she said. "It might help."

She was talking about Ricky again. Reminding him of all those sleepless nights he'd spent worrying about his family.

Now he knew what Erika had felt when Gia had told her that stuff about Alfonso. It wasn't a good feeling, the idea that someone could open your mind up like a can and peer inside.

He shook his head. "That's some gift you have." He watched her carefully. "Is that how you figured out Mimi Tran's security code? You read her mind? Or did you see that in a dream?"

"What?"

"The security code to the victim's house. You know it."

She gave him a puzzled look. "I most certainly do not. What gave you that idea?"

"During the first interview. You stood to act out the victim opening the door. She disabled her security system, punching in the code. Your hand, it was at the exact level of the actual keypad. The numbers you punched in—you know the code."

She still looked mystified. "Maybe my body knows the code."

"Your *body* knows the code?"

"It's like automatic writing," she said, trying to figure out what had happened, for all intents and purposes acting like someone who had no memory of the event. "It's a common form of automatism, muscular movement attributed to supernatural guidance." Suddenly, she glanced up, those blue eyes meeting his. "Do I need an attorney?"

The two of them sat staring across the tiny table, the silence absolute.

He answered by echoing back her own words. "Not yet."

She picked up the mailbag and started fishing through it coming up with her wallet. "I'd better go," she said.

He told her, "It's on me." And when she looked like she might argue the point, he added, "Hey, we're full service at Westminster Homicide."

He said it with a smile, trying to get back a lighter mood. But she wasn't buying it.

She stood up, watching him, and the look she gave him…it was almost as if the air were crackling around them with that static charge. Slowly, as if trying not to spook him, she reached out and touched his hand.

It was only the slightest touch—her fingertips brushing over his knuckles—but suddenly, he felt on fire.

An image flashed inside his head, he and Gia, naked in bed together, their arms and legs wrapped around each other so that he couldn't tell where one started and the other ended.

He pulled his hand away, shocked. He could feel himself trying to catch his breath, almost as if those passionate kisses had been real. He looked up to find her staring at him.

She said, "I have to go."

She turned and jogged into the parking lot. He could still feel his heart hammering in his chest.

He noticed she drove a hybrid. A Prius.

In his jacket pocket, his cell phone chirped to life. Taking a few breaths, he glanced at the display and saw that it was Erika calling.

"What's up?" he said into the phone, thankful that his voice sounded normal as he watched Gia drive off.

"No kidding," he said, hearing the news.

The archaeology professor, Murphy—he'd shown up at the precinct. And he'd brought the troops.

23

Seven walked into the Crimes Against Persons unit to discover it had been turned into a laboratory. The sight of microscopes, laptops, scales and calipers warred with the utilitarian office furniture where Professor Murphy and his minions had set up to examine the bead. Looking around, Seven hoped the professor hadn't brought along anything radioactive.

The troops turned out to be five grad students, one with a digital camera preparing to catalog the moment, until Seven shut down the impromptu documentary. The precinct had its own video equipment, thank you very much.

Murphy was at the center of the controlled chaos, practically rubbing his hands together in anticipation of "authenticating" the bead…while Erika made sure to dot her i's and cross her t's on the chain of custody. Seven felt a tad de trop in the hustle and flow. But given his discussion with Gia earlier, he was incredibly curious as to what the hell the professor might find.

At least Murphy was entertaining. A man used to the lecture podium, he hadn't stopped talking since Seven stepped into the room. The topic of the moment: the theft of a couple hundred artifacts from the Corinth Archaeological Museum.

"It was only a matter of time, really. With no more ancient treasuries to loot and a high demand on the black market, the thieves naturally turned to the museum collections themselves. There were 285 artifacts stolen in all, by a gang of Greek nationals, as it turned out. Several found their way to Christie's and were sold at auction. One of the pieces, a vase, was published in a catalog for sale. An Oxford professor recognized the piece and told the seller it had been stolen. Of course, the man immediately contacted the FBI."

The professor hovered over his microscope, talking as he peered through the binocular lenses. He kept referring back to the laptop, tapping in notes with two fingers, like Morse code.

"The FBI recovered most of the artifacts sealed in plastic boxes inside fish crates in a Miami storage facility. Can you imagine? Fish crates!"

"No kidding," Seven said, seeing a reaction was expected. At the same time he wondered what the hell any of this had to do with the damn bead.

"Except for just a few pieces," Murphy continued, "every one of the stolen artifacts was returned to the Greek government with the cooperation of the FBI."

"And the artifacts that were never recovered?" Erika asked, catching on to where the professor was headed.

"Estelle Fegaris believed that the very people who had those missing pieces also maintained possession of the Eye." The professor turned to Seven. "Have you ever been to Delphi, Detective?"

European vacations being such a big part of a homicide detective's lifestyle? "Can't say I've had that pleasure."

"It's considered the navel of the earth. Zeus let loose two eagles and they met at Delphi. One of the eagles dropped a stone from its beak and it made a hole in the ground. The *umphalos*—the navel of the earth. There's a stone still there to commemorate the spot. Tourists like to take their photographs showing their belly button in front of the stone."

Seven watched as Murphy removed the bead from the microscope and grabbed a tiny vial. He let fall a droplet of whatever was in the vial, then quickly returned the bead to the microscope.

"About the Eye?" Seven prompted.

"It's a colorful explanation for a location documented to have volcanic activity," Murphy continued, ignoring Seven's attempt to keep the conversation focused on the evidence. Apparently, a lecture on the classics was part and parcel of any relevant information the professor was giving up.

"Delphi, the home of the oracle, held the Panhellenic games every four years, called the Pythian games, their importance second only to the Olympic games in ancient Greece. It's also on the slopes of Mount Parnassus, rumored to represent Mount Olympus itself, the throne of the gods. It's truly an amazing place. The soil is purple from the bauxite mined there. The blue Ionian Sea meets what is called the green sea of Itea—a grove of five million olive trees."

Standing next to Seven, Erika gave the supervising tech a nervous glance that seemed to say, *What the hell is he doing to our evidence?*

"Mythology tells us that Zeus commanded Apollo to leave his sister and mother on the sacred island of Delos. So Apollo turned himself into a dolphin and traveled to Delphi. He fought the Python, Gaia's sacred creature, and killed it to claim Delphi for his oracle."

Murphy moved back to the laptop. Even from where he stood, Seven could see graphs light up the screen. He couldn't make heads or tails of it, of course, but he knew it would mean something to their own techs…which he figured was the point of putting up with the professor. Murphy was the expert here, helping to authenticate the damn evidence.

"In the ruins, you can still see where Apollo's priestess," he said, not missing a beat as he typed, "the Pythia, would crawl through a tunnel into the sanctuary of Apollo, chewing the leaves from the sacred laurel tree. Deep inside, in a place where only she was allowed entry, there bubbled up from the earth a poisonous spring. There she'd sit and chew her leaves. Many believe that the ethylene gas vapors combined with the juices from the laurel leaves to put the Pythia into a state of ecstasy, a trance, from which she would interpret the future. Estelle Fegaris postulated something different."

"The necklace?" Seven prompted.

"According to Fegaris, the Eye acted like a lens, magnifying the psychic powers of its wearer, a theory considered by many to be wildly out of touch with the evidence in the field. Fegaris needed to produce the necklace as proof."

"Is there a picture of this thing on some piece of papyrus somewhere?" Seven asked, thinking of Gia's sketch.

The professor shook his head. "That would be too easy. Only Fegaris claimed to know the necklace's appearance and origin, and she wasn't sharing. It was one of the many mysteries surrounding the Eye."

"So how do we know she didn't make the whole thing up?" Seven asked.

"We don't," Murphy said, suddenly stepping away from the stone. "But given her reputation, there were those of us who chose to believe in the Eye's existence."

The professor stood there, staring at the bead. He glanced back at the computer screen, a strange expression on his face.

"What is it, Professor?" Erika asked. "What did you find?"

"Dating ancient glass can be a tricky business." His expression now changed to one of reverence as he approached the tiny sample. "Frankly, the dating of an isolated piece like this is a near impossible task, particularly with no existing *comparanda*."

"Meaning?" Seven said, getting a bad feeling.

"I can't authenticate the artifact. Not here," he said, still focused on the bead. "It requires the kind of chemical and physical examination that can only be done in a major laboratory—if it can be done at all. Perhaps the University of Pennsylvania. Or the University of Washington." His expression visibly brightened, as if he'd just come up with a wonderful idea. "In fact, I have a colleague I could call there. I would be happy to accompany the piece myself."

"I just bet you would," Seven said. "Dr. Murphy, you knew before you came that you couldn't authenticate the bead, didn't you?"

"That would be correct, Detective." Murphy pressed his glasses back up the bridge of his nose. "Of course, if I had said as much before, I would have risked never seeing the bead…something I found completely untenable. What can I say, Detective? I took my shot."

Before Seven could take *his* shot, Erika stepped between the two men. "Come on, Professor. The last hour wasn't just for show. You found something."

"I *can't* categorize the sample, Detective."

"For someone who just came up with a blank," Seven said, "you look incredibly pleased."

"The fact is, I am, Detective. This stone, its unique ability to change color—the cat's-eye slash of light down the center—Fegaris described it perfectly."

"And?" This time, Seven didn't even try to keep the impatience out of his voice.

"There is a family of crystals here on earth called chrysoberyl that exhibit similar traits to this stone. Alexandrite, named for the Russian tsar, Alexander II, can change from red to green, the colors of Imperial Russia. A cat's-eye variety also exists. Microscopic inclusions occur in an orientation parallel to the c-axis, producing the effect. This, however, is nothing like that."

"So what is it?" Erika asked.

"I'm not sure, but after a cursory examination, I am convinced more than ever that this bead is part of the Eye of Athena. Which means Estelle Fegaris was right. The Eye exists," he said, indicating the bead was proof of just that. "And if she was right about the existence of the Eye, then I tend to think Fegaris was right about its origins. This bead, Detectives," he said, turning to look at both Seven and Erika, "is not of this earth."

24

Seven found himself back at the Coffee Factory, this time with Erika across the bistro table sipping iced coffee through a straw. It was almost three o'clock in the afternoon. Other than a table of Vietnamese men in business attire, they were the only people in the place.

Seven watched a middle-aged woman power-walk through the parking lot wearing a conical hat made from braided palm leaves. The hat, a *non la,* was typical here. He looked around the pastel minimall. The clapboard storefronts all carried Vietnamese names; billboards pitched their slogan in the same language. Everything looked clean, upscale—a glimpse, perhaps, at what might have been if the Americans had won the war decades ago.

It still surprised him, this small enclave of the exotic. If you were Vietnamese, you might live as far away as Irvine, but come the weekend, the diaspora descended here. And why not? Little Saigon provided *Pho* noodle shops and *banh mi* eateries, block-long supermarkets and jewelry stores, not to mention the latest that Vietnamese pop stars had to offer—all in a shiny new home away from home.

He thought of his own background, French-Canadian. Erika was right, he'd been whitewashed long ago, assimilated into the SoCal culture of burgers and surfing. His father barely spoke French, Seven spoke none at all. Traditional meals at home had long ago given way to Kentucky Fried Chicken and Hamburger Helper.

"I noticed you passed on the avocado smoothie again," Erika said.

"Big mistake there," he said, choosing to tank up on hot coffee sweetened with condensed milk.

He glanced down at the spiral notebook on the patio table, a mishmash of dashed-off notes and underlined names connected by arrows, the mind map they'd been working from. He and Erika had spent the last half hour piecing the story together.

Estelle Fegaris, renowned classical archaeologist from Harvard University, believes in the existence of the Eye of Athena, a crystal that supposedly allows its wearer to amplify psychic abilities. Fegaris postulates that the Eye, a crystal from outer space, was worn by the oracle at Delphi in the form of a necklace. Only, she can't reveal how she found out about the Eye or why she even believes it exists. Despite this, Professor Murphy recognizes one of the beads from the oracle's necklace.

Fegaris, according to the professor, asks for the archaeological community to take a leap of faith. When that doesn't happen, she sets out to find the damn stone to prove she's right.

She claims the Eye is part of the Treasury of Atreus, looted from the Beehive Tomb during ancient times. Fegaris discovers a connection between the looted Treasury of Atreus and artifacts stolen from the museum at Corinth during the 1990s.

Eventually, Fegaris reveals her dark side, giving in to the psychic within. She becomes very active in psychic archaeology. She takes part in a series of experiments conducted by Morgan Tyrell on the human brain. The connection ends up costing Fegaris her job. Harvard gives her the heave-ho.

But Fegaris doesn't seem to care. For the next decade, she is a woman on a mission, tracking down the Eye. She ends up in Greece, presumably dealing with the shadier side of archaeology, the black market in antiquities, desperate to locate the object.

"But she can't prove a thing," Erika says, tapping her finger on the mind map where the words *The Eye* appeared underlined. "She has no methodology, no proof. Nothing. Only a bunch of ragtag amateurs ready to believe what she's selling."

"Not just amateurs," Seven said, pointing out the obvious. "I think we're talking acolytes. And Fegaris has enough credentials

o sell her vision to the likes of our man Murphy…and others in
he field."

"So what does she want with this Eye of Athena? And why
sn't she telling what she knows?"

"Maybe she wants to use it. You know, dangle it from her neck
nd become Super Psychic. I-will-use-my-power-only-for-good
ort of thing." He cocked his head, staring down at the mind map
n the notebook page. "Or maybe she just wants to get her ducks
p in a row before she reveals what she knows and gives her col-
eagues a chance to pooh-pooh her ideas."

"I don't know, cowboy. After reading that Web site, I think
his is more about some cult figure than any serious work."

"Maybe."

When Estelle Fegaris is killed, purportedly by the very an-
iquities dealers she sought out in tracking the Eye, the whole
hing takes on new life. Fegaris becomes a martyr for her cause.
Ier acolytes go to ground, spawning Web sites and a legend wor-
hy of Camelot. They call themselves Lunites. Others in the field
all them Lunatics.

"Fegaris left clues about her killer's identity," he said. "Pre-
umably a student. But the charges don't stick, so twelve years
ater, we're left with a cold case somehow connected to Mimi
ran's murder."

"And now, Murphy claims the Eye does exist. That someone
as it—'something not of this earth,'" Erika murmured, quoting
rofessor Murphy.

"And darned if it doesn't end up stuck in the mouth of our
ictim."

Erika shook her head. "It's all too Erich Von Daniken for me."

"Erich Von who?" Seven asked, wondering if he would ever
et to sleep tonight after downing his second *ca phé sua nong*.

"Von Daniken? You know, the *Chariots of the Gods?*" And
vhen he still drew a blank, she muttered, "Jesus, Seven. Don't
ou ever watch the Discovery Channel?"

"Hey, I have seen every Freddy Krueger movie ever made, at
east *twice*, so don't you even try to say I lack culture. But look,

I'm actually impressed. I think I should start calling you the Amazing Supernatural Sleuth."

She pursed her lips. "You're going to call me ASS."

"Would I do that?"

She gave a long, loud slurp on the straw. "I was thinking maybe your psychic is right, after all."

Your psychic.

Seven hadn't mentioned anything about his conversation with Gia after Erika left the interview room—especially the part about him having a vision of the two of them in bed together. But here was Erika with her sixth sense, pushing him.

Your psychic.

"What exactly is my psychic right about?" he asked.

Erika slid the empty cup away. "She said whoever had the necklace wouldn't want us to know they had it…because it was part of some stolen collection. That's starting to sound a lot like what the professor said when he mentioned Fegaris and the stolen goods from the museum in Corinth. Think about it, Seven. It's the perfect crime."

"Who's going to report that the damn thing is missing if it's stolen in the first place?"

"What about Murphy's claim that the bead we found comes from outer space?"

Seven made a rude noise. "The guy would say anything to get his hands on that artifact, so he drops some theory on alien visitation. We're supposed to freak out and hand him the bead so he can fly it up to some lab? You saw how he played us today. I don't care what Guru Lois said about the guy's impeccable credentials. Any more testing gets done by our people alone."

Erika shut the notebook. "So we focus on the bead and its connection to the Tran murder—like the possibility that the damn thing was bait. The killer leaves a single bead at the murder site."

"It's like advertising."

She nodded. "A sensational killing, guaranteed to get lots of press. Whoever wants the necklace knows the killer has the rest."

Seven thought it made sense. Only, there was this other theory bumping around his head.

The killer will keep giving you bits and pieces of it, like bread crumbs.

That's what Gia had told them. That this was just the beginning…there would be other killings, each with its own piece of the necklace.

Erika tossed her plastic cup into the garbage can. "Me? I still like the psychic as a suspect."

"Yeah." He looked away. "So you said."

"But not you?"

He sighed. "I'm stuck on the fact that she came to us. I mean, come on."

"You're really going with the no-one-could-be-that-stupid defense?"

"It's just a gut feeling. You saw that crime scene. You really think she's the perp?"

"Wouldn't be the first time some sweet little thing done someone wrong," she countered.

Seven stood and threw his own cup into the trash, making the bank shot. Despite the hot coffee he felt chilled by the direction the case was taking.

"All righty then," he told Erika. "In the meantime, what do you say we actually find the asshole who did this—before anyone else dies."

David stared down at the velvet-lined drawer. He felt himself hyperventilating.

The necklace had been decimated, its precious beads tossed around like dice inside the drawer. The central crystal, the Eye, was missing.

No, not missing. Stolen.

The Eye of Athena, a crystal worn by Apollo's Oracle, had been stolen from right under his nose.

After the first break-in, he'd had his security team go over the place with a fine-toothed comb. Jack had juiced up the safe room to just a notch below Fort Knox. No way anyone was getting into his vault again. Guaranteed. Not without triggering multiple alarms and safety devices.

David had just got off the phone with Jack to hear that, according to the motion sensors and video cameras, there *hadn't* been a break-in. Every damn piece of equipment showed that the only person to enter the safe room had been David himself. Jack would messenger over the DVDs for him to look at.

And still the necklace lay in pieces, completely disassembled, the central crystal, the object of power, gone.

He sat down on the couch, trying to catch his breath. He remembered his last meeting with Mimi, their lunch at Le Jardin.

That which is invisible is always the most dangerous.

Shit. Shit!

Twelve years ago, he'd been on top of the world. He'd acquired the thirteenth tablet of the Gilgamesh saga, the *Odyssey* of the Ancient Near East, that had been discovered in the ruins of Niveveh, the capital of ancient Assyria. Only David knew of the existence of the thirteenth clay tablet.

He had been captivated by the story, a tale that gave voice to man's grief and fear of death as Gilgamesh, the king, searched for immortality. David saw himself as a Gilgamesh figure, a king who was part god, part human.

All twelve original tablets were hidden away in the British Museum in London. Many scholars didn't even include the twelfth one as part of the original story. Inconsistencies within that tablet made it an independent tale in the eyes of many—particularly because Enkidu, one of the main characters, who dies in the original eleven tablets, is alive and well in the twelfth, traveling to the underworld to retrieve objects of power for his friend Gilgamesh.

The tablet David possessed continued the story written in that last tablet. In the thirteenth tablet, Enkidu takes to Gilgamesh precious objects that "rained down from the heavens." The first tablet in the original story hinted of the existence of these objects, referring to a dream Gilgamesh had in which a magnificent meteorite falls to earth. The fourth tablet referred to dreams of the sky lighting up in a storm, lightning smashing to the ground and setting it ablaze. Death flooded from the sky. David's translation of the thirteenth tablet mentioned both dreams and continued to describe the Eye in detail.

That's how he knew Fegaris was doing righteous work. The thirteenth tablet described the Eye exquisitely.

So he'd contacted Fegaris, became a silent partner in her quest. He'd told her then and there he was willing to do whatever it took—*whatever*. He'd said everything she wanted to hear, giving her some bullshit about the Eye's importance to the field of psychic archaeology.

And now it was gone, the necklace destroyed.

He shut the vault, using the remote control. He dropped the device and headed out the door. Rounding the corner, he almost slammed into his wife, who was looming at the top of the stairs.

For a minute, he had to fight back the urge to just grab her and shake her. He could see it like a movie in his head: he'd shove her down the stairs, watching as Meredith toppled head over feet. He could see her lifeless body at the foot of the stairwell, her limbs in disarray.

It was an accident, Officer....

He gulped down another breath, squashing the urge. Fuck. The last thing he needed was to have another dead body pointing the finger at him.

"What is it, Meredith?"

"You've done something," she said in that fragile voice, her eyes darting up and down the hall. "The police, they're going to come after Owen, aren't they?"

When he ignored her, stepping around her, she curled her fingers into his biceps, hanging on. She looked up at him in a wild-eyed stare. "Don't send him away again, David. I couldn't bear it."

"Don't you have some church meeting to go to?"

"He's your son. Our only child. Don't you think he's been punished enough for your suspicions?"

He yanked his arm free. "It was more than a suspicion, Meredith. Don't try to make me out to be the villain here. I *saved* his ass. And I'll do it again, if I have to."

She seemed to collapse with relief. "Thank you," she said, getting the answer she wanted.

She slipped away down the hall like a wraith. It was all she'd needed to know, that he'd keep her little boy safe. And damn if he wouldn't.

No one was getting their hands on Owen.

That pleasure would be entirely his.

25

Erika stared up at the column of reflective black glass. She'd read on the Internet that the building had been designed by some famous Dutch architect to resemble an Egyptian obelisk. Here in Newport Beach there were no skyscrapers to speak of. Only the offices of Gospel Enterprises at Fashion Island even came close.

"I bet it's a hell of a view from the top," she said.

Seven headed for the entrance. "Haven't you heard? The view's always better from on top."

She shook her head, following her partner.

Scant decades ago, Fashion Island was just a nice little outdoor shopping mall with a sweeping view of the ocean. Today, the indoor-outdoor center included the OC's only Bloomingdale's and Nieman Marcus, along with an upscale farmer's market, restaurants for every pallet and a Venetian carousel. The mall was surrounded by posh hotels and had its own summer concert series. Come November, it would be home to the tallest decorated Christmas tree outside of the Rockefeller Center. Erika brought her nephew and niece here every year to take their photo with Santa Claus.

Stepping into the marbled entry of the Gospel Building, Erika tried not to act intimidated as they checked in with security. She glanced at her partner. Seven looked loose, his body language saying it all. As far as he was concerned, he could have been walking into Wal-Mart.

Erika grimaced. She figured Ricky, the plastic surgeon, had

given Seven a taste of this kind of opulence. But that's not where Erika was coming from.

In preparation for their meeting, she'd read up on David Gospel. Rumor had it that "The David" was at this moment negotiating with "The Donald" to build a posh new golf resort for Trump down south. Gospel Enterprises was over a hundred years old and privately owned. Its holdings included office buildings, residential villages, retail centers, marinas and golf clubs.

You name it, Gospel owned it.

On the Web site, Gospel's mission statement talked about "a land of riches," something not to be "misused" for short-term gain. Landlord, builder and investor, Gospel Enterprises planned communities. They were *ecologically sensitive*—whatever that meant to someone who made money mowing down wetlands and building malls and homes in cities that already didn't have the infrastructure to support their bulging populations.

For the last thirty-five years, David Gospel, Chairman of the Board, had been the company's master planner. Like many of the OC's elite, Gospel was USC-educated. After he'd done a stint in the marines, he'd returned to USC for his MBA. The last ten years, he'd made the list of top philanthropists in the country for his commitment to education and the environment.

He was also an avid skier…and a collector.

It was the latter entry that had interested Erika the most. As Seven said, it was time for some real police work.

To that end, she had called Gospel bright and early in the morning, letting him know they wanted to talk about his relationship with Mimi Tran. His personal assistant thought she could *maybe* squeeze the detectives in before Gospel's noon helicopter ride to Malibu.

Erika took a deep breath, straightening her suit jacket. She'd put a lot of thought into what she was wearing—a dark blue Tahari suit she'd bought on sale at Nordstrom Rack. God knows how many different styles she'd tortured her hair with before she'd decided to just wear it down.

Watching her, Seven elbowed her in the ribs. "Don't," he said.

"What?" she asked, acting as if she didn't have a clue what he was talking about.

He gave her a look. "You're worth ten of these guys."

"Ya think?"

The elevator doors opened onto a reception area worthy of *The Apprentice,* complete with a stunning view of Newport Harbor. Erika stared out at the white sails floating on a plate of brilliant blue water, the hump of Catalina Island off in the distance. Again, she tugged at her suit...only to get her arm pinched by Seven.

"Right," she said, stepping ahead of him to take on the receptionist.

Gospel didn't keep them waiting.

His office was tastefully decorated, the walls painted a tranquil salmon, the furniture a butter-soft leather complimented by natural woods. Erika was pretty damn sure that was an original Dalí hanging behind his desk.

Gospel himself wasn't too hard on the eyes. Tall and very distinguished-looking, he had pewter hair and hazel eyes. And while she clocked him in at his early sixties, he could still fill out a suit. The man worked out.

"Please, have a seat," he said, indicating the leather sofa after introductions. His secretary hovered as he asked, "Would you care for coffee? Water, perhaps?"

"No, thank you," Seven said. "We'll try to make this quick, Mr. Gospel."

"David, please," he said, dismissing his secretary with a nod of his head.

He took a seat opposite the coffee table, unbuttoning his suit jacket as he sat down. The suit looked expensive. Prada, Erika thought. She noted the museum-quality pieces scattered about the room—African masks, idols from the Far East, rugs with geometric decorations and faded colors. It all reeked of money.

"I assume this has to do with Mimi Tran?" he asked.

Like any good tactician, Gospel knew the best defense was a strong offense.

"Your lunch with Ms. Tran on Tuesday in particular," Seven said. "We believe you were the last person to see her alive."

Gospel held up his hand. "I beg to differ, Detective. The last person to see Mimi was her killer." He shook his head. "It's just such a damn shame. She was so exceptionally talented."

"As a psychic?"

"Yes," Gospel answered. "As a psychic."

Seven kept a close watch on the man's face, wondering what he might give away. But Erika couldn't get a handle on it. Normally, she was all business. But today she felt antsy and out of her league. The research she'd done in preparation only made her feel intimidated. She was a little girl from Santa Ana taking on the man who lived in a glass fortress.

Worse yet, she couldn't stop comparing him to Alfonso. How Gospel was the kind of man her father had always pretended to be. Someone important—a leader. But Alfonso had been all talk...until Costa Rica, of course. That's when he'd made a small fortune in the import-export business. Now, Alfonso was back in California with enough money to retire and give his new family—the better family, the one he actually loved—the absolute best. A house in Santa Ana Heights and designer duds for Consuelo...while Erika's mom still lived in an apartment in Garden Grove and shopped at the discount stores.

As if he could read her thoughts, Gospel turned to look at Erika, focusing on her rather than Seven.

She felt herself blush hot. *Jesus.*

"So you saw Ms. Tran in a professional capacity?" Seven asked, taking the lead.

"I was a client of Ms. Tran's, yes," he said without hesitation.

"You get a lot of business advice from fortune-tellers?" Erika asked.

Her tone showed a healthy dose of suspicion, trying to put him on the defensive.

But Gospel didn't bite. "Actually, it was my personal affairs where I sought guidance. Of course, I don't make my sessions with Ms. Tran public knowledge. But then, as you know, Detectives, even President Reagan sought unorthodox advice at times."

He was referring to one of the greatest scandals of the Reagan administration: the revelation that then President Reagan had acted on advice from his wife's astrologer, Joan Quigley.

Erika sat up straighter. She could feel herself perspire. She didn't like the fact that Gospel made her think of her son-of-a-bitch father. She liked even less that her response was anger.

"David," she said, crossing her legs, leaning toward him. "I can see that you're quite the collector." She motioned to the room filled with objets d'art. "Are any of these artifacts?"

It was a wild stab in the dark. But it scored.

"Artifacts?" he repeated, as if the question needed some sort of clarification.

For the first time, she saw the man nonplussed. She pressed her point, gesturing to an idol on the coffee table. "Like this little guy, for example. What are we talking about, a couple of centuries old, maybe?"

He took a moment, appearing to smile to himself—almost an unspoken touché.

"This is Kali," he said. He picked up the small statue and handed it to Erika. "And you're quite right. The piece is quite old."

The figure wore what looked like a garland of skulls around the neck and held in its four arms a sword, a trident, a skull and a conch shell respectively. The tongue protruded snakelike, reminding Erika of the lead singer of the band KISS.

"She is standing triumphant over the demon Raktabija," Gospel continued. "In the Hindu religion, Kali is worshipped as the goddess of destruction, a fearful manifestation of Parvati—an incarnation of the Mother Goddess. The gods become troubled by the demon Raktabija because every drop of his blood that falls to earth creates another demon. But Kali spread her tongue over the battlefield to ensure Raktabija's blood never touched the ground. Intoxicated by the demon's blood, she destroys his army and takes the skulls and limbs of those she kills. I bought that particular piece at Christie's for a little less than two hundred thousand. It was an extraordinary bargain."

Erika tried to act as if it was her custom to hold $200 K in her hand as she set the idol back on its stand.

"Is that something you and Mimi Tran shared in common?" Seven asked. "An interest in the occult…demons in particular?"

David Gospel slowly turned to look at her partner. Erika thought she caught another whisper of a smile. She didn't like it, that expression of absolute confidence on Gospel's face.

"Yes," he said, "as a matter of fact."

He stood and walked over to his desk, where he picked up a wooden figure about as tall as his hand was long. Erika frowned, finding the statue somewhat familiar…until she remembered. It looked just like one of the three wooden idols they'd found on Mimi Tran's desk back at the murder scene.

He set the figure down next to the statue of Kali. "I admired this in Mimi's office once. She had four of them lined up on her desk. She immediately gave it to me as a gift. It's Enkidu, the wild man of Sumerian mythology. 'The whole of his body was hairy and his locks were like a woman's,'" he said, appearing to recite a poem. "That's from the Epic of Gilgamesh, presumed to be the oldest written story on earth. It was originally written on twelve clay tablets."

"You have those, too?" she asked. "The tablets, I mean?"

Gospel didn't hold back his smile this time when he looked up to meet her gaze. "Unfortunately, Detective, some things are out of reach for the private collector."

Erika couldn't image that there were many things on this earth denied David Gospel. From inside her purse, she withdrew the photograph of the bead and showed it to him.

"Are you familiar with anything like this? We found it at the crime scene. We're wondering if it belonged to Mimi Tran?"

He took the photograph, but gave it only a cursory glance. "I wouldn't know anything about that, Detective. In my own collection, anything I purchase is through a reputable dealer and carries all the necessary paperwork authenticating the purchase."

He was letting them know before they asked: *Bring it on.*

"Now. Is there anything else I can help with?"

A hell of a lot, Erika thought to herself. She would particularly like an explanation for that cat-who-swallowed-the-canary. expression on his face. But here he was showing them the door, apparently not wanting to keep his helicopter waiting.

"We'll stay in touch," Seven said, standing as well.

Erika followed her partner out, still wondering what it was about the interview with Gospel that had set off all these alarm bells inside her head. She was about to mention that to Seven, listen to his take on things.

Only the minute they stepped outside the building, Seven's cell phone went off.

It was the chief. He needed them both back at the station. Pronto.

26

Chief Flagler sat behind his desk with a frozen expression on his face. No, Seven thought, frowning. *Frozen* was the wrong word. *Wooden*, now *that* would be more accurate.

Mayor Condum-Cox, aka Dr. Ruth, stood directly behind the chief and slightly to his left. Her position and the chief's stiff posture made Condum-Cox look like a ventriloquist. The chief was the dummy, letting Condum-Cox do the talking.

Her message came in loud and clear: back off David Gospel.

The whole day felt a little like one of those amusement park rides right after some acne-challenged kid straps you in and the car bucks forward. You look at the torture you just committed yourself to undergoing for the next three minutes and think, *Oh, shit....*

Seven was already feeling itchy about the case, sensing a growing divide between himself and Erika. Now the mayor was waking them up to other considerations, like her sorry hide and how she didn't like hanging it out there as a target for Gospel.

"The last time this office took on Gospel," the mayor said, sounding spitting mad, "he sued the snot out of the city. You remember McGinnis, don't you, Roy? Your predecessor? Exactly. *Nobody* remembers McGinnis!"

Seven assumed the liberal use of the chief's first name was tactical. Dr. Ruth was hoping to remind *Roy* of their relationship both in and out of the office. *You're going to help me here—Roy—aren't you?*

"Gospel made sure his career was wiped off the face of the

earth," Condum-Cox continued. "He *buried* the man. Now, McGinnis owns one of those mow-and-blow gardening services. Runs it with his cousin in Stanton. Let me tell you something, Roy, after twelve years of public service, I am not ending up the proud owner of a gardening service."

"Hold up, Chief. Why was McGinnis investigating Gospel?"

This from Erika, who seemed to have given up on the Little Bo Peep act she had going back at Gospel's. His partner was all business again, addressing her question to the chief as if the mayor wasn't pulling the strings right there in front of them.

Condum-Cox, of course, was having none of it. She came around the desk to direct a blistering glare at Erika...who just loaded one of her patented smiles, aimed and fired.

"Roy," the mayor said, addressing the chief but staring right at Erika as she spoke. "I didn't call this meeting to open *that* can of worms. David Gospel is a pillar of this community. And let's not forget those unlimited resources. I consider him a personal friend and I will not have his family suffer any further harassment from this office."

Condum-Cox stood with one boney hip jutting out, her arms crossed. In her cherry-red suit and matching lipstick, she was the urban warrior. She didn't even blink as she stared at Erika.

"Get your investigation under control, Roy," she said.

As she walked out of the room, everyone left behind knew what she'd meant.

Get your people under control, *Roy*.

The door didn't even click shut before Erika asked, "What can of worms?"

The chief gave it some thought, like maybe he was considering his odds on getting Erika out of the room without answering.

"Michelle Larson," he said at last. "The murder took place seven years ago. Long Beach. But the victim's mother lived here and Larson had an office in Little Saigon. McGinnis started throwing some weight around. He thought Gospel was going down and he wanted in on the headlines. Well, he got headlines all right."

"An office in Little Saigon?" Seven thought about it. "This victim...she wasn't a psychic, was she?"

The look on the chief's face...

Holy shit, Seven thought.

"Holy shit," Erika said, rising out of her chair. "No way. Gospel was a suspect in the murder of a psychic?"

"Not David, no," the chief said. "The son. Owen Gospel."

Erika sank back into her chair. She glanced at Seven, then turned back to the chief. "Can of worms officially blown wide open."

Seven might not be psychic, but he could read that expression on the chief's face just fine. He was thinking he never should have brought Erika up the ranks to detective.

And she wasn't done. "Gospel must have checked in with the mayor first thing this morning—right after we made an appointment to discuss his lunch meetings with Mimi Tran. That's why Gospel was so cocky during our interview. The man owns half of Orange County and has half the politicicans here in his pocket. He knew he had the mayor covering his ass."

The chief appeared suddenly very uncomfortable. "I've looked into the matter, Detective, and while it does seem to raise some red flags, the Long Beach case was solved years ago. A transient confessed to the killing."

Erika nodded as if in agreement. "Right. The old a-transient-did-it defense." She gave Seven a wink. "That's my personal favorite."

"The man confessed, Detective."

"And Gospel wouldn't have the *unlimited resources,*" she suggested, using the mayor's words, "to make that happen?"

"Chief," Seven said, trying to stop the Latina's momentum before she crashed and burned with her accusations. "You can't really ask us to stop an investigation."

"No...but I'm not ignoring the mayor's concerns, either. We *do* need to tread carefully here. Meredith Gospel had some sort of nervous breakdown because of harassment from this department during the Larson investigation, and we didn't even have jurisdiction. My opinion? The Gospels had a legitimate case against McGinnis and the city. Luckily," Roy said, propping his fingertips together, elbows resting on the padded arms of his chair, "we're getting a break with the case."

Seven glanced at Erika. "A break?"

"The FBI is taking over. Special Agent Carin Barnes of the National Institute for Strategic Artifacts contacted me yesterday."

Erika almost jumped to her feet again. "The National Institute for what? What the hell is that?"

"National Institute for Strategic Artifacts. Apparently, your expert, Professor Murphy, recognized the bead as an object that is at the center of an international investigation. He contacted NISA."

"Jesus, Mary and Joseph. That's unbelievable!"

"What exactly will our involvement be?" Seven asked, trying to figure out why this little powwow was happening out of the presence of the ever-present FBI—conspicuously so.

"I've assured Agent Barnes that the FBI will have our full cooperation. She, in turn, assures me that she intends to keep us involved. Now, I have no idea what the hell that means, but I want to keep our involvement low-key, understand? Let the FBI lead the charge."

And don't draw attention to Gospel, Seven read as a heavy subtext.

Erika rolled her eyes and mouthed to Seven, *What bullshit.*

"I don't mind telling you both," the chief said, sealing it, "I'm glad the feds are stepping in. So. You two on board?"

Seven stood. "Whatever you say, Chief."

He caught Erika's eye and motioned toward the door. When she hesitated, keeping that stubborn jut to her jaw, he took her by the arm. With one last look of disappointment aimed at the chief, she shook her head and headed out.

Erika kept glancing over her shoulder as they marched down the hall, giving the impression that she might just turn on her high heels and head back to give the chief a good talking-to. Seven could almost see the steam coming out of his partner's ears.

"We should have given Murphy the damn bead," she said, arms pumping at her sides. "Maybe he wouldn't have sicced the FBI on us."

"It wouldn't have made a lick of difference. You heard the chief. He's happy to lob this grenade."

But Erika shook her head. "Nuh-uh. I don't care what the chief says. I'm not covering Gospel's ass with the FBI."

Seven stopped in his tracks, forcing Erika to do the same. She turned to face him with her arms crossed.

"Listen to me. We're not covering anyone's ass, Erika. Not even our own. But we don't have to go in with guns blazing. *Capice?*"

"But?" she asked, knowing him too well.

"But…while we're waiting for instructions from the FBI…"

"We have a little time on our hands without some agent breathing down our necks?"

"Maybe a lot of time," he said, continuing down the hall. "I'm betting this Agent Barnes is holed up with the professor and the bead in some underground lab in Quantico. It's a judgment call." He opened the door for his partner. "But I say we go talk to this guy who confessed to the other murder. See what seven years in the pokey has done to jog his memory."

Erika walked through the door, this time with a smile on her face. "Go, Yoda."

The only problem being that Benjamin Bass, the self-confessed killer of Michelle Larson, had died shortly after his incarceration.

"Hanged himself his first week in jail." This information was delivered by the warden of the correctional facility over the speakerphone back at the Crimes Against Persons unit.

"Any suspicious circumstances surrounding his death?" Seven asked.

"Not really."

"He hanged himself," Erika said. "Surely there were signs about his mental state. He wasn't on any kind of suicide watch?"

The silence that followed reeked of a man grappling with his conscience.

"Warden," Seven said, helping the guy along. "The man's dead."

"From what I understand," the disembodied voice said, "Bass was a total schizo. Heard voices telling him to do bad things.

These guys go off their meds and end up on the streets. Nobody gives a shit until they start burning down bridges with their campfires or stab some poor civilian they think is an alien trying to control their mind."

"Did anyone come for his effects?" Erika asked, hoping to salvage something from this fiasco.

"What effects, Detective? The man had nothing. Just another lost soul."

After they hung up, Erika looked at Seven. "He was lost, all right."

They both sat in a minute of silence for what was surely a miscarriage of justice. It didn't slap you in the face that often, but when it did, it stung.

Erika tapped the file from the Larson murder. It had taken some smooth talking to get the records here, pronto, but Erika had managed. "There were no signs of a break-in. You're telling me Michelle Larson just opened the door and let some stinky bum walk in?"

"His story was that he was panhandling. She walked by his regular spot every day and felt sorry for him. He followed her home. When she went into the kitchen to get her purse, that's when the voices told him to follow her inside and kill her."

"Bums going door-to-door. Now that's a new one on me."

"He said he'd been watching her for weeks," Seven said, repeating the bullshit in the police report—bullshit he believed about as much as Erika did.

"Cover-up, much?" Erika pushed away the file. "So. Time for Plan B, right?"

"I'm afraid to ask." Seven gave a long, tired sigh. "Okay. What's Plan B?"

"That's where you grow a pair and agree we should have a little talk with Owen Gospel."

Seven looked over at his partner. *Shit.* "You heard what the chief said."

Erika grabbed her purse and shrugged. "So we'll be gentle."

27

They tracked Owen Gospel to the Asian Garden Mall. Erika hiked up the steps alongside her partner, dreading what the concrete would do to her Jimmy Choo heels. At least she'd bought them on sale.

The mall reminded Erika of those ant farms you kept as a kid. From the artery of Bolsa Avenue, a wall of glass showed the two-story enclosed mall, complete with escalator. Gift shops, hair salons, jewelry stores and restaurants vied for the all-important dollar, but that's where the American influence ended.

Entering the air-conditioned building, you were no longer the uninvolved observer watching the ants toil. The energy of the place surrounded Erika. Vietnamese wafted on a current of climate-controlled air. Paper lanterns and incense teased the senses as neon lights and colors swept her up and transported her into the exotic.

She thought of Calle Ocho in Miami, a place where Cuban immigrants had recreated their homeland. She remembered going there once with her mother on vacation. She'd read a sign on a shop door that said English Spoken Here. The Asian Garden Mall felt the same. They'd stepped through the looking glass and dropped into a mixed-up world created by émigrés, a movie backdrop of old Saigon, cleaned up and polished for its American audience.

The second floor was almost exclusively dedicated to jewelry. Block-long display cases manned by eager salesmen and women housed the largest selection of gold, jade and diamonds to be found in the Southland. That's where they found Owen Gospel being waited on, hand and foot.

Even if he weren't one of a handful of Anglos in the mall, Owen Gospel stood out. He made sure of it, wearing a tailored silver-blue suit tailored within an inch of its life with a T-shirt. He'd accessorized with yellow-tinted glasses and groomed his blond-streaked hair into one of those fauxhawks, looking outrageously stylish for an afternoon at the mall.

He stood over an emerald bracelet, the stones so big Erika could size them from fifty feet away. He was working the saleswoman, a pretty brunette in a simple black suit. He smiled winsomely and laughed with her as he picked up the bracelet and draped it over her wrist.

Must be tough working for Dad, Erika thought. The middle of the afternoon and Owen was out for a grueling day of shopping. At least he'd kept it local. Hell of a drive out to Rodeo Drive on the 405 at this hour.

She knew the precise moment Owen spotted them. He leaned back against the display case, zeroing in. From that cocky smile, she figured dear old dad might have given him the heads-up. He knew they were cops. She tried not to take offense. *Must be time for a new wardrobe.*

Erika flipped open her badge. "Owen Gospel? My name is Detective Cabral. This is my partner, Detective Bushard. We're from Westminster Homicide, investigating the murder of Mimi Tran. Would you mind answering a few questions?"

The saleswoman made herself scarce. That was the problem with immigrant communities: people were a little too used to the turmoil of cops and robbers.

Owen made a show of checking Erika out. Her mother always told her she was too quick to judge. But in her line of work, she knew it was an asset. The kind of carnage she'd seen at the Tran crime scene wasn't everyday stuff. Whoever killed Tran was pure evil. Her instincts told her this kid in his fancy suit and John Lennon glasses didn't have the balls to pull it off. In her opinion, Owen Gospel was just a punk.

Peering over the top of his glasses, he said, "I'm not supposed to talk to you guys without an attorney." He gave Erika an insolent smile. "But it's hard to resist a woman with a gun."

"No kidding," she said. "Never heard that one before."

A tall block of muscle in a spectacular Armani suit walked up to stand alongside Owen. He wore his head shaved to show off a tattoo of a cobra at the nape of his neck. Erika immediately pegged him as Special Forces.

"Can I help you, Officers?"

Erika stared up, craning her neck. Really, the guy gave her chills. The good kind.

"That depends," she said. "Who, exactly, are you?"

Before the man could answer, Owen stepped in close to whisper in her ear, "He's my babysitter." Still leaning into Erika, he glanced over his shoulder at the Special Forces guy. "My father pays him gobs of money to make sure I don't do…bad things."

Seven grabbed Owen by the sleeve of his designer suit and pulled him off Erika. She made a mental note to tell her partner she didn't need help handling the likes of Gospel.

"Wow," Seven said, making a show of brushing off the suit. "Aren't you something."

"You're familiar with Dolce and Gabana, Detective?" Gospel asked, amused.

"You're kidding, right?" The look Seven gave was priceless— like he was thinking more Barnum and Bailey, but was just too polite to say so. "So, how well did you know Mimi Tran, Owen?"

"I didn't know her at all."

"But she was an associate of your father's?"

"I couldn't say."

Seeing that Gospel was giving Seven the runaround, Erika took a different tack. She turned her back on Owen, acting as if he mattered about as much as a flea on the ass of an elephant.

She said to the muscleman in Armani, "*Has* he been a good boy?"

The man just managed to hide his smile. "The best."

"Good." She reached inside her bag and pulled out her notebook. She flipped it open. Still ignoring Owen, she asked Mr. Armani, "Then you won't mind telling me when and where your charge—" just a touch of emphasis on the last word, nothing too obvious "—was on the evening of April nineteenth?"

Immediately, the man's friendly manner shut down. "Mr. Gospel is correct. That is a question for his attorneys."

"Really." Erika made sure the guy got a whiff of her disappointment. "That's not a problem." She flipped her notebook shut. "We'll meet you down at the precinct in, say—" she made a show of examining her sensible Citizen watch "—half an hour?" She looked over at Owen. "Does that work for you, Mr. Gospel?"

"Actually, it's entirely inconvenient."

But Seven was already punching a number into his cell. He said into the phone, "I'd like to speak with Judge Odin. It's about a search warrant for the residence of one Owen Gospel. The spelling is *O-w-e-n*. Gospel, spelled just like in the Bible."

"You're bluffing." But suddenly, Owen wasn't looking so confident.

Seven didn't flinch. "The basis for the warrant is new evidence linking the Tran murder to a case seven years ago." He turned away from Gospel. "Another psychic in Long Beach—"

"All right," Owen said, a touch of desperation lacing his voice. "All right." Then, flashing an insolent smile, he said, "It so happens, I have a few minutes."

Seven slapped his phone shut in his hand. His expression gave nothing away. "Great. How about we take a seat over there?" He motioned to the railing overlooking the first floor.

"Owen?" the block of muscle warned.

"Shut up, Rocket."

Erika liked her partner's style. Seven had imagination. She knew for a fact that there was no Judge Odin on the court.

They sat down and made themselves comfortable on a bench that looked down from the second floor to the food court below. The layout reminded Erika of a pinball machine. A lot of neon lights and flashing colors with tiny shoppers bouncing back and forth from one side of the mall to the other.

"You people," Owen said, taking out a bottle of eyedrops and squeezing some into his eyes. He carefully replaced the tinted glasses. She noticed he had curious eyes, nothing like his father's. They were a pale blue, shiny and unblinking. "Can't you let a man rest?"

"'You people'? That sounds a little insulting," Erika said, pulling out her notebook again. "But then, maybe you have an issue or two with law enforcement?"

He looked as if he was going to argue with her, thought better of it. "You have five minutes, Detective."

"Like I asked your babysitter, where were you on the evening of April nineteenth?"

"I was at a meeting. There were several witnesses."

Owen reached inside his coat pocket and pulled out a silver case, the kind that might hold business cards, only bigger. The initials D.O.G. had been engraved on the front, making Erika smile. *All that money, and your initials spell dog?*

He opened the case to show it contained a pad of plain paper. He began writing on the top sheet.

"Gee, isn't that nifty, Seven?" she asked, staring at the case.

"And you with a birthday coming up."

"Oh, I don't know. I like my little spiral," she said, holding up the dimestore version of Gospel's Tiffany case.

He ignored the ribbing and ripped out the sheet, handing it to Erika with that canary smile she'd seen on his father's face just that morning. Only David Gospel, the senior, had showed more finesse. Owen was rubbing their noses in it with that smile.

"These are three of the people who saw me at the meeting. They can vouch for my whereabouts." Again, he leaned in close to Erika to whisper, "And that, Detective, is all I have to say. Even to someone as delectable as you."

Erika could swear he hovered there, taking in her perfume with a sigh before pulling away.

Seven and Erika watched him saunter back into the jewelry store, the saleswoman at the ready as his self-proclaimed babysitter vanished as quickly as he'd appeared.

"There's something wrong with his eyes," Seven said.

Erika glanced up, surprised by the abrupt observation. "What?"

"His eyes. He's wearing glasses, but they're not prescription. The tint is light enough to allow him to see with indoor lighting, but still be fashionable. And he needed drops."

Erika turned to look at Seven, having herself noticed that unblinking stare of Owen Gospel's. "Mimi Tran's eyes were missing."

He shook it off. "It's a bit of a stretch. Certainly nothing we can take to the chief."

Erika frowned at her partner. Whatever he was thinking, he wasn't ready to share.

She stared down at the paper in her hand, Owen Gospel's alibi. "What do you want to bet these are ironclad?" she said with no little disgust.

Seven nodded, putting on his sunglasses before heading out. "I'd say they're the best money can buy."

28

Velvet stared down at the yarrow stalks on the table. The fifteen-inch-long dried stems lay carefully counted out in small, discreet piles, finishing the last line of her hexagram in the I Ching ceremony.

My future, she thought.

In Vietnam, it was believed that people did not simply pass away. Instead, they traveled to another world very near that of the living. The spirits of the dead, if properly worshipped, would happily stay in their realm, watching over their progeny, even passing along the good fortune they had accumulated during their lives on earth.

But restless spirits could prey upon the living, haunting them. They could pursue their victims into a wretched existence. There was even a celebration held on the seventh month of the lunar year, the Feast of the Wandering Souls, a time to appease those who died alone or neglected, the idea being that such spirits could be dangerous.

A week after Mimi's death, Velvet had begun to feel her presence.

Last night, she'd dreamed of Mimi dressed in one of her beautiful St. John suits. She'd looked perfectly normal but for the fact that her eyes had been gouged out, their empty sockets meaty and bloody. Closer and closer Mimi came. When she was just a few feet away, she held up her hands toward Velvet.

Cupped in her palms, Mimi offered her two bloody eyes.

"Don't be blind," she told Velvet in Vietnamese. "Use my eyes."

Velvet had woken with a start, completely shaken. Luckily, David rarely spent the night. Velvet had gotten up then and there, slipping barefoot into her living room, where she'd fallen on her knees before her mother's altar. She lit three joss sticks and begged Má to intervene on her behalf against the spirits.

That which is invisible is always the most dangerous.

She knew well Mimi's last prediction to David. What Velvet didn't understand was the sense of dread that had come over her these last days. The idea that she, Velvet, was part of David's prophesy.

And here was Mimi, invisible—a ghost—haunting Velvet, seeking retribution for…

For what? Velvet thought.

That's where the logic dissipated into superstition. Velvet was well-versed in the traditions of her ancestors. Some beliefs were harmless, like the idea that if a woman's left eye twitched it was a sign of bad luck, or that the first person you encounter in the morning sets the tone for the day.

But some superstitions had more haunting possibilities. The Vietnamese, the Children of the Dragon, believed that if any part of the body was missing at the time of death, that soul could never enter the hereafter. Like Mimi and her eyes.

And there were other reasons to believe that Mimi lingered, watching over Velvet, haunting her every step. It took forty-nine days for the soul to reach the underworld. Mimi had only been dead less than a week.

Sometimes, Velvet had the sense that if she turned around quickly and looked over her shoulder, she'd see Mimi there, holding out those two bloody eyes.

And yet she knew she had never done Mimi any wrong. She had, in fact, had little contact with the psychic, seeing her for only an occasional reading. But the idea that something was very wrong—that Velvet somehow bore responsibility for Mimi's death—wouldn't leave her.

That's why she listened with great trepidation to Xuan Du, the psychic promised to David as a replacement for Mimi. Velvet had asked Xuan to come an hour before David was due to arrive here at her condo. She'd wanted a reading, thinking to dissipate or at least clarify the sense of dread hanging over her. Now she waited for Xuan to interpret her hexagram.

They'd already had tea in the traditional manner, Velvet having bought special rice cakes for the occasion. They'd retired to the dining room, the table giving them the necessary space for the ritual drawing of yarrow straws.

I Ching was an ancient form of divination. It worked by dividing piles of yarrow sticks or flipping coins while meditating on a question. These days, there were even computer programs. But Velvet preferred the ancient ways, the yarrow oracle.

She liked the feel of the straws in her hands, enjoyed meditating on her question as she set aside the first stick, the straw representing unity. As she divided the remaining straws over and over, slowing creating the six lines of her hexagram, the ritual felt weighty and organic, conducive to contemplation.

In I Ching, the hexagram was always numbered one through sixty-four, using an order known as the King Wen Sequence. Afterward, the soothsayer would consult the *I Ching,* the *Book of Changes,* and read the text associated with the hexagram to interpret the future. Xuan Du was considered quite proficient in the craft.

There were four possibilities in drawing the straws: old yang, young yin, young yang, old yin. Old yang and old yin were about change. But young yang and young yin were static. Today, Velvet drew a static hexagram.

There were sixty-four possible archetypes. This one was number twenty-nine, Water.

"Water over Water," Xuan Du said ominously.

Velvet stared down at the yarrow straws, that sense of dread growing darker and more defined. She had almost drowned as a child of five in a friend's swimming pool. Afterward, she'd maintained a kind of phobia about water, refusing even to learn how to swim.

As Xuan talked about life's darkest moments and the repetition of danger in her hexagon, Velvet felt a strange sense of panic rising up inside her, making her breath tight in her chest. *I feel like I'm drowning....*

"You have grown used to the danger in your life, Velvet," Xuan said, looking up from the hexagon to meet her eyes. "You have become complacent."

In the words of the I Ching, Velvet had grown too familiar with evil. She had lost her way. Misfortune would be the natural result.

"But you are not in a position to save yourself," the older woman continued. "Like water, you must bide your time and try to slowly climb out of the abyss into which you have fallen."

Every step led to danger, Xuan Du pronounced, and thus Velvet must act judiciously. She should not overreach and flee, courting disaster.

"You have not been honest." Here, the woman looked up slyly to meet Velvet's gaze. "You are handicapped by your sins."

Xuan explained that Velvet's insincerity had brought darkness where there should be light. "You have surrounded yourself with darkness. You are blind to the danger around you."

Because Velvet had made the danger a part of her life, she couldn't see it there hovering, waiting to bring her down.

"Take great care, Velvet. Your ambition is leading you to disaster."

Velvet stared down at her manicured hands. Xuan, of course, knew of her involvement with Sam and David.

The logical part of her, the woman who had toiled at law school, burned with anger. She could see clearly how Xuan's knowledge of her situation had leached into this reading. She wondered if the soothsayer might have manipulated the hexagram, guiding her to Water. Judging her.

Hadn't Xuan herself agreed to help in Sam's schemes? And here she was judging Velvet? Pointing a finger at her actions?

Xuan asked, "Do you want to hear more?"

Velvet swept her hand across the table, sending the yarrow

sticks to the floor. She stared down at the mess she'd made, littering the carpet.

"I don't believe your judgment," she told Xuan.

But she didn't raise her head to look at the fortune-teller, the Vietnamese side of her knowing better.

Again, she had the sense that Mimi was just behind her. The feeling was so distinct, a chill raced through Velvet. And then the realization came. Mimi's prediction for David, how much it mirrored Xuan's warning now.

Velvet jumped to her feet, the motion a reflex, like a deer hearing the sounds of a predator in the brush. She wanted to run. Wanted desperately to call David and tell him not to come—

But just then, the doorbell sounded. Velvet stood frozen, paralyzed by Xuan's predictions of doom. Again, the air seemed to freeze up inside her chest, reminding her of when she was only five….

The door sounded again, David growing uncharacteristically impatient.

Too late….

"You will excuse me, Xuan?"

She spoke to the woman respectfully, wanting to convey more than a simple courtesy before leaving to open the door. She wanted to admit how poor her behavior had been, to apologize for her outburst. She stood waiting until the older woman nodded her head, dismissing her.

But even walking into the front room, Velvet heard Xuan's prediction echo inside her head, the warning dogging her like Mimi's ghost. Her meaning had been very clear: Velvet could not escape from disaster. She was trapped, incapacitated by her duplicity.

Standing at the door, she told herself to take a breath. If she were ever to become counsel for Sam, as he wanted, duplicity would be part of her everyday life.

She reached for the door, forcing a smile, expecting David.

But it wasn't David standing on the other side. As the door opened, all those nebulous fears of the week coalesced into the picture standing before her, and Velvet knew why she'd felt weighted down with dread.

That which is invisible is always the most dangerous.

No truer words.

29

Rocket stared down the corridor of crowded storefronts. He felt as if he were stuck in some Asian convention center or rock concert. The ebb and flow of bodies kept him on his toes.

No sign of Owen.

The little fucker had given him the slip.

He elbowed his way past a milling crop of teenagers at a music store featuring Vietnamese karaoke. The flock crowded around a cinema-size flat screen showing the newest in Vietnamese rock stars. Each and every teen was mesmerized. They didn't even notice Rocket as he barreled past.

It was damn embarrassing, him chasing down the kid. Rocket had made a pretty good career for himself in the marines. He'd been right there alongside Oliver North when they'd rescued those medical students off Grenada. Unfortunately for Rocket, he'd also been with Ollie during the whole Iran-Contra bullshit, the result of which had been Rocket's dishonorable discharge.

But shit, did he have training. He'd been Special Ops for more than half his military career. He couldn't believe that, with his background, the kid could ditch him.

Rocket stopped at the Buddhist temple, where mall visitors could light a taper for their intentions, and scanned the floor below. The problem was, he'd been distracted by the cops showing up. He'd been watching them, and not Owen, to make sure they made it all the way out the doors of the mall. Rocket was on the phone to Mr. David, telling him what had happened, when he'd turned around and the kid was gone.

Mr. David wouldn't like it. Not one bit.

And that *was* a problem. Something like this was major. Rocket wasn't so sure Mr. David could handle any more problems with his son—or anything else, for that matter.

These days, it seemed to Rocket that Mr. David had lost his way. More and more, he was becoming a different man, one Rocket hardly recognized.

When he had first come to work for Mr. David as his bodyguard, when Owen was just a little guy, Mr. Gospel was all about the business, Gospel Enterprises. Shit, Rocket could even remember a time when he'd been happy with the Missus.

But that was a long time ago. Before Mr. David's *collection* had taken over their lives. Now all his boss seemed to care about was finding a bunch of sacred objects mentioned on an old clay tablet he'd bought through some shady dealer.

Sometimes, the way Mr. David talked, Rocket worried he was doing the all-knowing and all-powerful thing. What did they call it? Megalomania. Yeah. That sounded right. He was just like those dictators, like Noriega, drunk on some power kick. Jesus, the guy hadn't even figured out his kid was a sociopath.

Or was it a psychopath? Rocket wasn't sure about the terminology, but he'd met all kinds when he'd been training mercenaries in the jungles of Nicaragua. Men who liked it, the killing—and those who didn't feel a damn thing. Chopping off a man's head was about as meaningful as stepping on an ant.

Maybe it was the thing with Owen's eyes. All those surgeries. There were a few years there when Rocket couldn't remember him without some patch under his glasses. Like a miniature pirate.

And the pupils. Always enlarged. Like he was on drugs 24-7.

Back then, when the kid was young and struggling with the surgeries, Mr. David and his wife, they'd been on the same page about the boy. Those days, the Missus couldn't keep up with Mr. David. She'd been cute and flirty, but a real lady—a hard combination to pull off, in Rocket's opinion. But then Mr. David bought that tablet. It was like the whole family had fallen under some curse.

Rocket felt good and sorry for Mr. David's wife. Imagine your son's a freaking nut, burying pieces of animals in the back yard like trophies, and your husband's cheating on you. It just wasn't right.

The whole situation got to Rocket. Rich folks screwing up their lives. Like maybe you needed the struggle of putting bread on the table in order to keep your head on straight sometimes.

Rocket figured his own baby brother and his wife had it right, middle class with two great kids. Sometimes, he wished he could just walk out on the Gospels. Get on back to Ohio and those two nieces of his.

But Rocket had never walked out on anything in his life. And now, he was good and fucked. Because there was no sign of Owen.

He'd done it before, disappeared on Rocket. Sometimes, it turned out okay. He'd catch up with Owen, or the kid would just show up at their digs as if nothing had happened.

But a couple of times...well, Rocket hadn't seen shit like that since his days in Nam.

Once, he'd found the kid with an eye in his pocket. An honest to God human eye. He kept it in a Baggie.

When Rocket asked him what the hell it was doing in his pocket, Owen had looked straight at him and said it was for good luck. Good fucking luck.

Rocket had talked to Mr. David about it. The really strange part? Mr. David couldn't be bothered. He just sent the kid to a shrink, who put him on pills. Owen became someone else's problem...while the Missus grew all quiet and religious and so thin you could practically see through her.

Hell, if someone told Rocket his kid had somebody's eye in his pocket, that sure would rock *his* world.

And then there was Michelle. Rocket was pretty sure Michelle had been the first time Owen had gone all the way.

That's when Mr. David sent his son away, with Rocket as his "insurance." Rocket had done his best keeping an eye on Owen. The places they'd gone, it was easy enough to bribe officials if the kid ended up in trouble. Darfur, the Balkans, Rwanda, Haiti—

places where human rights violations and a political void made it easy for Owen's kind of "missionary" work.

Once, Rocket found Owen with a ten-year-old prostitute. He had her all tied up and scared shitless. Seeing that, Rocket lost it, just lost it, thinking about his nieces back in Ohio. That night, Rocket beat the shit out of the little fucker. He'd stopped only when he got the sense that Owen liked it, that the kid wanted more.

Seven years Rocket had followed the little prick around the world. That's how long it had taken. Seven long years and finally, Rocket started seeing a change. Like maybe even Owen could grow up. Sure, he was still a creep, giving Rocket the willies. But the sick stuff—the eyeballs in the Ziploc bags, the ten-year-olds bound and gagged—that stopped. Rocket thought, good enough, right?

Only, there were those times, late at night, when Rocket wondered if Owen was just getting better at hiding his shit.

And now the papers were full of stories about this dead fortune-teller. *Just like Michelle.*

Searching the mall for any signs of Owen, Rocket reminded himself that Michelle's death was different. Michelle had been a young, beautiful woman. She'd been in love with Owen, but indebted to Mr. David. The whole father-son thing had been a little weird, maybe pushing Owen over the edge.

And the way she'd died, a broken glass across the jugular—that was definitely a crime of passion. From what Rocket had read, this Tran woman was killed in some kind of ritualistic fashion. He'd never known Owen to be tidy enough for any sort of rituals.

After a fruitless twenty minutes, Rocket ended up at the security desk. He'd done his time in Nam. If he was lucky, the underpaid rent-a-cop behind the desk would know what was up.

Sure enough, the kid took the Benjamin Rocket offered. The security desk had cameras all over the mall—a pretty slick operation, really. From here, Rocket could case the place and target Owen.

Only, there was one little problem. From every camera and at every angle, he couldn't find any sign of him.

The kid had disappeared.

* * *

Gia stood before the enormous canvas, completely covered in paint splatters and sweat. Like a marathoner nearing the end of the race, she was in the *zone,* unaware of anything other than the images crowding her head.

Gia had not started out as a painter. Long ago, during another life—a life that belonged to a woman with a different name, one with an alphabet of degrees behind it—Gia hadn't even owned a sable paintbrush. She didn't have a mortar and pestle to grind her own pigments, or know how to stretch a canvas over a wooden frame. She didn't own palette knives to mix colors, or dozens of sketchbooks shoved into the nooks and crannies of her house.

Gia Moon, the artist, didn't have a famous mother. In fact, she didn't have a mother at all—because she didn't have a past. She had started shiny and brand-new a dozen years ago.

Now, Gia Moon, the woman born twelve years ago with the arrival of her daughter, was consumed by her calling. She had a gift, one she'd honed and fed until she could do exactly this: stand before an empty canvas and fall into the story in her head, bringing the characters to life with paint and brush.

The painting was full of color and motion. Gia's paintings were seldom static pieces. Instinctively, she knew this would be some of her best work. It was a story of talent and destiny, the tale of a young woman named Kieu.

Beautiful and talented, Kieu came from a royal family. One day, a spirit came to visit her under the moonlight. The spirit cursed Kieu, who had been jealous of the spirit's beauty when she was alive. In revenge, the spirit told Kieu her name appeared in the book of the damned. She predicted a miserable life for her.

The images came faster than Gia could paint. She felt almost betrayed by her body and its inability to move faster, catch up with what she saw inside her head before it dimmed from memory. She used multiple brushes, holding one in her teeth as she painted with another. She mixed blues and greens and umber colors, the palette in her hand becoming an enormous rainbow mess.

This was a story for the ages: beauty betrayed.

The well-bred Kieu did indeed come to ill. Her fiancé was forced to abandon her and, in his absence, Kieu was tricked into prostitution in order to save her family, who had fallen on hard times. At the brothel, she eventually fell in love with a married client. But theirs was only a physical love, and in her heart, Kieu knew that their attachment was doomed.

Mommy?

Gia ignored that whispered voice. She couldn't stop painting now, in the grip of great inspiration. She needed to stay faithful to the images inside her head.

Though her lover bought her out from the brothel, disaster once again befell the lovely Kieu. The beautiful courtesan became prey to her lover's jealous wife, a cunning woman prone to physical violence. Kieu was a captive once more.

Mommy, please stop. You're scaring me.

Cruel fate put Kieu in a position where she must choose between what was right and what would make her happy—

"Mom! Stop it! What's wrong with you?"

Gia felt herself caught between two worlds. Her daughter, Stella, was holding her by the arm, her tiny fingers clawing into her skin, trying to stop her painting. At the same time, the beautiful Kieu sat holding her lute, her skin polished with moonlight. The image called to Gia there on the canvas. She had to work, bring Kieu to life!

"Mom, please. Please stop!"

Gia dropped her paintbrushes. She stood frozen in place. She couldn't move—couldn't breathe. She wanted desperately to turn and reassure her daughter. She could see Stella standing there at her side, looking young and frightened, shaking her by her arm. And still Gia couldn't catch her breath.

I can't breathe! I...can't...breathe!

She kept wondering when it would happen. When her lungs would fill with air and she could finally move and wrap her arms around her daughter. The words of comfort would come then, letting Stella know that everything would be fine.

Only, everything stayed hard and frozen.

Can't...breathe!

Standing there, watching her daughter, the realization came. *This is what it feels like to drown.*

She was familiar with the sensation. It wasn't the first time she'd felt like giving in. *Why fight it?* She was like Kieu, her name written in the book of the damned.

"No, Mom! Look at me. Not the painting. Look at me!"

Suddenly, Gia took in an enormous breath, filling her lungs with air. Whatever vise had been holding her in place suddenly released its hold, so that she fell down like a puppet with its strings cut.

"I'm okay," she said when she could finally speak. There on the floor, she took Stella into her arms. "I'm okay."

Gia realized her arms ached. She had no idea how long she'd been painting, but the cramped muscles said it had to be hours.

Over her daughter's shoulder, she looked up at the canvas. She'd been expecting to see a painting of Kieu playing her pear-shaped lute, the moon and her lover in the background. That was the image she'd had in her head, the vision that had held her in its grip as she'd painted.

The canvas was completely covered with color. But the image there looked nothing like the vision she'd imagined.

She turned her gaze from the painting to her hands wrapped tightly around her daughter, and frowned. She remembered mixing blue for the glowing moon and a warm umber for the lute Kieu had been holding. But there was only one color on her fingertips and under her nails.

Red. A deep bloodred.

Everywhere in the room, dripped onto the concrete floor of the studio, mixed in a frenzy on the wooden palette, there was only red.

Red mixed with white. Red so vibrant it glowed. Red approaching a near black.

Stella pulled away from her and stared up at the canvas. "W-what is that?" she asked in a whisper.

Gia thought she'd been painting the story of a young Vietnamese woman named Kieu. But on the canvas, there was nothing but death. The picture was of a woman hacked to pieces, the bloodied bits lined together afterward like a grotesque puzzle.

Her eyes were missing.

"Mom? Something's wrong, isn't it?"

"Stella," she said. "Go to the kitchen and get me some water."

"I don't want to leave. You'll start painting again—and I don't know if I can bring you back."

"I just need something to drink." She stood, forcing Stella to do the same. She turned her daughter away from the painting. "Please. It will help. I swear."

She gave her a smile, trying to reassure her daughter, when she felt nothing but rising panic inside her.

"Yeah, okay," Stella said. But at the door, she stopped to look back, checking on Gia, making sure she hadn't fallen again into her feverish painting spell.

"I'll be okay. Promise," Gia said.

The minute Stella stepped out of the studio, Gia ran for her purse. She pulled out her cell phone and the business card she'd tucked away in her wallet.

He picked up almost immediately.

"Detective Bushard? Seven?" she said breathlessly into the phone. "It's Gia Moon."

She stared at the canvas, sickened by the sight painted in shades of red and black. The woman in the painting had been gutted like a fish.

She'd never imagined anything like this carnage. The visions that had haunted her these last months involved only Gia and the danger to her daughter. But now she realized she was locked in a battle with a spirit who wouldn't stop.

The demon needed blood. Lots of it. And she was his voice into this world of terror.

He's playing with me. I'm part of the game.

"He's going to kill again," she said, trying to steady her voice. "A young woman. Her name is Kieu. Or maybe the letter *Q* is in her name," she said, unable to look away from the painting. "You have to find her, Detective. You have to find her *now*."

30

Life is always better when there are rules.

You understand how fundamental order can be. Rules instruct the dull muttons of this world, providing guidance on the sheep's place in society. The rules give a hierarchy, a plan. Without them, there can only be chaos.

But some people don't take well to instruction. They aren't satisfied with what they have. They consider themselves above the very laws of nature. They overreach, breaking the rules.

When that happens—when the common people usurp the powers of the universe—collapse will surely follow.

You understand how, throughout history, it's been the same. Plagues. Natural disasters. All of them consequences of man's inability to follow the rules. Destruction is the price man pays for disobedience and disorder.

But you are proactive, the one who sees the disaster that is coming, and acts. In this one thing, you must never falter.

When she opens the door, you strike down the concubine. The older woman runs when she sees the girl dead at your feet. She begs for her life. You act quickly. Amnesty is just another way of breaking the rules, making a travesty of justice.

It is your duty and privilege to weed out the practitioners of superstition, the deluders of the innocent. This is a test and you will not fail.

You drag both bodies into the center of the room, moving the furniture in order to make a proper sacrificial space. You are careful to wear surgical gloves so there are no prints. But it doesn't matter. The invisible leave no prints.

You do research. You want the moment to be perfect. You play the scholar, finding examples of what you must do. When Tu Duc ascended to the throne, he was forced to put his older brothers to death, lest they usurp his power. When the people of God forgot to worship properly, turning to idols, God sent a flood to cleanse the world.

These two women are not the people of God. Best to just do away with the vermin.

Now you are the enforcer—the wolf. Because you know the rules.

But David doesn't. He thinks he's safe in his Tower of Babel at Gospel Enterprises. In the end, you can no longer stand and merely watch someone try to circumvent the very laws of nature.

You *must* act. Quickly, decisively.

Of course, there will be penance for the cleansing you are about to commit. Just like Apollo when he killed the Python of Gaia. Or like the concubine who disposed of the rightful queen and all seventy of her ladies-in-waiting by entombing them alive. You will be seized by remorse. But that will come later. Much later.

You set out your instruments. Right now, you are surgeon and artist. You pick out the scalpel and make your first incision. You enjoy the precision of it. You're cutting into raw filet mignon.

The moment feels incredibly right. Better than the other time. It's clean and controlled. You read the words from the book you brought along, and smile. Everything is perfect.

Blood seeps into the carpet as the concubine's eyes stare sightlessly at the ceiling.

You haven't given yourself much time. You planned it that way. The ticking clock inside your head adds to the excitement. There's always the possibility that you will be interrupted.

When you reach the stomach cavity, the intestines pop out like springs, spraying everything. You feel baptized.

You stop and stare at the four walls, becoming almost lost in the pattern of the blood. The beauty of it.

There's something about blood on a perfectly white wall. You wonder if any artist has ever captured such perfection. To you it represents the very pattern of life.

You've never experienced anything so profound. You almost weep, thinking of the lost opportunity, the lack of time.

You get back to work.

You continue cutting. You are judge and jury, meting out the necessary penalty. Even though the time is too short, you understand you have passed a great test. You fulfill your duty and set balance to the world.

From now on, you make the rules.

31

David stood outside the door to Velvet's condo. The door was cracked open, as if maybe the last person to shut it hadn't been paying attention, and the door hadn't latched properly.

That in itself was strange. Velvet was usually so meticulous and extremely attentive. Normally, she would be waiting for him, wearing close to nothing and holding a chilled martini at the ready.

But he told himself today was different. Today was business. He was to meet Xuan Du, the new fortune-teller, the psychic Sam thought could take Mimi's place.

There was only one small problem, of course. David didn't fucking have the Eye of Athena. It was gone. Stolen.

He stuffed his roiling anger back into that corner of his mind where he'd contained it since he'd discovered the necklace had been disturbed in the vault room. It had taken him a day or two to decide how to deal with the disaster of the break-in. His security guy, Jack Lackey, had a top-notch operation. Jack had assured David it would just be a matter of time before he tracked down the Eye.

David pushed the door open. He would have to talk to Velvet about this lapse. Now wasn't the time to let their guard down. Someone was out to destroy him. Whoever it was had murdered Mimi Tran—they had stolen the Eye. Until David could shut down the danger, they all needed to keep on their toes.

For an instant, he thought about that kid, that student of Fegaris, the one David had paid to give him the Eye in the first place. Thomas Crane was his name. The thought occurred to David that Crane was somehow involved, the one calling the shots. But Jack and his people had looked into it. After Fegaris died, Crane had turned into a number-one nut job. Apparently, even though he'd been cleared of her murder, the accusations still haunted Crane's career, and the guy had snapped.

Or maybe it was his conscience, David thought.

Whatever the reason, Crane, a once promising archaeologist, was now nothing more than a shovel bum, working on a Native American site in New Jersey funded by the feds under the Archaeological Resources Protection Act. The guy was no threat at all.

David stepped inside the condo, calling Velvet's name. He paid for the damn place, right? In any case, he had a key. And while he'd always given Velvet the courtesy of ringing the doorbell, he thought he'd make his point better by surprising her.

But it wasn't Velvet who was surprised. His poor Velvet was well beyond anything of the kind. It was David who had the shit shocked out of him.

He'd walked into a fucking nightmare.

The first thing he saw was the blood. It was everywhere. Sprayed across the walls, painting the carpet, staining the beautiful Vietnamese prints Velvet loved so much.

Someone had moved the furniture, placing the pieces around the two bodies in the center of the room. For an instant, the pattern reminded David of Stonehenge or even one of those circular tholos temples in Greece. The bodies were at the epicenter, the focus of the room and the carnage there.

He almost didn't recognize Velvet, the body closest to him.

She'd been disemboweled. Her intestines were flung far and wide, reminding him of those novelty snakes released from a can. Her hands had been cut off at the wrist. They lay just a few inches away, like one of those dolls you pull apart, only to have the body parts snap back together when you let go.

She was wearing the jade ring he'd bought her. She'd picked

it out against his wishes. He'd wanted to buy her something more expensive, a Burmese ruby ring at the same store, but she'd insisted. The ring was simple, carved with Vietnamese calligraphy. Something about a bountiful future.

He remembered her smiling up at him and saying that sometimes simple things were best.

A book lay opened on her chest. Jesus, was there something stuffed in her mouth?

He turned away and vomited on the carpet.

When he'd emptied his stomach, he stumbled into the kitchen. Leaning over the sink, he splashed water on his face. He didn't know how long he stood there, staring at that white porcelain as the water funneled down the drain.

This wasn't anything like the time with Michelle. He'd never walked in to find her body eviscerated on the floor. He hadn't seen blood splattered on the walls.

He couldn't imagine anyone doing what he'd seen in that room. Who cut up bodies like puzzle pieces?

Velvet had been a special girl, bright and talented. A beautiful woman who someday would have accomplished great things.

He told himself to get a grip. He couldn't help Velvet if he fell apart. He needed to keep it together. Find out what the hell was going on.

He grabbed a couple of paper towels and scrubbed his face dry. He tossed the paper towels into the trash compactor and walked back to face the carnage in the living room.

The two women had been laid out in what was most certainly some sort of ritualistic manner. They were head to head on the carpet. Their hands had been cut off and lay just a few feet away. Both had been cut open, sternum to groin. But only the psychic, the one David assumed to be Xuan Du, had her eyes gouged out.

He turned away, unable to look at those empty sockets…at the same time thankful that Velvet had been spared that fate. But then he noticed Velvet really did have something stuffed in her mouth.

David stepped closer. Some sort of pastry?

"Jesus."

The room started to spin. He grabbed the back of a chair for balance. That's when he saw his shoes. They were covered in blood.

He looked back at the carpet, saw where his footprints led to the kitchen in patches of red.

"Shit!"

Suddenly, he wasn't thinking about Velvet lying there in pieces, her body violated.

He was thinking about the O. J. Simpson trial and his Bruno Magli shoes, the very same brand David was wearing now.

The vomit. The bloody footprints. No way in hell he could ever clean this up.

And then there was Velvet. The condo was in his name, for God's sake. She was his mistress. Just another bread crumb leading the trail straight to him.

Someone was trying to set him up.

They'd broken into his collection. They were killing the people trying to help him....

He forced himself to scrutinize the scene without emotion. Looking closer, he thought he recognized the pastry stuffed in Velvet's mouth. It looked like one of those cakes sold for the August festivals here in the bakeries of Little Saigon. Moon cakes.

Sam had filled him in on Mimi's murder. She, too, had had something stuffed in her mouth. The head of a parrot. That's where the police had found the missing stone from the Eye of Athena. Inside the parrot's beak.

David knelt over Velvet. He took out his handkerchief. Very carefully, he pried the pastry loose.

He hovered over her for a minute more, holding the moon cake. Velvet, her eyes and mouth open, stared up at the ceiling as if frozen in a silent scream.

He stood and turned quickly away. He focused instead on the cake. He could see clearly that something had been forced inside. He almost put it in his pocket before thinking better of it. He didn't want to get caught with the damn cake on him.

He had to hide it somewhere. Keep it safe.

But first, he needed to make sure he wasn't missing anything.

He took out his handkerchief and wrapped up the cake. He placed it gently in his coat pocket. Back in the kitchen, he started searching through the drawers. She was his mistress; that would explain his prints. He found a small flashlight in the third drawer down.

He came back into the living room. Leaning over her, careful not to disturb the body, he flashed the light inside Velvet's mouth.

Suddenly, she exhaled.

He screamed and fell backward, dropping the flashlight.

He crab-walked away from the body on the heels of his hands and feet. Even with her guts spilling out on the carpet, he half expected Velvet to sit up and ask him what the hell he was doing.

He was panting for breath, really shaken. He'd read somewhere that a body could do that postmortem. They called it a death gasp.

He looked at the now-bloody flashlight and the pattern it had made rolling across the white carpet—the mess of his prints on the carpet.

Shit!

It took him another few minutes to calm down. He couldn't undo his mistakes, but he could come up with a good story to cover for them. In the meantime, he needed to do some damage control.

Back in the kitchen, he grabbed a dish towel hanging on the handle of the oven. He used it to pick up the bloody flashlight, and wrapped it up tight. He put it inside the pocket of his trousers.

The condo didn't have a parking complex. Each unit had a place out back for vehicles. He was sweating like a pig, worried that someone might see him there—which was exactly what happened. Some kid on a mountain bike came speeding by, giving him a suspicious look.

David tried to act nonchalant, as if nothing unusual was happening. Which it wasn't. Really, how many times had he parked right here on his way to see Velvet? What would the kid report to the police even if they thought to ask?

Eventually, he put the cake and flashlight in the trunk of his Mercedes.

When he thought he could handle it, he returned to the condo with its two dead bodies. He sat down on the couch.

He cried, long and hard.

When he could finally manage it, he pulled out his cell phone.

He took a deep breath and dialed 911.

32

Carin Barnes sat cross-legged on the hotel bed, looking down at the file folders lined up before her. She was wearing running shorts and a T-shirt emblazoned with her alma mater, the University of Michigan. In the weeks since she'd contacted Professor Murphy about the bead found at the murder site, she'd been gathering information on the players involved.

The first file folder, to her right, she'd labeled "David Gospel."

Gospel was connected to the Eye through the murder of one Mimi Tran, the fortune-teller who'd been found stabbed to death with her eyes gouged out, and a bead from the oracle's necklace stuffed in her mouth.

Not so coincidentally, his son, Owen Gospel, had been implicated in the separate death of another fortune-teller. To Carin, it looked to be a slam-dunk case…before a transient confessed to the murder. Even without FBI training, anyone could tell the file on the death of the Long Beach psychic, Michelle Larson, reeked.

Another interesting fact penned in the file: Gospel collected psychic artifacts.

"Imagine that," she said, shutting the Gospel file and taking another drink of the ridiculously bad hotel coffee. From past experience, she knew no sugar or white powder that passed for cream could make a dent in it, so she drank it black.

Thus far, she hadn't been able to connect Gospel with Estelle Fegaris or Thomas Crane, two of the other files set out before her.

Carin stared down at the file for Estelle, and smiled. After all these years, it would all come together—just as Estelle had predicted.

Carin knew Terrence, her boss at NISA, did not consider her the subtle sort. He'd spent most of their lunch together—before he'd given her the green light to head up the investigation here in California—he'd talked about her bull-in-a-china-shop approach. Finesse had never been a big part of her work at the FBI, which was exactly why she'd never been considered for covert operations.

Carin looked up into the mirror straight ahead. Clocking in at just under six feet, she had an athlete's body. She wore her blond hair short and choppy, and hid her steel-gray eyes behind sensible lenses.

She'd lost count of how many times some random person had stopped her on the street to ask if she were interested in a career in modeling. There was even a time in graduate school when a short, balding man had run after her huffing and puffing down the streets of Old Town in Pasadena. He'd kept screaming that he *really* was an agent with the connections to get her on the cover of *any* magazine and she was going to be very *sorry* if she didn't stop to talk to him.

Carin couldn't have been less interested.

The way she saw it, she could either be one of those tall, skinny women with hunched shoulders who felt awkward in her own skin…or she could stand to her full height and ignore the gawkers. So, no, Terrence, Carin Barnes didn't have an ounce of subtle in her.

She looked down at the files. But she did know how to keep secrets.

She opened the file labeled "Estelle Fegaris."

Carin had always been fascinated by the brain. From the first time she'd studied biology in high school, she was determined to learn everything she could about the workings of the human mind. How was it possible that the chemical and electrical interactions of cells led to conscious thought? And if it's true that we only use a small percentage of our mental capacity, what then was the purpose of the dormant sections?

These were questions that fascinated Carin Barnes. Particularly after Markie's birth.

Her parents had been trying a long time for another baby, a sibling for Carin. They didn't want her to be raised an only child. But it soon became clear that it just wasn't in the cards. Even after costly and painful fertility treatments, her mother hadn't been able to conceive.

And then, a miracle. After twelve years, when they'd given up on the possibility, they'd been blessed with a son, Markie.

It wasn't until Markie turned three that they began to realize there was something different about him. Carin had been fifteen when he'd been diagnosed with autism spectrum disorder.

Suddenly, Carin's interest in the brain had a purpose.

It turned out that autism was her generation's new cancer. The incidence had increased to the point that the disorder was the topic de jour on all the talk shows, as well as headline news in the health section of the major newspapers. Every other grant had some neurobiologist claiming to have a finger on the cause or the cure.

Carin had her theories about the increase in autism in the general population. She wasn't a fan of the "environmental causes" or the "over-vaccination" theories perpetuated in the media. Carin believed that autism was more like the high incidence of hemophelia in the royal bloodlines. The basic fact was that, when people married, they kept to a certain socioeconomic class. Autism, Carin believed, was just another case of inbreeding, like the Russian tsars right before the Bolshevik Revolution. It was a theory that was gaining some popularity in scientific circles.

From the University of Michigan, she chose Caltech for her graduate studies in order to work with Nobel Laureate Roger Sperry on the emergent properties of the brain. But Carin soon found work in the laboratory slow and unrewarding. It wasn't getting her any closer to helping people like her brother. She was losing hope of making any substantial headway when fate introduced her to Estelle Fegaris.

For years, Carin had closely followed research being conducted on the effects of meditation on the brain. It appeared that brains of yogis who had meditated for fifteen years or more showed a significant difference from the activity found in those of individuals who did not practice consistent meditation. Specifically, using electroencephalographs, or EEGs, researchers determined that meditation in longtime practitioners like the Tibetan monks activated a higher frequency of gamma wave activity. Even more significant for Cairn's purposes, the trained brains of these yogis had higher gamma wave activity even when *not* meditating.

Gamma waves, Carin knew, had been associated with a higher level of mental activity, such as increased awareness and focus. That's when she made the connection. Carin measured the gamma wave activity in her brother's brain and discovered it was far below average. She began to wonder if stimulating such activity in Markie's brain could have some kind of impact on his autism.

She began corresponding with Morgan Tyrell. At the time, Tyrell had still been at Harvard, a maverick in the field of the "evolving brain," a term he claimed to have coined. Interestingly enough, in his work with psychics, Morgan, too, had measured gamma waves in the brain. He discovered that those with claimed psychic powers had the same high levels of gamma wave activity as the yogis in the published studies. But Tyrell took it one step further. He claimed that a strong psychic could actually *stimulate* gamma wave activity in the brains of *others*.

It was Morgan who introduced Carin to Estelle Fegaris.

Carin, a skeptic of the highest order, couldn't be bothered with the hocus-pocus part of Morgan's practice, which included people like Fegaris. But she was more than intrigued by the possibility that a woman like Fegaris could help Markie.

The day Estelle came to see Markie was the day Carin became a convert.

She remembered Estelle as a handsome woman with bright blue eyes and dark black curls. She could see by the way Morgan interacted with her that the two were involved sexually. Carin couldn't blame Morgan. There was something so inviting about the woman. Having learned that Carin's interest in the brain stemmed from her brother's condition, Estelle asked to meet Markie, and Carin agreed.

If she closed her eyes, Carin could remember the scene almost frame by frame: Estelle sitting in front of Markie, while her brother stared into space, swaying rhythmically in his chair.

And then Estelle reached across the table and touched him.

Markie's reaction was immediate and dramatic. He'd stiffened, as if shot by a jolt of electricity. Carin had thought he was having a seizure of some sort. She had been on the viewing side of that two-way mirror, with Morgan, a tall, stately man, standing beside her. Before she could move, Morgan had grabbed her arm, stopping her from running into the room and interfering.

He'd said only, "Wait."

It took just a minute or two…but the time seemed an eternity to Carin. Estelle had touched the flat of her palms to Markie's head and chest before closing her eyes in concentration. Soon enough, her brother's breathing matched Estelle's and his stiff body became limp, slipping back into the wooden chair.

Estelle opened her eyes and asked, "What do you want to tell your sister, Markie?"

He'd said, clear as a bell, "I love you."

Just those three words. *I love you.*

After that, Estelle had walked out of the room, leaving Markie in a sort of slumber, his body in a fetal position on a futon set on the floor for that very purpose. Estelle herself didn't look so great when she walked out: chalky white skin, perspiration and shaking hands.

Carin had immediately launched into plans for another session, but Estelle had given her this defeated look. There'd been tears in her eyes.

"I've worked with autistic children before," she said. "Most times, I can't even reach in as far as I did with your brother. I'm sorry. Really I am."

Markie was too far gone. He was beyond the reach of even her psychic powers. That short communication had come at a great price for Estelle and Markie both. There had been too much stress on his system to reach out. Estelle didn't recommend a repeat performance.

But there was hope. Estelle was of the opinion that the Eye, an artifact that magnified psychic abilities, could help children like Markie.

Since that day, Carin had been on a quest. She'd joined NISA. She used their resources to track down the man who had murdered Fegaris and stolen the Eye. But from there, the artifact just seemed to disappear into thin air. She'd lost track...until now.

And now, she had the homicide team at Westminster at her disposal. She'd assured the chief of police and his people that she wasn't here to take over the case. No way. And basically, that was true—but not for any charitable reasons. NISA had zip in terms of funding, and Carin desperately needed the department's manpower and resources.

She'd looked over the files she'd been given, reading the autopsy reports and witness accounts. It all seemed fairly mundane until she came across the name: Gia Moon.

Carin pulled the final folder on the desk toward her. On the tab, she had typed *Gina Tyrell*.

According to the folks at Westminster Homicide, Gia Moon, a local psychic, had approached the police about the murder of Mimi Tran. In Ms. Moon's own words, she'd had a "vision" about the murder.

"I just bet you did," Carin said with a smile.

Carin's file on Gina Tyrell was a little more comprehensive than what the Westminster police had presented.

"Hello, Gia Moon."

The fact that Gia Moon, an artist, was here—able to own a home and send her daughter to school—let Carin know the psychic had help.

Before she could pick up her phone to call Morgan Tyrell— not really expecting him to reveal any secrets, but willing to give it a try—her BlackBerry danced across the surface of the night-stand. She'd set it to vibrate, and watched it now, acting like a wind-up toy. She frowned, recognizing the number: Westminster Homicide.

She picked up. "Agent Barnes speaking."

Her heart hitched into her throat as she listened.

She pulled the pen and pad of paper provided by the hotel toward her and wrote down the address. "I'll be right there," she said.

She jumped off the bed and changed quickly. Not familiar with the area, she'd made certain her rental car had an OnStar GPS unit. She'd just need to punch in the address and wait for instructions.

Carin holstered her gun and her BlackBerry. Before leaving, she tidied up the files and put them in her briefcase, turning the dials on the locking mechanism. At the same time that she'd been dreading the news, she'd half expected the call. She was more than ready.

Another grisly murder.

33

"**W**ell," Erika said, staring down at the two bodies lying on the carpet. "It's not a horse."

She was referring to the nursery rhyme—the one about the woman who had eaten the fly. The rhyme Gia Moon had recited after her second "vision."

But Seven was thinking about something altogether different. He was remembering that frantic call he'd received just before David Gospel dialed 911.

Her name is Kieu. Or maybe there's a Q in her name. You have to find her....

Seven stared at the bloodbath before him, the very definition of too late.

The two bodies lay boxed in by furniture. The coffee and end tables, sofa and love seat, circled the corpses of the women like covered wagons. David Gospel had identified Velvet Tien, the name on the mailbox downstairs. They'd found ID for Xuan Du in the purse on the dining room table.

Gospel had made mincemeat of the crime scene, trampling over the bloody carpet and trailing blood back and forth to the kitchen and door. He was in the kitchen now, sitting at the table with a uniformed officer watching over him.

To complicate matters, Special Agent Carin Barnes was on the scene. *The fucking FBI,* Seven thought.

Apparently, Agent Barnes was not holed up in some secret FBI lab in Virginia, analyzing the bead she'd confiscated from Westminster Homicide. The FBI agent had, in fact, arrived long before Erika and Seven, apparently alerted to the murder and its connection to Mimi Tran and the "illegal trade in antiquities," the FBI's toehold on the case. From what Seven understood, the National Institute for Strategic Artifacts was connected to Customs, the idea being that there were artifacts that could be of interest to the government due to their possible military or diplomatic implications. Who knew?

A sleek-looking blonde, Agent Barnes had the long, lean body of a high jumper. She couldn't be older than the midthirties, but wore the requisite black suit of the Bureau. She had been standing almost motionless next to the bodies while the crime scene techs did their work, every once in a while checking with a BlackBerry device that seemed melded to her hand.

Erika knelt down next to the younger victim. She looked closer, spotting something.

"Seven?"

Seven came to stand over his partner. Using the tip of her pen, Erika pointed to the woman's mouth, where several particles clung to her lips.

"They're crumbs," Special Agent Barnes said, still focused on the screen of her BlackBerry, like maybe she had eyes in the back of her head. "I assume she had something stuffed in her mouth. Just like Mimi Tran."

Seven peered closer. Around the victim's mouth and on her chin, there did indeed appear to be crumbs.

"Hey, Dan," Erika said, calling the crime scene tech over to the body. "Sample these, will you?"

"It's been done," Barnes said before Danny could respond.

Erika gave Seven a look. She stood. "So what was in her mouth?"

Agent Barnes glanced up, her glasses somehow making those gray eyes look bigger. "I couldn't say until we analyze the crumbs. The object itself is gone." Still keeping to her spot on the other side of the bodies, Barnes pointed her chin toward Velvet Tien. "You can see by the crumbs on the victim's chest that it was removed *postmortem.*"

"Danny, can you come here a minute," Seven called to the tech.

Daniel Ngo stopped what he was doing. He took a second before stepping over to the bodies. This wasn't your normal crime scene—the blood and body parts could make even the most seasoned warrior lose his composure.

"The book on her chest," Seven said. "It's in Vietnamese. Do you recognize it?" he asked.

"Not a clue," Danny said.

"The literal translation is 'The New Scream that Cuts Your Guts,'" Agent Barnes offered, "which I assume is why both victims have been cut open, thus spilling their…guts."

"You know Vietnamese?" Danny asked in surprise.

The agent lifted her hand, displaying the screen of her Black-Berry. "I found it online. It's an epic poem written by Nguyen Du of the Le Dynasty." She spoke in the voice of an intellectual rather than a cop. "Some say he plagiarized from the Chinese, and certainly the Vietnamese are highly influenced by Chinese culture. But it was written in six-eight verse, a popular form in Vietnam. Du used the story to convey the political turmoil at the end of the eighteenth century, but I suspect our killer had quite a different purpose."

Agent Barnes stayed outside the ring of furniture, playing the detached observer. Or maybe her placement had more to do with the view. From that angle, she could see both bodies in situ.

"The killer, I believe, is trying to underscore Mr. Gospel's relationship to one of the victims. The main character in the poem is a woman tricked into prostitution. I've already interviewed Mr. Gospel. Velvet Tien was his mistress."

"Listen to fucking Sherlock Holmes," Erika said under her breath, so that only Seven could hear.

"It's an extremely famous piece of Vietnamese literature, more commonly known as the Story of Kieu."

"What?" Seven asked, suddenly alert.

Agent Barnes cocked her head, her eyes now focused on him. "Does that mean something to you, Detective?"

Her name is Kieu. Or maybe there's a Q in her name.

He looked around the scene, trying to remember exactly what Gia had told him over the phone.

She's in some sort of prison, or maybe there's a barricade keeping her from getting away. He glanced at the furniture circling the bodies. *Her hands, she's reaching for help.* He stared at the hands cut off at the wrist and placed just a few inches away. *She's screaming but no one can hear her.* Velvet Tien's mouth gaped open, frozen in a silent scream. *Her eyes...they're gone. Taken.* Velvet Tien's eyes remained undisturbed. But the other woman...

He hadn't told anyone about the phone call—there hadn't been time. That little gem had slipped away in the hustle over to the crime scene.

Now he told himself he needed more information. He stood in the middle of the very nightmare Gia had described. Everything she'd told him on the phone looked to be right there in front of him. He couldn't just spill out the story. He needed to figure things out first.

"The eyes," he said, addressing Agent Barnes. "Only one of the bodies had her eyes taken."

Barnes stared down at them. "That's Xuan Du, a psychic, just like Mimi Tran. Psychic ability is often referred to as the third eye. I imagine it has something to do with that."

"How do you know the victim is a psychic?" Erika asked, ever the skeptic.

"The yarrow sticks on the dining room floor," Special Agent Barnes answered readily. "They are used in the I Ching ceremony, an ancient form of divination. It's quite popular, actually, especially in Asian communities. Judging from the fact that the yarrow sticks were scattered across the floor, I'd venture to say either the killer or Ms. Tien didn't care for the reading."

Seven nodded, as if everything she'd said made perfect sense. But his heart was racing. All he could think about was that call from Gia.

"You can handle things here?" he asked his partner.

Erika looked nonplussed. Seven didn't give her the chance to argue the point, taking advantage of her uncharacteristic silence.

As for Agent Barnes, he made sure he was out the door before she could start in on her next theory.

* * *

The blond giantess stared at the door where Erika's partner had just made a quick exit.

"He left in a hurry," Barnes remarked.

Didn't he just? Erika thought, wondering what the hell was going on.

Erika kept her expression deadpan as she answered, "What can I say? He's been battling the trots all day, poor guy. Some bad crab salad, I think."

She stared up at the Viking princess, daring her to contradict her story. She didn't even crack a smile. And here Erika thought she'd been downright clever.

It's not that she had anything against blondes, but throw in tall, skinny and horning in on her case, and yeah—she wasn't feeling so generous toward Barnes. Not to mention the fact that the agent appeared to know what she was doing as she studied the bodies. Shit, it would be a real pain in the ass if Erika had to show Barnes respect on top of everything.

Agent Barnes crouched down beside the body, studying Gospel's mistress, Velvet Tien. "The position of the bodies, the Story of Kieu…the killer did his research, leaving perfect clues."

"Okay, I'll bite," Erika said. "What clues?"

Barnes stood. "Not only does the Story of Kieu refer to Mr. Gospel's relationship to one of the deceased, it also brings in the *Nguoi Viet Kieu,* the name given to the Vietnamese diaspora, the immigrants who moved here." She raised a perfectly plucked brow. "*Kieu* is the Vietnamese word meaning 'to reside.' The killer is pointing the finger—at who or what is the question."

Erika glanced at the BlackBerry in the agent's hand. She was thinking the damn thing came in mighty handy, wondering if the FBI had popped for the little machine.

"We're dealing with a crime scene that has been compromised, of course," Agent Barnes continued. "Mr. Gospel has already given me his statement. Apparently he had an appointment with Ms. Tien. He claims to have no idea who the other woman is, and did not expect her to be here."

"You think he's lying?"

"About so many things, I wouldn't even know where to begin."

Erika couldn't help her smile. Barnes's expression of insouciance… She liked it. And agreed. The bastard was lying, all right.

"He found the door open," Barnes said. "He immediately sensed something was wrong."

Erika thought of the two bodies gutted like fish on the floor behind her. "Nailed that one, didn't he?"

"He came in and, upon recognizing Ms. Tien, vomited on the carpet," she said, indicating a stain just a few feet away. "He then washed his face in the kitchen and called the police, which explains his footprints on the carpet leading back and forth from the kitchen."

"But?"

Barnes glanced back at the bodies. "It's the back and forth part that has me curious, Detective. As well as these."

She pointed to partial prints that disappeared in the direction of the front door.

Erika nodded. "He left the condo after seeing the bodies. Did you ask him why?"

"Not yet." She gave a small smile. "But I'm sure he has a good story."

Erika studied the agent. She hated to admit it, but the woman was starting to grow on her.

"There's evidence that something was removed from Ms. Tien's mouth. Not the killer's doing—he would be responsible for putting it there in the first place."

"Maybe he changed his mind?" Erika suggested.

"Or someone else removed it. Someone who knew—possibly because of what was found in Mimi Tran's mouth—that it might be important. The previous bead was inside the beak of a bird. Whoever took the object—pastry, I'd say from the crumbs— might have believed there was yet another bead to be found."

"No one knew about the bead in the bird's beak."

But even as she said it, Erika was thinking about Gia Moon.

"No one?" Barnes repeated almost to herself. "I beg to differ."

The agent pointed out another section of the carpet. It looked like someone had rolled a stack of quarters over the blood, creating a strange pattern on the cream Berber.

"And then there's this."

Suddenly, Barnes's eyes widened. The smile that followed was brief but blinding. For a second, Erika thought maybe she should invest in those Crest White Strips.

Barnes jumped to her feet. She made for the kitchen, where Gospel waited, with a cop babysitting. Erika followed close behind.

"Mr. Gospel?"

Gospel looked up at Barnes. Erika tried to connect that tired face with the man she'd seen just a few days before in his office. She couldn't. With his thousand-dollar suit crumpled and stained with blood and vomit, his face dead-white, Gospel looked like shit.

"Yes?"

"Do you have a handkerchief, by any chance?" Barnes asked.

Gospel didn't even flinch at the strange question. "Not with me, no."

Barnes nodded, as if that made sense. "I'm afraid I'll have to ask for your coat."

Suddenly, Gospel bristled, sitting up in the kitchen chair. "Am I a suspect here?" he asked, sounding a little too irritated.

And then this idea struck Erika. If Gia Moon knew about the bead, then anybody could be privy to the information, through Gia or even another source. Gospel was a collector. Even if he didn't originally have the necklace, he'd be interested in possessing any part of such a valuable artifact.

The missing object. The footprints leading back and forth to the door. And now, Agent Barnes asking for his handkerchief, something a gentleman like Gospel would most certainly carry—a handy container for a crumbly pastry pulled from the victim's mouth.

Erika flipped open her phone. "Mr. Gospel, we can have a search warrant issued over the phone if necessary."

He seemed to think about it. Strange how the question energized him. A second ago, he was a man defeated. But now he stood, straightening his jacket, ready to make it a good fight.

"Well, then. I'm afraid it's time for me to seek counsel."

Barnes nodded, as if she expected as much. "Make the warrant for his car as well, Detective."

Erika walked into the main entry as she punched in the number. "Fucking *great* Sherlock Holmes," she said under her breath with a smile.

34

Seven didn't bother with turn signals or speed limits, just using the siren, the light built into the rear window of the Crown Vic flashing. One of the perks of the job, he figured. After a quick call to the precinct, he had her address in hand. Now he was speeding to Garden Grove, not really sure how he'd handle the situation once he got there.

He told himself he'd heard about this sort of thing before. He'd even seen a couple of shows on cable TV. *Psychic Detectives* or something.

He remembered this one case. A cop brought mug shots and placed the photos facedown in front of the psychic working on the case. She picked out one photo, saying something about how it made her feel strange, as if she couldn't catch her breath. Turns out, she'd singled out their number one suspect. The police pressed him on his alibi. Next thing you know, the guy confesses.

Seven parked the car in front of Gia's place. It was one of those little houses that looked like it was made out of gingerbread, complete with white picket fence and lots of flowers. There was even an arched trellis dripping with wisteria. Swear to God, she was growing a freaking English garden.

Seven had a black thumb. He'd even killed one of those indestructible philodendrons. He remembered his mom commenting on it, giving him this look. Maybe he was being sensitive, but from the expression on her face, he'd had the idea that she was thinking about Laurin. How he couldn't keep anything alive, even his marriage.

He'd been thinking about that a lot lately. How maybe, because of his job, death could seep into his bones and slip out his fingertips.

"Screw it," he said, getting out of the car. Now wasn't the time for personal ruminations.

He was about to push the doorbell when the door opened. Gia stood there looking at him with those vibrant blue eyes.

The idea came to him: her "psychic" self already knew he was on his way. She'd seen it all in one of her "visions." Wasn't that how it happened in the world of the paranormal? She would always be one step ahead.

"The victim's name was Velvet Tien," he said, this time trying to beat her to the punch. "She had a book opened on her chest," he said. "The Story of Kieu."

He told himself to take a breath. He was acting crazy, driving here like a maniac, making outbursts to a potential witness-suspect. A very silent witness-suspect.

He couldn't read the expression on her face. Standing there in her T-shirt and jeans, she was the proverbial blank slate. Apparently, life kept on going for Gia Moon. Have a vision of two women eviscerated? Not a problem.

Her hair was wet; obviously, she'd just stepped out of the shower. It made the color even darker, a pitch-black.

He remembered reading the term Black Irish in a book once. He'd been just a kid and thought it meant someone part African, part Irish. He'd come to learn the term referred to Irish people with pale skin, black hair and blue, blue eyes. That was Gia Moon to a T.

She opened the door wider. She leaned against the doorjamb, motioning for him to enter. "You'll want to see the painting."

He followed her through the living room into the kitchen. The place looked like an artist lived here, all right. Nothing was your normal interior decor. The top of the coffee table was made of broken pieces of china pieced together. The sofa had green papier-mâché leaves sprouting from the back and the arms, as if it were alive and growing.

There were children's paintings on the walls, the kind of thing that normally would be held up by magnets on the refrigerator. But here the drawings were set in ornate wooden frames, displayed like valuable works of art.

Every corner had something of significance. A lot of it religious. There were skulls made out of tissue paper to celebrate the Day of the Dead. A crucifix with the bleeding image of Christ on the cross. A set of icons hinged together. Lots of candles in all shapes and sizes.

And photographs. Everywhere there were pictures of a girl in different stages of life, from birth to her early teens. She looked a lot like Gia, except her hair was a tangle of wild curls.

The kitchen was bright and sunny, the walls painted in vibrant yellow. The counter tiles were a kaleidoscope of red and orange.

He wondered if that's how she got through the day: painting her surroundings in bright, shiny colors.

"Do you want some coffee?" she asked. "Or would you prefer to go straight to my studio?"

"Coffee? Sure, why not," he said, finding his voice. *Drink a little caffeine and freaking wake up!*

She had one of those French presses. He watched her pour, looking at those delicate hands—artist's hands. She never wore makeup, and still she was stunning.

He thought about Beth. How hard she worked at everything, always looking "just so." Even when she was drunk off her ass, she had her perfect nails, her sweater sets and immaculate hair.

The kitchen was small. There was only room for a tiny, round table and two chairs. Gia gestured to one and handed him a mug.

"I'm sorry I called you in such a panic," she said, sitting across from him. "I'm not sure what I expected you to do."

"I believe your words were something like, 'you have to find her, Detective,'" he said, having an excellent memory for such things. "'You have to find her *now*.'"

Gia looked down at her cup, as if reading tea leaves. "I'm sorry. I really don't expect miracles. I didn't give you enough. There was no way you could find her in time."

He flipped open his notebook, refusing her invitation for a pity party. Pulling out his pen to take notes, he noticed his coffee cup for the first time. The mug showed a cartoon image of two women. One looked like a gypsy, with a scarf around her hair and wearing a long, flowing skirt. The other woman was seated across the table, waiting anxiously. The gypsy stared into a crystal ball. The bubble over her head read, *I got nothing*.

"A gift from a client," Gia said, catching his gaze.

He wondered if that was her real "gift," just being observant. He said, "You said your visions come to you in dreams."

"Usually, but not always. Like today. I was painting in my studio. I thought I was in the middle of making something truly amazing. I didn't even know how long I'd been at it, but my arms and back hurt from the effort. When I stopped, I expected to see this beautiful piece. Only, that's not what was on the canvas."

"Are you saying you went into some sort of trance?"

She seemed to think about it. "Yes. I suppose I did. Or the spirit somehow possessed me. I told you before, powerful spirits are drawn to me. Just like my mother."

"So it runs in the family?"

"Like cancer."

"You see your gifts as a disease?"

She leaned across the table toward him. "Do you ever have a case go bad, Detective?"

He paused, seeing the feelings so clearly on her face. "None of us is perfect."

"Then you know about the guilt," she said. "I'm in their heads, the minds of the bad guys. It feels weighty and tough. I'm supposed to stop them. If I get it wrong, someone dies...."

He could see what she was getting at. What happened today, she saw as a personal failure.

She smiled. "Is there any other way to see it?"

He nodded, but said, "That mind-reading thing of yours...not my favorite."

She took his coffee cup and stood. She put both cups in the sink. She turned and stood there, looking back at him.

Finally, she said, "The painting. I'm ready to show it to you now."
He stood, as well. "Lead the way."

They found the moon cake wrapped in Gospel's handkerchief, hidden in the trunk of his Mercedes, right alongside a
bloody flashlight.

The pattern on the handle of the flashlight was a perfect match
to the blood splotched along the carpet.

Erika shook her head as the techs bagged and tagged the evidence. "How did you know?" she asked Barnes.

The Viking queen watched the crime scene techs do their job.
"There were two sets of prints going back into the kitchen. That
meant Gospel didn't just go in there once to clean up, as he
claimed. And then there were the prints leading to the door. You
noticed he had on his suit jacket?"

The lightbulb flashed on for Erika. "Still elegantly dressed at
the grisly murder of his lover…which, no doubt, would include
a handkerchief?"

Barnes cocked her head. "Monogrammed, I would think. Men
like Gospel like to keep their hands clean."

Erika nodded. Once Gospel refused to hand over his handkerchief, Barnes guessed he'd used it to grab whatever had been in
the victim's mouth. The prints leading to the front door showed
he had some business outside, perhaps at his Mercedes.

"Not bad," Erika said, giving the devil her due.

Barnes turned to her. "Detective, let me be perfectly clear. I
am not here to usurp your authority. NISA is not a typical branch
of the FBI."

Glad to hear it. "Meaning?"

"We work behind the scenes, taking a back seat to local law
enforcement. The unfortunate murder of these women is not the
focus of my investigation."

"You want the Eye," Erika said.

"I believe Mr. Gospel, with his financial wherewithal, could
very well have purchased the Eye from unauthorized sources.
The very fact that he took the moon cake out of the victim's

mouth—given the information that part of the necklace had been found inside Ms. Tran's mouth—leads me to believe Gospel was after another bead."

"Okay, call me thick, but I don't get it. Does he have the necklace or not? Why is he searching for pieces of it inside the mouth of a dead woman?"

For the first time, Agent Barnes gave Erika a very wide smile. "That is the question, isn't it?"

And with that, she walked away, leaving Erika to make sense of it all.

35

Stolen artifacts, dead fortune-tellers, millionaires and their private—and possibly illegal—collections. Erika sat bellied up to the bar at the House of Brews, trying to figure out what connected the dots.

She punched the speed-dial number—her third time. She pushed End before his voice mail could pick up.

And now Seven wasn't answering his phone.

It probably had something to do with his sister-in-law, Beth, Erika mused, sipping on the cosmopolitan. Now there was a black hole of need if Erika had ever seen one.

Not my problem, she reminded herself. But still, she worried. Seven wasn't thinking straight, still carrying the cross of his brother's sins. Only now, they had this fat case. A career maker—or breaker. If Seven wasn't careful, it would be the latter.

As she picked up her cosmo for another sip, wondering if maybe she should order the sashimi salad, a man sat down on the stool next to hers. It was early, the place was almost empty, with just a couple playing pool behind her. Erika frowned. She wasn't in the mood for a pickup. She didn't take it as a good sign that the guy had chosen the seat next to hers.

The mere fact that he was under six feet tall scratched him off the list of possibles. Not to mention the glasses and the less than Gold's-gym physique. She ignored him, hoping he'd get the message.

"I come here almost every night," he said, wrapping his hands around the beer bottle in front of him. He had curly brown hair he tried to tame with a short haircut. She thought she detected hazel eyes hidden behind thick glasses. He was also hairy. His five o'clock shadow looked more like next-day stubble.

"I figured you'd show up sooner or later," he said. "By the way, what's your real name?"

Caught off guard, Erika turned on her stool. "What?"

"Your name? I've heard quite a few variations. Some nights you're Suzy. Then there's Sophia. And Sonia." He took another drink from the bottle. She noticed it was one of those low-carb beers. "You seem to stick with the *S*s."

She didn't say anything. It sort of pissed her off that she was actually embarrassed. It wasn't as if she was hiding her life-style—not that it was anybody's business. But she'd never had anyone call her on it.

She took a swift drink from the cosmo. "As it so happens, my name *is* Sophia."

"That's your story and you're sticking to it?"

"Yeah. I guess I am."

He held out his hand. "Frank."

She gave the outstretched paw a withering look. "Lovely to meet you. Now, why don't you just go away…Frank?"

He put the hand back on the beer and gave her a big smile, as if she hadn't just blown him off, big time.

"Are you kidding?" he asked. "Do you know how long it's taken me to get the courage to get this far?" He took another swig from the bottle. "Let me savor the moment…Sophia."

When she went to stand up, taking her drink with her, he grabbed her hand so that she would be forced to spill the cosmo-politan if she wanted to leave.

"Is it my breath?" he asked.

She rolled her eyes. "I got to tell you—that's not much of a line."

"But is it working?"

She didn't like it. She never slept with guys like Frank, the kind that had lovesick written all over them. The nesters. Sure, they hovered at bars, thinking they were players and might get lucky. But in reality, they were always looking for Mrs. Right, someone to bear their babies. You get drunk, they drive you home and tuck you into bed with two aspirins and a bottle of water. You give them your number, and they call and call.

God forbid you have sex. That was practically a ring on the finger to Frank's type.

Erika preferred the jerks who knew the score. It was one night; it was sex. He wouldn't need her real name.

Or maybe it was the fact that she was feeling a little too vulnerable. A lot was going on right now. Her father was back in town, her partner was MIA. And some asshole was ripping out women's guts. Tonight, it might be to easy to make a mistake with the Franks of the world.

He made a show of looking at the watch on his wrist. "Give me fifteen minutes? I could buy the next round…make it worth your while? You look like you could use it."

"Ah, that's so sweet, Frank. Telling me I look like crap? I bet you say stuff like that to all the girls."

"Hey, 'Bad Day' is written in neon across your forehead."

She thought about it a minute. Agent Barnes had made it clear they were done for the night, and Seven wasn't answering his phone. Just about now, her partner was probably cooking dinner, trying to hide from his nephew the fact that Beth was drunk.

"Suit yourself," she said, sitting back down. If the guy wanted his heart broken, that was his problem. "By the way? I'm not sleeping with you."

He nodded with mock solemnity. "If you're sure."

"Yeah." Suddenly, she felt a little better. "I'm sure."

"Phew." He acted out wiping the sweat from his forehead with the back of his hand. "So, now that we have *that* settled, what are we doing for the rest of the night?"

"What happened to fifteen minutes?" she asked.

He shrugged. "I got my foot in the door. It's human nature to want to crack it open a bit wider."

She'd come to the House of Brews to get good and plastered, maybe even power down some real food, like ribs—screw the salad—with her booze, then take a taxi home.

But suddenly, she was actually tempted by a night of talking over taxes or airplanes, pegging Frank here for an accountant or an engineer. Maybe after a day like today, she could give herself a break. Maybe she could just sit with a nice guy she'd met at a bar and pretend she had a normal life.

"Have you had any dinner?" she asked.

He grinned. "Nope."

"The ribs here are great."

"I'm a vegetarian."

She gave him a look.

"Just kidding." He said it like that was the most brilliant thing he'd ever heard.

She grabbed her drink and headed for one of the tables. "You know what, Frank? We're going to have to work on that sense of humor."

Seven stared up at the painting, transfixed. The canvas stretched across its five-by-five-foot wooden frame, the colors all shades of black and red.

The image of Velvet Tien was life-size and amazingly accurate, the details of the face so precise that he could have recognized her on the street.

The painting showed only her head and torso. At the same time, it looked as if she'd been torn to bits and pieced together like a macabre puzzle. Her arms stretched off the edge of the canvas, disappearing at her wrists. With its black-and-red palette, the painting was a surreal rendition of the murder scene he'd just left.

There were a few differences. Gia had painted a black crescent moon almost like chocolate candy on the victim's red tongue. It reminded Seven of communion. And in the middle of her stomach cavity was an enormous human eye.

There was no sign of Xuan Du, the second woman.

"Her eyes," he said, pointing to the dark, empty holes. "The killer left her eyes intact."

He didn't mention the other woman, the psychic. The fact that the killer had taken *her* eyes instead.

"As I said, Detective, it's not an exact science."

Gia had converted her one-car garage into a studio. There wasn't much in terms of furniture in the room. Mostly, it was space for her paintings. They were lined up against all four walls. Her talent was spectacular and engrossing.

He thought about those shows he'd seen on cable, the psychics who helped law enforcement. This wasn't anything like that. It felt like a magic trick when you stop and think, *How'd she do that?*

She came to stand in front of the butchery on the canvas. The contrast between the woman and the painting struck him as an odd juxtaposition. She looked small and feminine, incapable of producing such a chilling scene.

She looked up at Velvet Tien. "In my mind, I was painting something completely different. A beautiful image of a young woman playing a lute. There was a full moon in the background." Gia shook her head, almost as if she couldn't quite believe what she was seeing. "There was so much *color*."

He was used to seeing dead bodies; it was part of his job. He could pore over photographs of the dead and testify about the details in court. *Here are the ligature marks…notice the cigarette burns.* He'd dutifully woven this kind of violence into his life.

But there was an element here that unsettled him. The possibility that someone had a gift to see this kind of horror.

Again, he thought of Erika's explanation. *She did it, or she's somehow involved.*

"The victim's hands," he said, "they're not on the canvas. You told me she was reaching out, asking for help."

Gia frowned at the painting. "He cut them off, didn't he?"

She hadn't even hesitated.

"Yes," he said.

She nodded. "Again. It's a matter of interpretation."

"Right." He told himself not to make any judgments. He was here to gather information. "What about the moon on her tongue? What does that symbolize?"

"It tasted sweet," she said. "That's why I put it on her tongue."

Like a cake, he thought to himself, remembering the crumbs found on the victim's lips.

"And the eye inside her stomach? Why there?"

She shook her head. "I'm not sure." She pushed her hair back, looking suddenly tired. "I'm sorry. I wish I could be more helpful."

He wanted to press her. She could very well be hiding something. He was here to make sense of her story—and if the facts didn't jibe, that, too, could be significant.

Suddenly, she sat down cross-legged on the floor. In that moment, she looked incredibly vulnerable. A woman carrying the weight of the world on her shoulders.

"Are you okay?" he asked.

"His lover was pressing your brother to leave his wife," she said. "But your brother needed to be perfect. The perfect husband, the perfect father, the perfect surgeon. The affair was his only vice. He didn't want anyone to know he was a homosexual. Especially his son."

Everything she said was like a blow to… Like she'd dipped her hand inside his chest and squeezed. Seven couldn't catch his breath.

"I'm sorry," she said, looking up at him. "You were…projecting. Sometimes, it's hard to hold back."

He forced himself to take deep breaths, tried not to be conspicuous about it. He thought about what Erika had told him. *Next, she'll be saying your brother murdered somebody.*

It wouldn't be hard to piece it together. Even *Nightline* had contacted Ricky's attorney. Between the newspaper articles and what was available on the Internet, there wasn't much left to the imagination.

Gia gave him a tired smile. "You really should go see him."

Seven took a step back. He hadn't visited his brother in months.

"Mom? You okay?"

He looked toward the door. There stood a young girl, the one in the photos—almost a carbon copy of her mother, except for the curls. Gia rose as her daughter came to stand next to her.

The girl looked at Seven with such a fierce expression, he almost burst out laughing.

"You a cop?" she asked.

That brash expression, as if she wasn't under five feet and wearing Keds... He had to smile at her tone, all bluster and suspicion. She made him think about his nephew, Nick, and his dull expression. How different this young woman was from Ricky's boy.

Seven held out his hand. "Detective Seven Bushard, at your service."

The girl gave a firm shake while looking him over. "Seven. That's a weird name."

"It's a nickname. Just sort of stuck over the years. My real name is Stephen."

She nodded. "Stephen—Bushard. Seven letters. You're into numerology."

He looked at Gia. He couldn't imagine a kid coming up with that explanation so quickly.

"Not really," he said. "It was a friend of mine. He was into that stuff and gave me the name."

"But you kept it," she insisted.

He gave his most charming smile. "I thought it sounded cool."

She nodded. "It does. Sure as hell beats Stephen, anyway."

"Language," Gia said, taking her daughter's hand and giving it a squeeze. To Seven, she said, "I'll walk you to the door, Detective."

Seven found himself outmaneuvered. He wasn't done with his interview, and still he was following her out.

At the door, he was about to tell her as much, that he wasn't finished with her. Only she beat him to the punch, saying, "Your partner has a private investigator following me. He'll report your presence here. I thought you might want to know."

She shut the door before he could respond.

Gia collapsed to the entry floor. She shut her eyes and took a deep breath.

"You like him, don't you?"

Once again, her daughter watched from the doorway. She'd crossed her arms over her chest and held one hip jutting out. She didn't look at all pleased by the prospect.

"Yes," Gia told her. "I like him."

She hid enough from her daughter. She didn't need to keep such a trivial secret. Nor would it do her any good to even try. Once Stella had a bead on a particular emotion, holding out only made her dig in.

"You didn't have to do that," Gia said, referring to Stella's interruption in the studio.

Her daughter turned toward the kitchen. Over her shoulder, she said, "I was trying to do my homework, but you were giving me a headache. By the way, I'm making us spaghetti for dinner."

And there was the problem. Stella was too in tune with her mother. Emotions like the ones Gia was fighting with Seven being the worst kind to try and hide.

Gia followed her into the kitchen. She had been hoping to give herself more time with her daughter, but now she understood she'd waited too long already.

The spirit was closer. Stalking her. And despite any hedging on her part to Seven, Gia knew the killer. She wasn't waiting for him to arrive on her doorstep.

Time to find Stella a safe place.

36

Seven had taken Nick to Steve's Burgers on Warner, one of those burger joints, inevitably run by a Greek, where the food was piled high and served with a smile. They'd both indulged in pastrami sandwiches and chocolate shakes. He'd asked Nick about school and basketball, anything but the obvious—how his mother was doing. How Nick felt about his father.

Seven told himself Nick needed time to just be a kid, to forget all the darkness that was going on in his life. But he wondered if maybe it wasn't only his nephew who needed the break.

And it worked—at least for the span of a dinner. They tried to outdo each other on knock-knock jokes, and had a fry-eating contest. They even played thumb wars. Seven was pretty ruthless, never "letting" Nick win. Because it didn't matter. It was the good old days. Just he and Nick having a good time.

But driving back to the house, he could see Nick sinking into the passenger seat. They both knew what was waiting for them at home.

The minute they stepped inside Ricky's minimansion, with its perfect view of the main channel, they heard Beth crying upstairs.

Without batting an eye, Seven asked, "How's the homework situation?"

"I'm on it."

On his way to his room, Nick stopped to stare up the steps toward his mother's bedroom. The look on his nephew's face…suddenly, that kid seemed a hundred years old.

Seven knew what lay ahead—a night of hand-holding. But

now he wondered how many nights it was Nick who had held his mother's hand when Seven wasn't here to take on the load.

After he'd set Nick up with his math, frankly amazed the kid was doing pre-algebra—*algebra,* for cripe's sake—Seven walked up the stairs.

Beth had been drinking heavily, an empty bottle of some pricey chardonnay stood on the nightstand next to a Waterford goblet. He remembered shopping for his brother's wedding. Beth had registered at Nieman Marcus. A set of her china cost almost a week's salary.

He sat down on the bed next to her. He picked up the bottle of Xanax, the tranquilizer her doctor had prescribed.

"Hey," he said, brushing her hair from her face. "I don't think the pills mix with the booze. You want to end up in the hospital? You think Nick can handle that?"

She bit her lip, the tears still coming. "I know, I *know.*" She looked up at him, shaking her head. "Don't make me feel worse. I *try,* Seven. It's just…shit. I had a really bad day."

"Beth, you need to call me when you're like this."

"You're here now." She snuggled up to him, putting her arms around his waist and resting her head against his chest. "That's all that matters."

He rubbed her arm, feeling the weight of that burden. "Help me here, Beth. I have Ricky and Nick to think about. I can't worry about you, too."

She nodded, brushing away her tears. "I see a therapist. I'm *trying.* What more can I do, Seven?"

He remembered being jealous once, of Ricky and his perfect wife and family. The pride he'd brought to Seven's parents. They loved to talk about Ricky's newest accomplishments, the practice he'd opened in Newport Beach, his stock portfolio, the fifty-five-foot yacht. The private schools and sailing lessons for Nick.

But now, Seven couldn't help but make the comparison. Gia and that painting—her daughter and her fierce expression. The two of them stood against the world, propping each other up. No way Gia would let her kid down like this.

But he told himself he didn't know their story. Maybe it was just harder, falling from Beth's great heights.

He looked back at the bottle of wine next to the prescription medicine. "You're going to have to stop, Beth. If you need help, I can take care of Nick. Maybe you could go somewhere. A clinic, you know?"

She shook her head. "He's all I have, Seven. I can't. I just can't." She looked up at him, biting her lip. "I won't let him down. I swear to God I won't. Not after everything that's happened." She nodded, as if she was making a pact with herself. "Tomorrow, I start getting sober. No more trying to stay numb." She looked up again, her pale blue eyes weepy and needy. "But tonight, can you just hold me? Until I fall asleep?"

"Sure."

And why not? He'd done it before. Many times.

"He was never around," she said, her voice heavy with the meds and alcohol. "I thought it was the job. He was such a gifted surgeon. I didn't know he didn't love me anymore…if he ever did. I was so stupid."

"How could loving anyone be stupid?" he asked.

For a while, they didn't speak. He just held her, stroking her hair, waiting for her breathing to grow deep and rhythmic with sleep.

"Do you ever miss it?" she asked after a while. "Being married?"

He sighed, thinking about Laurin. They'd had a tumultuous relationship. She'd thought she was pregnant and they'd jumped the gun. It hadn't lasted. Big surprise.

"I got married too young and for all the wrong reasons. It wasn't ever going to work out."

"I miss it," she said, nuzzling closer. "A lot. I didn't know how much I loved being married. I was someone's wife and mother. Did you know I was running for PTA president when he killed Scott?"

"Hey. This wasn't your fault. Ricky made some bad choices, not you, okay?"

"I wonder sometimes," she whispered. "Maybe if I'd been prettier…smarter. Better."

"That's a bunch of crap."

"Really?" She looked up at him. "My husband left me for a man."

"What Ricky did was a huge betrayal," Seven told her, suddenly finding himself having the conversation he'd planned for Nick. "He betrayed you and his family. How is that your fault?"

The tears spilled. "Why didn't I know, Seven? How could I have missed the signs?"

"Come on, Beth. I'm a homicide detective and I didn't know there was anything wrong."

"I lived with him. I *slept* with him." She reached up and touched Seven's face. "You hate it, that I'm weak."

"That's the booze talking."

She bit her lip again, looking entirely too vulnerable. "Maybe it wasn't just Ricky who made some bad choices."

She was delivering the message loud and clear: *Did I pick the wrong brother?*

"I'm not such a prince," Seven told her.

"From where I'm sitting, you're looking pretty good."

Shit, he thought, remembering everything Erika had told him.

He pulled away gently. "Promise me something? You get sober, and then we'll talk, okay?"

She saw the rejection in his eyes. She rolled into a little ball on the bed. "Oh, God."

Again, that image of Gia flooded his mind. He couldn't imagine her falling apart like this. And that kid of hers, the two of them were like a mother lion and cub.

"Come on, Beth. What's Nick going to think if you and I can't keep it together? I'm his uncle—all he has besides his grandparents to make up for that image of his dad in an orange suit with his hands cuffed. He needs me…he needs you. What he doesn't need is us screwing that up, okay?"

She rubbed the tears from her eyes, sitting up. He could see she liked the idea that his rejection was something practical rather than personal.

"You're right, of course. I don't want to be that kind of mother—I don't want to be *this* kind of a mother," she added angrily. She shook her head, looking more sober. "I'll talk to my counselor." She brushed away her tears. "Maybe I do need to get away." She took his hand and squeezed it. "Your parents already offered. But you'll check in on him, won't you?"

"God, Beth. You don't even have to ask. You know how much you and Nick mean to me."

She nodded. "Yeah. I do, Seven. I really do."

He gave her a kiss on the top of her head. "We'll get through this. I promise."

He waited until he knew she'd fallen asleep. He checked on his nephew. Nick, too, was tucked into bed, homework finished and at the ready on his desk.

Seven locked the front door on his way out. He told himself they'd work it out. He had his parents to help out. No matter what, Beth and Nick were family.

Only, once he sat inside that quiet, empty car, all that emotion he'd kept in check exploded. It was like one of those laws of physics: nature abhors a vacuum or something. The anger he felt transformed him. He wasn't thinking about his brother or Beth or even Nick. Instead, all that emotion boiling inside focused in a different direction.

Your partner has a private investigator following me. He'll report your presence here.

Once she'd said it, he'd spotted the car immediately, a nondescript gray sedan. He recognized the P.I., Cedric Patterson. He was pretty well-known. Most of the defense attorneys in the area used him. When Seven decided to get his own take on what happened with his brother, he'd given Patterson a call.

Which was apparently what his partner had felt the need to do. A little extra investigating—not that she'd mentioned anything to him.

Erika didn't trust him.

And maybe she shouldn't. What the hell, it's not like he'd been honest, right? He was keeping secrets, fooling himself into believing that he just wanted to give it some time before he talked it over with is partner.

Well, it looked as if his time was up.

Suddenly, he felt this urge to *do* something. Like Beth, he didn't want to swallow back his anger anymore. He wanted to let that emotion flood over him and burn him up.

He jammed the key into the ignition and turned over the engine. He had a better way to deal with this.

Erika rolled over and stared up at the ceiling. She could hear Frank snoring in the bed next to her.

Shit.

Just as she'd thought. Frank was a nester.

She'd never considered herself needy. She knew better than to let some cute banter over ribs and a cosmo bring her to this point. But here she was, wishing she could at least pass out alongside him. Instead, she was wide-awake, already dreading the awkward morning after.

She knew exactly when it had all gone wrong. She hadn't admitted to herself how much the butchery of the day had gotten to her. Those poor women. She'd tried to keep it all professional, admiring the FBI agent solving the case with commendable precision. Snaps to Special Agent Barnes.

But that wasn't Erika. Her Latin soul prevented that kind of distance. All along, she kept wondering how they were going to stop this monster. Who might be next if they didn't? What good had it done her to think she could keep that cool head she projected to others?

It's like she always said. Denial—there was no stronger emotion.

And now she had Frank camped out beside her, business that she would have to deal with in the morning, when her emotional reserves were already shot.

Only suddenly—out of nowhere—the doorbell rang, the sound echoing through the quiet condo. She glanced over at Frank, still fast asleep. She glanced at the digital alarm clock at her bedside. *What the hell?*

It was well past midnight.

Again, the doorbell.

She grabbed a robe and headed for the door, wondering who would come a-knocking at this time of night. She gave a glance to the drawer where she kept her service revolver, the vivid image of those women stamped inside her head.

Maybe that's how it had all started for Mimi Tran and Velvet Tien? A simple doorbell?

But instead of grabbing her sidearm, she checked through the peephole to see Seven standing on the other side, looking none too pleased.

"Shit!"

She stepped away from the door. She turned to stare at the room. Clothes lay strewn across the floor, like bread crumbs leading to the bedroom.

Seven was leaning on the doorbell now. Any minute, the guy in her bed would wake up from the bender they'd just shared and wonder what the hell was going on.

She opened the door a crack.

"Jesus, Seven. What the hell are you doing—"

He didn't wait for her to finish the sentence. He pushed the door open and walked inside.

"Well, come on in," she said, shocked by the aggressive tactics.

He turned to look at her, absolutely fuming. "You didn't think you should let me in on your little gig with Cedric?"

She immediately put it together. "Well, well, well." She crossed her arms, leaning back on the door. She'd thought he'd left today to go put out some fire with Beth. But he must have gone straight to Gia Moon's from the crime scene. That's the only way he could know about Cedric.

"You went to see your psychic?"

The way she said it, it sounded like some strange accusation. Almost like some fishwife yelling at her unfaithful husband.

"I was following up on some information I had, yes. And imagine my surprise when I discover Cedric on her tail."

Erika shook her head. Maybe it was her own secrets that gave her special insight, but suddenly she understood.

"You didn't go see her about the murders. You're falling for this woman, Seven. A possible suspect in a high profile case."

"Bullshit. Jesus, Erika, what the hell were you thinking, hiring Cedric? If we actually end up putting a case together against this woman, and her attorney discovers your personal involvement, what do you think is going to happen? Our case goes down the crapper. What could possibly make you believe it was worth the risk?"

She locked her arms around her stomach, giving him a hard stare. "*My* personal involvement? That's what has you worried?"

"Are you telling me you didn't hire Cedric?"

"No, you're right. I put Cedric on her. And if I thought for a minute that you had your head on straight, I would have told you about it."

He looked as if she'd slapped him. But before they could really get into it, the guy—Jesus, what was his name?—walked out from the bedroom.

"Is there a problem here?"

Like two kids caught in the act, Seven and she turned their attention to Frank. It was almost comical, the way Seven's eyes grew huge as he stared at the men's trousers lying next to her bra on the carpet.

Frank stood there with a sheet from the bed covering him toga style. From their conversation at dinner, Erika was pretty sure he was an engineer and not an accountant. Too much imagination. He'd never looked more the part of the nerd, with his glasses and that stupid sheet wrapped around him like some Roman senator.

And now he was trying to stick up for her? Bring it on!

"Everything's fine," she said. She looked pleadingly at Seven. "We can talk about it tomorrow, okay?"

But Seven just stood there frozen, as if he'd been flattened by one of those big rigs, staring at Frank in his toga.

In perfect timing, his cell phone went off. That distinctive ring. Beth was calling.

Erika couldn't help her mocking tone. "Don't you think you'd better get that?"

He stared at her again with a strange disbelief in his expression—only to turn on his heel and flip open his cell phone on his way out.

"Hey, you okay?"

Frank again, coming to stand behind her.

She didn't even want to look at him. "Yeah. Just dandy."

Except that she felt like shit.

"He called you Erika."

She took in a deep breath. Jesus. The lightbulb hadn't gone on yet?

She turned to give him a wane smile. "You always knew Sophia wasn't my real name. And by the way, you look ridiculous in that bedsheet."

"Hey, if I knew you preferred me naked…"

She shook her head, looking away. "Why do I feel like I owe you an apology?"

He stepped up closer. "Because you're a woman. It's supposed to be the guy who lies and scams you into bed, not the other way around. That was your partner, right? You're a cop?"

Erika frowned. Okay, she'd had a lot to drink. But she quickly went over her conversation with Frank during the evening—nothing which included anything specifically about police business. She'd made damn sure of it.

She stared at Frank in his toga. "What makes you ask that?"

He walked over to a set of bookshelves and picked out a framed photo of her in uniform, hugging her mother. Erika remembered her brother had taken the photograph when she'd graduated from the academy.

"A cop, right?" he asked, holding up the photo.

"Well, aren't you the observant one." She thought about it a minute. She asked, "What did you say you do for a living, Frank?"

He put the framed photo back. "Actually, I didn't."

"Really?" Suddenly, Erika got this sick feeling in her gut. "Okay. So, what do you do for a living, Frank?"

He shrugged. "I'm a reporter."

She dropped onto the couch, her knees feeling like rubber...and it had nothing to do with the cosmopolitans she'd downed like punch. She tried to slow her breathing.

She was working on a red-hot case that was just about to blow open once these new murders were reported.

She laughed. "Wow. I must have drunk more than I thought, because I think I just heard you say you're a *reporter.*"

He sat down next to her on the couch, still wearing the toga. "For the *Register.* But what's the big deal? And by the way, for the record, I was sober the entire evening."

He reached over and took her hand in his. He started stroking her wrist with his thumb. She felt a tingle run up her spine.

He had that look in his eyes. She saw it all the time. He was falling for the exotic Latina, never knowing how much baggage that entailed.

She shrugged it off, forcing herself to focus on something other than Frank's broken heart.

"And here I thought you were an engineer," she said, almost to herself. So much for her powers of observation.

He laughed. "Why would you think that?"

She looked into his hazel eyes behind the thick glasses. His wardrobe alone—slacks with a not-so-matching shirt—had put the idea in her head. Not to mention his cell phone strapped to his belt like a gun holster. Really, all he lacked was the pocket protector. And wasn't Huntington Beach full of engineers, Boeing being one of the top employers in the area? She was used to them chatting her up at the House of Brews.

"Must be the name," she said. "Frank. Sounds so solid and engineerlike."

"And Erika sounds like a homicide detective?"

He said it with a smile, but again, she had this sinking feeling. She tried to think of any clues in the room that could lead him to believe she was a homicide detective, and came up empty.

He was still stroking her hand, his touch distracting as hell.

"Maybe you thought I was an engineer because I come off as such an intellectual."

"You got off, all right," she said. "Several times, if I remember."

"Wow. Keep talking like that and you'll definitely nail down that whole hussy thing you have going."

"What? You didn't see *hussy* tattooed on my ass?"

"Maybe I'd better take another look."

They sat in uncomfortable silence, Erika on pins and needles, almost afraid of what was coming.

"So," he began, sounding almost too casual.

Oh, God, here we go, she thought. The marriage proposal.

But instead, he asked, "Is there a break in the Tran case?"

Suddenly, whatever amorous feelings she'd had simmering inside went stone cold.

She pushed his hand away and stood. "I think it's time for you to leave."

"What did I say wrong?" he asked, standing, as well. "I was just making conversation. Smoothing over an awkward moment."

"Bullshit! You're an investigative reporter for the *Register*. How did you know I was involved in the Tran case?"

She could see him calculating his chances of talking his way through this.

"If you are honest with me," she said, "there is a *slight* chance I won't go and get my service revolver."

He nodded. "Okay. I may have asked the bartender your real name, and I may have Googled you." He shrugged. "I go to that bar a lot. I thought it was interesting, how you gave a different name every time. Like maybe you had something to hide."

She always used her credit card at the bar. She'd never thought she had anything to hide—or that anyone would come snooping around, slipping the bartender a twenty for information.

She couldn't believe it. Plain and simple, he was here for a story. All along, he'd known who she was—she was his ticket to headline news on the Tran murder.

And here she'd spent the night feeling sorry for the guy? Calling him a nester?

More like a nest of asps....

She grabbed the neck of her robe shut. "Get...the fuck...out."

"Geez. What happened to 'if I'm honest I might get another chance'?"

She walked over to the drawer where, indeed, she kept her service revolver. It wasn't loaded, but Frank wouldn't know that.

"The door. Now."

He nodded, sensing that she meant business. "My clothes?"

She kicked his trousers over to him. She figured they'd have his car keys and wallet. "I'll drop the rest off with your friend, the bartender."

He nodded, putting on his pants and leaving the bed sheet. "One bit of advice before I leave. The psychic—the one you hired the P.I. to investigate? I might be able to help you there."

What the hell? She quickly went over her conversation with Seven, a conversation Frank here had certainly overheard. *Fuck!* "You have thirty seconds to walk out that door before I shoot your sorry ass."

He was zipping the trousers, talking fast. "If you want information on this woman, the best way to flush out her past is to let me run the story. The tabloids do it all the time. Make an accusation and see what dross rises to the surface."

"Now you have ten seconds."

He took out his wallet and pulled out a business card. He held it up as he flashed what she'd come to think of as an extremely sexy smile.

"Just in case," he said, dropping the card on the coffee table.

She slammed the door shut behind him.

Erika dropped onto the sofa, still holding the gun. She didn't know if she wanted to scream or cry.

She'd never had anything like this happen. Her nightlife never followed her into the light of day. She should have stuck with the usual suspects. Instead, she'd let some nice guy with what she thought was an engineering degree buy her dinner.

She glanced down at the business card and frowned. Suddenly, she put the gun on the coffee table and grabbed the card.

He was indeed a reporter at the *Register.* But the name printed on the card wasn't Frank.

It was Greg. Greg Smith.

He'd lied about his name.

"Freaking great," she said, already trying to come up with some damage control.

37

Seven's conversation with Beth was short and sweet. Beth was embarrassed—*God, did I really make a pass at you?*

He was understanding—*That was the alcohol talking, Beth. You and I are fine.*

Only, he wasn't fine. Far from it.

He'd gone to Erika's place thinking he'd get some of it out of his system. He and Erika would have a fine old knock-down, drag-out like the good partners they were. They would come clean on their transgressions, all the secrets they'd been keeping from each other. Maybe they'd even open a bottle, and Erika would help him understand what the hell he was thinking, lusting after what might be their chief witness—if not suspect—on a triple homicide.

Instead, he'd walked in on Erika having a normal life.

Moving on....

Seeing Mr. Toga come out from her bedroom, Seven had felt as if he'd slammed into a brick wall. He hadn't realized how much he'd come to rely on Erika, the only other person who had no one else in the world.

After leaving her place, he'd driven in circles, first heading home, then thinking he'd just go grab a drink somewhere. Calm down.

He didn't want to face the fact that there was no one out there waiting for him.

So he made another mistake, ending up exactly where he shouldn't—back in front of Gia's house.

He told himself he'd just pull up alongside Cedric's Acura.

He'd signal Cedric to roll down his window, let him know his services were no longer needed. But, by the time he got there, Cedric was long gone.

Seven turned off the motor and settled back behind the steering wheel. What was it Erika always liked to say? Something about denial being such a powerful emotion.

Maybe that's what this was about. Denial. Acting as if he didn't feel those sparks between him and Gia. Ignoring the image of their tangled bodies, like a memory he wanted to wipe from his mind, when it had never actually happened. Trying to make sense of things that couldn't make sense.

He imagined this was what his brother had felt like. Out of control, wondering what he could do to make the circus inside his head shut down.

Suddenly, the porch light turned on and the front door opened. Gia stepped into the moonlight.

She was dressed in low-slung sweats tied at her hips, and a gray T-shirt. She wrapped her arms around her stomach, watching him from her porch.

He didn't want to think there was anything special about her. She couldn't read minds or tell him about his brother. She was just like the cute blonde at the grocery store or the bank teller who cashed his checks. *Nothing special.*

And still, he couldn't stop himself from stepping out of the car and slamming the door behind him.

By the time he reached her porch, he was out of breath.

"How do you do it?" he demanded, thinking about Beth. "How do you believe that you can raise your kid and take her to school and make macaroni and cheese and everything will be okay? How can you even…*imagine* those things you paint and still think that life goes on?"

He wanted so badly to have those answers. He wanted to explain it all to Nick and Beth and make them whole again.

Gia looked up at him. He thought maybe she would tell him to get lost. It's what she should do. Every minute he stood here, he was breaking all the rules.

But that's exactly what he wanted. To break the rules. Breaking the rules was normal. *The way life used to be way back when*.... He wanted to be the bad son to Ricky's perfection, just like before.

Break the rules!

Before he could change his mind, he took her face in his hands, almost grabbing her. He kissed her hard on the mouth.

He could feel her pushing him away, but he didn't care. He was breaking the rules. So he forced it, trying to convince her. It didn't take long. Her arms came up around his neck and she kissed him back. He wanted to make her as breathless as he felt.

Crazy. So crazy. Just like Ricky....

Just like Ricky.

Jesus!

Seven forced himself to pull away. He was still breathing hard. What the hell did he think he was doing?

"I'm sorry," he said. He shoved his hand through his hair, taking another step back. "I'm sorry."

But Gia was having none of it. She followed him, the move just like a dance step. She put her fingers over his mouth and shook her head. "It's okay," she whispered, those eyes gleaming in the moonlight. "Some things are meant to be. No matter how much we want to change them."

He thought about that image of them in bed together. But he shook his head. "I'm not sure I believe in the things you do. Fate. Destiny. That we lack control over our lives."

Her smile was beautiful and mischievous and alluring all at the same time. "Well, then. How about it's just sex...or two lonely people holding each other through the night? You choose."

She held out her hand toward his, waiting.

"See?" she said. "You're in control."

He sighed, realizing it was bullshit. He wasn't in control...because there was no way in hell he could walk away from her.

His heart racing, he placed his hand in hers. He followed her inside, watched as she shut the door quietly behind them. He wondered about her daughter, for a moment hesitating.

"Stella is asleep in my room," she said, holding his hand tighter. "But there's a guest room down the hall."

"Do you always answer questions before they're asked?"

She frowned, thinking about it. "No. You're…different. I hear you, but I can't *read* you."

He shook his head. "Why does that make perfect sense?"

She gave him that same smile, the one that made his heart catch right there in his chest. She led him down the hall.

Once they were inside the guest room, she shut the door and locked it. Her eyes on his, she pulled off her T-shirt. She shimmied out of the drawstring pants. She looked so vulnerable standing there in only her bra and panties.

"You choose," she whispered.

He took off his shirt, giving in—giving up.

He closed his eyes, taking her into his arms, kissing her. He told himself it wouldn't last. Soon enough, he'd have all those demons hammering at him. Beth and Nick. Ricky and his parents. The Tran case.

But for now, he had Gia in his arms. With his mouth against hers, the last thing he was thinking about was breaking the rules.

Sam was having dinner with Trudy H. A long, dull dinner, like so many they'd shared before.

The restaurant was called S. Trudy H. was downing a lychee tini, her third, while he sipped on a more pedantic martini.

Sam had been drinking Grey Goose martinis ever since he'd read somewhere that it was David Gospel's favorite. Of course, he never did it in front of David. Sam didn't want to give the old man the idea that he was somehow modeling himself after David. Hell, no.

Only he was. Very much so.

Gospel was a winner. Sam Vi planned to be a winner, too. In California, it was all about real estate and development. That's where the real money came from.

Like Sam, the restaurant S straddled two worlds. Enormous silk lanterns hung like gossamer webs over white tablecloths. The light combined with hardwood floors to give the place a warm, amber glow. Modernist pastels of lilies decorated the walls, alongside screens lit up like neon bamboo.

The decor was serene but modern, the food delectably the same. Really, the place was a thing of beauty, representing to Sam what was best about the community here. Set just outside of Little Saigon in the Westminster Mall, the restaurant held an equal mix of Asian and Caucasian diners. Sam knew that had been the idea. To bring Vietnamese cuisine to the white community that might not venture into Little Saigon.

Trudy looked bored with the food. Trudy, Sam noticed, was easily bored. Lately, he was beginning to wonder if she was bored with him.

That worried Sam. In fact, a lot of things were beginning to bother him about his "engagement." Like the fact that Trudy constantly denied the relationship to the stalkarrazi that followed her every move. Whenever a photograph of the two of them got printed in the tabloids, it appeared with a caveat attached, some comment from Trudy or her publicist about their "rumored" romance. Sam's engagement was starting to feel like a box of cigarettes with a warning from the surgeon general. *Do not believe what you see.*

Rumor my ass, he thought. A fucking six-carat diamond in a rare blue color wasn't a fucking rumor.

Tonight, she wasn't even wearing his ring. Sam took a swig from the martini. But, hey, maybe she was bored with that, too?

And here he was, trying to make himself over for her family? Well, Sam was starting to get the idea that Trudy didn't give a shit about Sam the business mogul. She much preferred Sam the gangster.

These were the thoughts nagging Sam as he ate a perfect Chilean sea bass, wondering what Velvet would say if she could see him now.

Velvet, he was certain, would be telling him that Trudy was just part of the package: Sam's attempt to make himself over into the image of David Gospel, the mogul on high. Sam had the money, sure, but now he needed legitimacy.

Velvet, Sam believed, would let him know that—like the Vietnamese businessmen who spoke only French, trying to become one with their colonial masters—he, too, was only mimicking David. Hadn't he bought a construction company? Wasn't he using Gospel to get coveted city contracts? Getting engaged to Trudy, a hot celebutante, was just another step in his transformation.

Well, fuck, Sam thought. *Maybe she's right.*

Velvet didn't approve of his relationship with Trudy. She'd told Sam more than once that Trudy was just pretty poison.

Just like David, she'd said, making the comparison more than once. To Velvet's way of thinking, Sam and she needed to stick to their community. They were outsiders in the world of people like David Gospel and Trudy H. And no matter how much they tried—no matter how many degrees she earned or blue diamonds he bought—they'd never fit in.

Velvet, Sam realized, wasn't bored with that old geezer, David Gospel. Quite the opposite. She was falling in love. And unlike Trudy, for Velvet, that wouldn't change.

So he was trying to figure out how to get her advice without the lecture he'd have coming right along with it, when he spotted his bodyguard coming toward his table.

The muscle that traveled with Sam kept their distance. Sam didn't care about being seen with an entourage—hell, he loved it. But that was part of it, see? The fact that they stayed behind the scenes made it classy. And Sam was all about class.

Trudy didn't even look up when his bodyguard leaned over to whisper in his ear. With no little irritation, he again noticed she hadn't touched her food. He'd ordered for her, knowing she would take only a few dejected bites of the *tom hum nuong,* grilled lobster tail topped with tamarind sauce. She didn't like Vietnamese food, even the gourmet feast prepared at S. Hell, who was he kidding? Trudy didn't like *food.*

But she liked her booze. She'd just sucked down her third cocktail, leaving only the lychee fruit at the bottom of her martini glass—damn thing looked like an eyeball, Sam thought. She was no doubt counting the minutes until they left for some hot club in downtown L.A. far away from Little Saigon...while Sam had been hoping for a quiet night at home.

That was another thing he wanted to talk over with Vee. Sam liked the community here. Okay, maybe it had all started as some dumb-ass attempt to become another David Gospel, but he *was* building an empire in Little Saigon. And it worried him plenty that Trudy, the woman he loved, wanted no part of it.

That's what had been going on in his head, how maybe he should start listening more to Velvet and less to David, when his bodyguard whispered in his ear that he had an urgent call. Sam almost rolled his eyes at the annoyance, but took the phone handed to him—he always turned off his cell phone at dinner with Trudy. Any emergency would come through his bodyguard.

He'd been sitting there, staring at that damn lychee at the bottom of Trudy's martini glass, when he'd heard the news.

Sam. It's bad. Velvet. She's dead.

At first, Sam didn't know how to feel. It was a joke, right? Some sort of mistake. Velvet was like a sister to him, the one person who wasn't afraid to tell him what a piece of shit he'd turned out to be and how he should do better. Be better. Over the years, he'd come to think of her as his conscience.

And now she was dead?

No, not just dead, the voice on the cell phone informed him. She'd been slaughtered. Gutted like the damn Chilean bass on his plate.

"What's wrong, Sam?"

He looked across the table at Trudy H. Suddenly, she was every bit the woman Velvet had warned him about: a spoiled, too-thin celebutante who would never, *ever,* marry him.

Sam stood. He swept the dishes off the table, sending everything crashing to the floor. He raised his face to the ceiling and howled.

Trudy stood as well. She wasn't scared. But she was embarrassed, looking around at the other diners.

The restaurant was family-run. Immediately, one of the owners, a woman, came over, completely solicitous. A busboy was cleaning up the mess on the floor. But the muscle didn't let anyone near Sam as he dropped back into his chair, the cell phone still in his hand.

"Go," Sam said to Trudy.

He didn't have to tell her twice.

What Trudy didn't know was how long he'd waited to say those words. Too long. Because her dismissal wasn't just for tonight.

Dong-bao. Born of the same womb. That was Vee.

Sam Vi. Velvet—Vee.

He could feel the tears roll down his cheeks. In that moment, watching Trudy H. tottering out of the restaurant on her heels, drunk and uncaring, dragging on the floor a mink that she didn't need, Sam Vi felt his life come into vivid focus. The one person who really mattered had been taken from him.

From now on, Sam would focus only on his lost sister, Vee. He needed to find the dumb fuck who'd killed her. He needed to make sure he paid.

38

You dream of Corinth.

In Corinth, there is a fountain named the Well of Glauce. It is a monument to the beautiful daughter of King Creon, Princess Glauce, who so famously donned the poisonous wedding dress given to her by husband-to-be Jason of the Argonauts, after he returned triumphant from his quest for the Golden Fleece. The gown was a gift from her rival in love, Medea, the mother of Jason's children, his barbarian bride.

It is said that Glauce threw herself in the well, believing that the waters there might cure her of the poison from the wedding gown.

There are holes in the porous rock of the fountain. The people of Corinth make offerings to Glauce, deified in death, stuffing them into the crevices of the rock.

Glauce, it is said, was named for her blue eyes, *glaukos* being the ancient Greek word for blue. *Glaukos* refers to man's fear of blindness—glaucoma and cataracts often giving that pale hue to the eye of the infirmed.

In a healthy eye, the color is seen as unnatural…something to be feared. Foreigners from the north often have blue eyes. It is something strange and maligned in the ancient world. Only Athena, the great protector, can possess such a color. And thus her eyes are the amulet against the Evil Eye. The blue eye of Athena.

Whenever you dream of Corinth, you remember the Eye. How you cradle it in your hands. The heat of it against your skin, branding you. You're reluctant to give it back. *She* believes it belongs to *the people* and is unwilling to listen to your plans.

So you make your own plans.

The anticipation is nice. Working alongside her, sharing her smiles—but knowing, just knowing.

Next week. Tomorrow. Tonight!

She tries to fight. That excites you. You're like Apollo fighting the Python, earning your treasure. When you loop the garrote around her neck, she falls to her knees. Her arms and legs flail like a trout on a rock. You hold on, pulling tighter.

That's right, you whisper to her. *You've seen this all before.*

Go easy. Die.

You kill her. You take the Eye, her eyes.

At long last, you begin your collection.

Gia sat straight up in bed. She clawed at her neck. She could *feel* the garrote around her throat, a man's body straddling her.

Beside her, Seven immediately woke up, the hair-trigger instincts of a cop kicking in.

"What's wrong?" he asked.

It was just like the time before, in the studio. Just like every time this demon brought her into his vision. Only it was getting worse.

I...can't...breathe!

Seven grabbed her by her shoulders and turned her to face him in the bed. "Gia?"

With the moonlight coming through the window behind her she could see him perfectly. She remembered what it was like to make love to him, how soft his lips felt against hers. She hadn't realized how much she'd wanted him. She hadn't made love to a man since she'd conceived her daughter. All these years of loneliness seemed to catch up with her in that moment of release, the surprise of that desire sweeping over her.

But now, she couldn't even move. Every muscle in her body remained caught in a vise.

"Oh, Jesus. Gia!"

He laid her out on the bed. Tilting back her head, he began to give her mouth-to-mouth.

She felt the air in his mouth fill her lungs. The action struck her so much like the act of making love that the same wave of desire swept over her.

Suddenly, every muscle in her body came to life. She sat up, pushing him away. She sucked in a lungful of air then collapsed back against the headboard.

She rested her cheek against the cool wood, waiting for the motion of breathing to come more naturally.

"What the hell just happened?"

Seven was naked, kneeling on the sheets crumpled beneath him. She could see she'd frightened him, his breath coming deep from his abdomen. A man who dealt with death probably knew what she'd just experienced.

She pushed the hair from her face and sat up straighter, taking comfort in that normal rhythm: breath in, breath out.

"Gia, what…the *fuck*…just happened?"

She shook her head, biding her time. When she was ready, when she could speak without struggling for oxygen, she told him, "I had a vision."

Only this time, what she'd lived through had been all too personal. Her spirit guides had taken her to the brink of death—her mother's death.

The vision had been so powerful. She felt as if she'd grabbed hold of a live wire.

Gia let out a long sigh. Seven was kneeling at the foot of the bed. She leaned forward, reaching for him. She placed her hand to his chest, feeling his heart beat against her fingertips.

He took her hand and pressed a kiss to the inside of her wrist. "Jesus, you scared me."

She closed her eyes, ashamed. He couldn't see the future. He wouldn't know what lay ahead. But she did.

He was still holding her hand when she said, "I think you should go."

He cocked his head as if he hadn't heard her right. "You almost died just now. You *stopped* breathing."

She held up her hand, cutting him off. "It's happened before. It's part of the process. I know you think I'm crazy, but I would have been fine."

"Bullshit," he said.

She smiled, giving him a mental thumbs-up for his instincts.

"Stella, my daughter." She knew enough about him to understand that only her daughter would be reason enough. "I don't want you to be here when she wakes up for school." Gia bit her lip, hating the lie. "Okay?"

She stood and took his hand. She picked up his shirt off the floor and slipped his arms into the sleeves. As she buttoned the front, she felt a warmth in her chest. She wondered what it would be like to have a normal life, one that allowed a man like Seven.

When he tried to speak, to tell her what he was feeling, she placed her finger across his lips. She shook her head.

Once they were both dressed, she again took his hand and led him to the front door. She rested her head against his chest.

"I'm sorry."

It was the only explanation she could give him.

"Gia?" His voice sounded soft and vulnerable. "If you know who killed these women... If you're somehow involved—"

"No."

She looked up at him, trying to leave it as ambiguous as possible. *No, I don't know anything. No, don't ask me.*

She kissed him, pretending for both of them that they could live in this moment and forget what lay ahead.

"Call me later," she said, hugging him.

Later, she told herself. *I can be honest later.*

Almost on cue, Stella coughed. Gia turned to find her daughter standing in the hall, watching them.

"You have to go," Gia whispered.

He stepped outside, the motion almost involuntary. He had this comical expression on his face, as if he didn't know what else to do.

Gia shut the door. Leaning back against it, she faced her daughter.

"Mom?"

"Hush, darling," she said, walking back to the kitchen. "We'll be fine."

39

Erika walked into the precinct, balancing her purse and a tray of coffee from Starbucks. She'd stopped on her way into the office for the peace offering, needing something to break the iceberg she was about to crash into, *Titanic* style.

Seven sat at his desk, hunched over his laptop, studiously avoiding her gaze. Erika sighed. Okay, he *was* going to be a dick about last night.

Theirs was a complicated relationship. That's why Erika had decided to be dead honest with her partner from now on, the operative words being *from now on*. No need for some futile confession about Mr. Greg—Frank—Smith, the reporter from the *Register*, she figured. Not if she wanted a career....

She sat down across from Seven and pulled out one of the Starbucks cups. She held it out for him. "Café Americano. Black."

He pushed away from the laptop and gave her a look. He shook his head. "A cup of coffee, Erika? Just that?"

"Best I could do on such short notice." She leaned forward. "Hey, I know. What if I let you call me the Amazing Supernatural Sleuth, like you've been dying to do? You know, ASS? Because I've been a bit of one lately?"

He remained silent.

"Wow," she said. "Look who suddenly lost his sense of humor."

She put down the cup and reached inside her purse. She pulled out the file on Gia Moon, the one put together by the private investigator.

She placed it on the desk in front of Seven. "That's everything

I have so far from Cedric. And, you'll be happy to know, I called him off the case. You're right. I am jeopardizing the investigation."

The reason being that anyone connected to the police, or working under their directive, had to follow all the rules and regulations as a cop—fourth amendment rights and such—which wasn't likely to happen with Cedric Patterson, private dick extraordinaire. He was damn good at digging up the dirt, not so good about how he went about getting the job done. If they ever did have to take Gia Moon to trial, Cedric Patterson's involvement could taint the evidence, making some defense attorney's day.

She watched her partner stare at the folder, frozen to his seat. She realized that he didn't want to know what was inside.

Jesus, Mary and Joseph!

"Okay." She reached across and turned the file to face her. She opened to the first page. "So I screwed up. But since we already have the information, let's take a look, shall we? Gia Moon turns out to be this *really* interesting person," she began. "But not for the reasons you'd think. Not because she's some famous psychic or this great artist. Gia Moon, it turns out, doesn't exist."

That got his attention.

Seven glanced at the file. Erika, being the patient sort, waited him out.

Eventually, he motioned for her to slide the file back.

"No social security number, no bank account," she said, recounting out loud what the file would reveal. "No mortgage. She paid cash for that house. I didn't even know you could do that in California."

Erika could see his body language change, the muscles across his back tightening. But still he kept quiet, just flipping through the pages of the report.

"I checked with witness protection—just in case," she continued. "Nada. Do you know how hard it is to hide from the government like this?" she asked, tapping the file. "To put it delicately, it's freaking impossible. But here it is. The invisible woman. My question is, why?"

She was thinking of her own foray into Google. How easily

she'd discovered that she, Erika Cabral, was the lead detective on the Tran case. Even her phone number and address had been listed, for God's sake. All of it there for the pillaging by little scavengers like Greg Smith.

"So here's this single mom—an artist—who is managing to do the impossible. According to all government sources—federal, state and local—she is completely invisible."

He slapped the file folder shut. "Last time I checked, that wasn't a crime."

"Not to mention, not the least bit suspicious." Erika leaned over the table, getting into her partner's face. "You want to hear my theory? She's hiding, Seven. From someone—someone powerful. Someone dangerous. Maybe even someone who could be killing psychics." When he looked up and met her gaze, Erika smiled. "And now she has a cop guarding her. She's using you. And you're falling for it."

"You know what, ASS?" he said, his voice on edge. "I'm a little confused. I thought I had a thing for my sister-in-law. Now I want a key witness in a case?" he said, sounding defensive. "Or do I want them both? Maybe I'll just take anyone, even someone I can pick up at a bar?"

She felt her face get red, and pushed back in her seat. She wasn't about to ask how he'd found out about her nightly habits. "You're right," she said. "It's none of my business. So how about you explain why you showed up at my place in the middle of the night?"

She could see him putting it together. They were partners; they relied on each other. This wall between them, it wasn't right.

She smiled. She lifted her latte in a toast. After a few seconds, he picked up the café Americano and tapped it against her cup.

"There's more to my theory on your psychic," she said. "Do you want to hear it?" She didn't wait for him to answer, already feeling as if she were walking on eggshells. "That first day she came to the station, she wasn't lying when she told us she thought she was next. But not because of the reasons she gave. She knows who the killer is. She needs him stopped—and she's willing to risk exposing her own involvement to get the job done."

Erika gave him a minute. But she could see he needed a nudge.

"So." She took another sip. "What were you doing at her house yesterday?"

He looked up and gave her the biggest smile. "Fucking her, of course."

She rolled her eyes, knowing that Seven would *never* do any such thing. That kind of screwup was completely within her province.

"I kept waiting for you to bring it up," she continued. "Say something like, 'By the way, Erika, here's the reason I raced out of a double homicide.' Come on." She stared at him. "Give."

The hard stare he gave her let Erika know he was through with the runaround.

"She called me," he said, "just a few hours before Gospel reported the killings. She said someone named Kieu, or who had a *Q* in her name, was going to die if I didn't find her first."

"Jesus." Never mind that he hadn't made an official report. "Why didn't you tell me?"

Seven put down his Starbucks cup and shouldered on his coat. "It's premature…and I have my own theories. I'm looking into something. Which reminds me, I need to be somewhere."

As he passed her, she grabbed his hand, stopping him.

"Seven," she said, now truly concerned, "what the hell are you doing?"

Right then, his phone went off with that special ring. Beth always did have good timing.

Without thinking, he turned it off.

Erika stared at the phone in his hand in shock. He followed her gaze, suddenly realizing what he'd just done.

It was the first time he'd ever cut Beth off.

"We'll talk later," he said.

Erika let him go, knowing to the depth of her soul it was the wrong thing to do. She should stop him, perform some sort of intervention.

Fucking her, of course.

"*Miercoles,*" she said under her breath, repeating her mother's favorite curse. The word actually meant Wednesday, but it was close enough to the real curse to be satisfying.

Erika closed her eyes, weighing her options. When she opened her eyes again, she was staring directly at Seven's laptop. He'd left it open on his desk.

Just looking at it had her Catholic guilt working on overdrive. But there it was, within easy reach…with no one in the room to see her.

She let out a deep sigh and put down her coffee. She stood and sat in Seven's chair. She pulled his laptop toward her.

"Dios, ayudame," she whispered. God help me.

She'd memorized his password about a month after they'd become partners. She'd watched him punch it in several times. It was LAURIN. His ex-wife's name. He'd never changed it.

"Such a romantic," she said to herself.

She clicked on the down arrow of the address line. Instantly, a list of the last Web sites he'd visited appeared. Erika scrolled down, seeing that the addresses were all associated with paranormal phenomena, including a few on psychic painters. He was conducting his own investigation, completely independent of Erika, his partner.

Maybe this was how it had all started with her mother, Erika thought. How she'd been taken in by people just like Gia Moon. That first time with the *espiritista* "saving" her little girl's life, making that personal connection.

Half an hour later, she was sitting at her own desk. In her hand, she held a business card. She'd been staring at the same damn number since she'd sat down. By now she had it memorized.

What were you doing at her house yesterday?

Fucking her, of course.

That big smile he'd delivered right as he'd said it, daring Erika to believe him.

She put the business card in her jacket pocket and stood. Grabbing her purse, she headed out.

She was thinking about her own nightly transgressions. About a certain reporter at the *Register.*

The tabloids do it all the time...print an accusation and see what dross rises to the surface.

That's what Greg—Frank—Smith had told her. It reminded Erika of something her grandmother always used to say when she thought Erika and her brother were up to no good. Loosely translated, it went like this: *When you turn on the lights, you can see the cockroaches scurry for cover.*

Erika was thinking that's what this case needed, for someone to shed a little light.

She drove herself out to Fountain Valley. It was a little paranoid for her tastes, but she needed to be careful. Whatever happened, she didn't want this call traced back to the department.

She popped the right amount of coins into the gas station pay phone. In just a few years, these antiques would become obsolete, what with all the cell phones glued to everyone's ears. But today, this pay phone was coming in handy.

"Get in contact with me," she said, not bothering to leave her name or number. If the guy was worth his mettle, Smith would know who was calling. "And this isn't about sex, you asshole." She took a deep breath, hoping she was doing the right thing. "I have your story."

Carin Barnes rang the doorbell and waited for the front door to open. Gina Tyrell wouldn't be happy to see her, but Carin couldn't help that. Coming here was the next logical step. Really, she hadn't hoped to get this far so fast. Apparently, fortune *did* favor the brave.

When the door opened, Carin said, "Hello, Gina."

Gina leaned against the doorjamb. She crossed her arms protectively in front of her.

"Excuse me. I forgot. I mean Gia," Carin said in an ultra polite voice. "Gia Moon."

"Hello, Carin." Gina opened the door. "Why don't you come inside? Although, if I remember correctly, you were never one to wait for an invitation. By the way, I expected you weeks ago."

Carin couldn't help just a small smile as she followed Gina out to what looked like some sort of garage studio. Once in the room, Carin felt her breath catch in her throat as she admired the painting leaning up against the wall.

She walked to stand in front of the black-and-red depiction of the most recent killings.

"Painting helps with the visions," Gina said.

Carin nodded. "Do you know where it is?"

"It? You mean the Eye?" Gina shook her head. "Can't help you. I hope the damn thing never surfaces again."

Carin could understand her anger. Gina had always hated her mother's dedication to finding the Eye. Carin couldn't imagine that after Estelle Fegaris died, Gina's feelings for the artifact had changed for the better. She'd no doubt come to blame her mother's death on her quest.

"But you know who has it?" Carin asked.

Nothing.

"Ah," Carin said. "Silence is golden." She pointed to that half moon on the tongue of the victim in the painting. "It was a moon cake. Whoever killed Velvet Tien stuffed it in her mouth. You did well."

"Encouragement from you, Carin? What is the world coming to?"

Carin ignored the sarcasm. The Lunites, those who kept Estelle's dreams alive, would always be a source of pain for Gina. But before she could ask her next question, Carin found the answer herself, in Gina's painting.

She looked closer, seeing that, indeed, Gina had placed the primitive image of an eye inside the victim's stomach.

Carin turned to look at her and raised her brows in question. "You don't know where the Eye is?"

Gina sighed. "You know how it works, Carin. I have no idea what that represents. It could be a clue leading to a clue that leads to another clue…or it could be my imagination."

Carin frowned. "You have a powerful talent. Just like your mother."

But Gina shook her head. "I am *nothing* like my mother."

Carin sighed. "I meant it as a compliment. Now, how about some coffee?"

"I was hoping you weren't staying that long."

"Well, you're wrong." She lifted up her leather satchel. "You and I have some business together."

Carin walked past Gina, heading toward the small kitchen they'd walked through on their way to the garage studio. "By the way, I take my coffee black."

"Shocker," she heard Gina say under her breath.

Gina didn't need to voice the subtext: *Like your black, black heart.*

Again, Carin let out a deep sigh. She didn't expect their meeting to improve Gina's opinion.

40

David Gospel stared down at the piece of paper on his desk. It was a perfect square, like one of those sheets used for origami. Even though it was spread open, it appeared crumpled, as if someone had grabbed it and crunched it into a ball—which was exactly what he'd done.

When he'd taken the moon cake to his car, out of nowhere a kid on one of those mountain bikes had sped down the street. In that instant, David had felt exposed to the eyes of a ready witness…and he'd panicked.

In one motion, he'd opened the trunk and dumped the moon cake wrapped in his handkerchief inside. The damn cake had rolled out. That's when he'd seen the edge of the paper sticking out.

When he'd stood over Velvet's dead body, looking into those dead eyes as he pried the moon cake from her mouth, he'd assumed a piece of the necklace would be tucked in that cake—just like the bead stuffed inside Mimi's bird. But that's not what he'd found.

Instead, a folded sheet had been forced into the moon cake. Once the kid had passed, David had taken the paper out and read the message with shaking hands.

There was one word scribbled on the paper: *Gotcha!*

Just that. *Gotcha!*

Actually, it was quite brilliant, forcing his hand like this. No doubt, the cops would figure out he'd tampered with the crime scene. Soon enough, some CSI asshole would come knocking on his door, shoving evidence under his nose.

He could just hear the district attorney during the trial on cross-examination. *Tell me, Mr. Gospel, why did you take that moon cake from the mouth of your dead mistress?*

Thinking just that—how *fucked* he was—he'd been so angry, he'd totally lost it. Somebody was pulling the strings, engineering his demise. He'd taken evidence from a crime scene, basically pointing the finger to himself as the killer.

In another rash move, he'd balled up the paper and thrown it into the bushes.

Which was exactly where he'd found it after the cops impounded his car and clothes.

Once he was home, he'd spread the paper open on his desk. He'd spent a good hour just staring at it, realizing his mistake.

He'd failed to see that whoever had left the note had written on both sides of the paper.

The second message was eerily familiar: *That which is invisible is always the most dangerous.*

Mimi's warning at his last reading.

Someone knew entirely too much about his personal life.

As surely as they knew that David would take that moon cake, whoever planted it there as a decoy most certainly had left something else behind. He thought about poor Velvet's defiled body, her intestines popping out from the stomach cavity. He'd made a couple of phone calls. His source at the police didn't have anyone inside the coroner's office. But it didn't matter. David would bet money that they'd find something in poor Velvet that he'd missed.

He'd already called Rose Fletcher, one of the top criminal attorneys in L.A. She'd gotten him out of hot water before and he was counting on her to pull another rabbit out of the hat.

Last night, he'd had a long talk with Rocket, who'd confirmed he'd been with Owen the entire time the murders had been committed, which was good. Surprising, but good.

Only now, the only person who didn't have an alibi was David himself.

That which is invisible...

As far as David was concerned, there was no one who could be that invisible. It was just a matter of time before he found the son of a bitch trying to destroy him. After that, David would be back in charge.

He'd been thinking just that—*you're the man*—when he felt a presence behind him. On edge, he jerked around.

Meredith stood in the doorway. He must have forgotten to close his office door, something he would normally do.

Talk about losing it....

She was holding a tray with a coffee carafe, cup and saucer, and all the trimmings. "Maria just made some biscotti," she said, in that breathy voice he hated. "I brought you some."

He picked up a notebook and placed it on top of the crumpled paper. "Fine."

She was wearing a flowing gown. Swear to God, it looked like a freaking muumuu on her. He wondered if she thought she could make up for her own lack with the yards of fabric.

He tried to recall those early years when her blond hair had been long and lustrous, her figure full. But he couldn't connect this bag of skin and bones to those memories.

She placed the tray on his desk. There was a china bowl with sugar cubes and a tiny silver creamer. She poured him a cup of coffee, added one sugar and lots of cream, just the way he liked it. She followed up with the plate of biscotti. Only, when she finished, she didn't leave. She stood there, hovering.

"What is it?" he asked. Shit. He didn't have time to deal with his neurotic wife.

"I spoke to Rocket last night," she said, surprising him. "He explained how you're helping Owen." She paused, the words almost too much for her. "I appreciate it, David. I most certainly do."

He stared up at his wife, trying again to remember the woman he'd married. Jesus, how many times had he seen her do a line of coke? How often had he heard her scream in orgasm? But these days, his wife spoke like a Puritan. *I most certainly do....*

"Rocket called you?"

She nodded. "He wanted to make sure I understood. We're all in this together."

David stared up at his wife, nonplussed. Someone had stolen

he Eye. They were trying to frame him for the death of three
women. And Rocket, dear Rocket, was trying to save his marriage?

"Meredith," he said. "Let me be very clear. At this point, I
don't give a shit what happens to Owen."

She looked as if he'd hit her. "Then why call Rose Fletcher—"

"It's me, Meredith. They think I killed those women."

She cocked her head like a bird, the very idea that he could
be any sort of threat completely foreign to her.

After a while, she spoke. "I know you don't love me, David."

Oh, shit. Here we go again.

"But we must stand united as a family, just like Rocket said."
She paused, as if choosing her words carefully. "Whatever you
need, David. As long as Owen is safe, you'll have my support."
Those dull blue eyes met his. "Do you understand, David?
Anything."

She reached out with an ice-cold hand and gripped his on the
desk, as if the statement needed emphasis. "I'll come back for
the tray later."

In shock, he watched her turn and walk out of the room. Had
she really said what he thought?

Anything....

But there was no mistaking her intentions. That tone, the look
in her eyes.

"Fuck me," he said under his breath.

Who knew the bitch could still be of use to him?

He picked up the phone and called Rose. Her secretary put
him through immediately.

He said into the phone to his attorney, "I have an alibi."

It took only one sip of Gina's coffee to let Carin know she was
dealing with a caffeine aficionado.

She put down her cup. "Wow. I'm impressed."

Gina didn't even pretend to care.

With a sigh of regret, Carin reached for the file she'd been
given. She turned to the first highlighted passage.

"'There were eyes everywhere,'" Carin read from the transcript of Gina's interview with homicide. "'And there was something in her mouth. Something very old—very powerful. And small. Blue. No red. Perhaps made of glass.'"

When Gina didn't respond, she said, "At that point, they began video taping you. You articulated a perfect description of one of the beads from the Eye." When Gina still didn't respond, Carin added, "There's also a sketch." She placed the pencil drawing on the table, the one Gia Moon had delivered to the police.

"It's very accurate," Carin said.

Estelle had confided in only a few people the intimate details of the Eye, what it looked like and how it worked. Certainly, her daughter was one of those people, but the drawing was almost too real, as if Gina had actually seen it, held it—something Carin had never had the opportunity to do.

The minute Carin had seen the sketch she'd begun to wonder. When and where had Gia seen the Eye? But her question was met with only silence and an almost obstinate glare.

"Of course," Carin said, "you would have to pretend you knew nothing about the artifact. Obviously, you've gone to great lengths to hide here." She indicated the kitchen, the house. "In plain sight, as they say. I just want to know what else you're hiding."

Gina turned her coffee cup in her hands. Carin could almost see the wheels turning. *Do I trust her?*

"Have you heard from Thomas?" Carin asked, pushing a little.

Gina glanced up at the clock in the kitchen above Carin's head. "I think it took you all of fifteen minutes to bring out the heavy artillery. That's got to be some kind of record for you."

Carin could see immediately she'd made a mistake. "Have I ever held back?"

"I don't know where the Eye is, Carin. If that's why you're here, you're wasting your time. So don't bother with the veiled threats."

Carin didn't know how she'd expected Gina to react when she mentioned Thomas. But she wasn't here to threaten anyone. "Your mother was the only person in this world who gave me hope. If Thomas finds you, it won't be through me."

"You have what you came for, then," Gina said, referring, no doubt, to the painting. "You can show yourself out."

Carin nodded, seeing that her olive branch had done no good. She packed up the sketch and transcript. "We'll keep in touch."

Terrence had warned Carin. *Don't go in like a bull in a china shop.*

Outside, she took out her cell phone as she walked toward the rental car she'd parked outside Gina's house. She punched in the number for the coroner's office. She knew how to cut through the red tape.

In less time than it took for Carin Barnes to get inside her rental and start the engine, she was talking to the coroner.

"Check everything in the stomach cavity of Velvet Tien," she said into the cell phone. "Call me as soon as you find it."

41

Thomas Crane was reading through The Lunites Web site. The board had lit up like the Fourth of July with the breaking news: there'd been another killing in the case of the fortune-teller.

Two murders, actually, from the accounts picked up by the wire services. This time, it was the fortune-teller and her lawyer client who'd been slaughtered...in the middle of a reading, judging from the I Ching yarrow sticks found on the floor.

The murders were incredibly brutal, including what looked like a ritual evisceration. But what captivated Thomas the most was the fact that the police were working with a psychic by the name of Gia Moon.

"Aren't you a clever girl, Gina."

After all these years, he'd fucking found her.

Even the thought of seeing her again, the anticipation, was laced with rage, No one could make him angrier than Gina.

They'd met that summer at Estelle's dig site. Gina didn't advertise that she was Estelle's daughter. It was Estelle herself who had given him the news.

He remembered as if it was yesterday, instead of twelve years ago. *Don't you break my baby's heart,* Estelle had said with a wink.

At first, he thought the relationship could be advantageous. No way would Estelle play ball with the likes of David Gospel, selling the Eye to a private collector if she should ever get her hands on it. Thomas had thought that if he had Gina on his side...

As things turned out, Gina's love was worth shit. Pure shit. She'd crapped all over him.

Ever since he'd met that bitch it was like someone had dropped the fucking A-bomb on him. Wasn't it her fault Estelle was dead? She'd filled her mother's head with these great aspirations. Estelle wanted to find a place for psychics in society, trying to make a "better world" for her little girl. Once she found the Eye, Estelle planned to use it to give normal people "the psychic experience," as she called it. Forget faith; once and for all people could see it up close and personal. Psychics would no longer be those bizarre beings nobody believed. With the Eye, the paranormal would practically be a science.

But thanks to Gina, Thomas ended up losing both Gospel's money and the Eye. He hadn't counted on Estelle leaving her "psychic" clues for her daughter. Here she was carrying his child, but did that stop Gina from turning him in? To get his ass out of jail and back home in one piece, it had cost him almost every penny Gospel gave him.

As his anger grew, Thomas noticed the creeping scent of sulfur filling the air. He closed his eyes and lifted his hands off the keyboard, knowing what was coming. The last thing he saw was that photograph of Gina on his screen saver.

He woke up on the floor. As he slowly rose to his feet, the memory of what had triggered the attack came over him.

He groggily climbed back into his chair. He checked the postings again, making sure he had it right. That the name Gia Moon on the screen wasn't some sort of delusion.

Thomas smiled. Sometimes, if a man was patient, life might just hand him a gift. And this was a gift.

He'd been forced into this low, hidden life by Gina. She'd stripped him of everything. Even his dreams. He could close his eyes this very minute and she'd be there, taunting him, always whispering with a beguiling smile, *One day I will be the end of you, Thomas.*

"Not if I get to you first."

In Greece, he'd found out she'd been the one to tip off the police before she'd disappeared. If she'd stuck around—if he'd killed her in the heat of passion—that mistake could have earned him a life sentence. Now, he had time to plan.

Like mother, like daughter.

He smiled. Someone was killing psychics?

He picked up the phone. "Imagine that."

Stella was crying. That in itself made Gia's job more difficult. Stella never cried.

"I don't want to go. Something horrible is going to happen. That's why you're sending me away. You're trying to protect me. And you can't."

Stella had refused to pack, but her mother had been way ahead of her, doing the packing for her. She'd contacted Stella's school, completed the necessary forms for her daughter to attend school where she'd be staying.

The hardest part: calling Morgan and setting the rules. *She doesn't even accept her gifts—don't push her.* Gia didn't know how much she could trust her ambitious father and his band of psychics-with-doctoral-degrees.

"You won't even tell me what's going on!"

Gia pulled her daughter into her arms, hugging her. "Because it's nothing."

"Nothing" that came in the form of a newspaper article, exposing Gia Moon to the world.

"I can handle this," she whispered. "Okay?"

But when she looked into her daughter's eyes, she only saw Stella's fears.

"What if I could help?" Stella whispered.

Gia smiled. "A mark of true desperation—you admitting you actually have psychic abilities."

The girl knuckled the tears from her eyes, impatient with her own emotions. She was the little warrior, ready to take on anyone. "If you need me, yeah. Okay."

Gia kissed the top of her head. "Of course I need you, sweetheart. But not like that. I'll be fine. I swear."

A necessary lie, she told herself. What good would it do to worry Stella?

But Gia knew she was on shaky moral ground…not exactly new territory for her. Not since her first vision with Mimi Tran through the eyes of her demon killer. She hadn't been able to help those women. Her gift—knowledge of the future without the power to change it—made her that much more culpable.

Now Carin was on the scene, threatening her. Because Carin was dead right; there were things Gia couldn't tell Stella or Seven or anyone else, for that matter. Not if she wanted to keep her daughter safe.

Still holding her, she made a silent vow that she would be ready…and she had little enough time to prepare. She'd read the article in the paper this morning, just like everyone else.

Cops Use Psychic in Fortune-teller Murders.

By now, the information would have spread through blogs and Web sites, delivered with the ease of a high-speed connection.

The truth was, ready or not, he would come.

42

Seven stood next to Erika before the chief's desk. They'd been called in—one of those special invitations every cop learned to dread.

Apparently, Gospel had been filing motions all morning—cease-and-desist; unlawful imprisonment—threatening to sue anything that moved.

The mayor's rage over headlines and lawsuits still lingered in the room with her designer perfume.

I told you to handle things—Roy—and trust me when I tell you that flagging down Gospel's son and harassing him in a public place in front of witnesses does not help the situation!

The chief was rubbing his temples, looking to fight off a migraine. "I told you to let the FBI handle this."

"Excuse me for saying so, Chief, but Special Agent Barnes made it very clear that she has a hard-on for some artifact we promised the Greek government," Seven said, failing miserably to keep his own anger in check. "Finding the bastard who did this wasn't exactly her focus."

"Gee, Seven. And here I thought it was justice for all?" Erika said.

"That's enough," the chief snapped, banging his hand on his desk.

But Seven didn't think so. "The kid looked awfully good for the murder of Mimi Tran. For God's sake, we're cops, not politicians."

"Good for the Tran murder?" the chief asked, now seeming to pack it in with the mayor. Despite a shock of white hair and ten pounds he didn't need, he could be pretty intimidating. Now he rose slowly to his full six feet two inches from behind his desk. "Where's your evidence, Detective?"

"I think that's why it's called an investigation, Chief," Erika said, moving in like a bulldog.

"I expect anyone on my force to act professionally. Harassing Owen and David Gospel is *not* professional."

"That's right," Seven said, turning to Erika. "We only shake down gangbangers and the homeless—"

"And *not* law-abiding citizens," the chief finished, starting to look a little purple in the face. "Jesus. All we have is some asinine psychic and now she's front-page news? Do you have any idea how much damage control I've been doing this morning? If you ever think you've seen the shit hit the fan before, Detective Bushard, think again, because that time is *now!* It's all our necks on the chopping block. So stop dicking around with Gospel and go get me some righteous evidence!"

Seven recognized the last word when he heard it. He didn't like it, but he and Erika headed out.

Once they hit the hall, he flipped open his cell phone.

He'd been calling steadily all morning. He'd left messages, but Gia wasn't picking up or returning his calls…and he could well imagine why. Like the chief, she'd be getting calls from the press to the crazies. There was probably just a little puff of smoke on her counter where her answering machine had sat.

Around the fifth time he punched in her number, Erika grabbed the phone from his hand and shut it.

"Jesus," she said, handing it back to him, "will you give it a rest?"

Only he couldn't. He hadn't spoken to Gia since waking to find her unable to breathe in the bed beside him. Bringing her back from the brink like that—her assertions that she would have been fine even if he hadn't been there…that it was all part of the process. Her visions.

What was it Nietzsche had said? Something about the irrationality of a thing being no argument against its existence, rather a condition of it?

Well, Gia's condition was blowing his mind. What he'd seen that night, that *couldn't* be an act. Yesterday, he'd spent hours on-line, reading up on psychic phenomena. Then Erika shows up throwing information in his face that Gia Moon can't exist? What the hell was Gia hiding from? His head was spinning.

When Erika started honing in with her Latina sensitivity, he'd taken off. Most of the morning he'd spent just driving around. When Nick got out of school, he'd taken him fishing down at the pier—nothing like fishing to give a man space to think.

Last night, he'd had it all straightened out. He'd confront Gia. Make her talk. If she was in trouble she could trust him.

Only, when he woke up this morning, the world was upside down again.

And now he couldn't reach Gia. And he needed to. He had to find out if she was okay. That she and her kid weren't being harassed. Or worse.

I'm next. That's what she'd said the first time she'd come in. Maybe now she would be.

"You're right," he said, shoving the phone back into his jacket pocket. "This is useless."

With that, he headed for the nearest exit.

Sam watched Owen Gospel from across the room, sizing him up. Owen had been at the Net High before, many times. He'd struck Sam as the type who was always in-the-know. Hot new club? Owen Gospel was the first through the door. If you wanted to make *US Weekly,* you invited people like Gospel.

Right now, Owen was enjoying the attentions of two lovely ladies, friends of Sam's, as well as his employees. Owen liked the ladies. He also had a reputation for liking it rough.

Sam made sure to be accommodating. More often than not, the girls Owen used showed up with burns or needing stitches. Sam would take care of the situation, smoothing things over with cash. It didn't take much. A lot of these girls were fresh off the boat and desperate. In Vietnam, human trafficking was practically a percentage of the gross national product.

Sam didn't consider it taking advantage—he figured he had more to offer than what usually awaited the flotsam and jetsam of illegals arriving on the shores of opportunity. Shit, sometimes they found the girls half-dead inside metal cargo containers at ports in Long Beach or Los Angeles.

When Owen Gospel had first started coming to the Net High, Sam had seen it as a plus. The kid's father was one of the most influential men in Orange County. It couldn't hurt to get in good with his only child, right? A son, no less.

But it didn't take Sam long to figure out there was no love lost between father and son. It was something he couldn't understand, Owen's disrespect for his parents. Shit, if only Sam's father had lived. As it was, Sam honored his father daily in death.

Owen struck Sam as a punk. But Sam didn't underestimate him. Too many people had done the same to Sam over the years, discounting him as so much gang trash.

Catching Owen's gaze, Sam headed toward him. The girls scattered as he approached. He motioned for Owen to join him in a private booth. It was early, just past noon. The Net High wouldn't open officially for hours.

Sam smiled as he shook Owen's hand. He knew how to put on a good show.

After Velvet's murder, Sam had started to think about strategy. It was weird, how he'd always thought he had a purpose in his life. A goal. He was going to be swimming in money. And power. Oh, yes, that most of all. He hadn't understood until now just how shitty his "grand plan" had been. Trudy H.? A distant memory since Vee's death. Making himself over in the image of a man like David Gospel—not even an option.

Velvet had always told him they were Children of the Dragon. Now, Sam thought he finally understood what she meant. No more making pacts with the devils of the world like the Chinese triads and Gospel.

So he'd called Owen Gospel, hoping to mine that rift between father and son.

Sam knew in his gut David Gospel had killed Vee.

Oh, maybe Gospel hadn't gone over to her apartment and personally gutted her open with Xuan Du. But he was responsible. Nothing had ever gone wrong for Vee before Sam brought her into Gospel's life. And Mimi? What about her? No, Gospel was the thread pulling it all together. Him and his damn artifacts.

Owen sat across from Sam. Both men waited, sizing each other up.

"So," Owen asked. "Am I here to talk about dear old Dad?"

Sam shook his head, knowing that would be too easy. "Of course not." He frowned. Sam had always been good at this. "What makes you ask?"

Like he said, he didn't underestimate Owen Gospel.

"Just a hunch," Owen replied.

"I wanted to talk," Sam continued, "because I have a business proposition."

Sam knew what it took to succeed. He'd been at this game for years. Rule number one: take it slow and don't fuck up. That's how Sam planned to get justice for Vee…that's how he would honor her spirit. *Take it slow and don't fuck up.*

Sam leaned forward on the table, toward Owen, knowing the importance of body language. He needed to act pumped. The story was he couldn't get David Gospel on board in his big plans. So what was the next best step? Gospel's kid, Owen.

"I've been trying to make things work with the old man," he told Owen. "But you know how it is. He's like God or something."

He wanted to rub it in, get the son good and mad. *Daddy is way out of your league.*

Sam had thought about it all night. He would talk to Owen, let him know that things weren't happening fast enough. He wanted a piece of Westminster. Little Saigon was his home turf and David had promised him part of the new expansion plan.…

Only, the project had been tabled—some problem with the city planning commission, pissing Sam off but good. Hadn't Sam been buttering up the old man to solve just these kinds of roadblocks with his connections in the mayor's office? Gospel couldn't call in some favors?

Sam knew how to play stupid thug for Owen. On the phone, he'd explained how he needed that pot of gold at the end of the rainbow faster than *dear old dad* was promising. Could Owen help him out?

So it pretty much shocked the shit out of him when Owen gave Sam a big smile and said, "This is about Velvet Tien, isn't it?"

Sam took a moment, reminding himself, *Don't underestimate Gospel's kid.*

"Wow." Sam shook his head. He pushed away from the table and met Gospel's strange blue eyes. He'd noticed from the first there was something wrong with the kid's eyes. The glasses and the constant eyedrops. That unblinking stare.

"She's my cousin, you know," Sam said, seeing how far the truth would get him. "And I loved her, very much."

"He did it," Owen said with that startling gaze. "He killed her. I'm not saying he planned it. Daddy *never* thinks anyone is going to get hurt. He just knows what he wants."

Owen sat across the booth with the weight of regret on shoulders fitted perfectly in a sleek-but-rugged Belstaff shirt, the body language said it all: what could he do? He was just the son, a powerless observer.

But Sam wasn't buying it—but he was listening.

"They died, Mimi Tran, Velvet Tien and the other fortune-teller, Michelle. They died because of Dad—oh, yeah. I know all about that. You see, Sam, you're just another tool to feed my father's obsession with immortality. They all died, even your poor cousin. And you know why?"

Here, Owen leaned forward, resting his elbows on the booth table, making Sam think of his own strategy about body language. Owen was letting Sam know he was pumped, ready for action against the old man.

"You said it yourself, Sam. He's like God. Only Dad, he actually thinks he can do it. Become immortal."

Owen gave a short laugh, as if it were the most ridiculous thing he'd ever heard. But Sam heard something else. Admiration. Or maybe it was a desire to beat the old man to the punch on the immortality gig.

"He used to tell me these bedtime stories," Owen continued. "Each and every one talked about changing the rules and living forever. My favorite was the story of the Moon Fairy. It's Vietnamese, you know? Are you familiar with it?"

Sam nodded. Every kid had heard the story of the king who married his fairy princess, only to betray her by trying to sacrifice their child in his quest for immortality. According to the story, the Moon Fairy turned her daughter into a rabbit and took her to the moon to keep her safe.

Sam frowned, making another connection. Those eyes of Owen's. How they never blinked. They kind of reminded him of a rabbit's eyes.

Here, Owen leaned over the table eagerly. "The thing about these stories, Sam? There's always a sacrifice."

Sam didn't answer right away. This was a chess match. *Pawn to queen's four....*

"You're saying Velvet was his sacrifice?" Sam asked.

Owen smiled. They were on the same page now. Two men who didn't trust each other, but hoped to bring down their nemesis. The enemy of my enemy *is my friend.*

"I know you want revenge for your cousin. You called me because you thought I could help. You want to destroy the old man. You're playing him," Owen said.

The punk's unblinking stare sent a shiver up Sam's spine.

"I'm here to tell you, Sam, I want to play along."

43

Gia pulled back the blinds and stared at the crowd of reporters. She'd unplugged the phone, hoping for a little less volume to the day. Mission accomplished. Despite the throng just outside her door, she felt absolute silence—and not in a good way.

Stella, she thought to herself. Without her daughter's presence, Gia felt empty.

She remembered having a similar connection with her own mother, the famous Estelle Fegaris, psychic archaeologist. Only, to Gia, Estelle had been so much more.

Gia sighed, staring through the window, searching the faces outside for the one she knew was coming. She wondered if he was already there in the shadows, even now watching her.

I'm next.

It's what she'd always believed. Maybe this time, with the morning's headlines, it would prove true.

By now, Thomas's psychosis had focused to the point that killing her would be a compulsion he could not refuse. She couldn't be sure why he'd ended up here in California. Possibly it was the Eye that had brought him; she'd always thought that thing was corralling them all closer for its own inevitable purpose.

He was experiencing seizures, she knew that much from her visions. How it connected to the Eye, she wasn't sure. Estelle had once told her exposure to the crystal wasn't always safe.

Gia continued to watch from behind the blinds. The man she was looking for was tall with thinning blond curls.

But it wasn't Thomas skulking in the shadows who caught her eye. Instead, she focused on another man, one pushing past the reporters, flashing his badge, making his way to her front door.

Seven.

She sighed, dropping back the blinds. She'd been thinking about him all morning.

It happened so often like this. She'd have this feeling that reminded her of those lava lamps with the oil heating up until an opaque bubble rose to the surface. Anticipation—for what or whom, she didn't always know.

She'd thought it had been Thomas she'd been expecting out in that crowd.

She couldn't help a small sigh of relief.

Seven gave a sharp knock at the door. She let him in and he quickly shut the door behind him.

"You okay?" he asked.

She could see that he was trying to catch his breath. She knew this was difficult for him. He'd be making choices that warred with his values as a cop, choices she had forced by allowing events to proceed as they had.

"I'm fine," she said.

"Liar," he declared.

"What does it matter how I feel?"

"It matters to me."

Before she could think better of it, she stepped into his open arms. She rested her head on his chest, just breathing in the smell of him, soap and a spicy aftershave.

Seven took her face in his hands. Their eyes met.

But this time, when he leaned down to kiss her, she turned away.

He let her go, looking almost relieved as he stuffed his hands into the pockets of his trousers. The action made Gia smile. He looked suddenly ten years younger, an awkward boy who didn't know what to do with his hands.

"How's Stella handling all this?" he asked.

"I sent her away." And because she could see the questions on his face, she said, "It's just too much for her." Gia had never

een a good liar. Stella had left yesterday, long before the head-
nes. "I sent her to stay with some relatives."

"Good thinking."

He didn't say it with suspicion. Instead, he took her hand in
is and pulled her toward the kitchen. "Got any coffee?"

"I can make some," she said, suddenly finding herself just as
reathless.

A few minutes later, he was holding a cup between his hands,
tanding next to her at the counter. "About the other night—"

"Please, Seven. I'm a big girl. I know that a relationship be-
ween us is impossible. I don't regret what happened, but no re-
eat performance. I promise."

He watched her for a minute. "Well. That sounded a little
ehearsed."

She hid her smile behind her coffee cup. "Okay. Maybe it was
ust a little. I'm sorry."

"No, that's okay. I had my own canned speech going back in
he car on the way over. Only mine centered around the fact that
ou stopped breathing. The sex, I kind of liked."

She kept her gaze on his. He was an incredibly handsome man,
he type women swooned over. Hazel eyes and a crooked smile.

She could imagine how lonely it must be for him as a homi-
ide detective. The home life couldn't be easy.

Which was part of the problem. That she could relate so well
o his situation.

She put down their coffee cups and leaned into him, just let-
ing him hold her.

He brushed his hand up and down her back. "I'm here now.
'm listening. Me. Not Detective Bushard." He whispered in her
ar, "Tell me what you're hiding. I'll keep your secrets. I'll keep
ou safe."

The offer broke her heart. "If only it were that simple."

He rested his forehead against hers. They stood there, the two
f them, holding each other. After a minute, he asked, "Is this
vhat they call a meeting of the minds?"

"Ha, ha."

He brushed her hair back, and seemed to be searching her face for answers. She knew how badly he wanted her to reassure him. *It's okay, Seven. I'm one of the good guys....*

"I'm sorry." She stepped away and tucked her arms around her stomach. "I have more than myself to think of, Seven."

"Stella. This is about your daughter, then?"

Gia walked over to the window and pulled back the blinds to look at the crowd of reporters waiting outside. She needed to remember what was at stake.

"In my old life, I was a scientist. I even have a doctorate." She shook her head. "I could explain things in a way that made *sense,*" she told him. "Now I have to go on faith."

She could see that someone had trampled her impatiens. Seven came up behind her. He put his hands on her shoulders.

"I was reading some articles on the Internet," he said. "There's this theory that kind of made sense to me. That maybe psychic ability isn't any different than being a concert pianist or a rocket scientist. It's a talent. Some people, they just notice things in a different way than everybody else. It's like their computer program is just more sophisticated for predicting patterns. They stick the pieces together and come up with a story. More often than not, they're right."

"You're starting to believe."

He turned her around, looking puzzled. "And why don't you sound happy about it?"

She took his face in her hands. On tiptoe, she leaned up and kissed him. One deep kiss.

She stepped away. "I have to do something, Seven. I'm going to see a friend of mine. He helps put me into a trance state."

"What are you talking about? What are you planning?"

She could already hear the alarm in his voice. "I have to know what's going on," she explained. "I can't afford to let the killer be in charge of my head anymore. I need to stay a step ahead of him."

"Him?" Seven said, catching the slip. He grabbed her shoulders, not hard, but enough to keep her there. "You know who did this?"

She shook her head. "I can't be sure. Not without going under

It's not...pleasant. But I can't avoid it any longer. Maybe if I'd had the courage to do it before, those women would still be alive."

He dropped his hands away. "How can you stand here and not tell me?"

"That's the responsibility that comes with my gift. I can't tell you what I don't *know* to be true."

"Bullshit. You're holding something back. And now I'm wondering why?"

She could see the physical transformation: Seven becoming "the cop." Well, it was probably for the best. They both had their roles to play in the drama ahead.

"Of course, you'll want more than an audiotape of the session," she continued, trying to avoid what was coming next. "I thought perhaps Special Agent Barnes should stand as a witness."

He closed his eyes as if she'd struck him. He shook his head and opened his eyes, looking like a man just waking up. "Right," he said, nodding his head as if it all made sense. "Okay. Oh, and—how the hell do you know about Agent Barnes?"

"I know Carin Barnes. I've known her for years. If she hasn't already said as much, she's shown more restraint than I'd anticipated."

He took another step away from her, shaking his head as if he still couldn't believe what was happening.

"Agent Barnes has a special expertise in the field of paranormal phenomena," Gia said.

She knew it wasn't helping, these pathetic attempts to explain, when she could only tell him half-truths.

But suddenly, he wasn't paying attention. His eyes focused just above her as he frowned. He brushed past her, shoving open the curtains to stare at the crowd of reporters.

"What the hell?" he said under his breath.

The next thing she knew, he was heading for the front door.

"Where's today's paper?" he asked. "The one with the article?"

"It's right over there," she said, pointing to the stack on the coffee table. The pages were folded back to the fortune-teller murders and her involvement as a psychic.

He picked up the page and walked out the front door. She hurried after him.

She could see he was gunning for one man in particular. Seven must have seen him through the window in the kitchen. The reporter seemed to recognize Seven, as well. He motioned for his cameraman to follow, and headed for the street, away from Seven and the line of fire.

Before he could get away, Seven grabbed his arm. He pushed the paper into the man's chest.

"Is your name Greg Smith?" Seven asked.

The man smiled. "It's good to see you, Detective Bushard."

The next thing she knew, Seven's fist connected with the man's smug expression.

Rocket stared at the surveillance tape playing on the television screen. He had a cup of coffee in front of him, but the coffee had long since gone cold. He'd been at this most of the morning, staring at the same three minutes of footage. Rewind—play. Rewind—play.

He knew he should have told Mr. David about what had happened at the mall, those few hours Owen had given him the slip. And still he hadn't said a thing. From the beginning, Rocket had had a bad feeling about Owen's request to go to the Asian Garden Mall. Rocket kept wondering, *Why Little Saigon?* Hell, Owen was a Rodeo Drive boy, through and through.

After he heard about those poor women getting killed, it all made sense. The mall wasn't that far from the scene of those murders.

Damn punk would have had just enough time....

Rewind—play.

And now, more bad news.

Rocket knew he needed to be very careful about how he approached Mr. David with the facts. He didn't want to just dump a bunch of information on the man.

Mr. David might overreact. Rocket knew what it felt like to be pushed into a corner. That time with Ollie North, maybe if he'd handled things differently, if he'd been better prepared, he might still be part of this country's great military.

The fact was, Mr. David and his wife were like family. Rocket needed to watch out for them. Make sure that things worked out. And he knew Mr. David. He was a hothead. Especially when it came to his kid.

In fact, the more he thought about it, the more Rocket knew it wasn't Mr. David he needed to talk to.

44

When Seven barreled into the office, he could practically feel the steam coming out of his ears. Erika, no slouch, was ready for him. She swiveled around in her chair to face him.

"Did you really punch him?" she asked.

"I hope I broke his fucking jaw," he said, seeing that she'd already gotten wind of what happened. No doubt that bastard, Smith, had called Erika from his cell. The fact that the reporter had robbed him of the element of surprise only heated up the fire in his gut.

Erika stood, chin up, ready to take him on. "You're lucky he's not the type to sue."

"Are you kidding? After the story you just handed him?" He stepped toe-to-toe with his partner. "Why would he bother?"

Erika gave him a steely look. "And now you're pissed?"

"Why'd you do it, Erika?"

She rolled her eyes. "Come *on,* Seven. She has you by the balls. I'm supposed to stand back and let her take advantage?"

"So that's what this is about?" he asked. "You think you're protecting me? You have got to be kidding!"

"I'm talking about our partnership, okay?" she whispered. "The fact is—"

She stopped herself and stepped closer. Lowering her voice, she continued, just as steamed as Seven, "The fact is, *mi amigo,* you've been screwing a witness-slash-possible-suspect and I'm *not* supposed to do dick about it? Listen up, Bucko. It's not just your career you're throwing away. This is my case, too, you know."

"Okay. I cop to that—I screwed up. But come on, Erika. You're not the type for pillow talk. You called the bastard. You fed him the story—"

"Damn straight, I called him," she said. "And I'd do it all over again." She jabbed a finger into his chest. "You just don't get it. I have an instinct about this woman. You used to believe in my gut. Gia Moon is playing you. But suddenly, what I think doesn't matter? Jesus, Mary and Joseph. How many years have we been partners?"

"Maybe too many," he said, half meaning the threat.

Suddenly, she stepped in close, almost pressing against him. "*You* compromised yourself for this woman." Again, she lowered her voice. "Remember your brother, Seven."

And there it was, the idea that he could never really trust anybody, just like Erika.

She reached across him for her desk and picked up the folder that she'd been reading when he'd stormed in. "Agent Barnes dropped this by earlier. I just started reading, but I got the gist." She slapped the folder into his chest. "Besides, I think you should read it first. It explains a lot."

He looked down at the folder. It had the name "Gina Tyrell" typed on the cover like some dossier.

Erika picked up her jacket and purse from the back of her chair. "I'm heading out." She looked him up and down. That expression on her face made him feel about as big as a cockroach.

"The fact is, Seven," she said, brushing past, "I don't want to be here when you read it."

Seven stared down at the folder.

Her name wasn't Gia Moon.

He felt as if his legs had turned to rubber as he dropped down into Erika's chair.

Gina Tyrell.

Suddenly, all that information from Professor Murphy and Erika came slamming back into his head. The Lunites, the cult following for that psychic archaeologist, Estelle Fegaris, Harvard professor and self-proclaimed psychic. Her search for the Eye of Athena, claiming it had the power to tell the future.

Fegaris. It was similar to the Greek word for moon: *feggari*. That's why her followers called themselves Lunites.

Gia Moon.

Stella, her daughter. Short for Estelle.

Gia Moon was the daughter of Estelle Fegaris and Morgan Tyrell, the famed parapsychologist who got kicked out of Harvard and started up his own center for the study of paranormal phenomena and the brain.

And there was more. A lot more.

The student implicated in Fegaris's murder? His name was Thomas Crane. He'd claimed he was Gina's fiancé. Twelve years ago.

Stella was twelve years old.

Thomas Crane stepped off the Gulfstream V. There was a nice breeze coming off the tarmac of John Wayne International Airport. He looked around, taking in a deep breath. Flying over, California reminded him of Greece. The rugged hills—the blue waters.

It was nice of Gospel to send his jet. And yet the flight over had a bittersweet quality for Thomas. He'd been thinking how this could have been his life if Gina hadn't screwed him over. He would still have his reputation as a top classical archaeologist *and* the half million Gospel had paid him for delivering the Eye. Maybe, if he'd played his cards right, Thomas might have even ended up with the Eye, too. That had been his plan, in any case.

But then, you couldn't beat that witch, Gina. She had the power to see the future. Without the Eye to guide him, Thomas had shit against her.

Not anymore, he thought, walking toward the waiting sedan and driver—another courtesy, care of Gospel. *Not ever again.*

Gospel hadn't taken his calls in years. But when Gia Moon hit the papers and Thomas made the connection, Gospel was the first person he'd phoned. Suddenly, the guy couldn't do enough for him.

Something there, Thomas thought. He could hear it in Gospel's voice. Even all these many years later, he could recognized the difference. No longer was Gospel some gazillionaire blowing him off as he had a decade ago. Gospel's voice was just like it had sounded that first time when he'd contacted Thomas and Estelle about the Eye. There'd been a hint of desperation there.

Thomas smiled, getting it. Fuck! What if Gospel lost the Eye? What if Gina somehow managed to take it from him?

Watching the driver dump his duffel into the trunk of the Lincoln Town Car, Thomas settled in the backseat. It's what made sense, he realized. That's why Gospel had been so accommodating. *Whatever you need, Thomas.* Just like in the good old days, when he had something Gospel wanted.

Thomas leaned back into the butter-soft leather. Well, maybe this time he would get it right. He'd get the Eye and kill the girl.

Now wouldn't that be a happy ending?

He looked out the window at the landscape speeding by. He knew Gina would be expecting him. She had her "gift," after all. But she wouldn't disappear. Not again. Not when she had what she'd wanted all along.

Now, she was important….*she* was headline news, taking her mother's place like some psychic royalty.

It was only a twenty-minute drive to Newport. Thomas waved off the bellhop and grabbed his duffel from the driver. He stared up at the impressive facade. Today, Thomas Crane was staying at the Four Seasons. In a suite.

After he settled into his room, he walked out onto the balcony. He'd already called room service for a massage and champagne. Now, he watched the sun set over the water.

He was thinking about the sunsets he'd watched with Gina in his arms. To think, for a minute or two there, he'd actually convinced himself he might be falling in love with the bitch.

He wasn't sure what he'd do about the kid. Maybe this would be one of those tragic double murders? He'd have to think about it, play it by ear.

He smiled at the knock at the door. Room service, with the champagne.

At long last, he was in charge. And he couldn't wait to see Gina's face when she figured it out.

45

Gia stared out the floor-to-ceiling window of the highrise, admiring the panoramic view of the San Diego surf below. Here at the Institute for Dynamic Studies of Parapsychology and the Brain, it was always a day in paradise…even for someone living through hell.

She'd arrived by car, driving down from Garden Grove. Morgan, of course, had offered the helicopter, but she preferred getting here on her own steam.

She remembered when Morgan had opened his San Diego office. Gia had been studying at the University of California at San Diego, getting her doctoral degree in neurochemistry, Morgan being the motivating force behind her choice. If they were going to be partners at the institute, Gia needed to develop an area of expertise. For her, it would never be enough just to be only one of the subjects, a psychic providing data on brain functions.

It was during one of his visits from back East that Morgan fell in love with San Diego. He'd promptly moved the institute here, claiming his old bones couldn't take the Boston winters any more. But Gia always suspected he just missed her too much.

She looked around the office, remembering well the Navajo rugs and colorful blankets accenting the institute's leather couches. Morgan had fallen hard for Southwestern decor. He'd said it energized the spirit. Kokopelli, the mythic being depicted as a humpbacked flute player, had become a talisman for the institute.

Morgan Tyrell was in his midseventies but looked a good

ten years younger. He had bright blue eyes and an athletic build. As well as a medical degree, he had a Ph.D. in psychology, and was a millionaire philanthropist. He was also Gia's father.

He came to stand behind his thirty-nine-year-old daughter, staring out at the surf with her. "It's been a long time, Gina."

"My name is Gia now," she said softly, reminding him.

Twelve years ago, it was Morgan who had helped her become Gia Moon.

"Stella." He shook his head. "She's amazing."

"I know."

Gia smiled. Stella had been staying with her grandfather just over twenty-four hours. But her daughter always made an impression.

"That's some peculiar curse I have," Morgan said. "To never meet my daughter or granddaughter until they're in their teens, fully formed."

"She's hardly that," Gia said. "And neither was I when I decided to live with you instead of follow Mom on her travels."

He smiled benevolently. That was something she'd always loved about her father. That peaceful smile.

"I missed you," she said.

"Then why stay away?"

"It wasn't safe."

He frowned. "I could make it safe."

"Such hubris, Daddy." She turned to gaze at her father. "Besides. You look at me and you see Mom."

"And that's a bad thing?" he asked

She took his hand and gave it a squeeze. "It makes you sad."

He didn't deny it. He and Gia's mother had never married. Estelle had left without even telling Morgan she was pregnant, disappearing into her obsession to discover the Eye of Athena, Morgan claimed. But Gia had always thought there was more to it. A secret burden that her mother carried.

Only a handful of people knew the real story behind her mother's dedication to the Eye of Athena. Estelle had always been careful to keep the origins of the myth surrounding the artifact vague, the truth being much too difficult for the academics she valued so much to swallow.

Gia knew the tale like a bedtime story. *Once upon a time...* How the women of her family claimed to be direct descendants of one of Gaia's sybils. They called themselves the daughters of Sybil. That same oral history documented the existence of the necklace bearing a crystal with the power to enhance psychic abilities, a family heirloom lost long ago. Used for good, the crystal could help it's bearer achieve great things. Used for evil, it would destroy you.

For years, the Eye had remained just that, a bedtime story, part of her family's heritage. But for Estelle, the Eye had become something much different. She was driven to discover the true origins of the artifact. With her strong gift and advanced degrees in classical archaeology, she'd set out to prove the Eye existed, to find the object and put it to use. Estelle believed that once ordinary people experienced a psychic vision—something that would be possible with the Eye—the paranormal would become accepted as a new science, a field that could forward the cause of mankind.

When Morgan came into her life, as a colleague at Harvard, Estelle always assumed he'd been guided to her, so strong was her belief in fate. With Morgan's help—a man trained in hypnotherapy—she was able to fall into the deepest trances, delving into the art of psychic archaeology. She used her guides to help her find the Eye in much the same way that Frederick Bly Bond used remote viewing to guide the excavations of the famous Christian shrine in Glastonbury—the most famous case of psychic archaeology.

In return for Morgan's help, Estelle allowed Morgan to record and study her psychic abilities. She also became his lover.

"I adored your mother. Estelle was my soul mate. I never understood why she left."

"Hmm. I'm sure it had nothing to do with the fact that you were sleeping with one, if not more, of your graduate students. Daddy, you broke her heart."

Now he looked injured. That was the problem with Morgan. He tended to create his own reality.

Estelle had always maintained that Gia's father was dead. She'd mentioned a plane crash when her daughter was old enough to press for details. But when Gia started having visions about her supposedly dead father, she questioned her mother further. Gia could describe Morgan in such vivid detail, she refused to believe he was dead. He would talk to her in her visions, telling he was searching for her—which wasn't the case at all. Morgan had no idea she even existed.

On her seventeenth birthday, she'd confronted Estelle, who'd finally admitted the famed parapsychologist Morgan Tyrell—her biological father—was very much alive.

Hurt and angry, Gia left to go live with Morgan. It wasn't until years later that she forgave her mother, spending summers with Estelle at her dig sites as one of her mom's many shovel bums.

"After I had Stella," Gia said quietly, "I understood a little better why Mom did it, kept your identity a secret. I think she came to believe her greatest value to you was her work at the institute. And that's not what she wanted. She loved you too much to be just a data point. When she had me, I think she didn't want me to be hurt, like she'd been hurt."

He frowned. "Are you implying I would use my daughter, even my granddaughter? That I was some kind of threat like Thomas?"

"Not that, Daddy. Never that. But it did occur to me that you might push Stella to accept her gift before she was ready."

"Granted, I can see she's a powerful medium. But, honestly, I wouldn't push a child."

"Really? Isn't that what you did to me?"

"You were almost eighteen years old, Gia. An adult. Stella is different." And when she didn't comment, he nodded. "So your mother convinced you. I am the big bad wolf, after all. Fair enough." He gave her a tight hug, saying by the gesture that he forgave her doubts. He took her by the shoulders and tilted her head up to his. "You were blessed, and cursed, with ambitious parents. Nonetheless, you've sent Stella to me. So what's changed?"

"I need your help," she said. "Again."

Twelve years ago, she'd found herself pregnant and on the run, her mother murdered. She'd called Morgan, who—with his money and powerful connections—had given her a new identity. A new life.

It didn't take her father long to put it together.

"Thomas," he said. "He's found you?"

"Last night, someone called me in the middle of the night. Each time, the caller ID screen read Private Caller. They called three times, exactly twenty minutes apart—just enough time for me to fall back to sleep if I was so inclined, which I wasn't. There was music playing in the background, barely audible—'Stairway to Heaven.' Thomas called it 'our song.'" She shook her head. "The caller hung up as soon as I said a word. If I stayed quiet, the music just kept playing."

Morgan was familiar enough with her gift to understand she hadn't needed the familiar music to know who was on the other end of that line.

Any father would warn his only child against holding herself out as bait, hoping to catch a killer—which was certainly Gia's plan if she'd sent Stella to him. Any father except Morgan.

He sighed, stepping over to the audio equipment. He began setting it up for a session.

"Well then—" even with his hands shaking, he sounded upbeat "—we'll just have to stay one step ahead of him."

46

Carin had been given very specific instructions. She was to wait outside Morgan's office until Gina was completely under. Only then would she be called inside as a witness.

Spirit guides. The ancient Greeks called them daimons, spirits that intervened between man and the gods. Socrates was said to have had a daimon guiding him throughout his life. It was only later that the church changed all daimons into evil demons, and protector spirits became angels.

Channeling, remote healing, depossession work. Carin didn't care what label you put on what was about to happen. Communicating with nonphysical entities was as old as man himself.

There was even a branch of science, neurotheology, that studied the effect of religion on the brain. Carin was familiar with the work of Dr. Michael Persinger, who had stimulated the temporal lobes of volunteers, using a weak magnetic field. His subjects had sensed a spiritual "presence." People having temporal lobe seizures—temporal lobe epilepsy—experienced the same phenomena, religious revelations or hallucinations, even if they were atheists. In theory, the human brain was ready-made for a spiritual experience.

People like Gina took it one step further. In a deep trance, she could communicate with those who had passed over. Today, Carin would witness Morgan guiding just such a session, using Gina as a "medium" through which he could communicate with her spirit guides.

The door to Morgan's office opened and Carin was shown inside by his assistant. With the blinds closed, there was only a glow from one strategically placed light, giving the office the feel of a child's room with a night-light. The woman indicated a chair set to the side and a few feet away from a leather couch, where Gia appeared to be in a deep trance. Carin took her seat as the woman left the darkened room.

Carin knew what to expect. She'd seen Morgan act as hypnotherapist before. She would never forget his final session with Estelle.

After years of estrangement, the two had once again found each other as parents needing to interact for the welfare of their brilliant progeny. Carin had certainly benefited from their renewed relationship. So had Estelle, who again sought Morgan's help in finding the Eye.

During that last session, Estelle's spirit guides had given their final clues…as well as the possible consequences if she should find the Eye. Morgan was convinced Estelle's obsession with the Eye had become too dangerous, while Estelle had airily dismissed his fears, focusing only on her endgame.

Carin remembered Morgan grabbing Estelle by her shoulders and giving her a hard shake, saying, "What if I lose you again?"

For her part, Estelle had looked calmly into his eyes and said, "There must always be a sacrifice."

Morgan had stepped back as if she'd struck him. Carin had never seen such a look of pain and betrayal.

That was the last time Morgan saw Estelle, his lover and the mother of his child. Now, Carin watched Gia quietly on the couch, reminded of that final session, daughter and mother looked that much alike.

There was a strobe light aimed in Gia's direction. Morgan used it to facilitate a deep trance, assuring the brain-mind response necessary for a deep hypnosis. Sounds of the ocean played from hidden speakers, waves crashing, seagulls in the distance, the wind. Carin knew there would also be synthesized thetawave sounds playing behind the music.

"Gia, I want you to humbly request assistance from your spirit guides. Repeat after me. I call out to my spirit guides."

The exercise continued as Morgan led Gia deeper into her trance. But the greatest surprise came when Morgan asked his daughter to invoke her spirit guide by name.

In a soft, sure voice, Gia said, "I ask for your help, Estelle. I beseech it and mark it and so it is."

Carin saw the shock on Morgan's face. For a moment, she wondered if he might put an end to the session. Instead, he turned to Carin and gave a short nod.

She took the plastic bag from inside her satchel. She and Morgan had discussed their course of action beforehand, the most successful path to discovering the identity of the killer. They both knew the danger of what they were about to do.

Carin took the bead in her hand. In this light, it glowed a deep red, the cat's-eye line of white very distinct. This was the bead that had been inside the bird's beak, the one found in Mimi Tran's mouth. Carin handed it to Morgan.

He seemed to warm the bead in his palm. She began counting silently in her head, telling herself she had to give him at least sixty seconds before she intervened. This couldn't be an easy thing for Morgan.

Fifty-seven, fifty-eight, fifty-nine...

Still, he kept the bead, just watching his daughter.

Carin said softly, "It's what she'd want, Morgan."

He looked down at the bead in his hand. "Yes. It's also what her mother wanted and look what happened to her."

"Perhaps it would be easier if I did it?" Carin asked.

He shook his head. With a deep breath, he picked up his daughter's limp hand and placed the bead in the middle of her palm.

Immediately, her fingers snapped shut around it like a trap. On the couch, her body became rigid.

Suddenly, Gia arched, gripped by a seizure.

"You're at the beach house, your safe place," Morgan said in a surprisingly soothing voice, keeping his cool despite the sight of his daughter's distress. "You can hear the ocean, smell the salt air. Your mother is there, your spirit guide. Take her hand, Gia."

Again, Gia's back arched, coming completely off the couch, her teeth grinding together.

"Take…her…hand, Gia," Morgan repeated, urgently now. "Your mother is right there. Take her hand. Take your mother's hand."

Just as suddenly as the attack came on, Gia's body fell limp onto the couch.

"Your mother is there, isn't she?" Morgan continued, his breath coming hard. "She's helping you."

Gia's eyes opened wide.

"There must always be a sacrifice," she said, in a strange, gutteral voice Carin didn't recognize. "This much, you know."

Carin glanced at Morgan.

There must always be a sacrifice. Estelle's final words to him.

"Sometimes," Gia continued in that same contralto, "the sacrifice is planned, a formal occasion to honor the gods. The Mayan priests draw their own blood by piercing their tongues, ears or genitals. The Aztecs dedicate their sacrifice to the god Huehueteotl, the god of fire. Victims are drugged and thrown into a blaze at the top of a ceremonial platform. Before they die, they are dragged out with hooks. Their living heart is pulled out and thrown back into the fire."

Gia made the gesture of grabbing her own heart from her chest with the hand not holding the stone. She still kept a death grip on the bead. There was a fierce smile on her face.

"But sometimes, the sacrifice isn't planned. The victim presents herself. The divine becomes understood only in that moment of pure clarity. Puerto Rico, the young Madonna drowning in the waters of St. John."

"Gia, I want you to wake up now," Morgan said. "I'm going to count to three slowly."

Carin could see Morgan had had enough. He was pulling Gia out from the trance. "Morgan, are you sure?"

"She's nonresponsive," he said. "One." He glanced at Carin, saying with a look what he thought: *I can't do this!* "Two."

"Morgan. Those women, they're dead. And there will be more."

"Three."

"Rocket lies at your feet." Gia kept speaking in that odd voice, sounding almost sad now.

"Three, Gia. I said three! You must wake up now!"

"He isn't going to fight as much as you thought. Such a big man. You thought he would at least fight for his life. But he kneels before you like a lamb to the slaughter."

Carin rose. She came to stand next to Morgan, grabbing his hand, stopping him from his futile attempt to waken Gia.

"It's him," she told Morgan. "She's in the killer's head."

Another killing?

"For the first time, you use a gun," Gia continued.

"Shit," Carin whispered.

"You shoot him in the back of the head. Brains spray across the white carpet. That's what you like best. The art of death."

"Who are you?" Carin asked.

But Gia ignored her. "But you don't see the beauty this time. You don't understand the pain you feel. Do you actually care for Rocket? Is this regret?"

Morgan pushed Carin aside. "Sit down and shut up," he ordered. "Or I will personally haul you out of this room."

"But he is David's underling and therefore tainted." The voice seemed to argue with itself. "Only now, standing over his body, you feel no triumph." Gia reached up and touched her own face. "And there are tears in your eyes. Poor Rocket. Poor, lovely man."

Carin walked to a corner, ignoring any protest from Morgan. She was calling the police station. "Detective Cabral. We have a problem. It's happening now. I mean right *now!* Another killing. Does the name Rocket mean anything to anyone?"

"You remind yourself that suffering *should* be part of the experience." Gia's voice was higher pitched, her breath coming harder and faster. "Your pain emulates the suffering of those who came before you."

"Help me, dammit!" Morgan stood. He grabbed Gia's hand, trying to dislodge the stone she held in her grip.

"They, too, evolved into gods. Without proper suffering, you cannot reach the next level."

On the couch, another seizure gripped Gia's body. Morgan held her down by her shoulders. He looked at Carin. "Please!"

Estelle's daughter, Carin thought. She dropped the cell phone and ran to Gia's side.

"You know that there must be more pain—more sacrifice!" Gia was screaming now in a strange, high-pitched voice.

Carin tried to pry her fingers apart and grab the stone. When that didn't work, she attempted to slip her own finger inside, to push it out.

Morgan was whispering into his daughter's ear, beseeching her to look for her mother. That he knew Estelle was there. That Estelle would help her.

"And you are ready!" Gia screamed.

"I can't get it out of her hand," Carin told Morgan.

"Estelle," Morgan shouted to Gia. "Help me, Estelle. Help our daughter."

Suddenly, Gia sat straight up, the force of her body throwing both Morgan and Carin to the floor.

She looked like a mannequin, sitting in that impossible position, legs straight out, hands straight down, her back stiff as a board.

The hand holding the stone opened. The bead dropped to the rug.

Gia turned her head to look at Morgan and Carin, her eyes still wide open.

"Don't *ever* do that to our child again, Morgan," she commanded.

"Estelle."

"She's in danger," Gia said.

Morgan stood, catching his breath. Carin stayed where she was, watching in awe.

"I know, darling," Morgan said, returning to his daughter's side. He sat on the couch beside her. "But like you, she's quite stubborn."

Gia cocked her head, the gesture almost birdlike. "Well, then you'll just have to be stronger, Morgan. She needs you. Stella needs you. *I* need you."

Morgan sighed, a relieved smile on his face. "Then for God's sake, my love, help me. Tell me once and for all, so I can let Gia know and she can stop playing Russian roulette with her spirit."

He took Gia's hand in his. She moved like someone who was not familiar with her own body, watching with great curiosity as she let Morgan bring her hand to his lips and kiss it.

"It's time, Estelle," he said. "Well past time. Tell me. Tell us all so we can stop him." Holding her hand over his heart, Morgan asked, "Who killed you, Estelle? Who took you from me?"

47

Gia painted in broad strokes, her arm sweeping across the five-foot-tall canvas before her. Paint splatters covered her jeans, arms and hair. She mixed colors feverishly, returning to the canvas she could barely see for the tears in her eyes.

She remembered her mother's hair, the inky curls Estelle hid under hats and tortured away in sensible hairstyles. Gia had stick-straight hair courtesy of Morgan. But not Stella.

Gia and her daughter had Estelle's eyes. Sorceress eyes, Thomas had called them.

On the canvas, Gia painted two dark holes where Estelle had once had eyes.

That's what Thomas had done to her mother. He had taken her eyes; he'd put them in a plastic Baggie and kept them as a souvenir.

And now Morgan wanted her to believe *she* was wrong? All these years, tormented by visions that Thomas would find her, kill her and her daughter—just as he'd killed Estelle—and it didn't mean anything?

"*You're* wrong, Daddy," she cried out. "*You're* wrong!"

There was no one else in the room. She was talking to herself, as if hearing the assurance out loud made it true.

"It's Thomas. It's always been Thomas."

Her visions had started three years ago. But it wasn't until she dreamed of Mimi Tran's murder that she'd understood. She'd been given a choice by her guides—a terrible choice—but a choice nevertheless. She had this one chance to stop her mother's killer and save her daughter.

That's why she'd gone to the police. Estelle had reached out to her, letting her know how to save herself and Stella from Thomas.

But after the death of Velvet Tien and Xuan Du, Gia wasn't so sure. *What if I'm wrong?* In her vision, Thomas wanted to kill only her.

And now Morgan, her own father, claimed she'd made a terrible mistake.

She'd gone to him to try and understand. But instead of focusing the images in her head, her father only contradicted everything she'd come to believe. She'd woken to find Morgan holding her hand. Behind him, Carin was already listening to the recording of the session, taking notes.

One look into her father's eyes and she'd realized something was very wrong.

"It's not Thomas, sweetheart," he said. "It never was."

Now, she brushed away her tears impatiently. She focused on the painting, on those black circles she'd painted on her mother's face. She still believed she could find her truth here, on this canvas.

It was Thomas. He as much as admitted it to me through my visions.

That's what she'd told Morgan, who'd just sat there staring at her, shaking his head. That final day, the clues her mother had left. Everything fit together....

Gia had driven home from San Diego against Morgan's wishes. The first thing she'd done was pull out a fresh canvas. She'd mixed the pigments, searching deep inside her soul for answers.

Certainly, Morgan was wrong. Oh, he'd played the tape for her—she'd insisted on it. She recognized her voice.

Thomas didn't kill me. I died by the hand of another. Find my eyes and you'll find my killer.

"Gia?"

She didn't stop painting, focused only on the image she was painting. She didn't want to lose the thread of the story. She was close. So close.

But Seven wasn't waiting. He grabbed her hand, the one holding the paintbrush. He turned her around to face him.

"Or should I say Gina?"

She twisted her hand free. The paintbrush dropped to the concrete of her garage studio.

With both her hands, she shoved hard into his chest, pushing him away.

"Get out of here, Seven!"

He grabbed her wrists and pulled her to him. He looked just as out of control as she felt.

"Gina Tyrell. Daughter of Estelle Fegaris and Morgan Tyrell. Fiancée of Thomas Crane, the archaeology student once accused of killing your mother. Why didn't you tell me?" he demanded.

"Tell you?" She threw her head back, staring up at him. "Why should I tell you anything? Don't you get it? I haven't even told my daughter!"

But she could see he wouldn't stop. He had come here to have his say. She'd lied; she'd used him.

"What was it, Gia? This Crane guy starts killing psychics in some sick game to get you to reveal yourself? He tracks you here, but he needs to flush you out. So he starts with Mimi Tran, knowing you couldn't resist getting involved—because you've known all along who was behind the killings and why."

She shook her head. He tightened his grip on her wrists, giving her a hard shake.

"Was I part of the plan? Making sure a cop was right here with you, watching your back when the shit hit the fan? Let's just seal the deal with sex? Make sure he's on my side?"

"You don't know what it's like to make that choice," she whispered. "It's me or him. You could never understand someone believing that it's better to kill than be killed? That's why you can't go to see your brother. You can't look into his eyes and hear his side of the story. To you, it would all sound like excuses."

"Excuses?" His eyes grew wide in disbelief. "It's more than that, sweetheart. He *killed* Scott." He pulled her in close, hurting her.

"But Scott *would* have blackmailed Ricky. He would threaten to tell...expose Ricky. Let everyone know that he was having sex with his male nurse, not only cheating on his wife but flat broke because he'd mismanaged the business." She leaned into him. "That wasn't death to your brother? Losing everything he'd worked for his whole life—his marriage, his son...his reputation? That wouldn't have killed Ricky?"

"*Anything* was better than what Ricky did," Seven shouted. "He ended a man's life. He destroyed two families. He destroyed *his* family."

"That's right." She was screaming right back at him, the tears still there. "You can't even imagine it, can you? Someone crossing that line? Going from a normal, caring human being to a cornered animal? No one gets to cross that line. Certainly not your perfect brother. Only, what if that's what pushed him to it? All those years of being just that. Perfect Ricky. Perfect son. Perfect doctor. Perfect brother."

"Now you're psychoanalyzing Ricky?" Seven snapped his fingers, the lightbulb going on over his head. "That's right, your father was a psychiatrist before he went into all that paranormal shit. You probably picked up the lingo from him, right? I wonder, what did he say about you screwing your mother's killer and having his child?"

"Get out!" she screamed. "Get out!"

When he left, slamming the door of the studio behind him, she collapsed to the floor.

She'd pushed him to that edge, where he would want nothing better than to leave her alone. That's what she'd needed, to get him good and angry. To get him gone.

She didn't know how long she sat on the floor of the studio, crying. Like Stella, she never cried. But now the sobs consumed her. All those years, she'd refused to talk to Estelle, angry about the choices her mother had made. Keeping Morgan from her, dedicating everything to discovering the Eye, obsessed with finding the artifact, even if it killed her... Gia knew her mother had a powerful gift. She didn't for one minute believe her mother's spirit guides hadn't warned her.

She stared up at those dark, empty circles on her mother's face where there should have been eyes. She stood slowly.

Maybe it would always be like this, she thought. Maybe Gia would forever remain blind to the truth.

"Who killed you, Mommy?" she asked the blinded image. "Who took you from me and Stella?"

But the moment had passed. That passion she'd felt painting her mother's image, searching for answers, no longer guided Gia. Instead, she felt spent and completely empty inside.

She went back inside the house. She knew Morgan would be worried. She'd been so angry when she left, almost accusing him of botching the session because she couldn't believe the result. She should call him, let him know she was all right.

But once inside the house, she thought she heard something. A door closing softly?

"Seven?"

She walked to the front room, expecting to see him back—almost hoping that he'd returned for another round.

The door remained closed. There was no one in the entry.

Something crashed behind her. She whirled around.

On the floor at her feet was a framed photograph. The picture had fallen off the entry table.

The frame was facedown on the wood floor.

She stooped to pick up the photograph and turn it over. It was a picture of Stella. The frame's glass had shattered across her daughter's smiling face.

Suddenly, her instincts kicked in. She dropped the photograph and ran, heading for the door out to the street.

Too late.

Seemingly out of nowhere, a hand grabbed her foot. She could feel herself being dragged back, away from the door. She almost lost her balance and fell to the floor.

Like a vise, an arm squeezed her stomach, keeping her upright. A hand clamped over her mouth.

"Alone at last," a familiar voice whispered in her ear. "Looks like your boyfriend didn't stick around to save the day."

Gia pushed back with all her weight, slamming Thomas against the wall, shocking him into releasing her. But again he grabbed her ankle, and she tumbled to the floor. She kicked and flailed her arms and legs, trying somehow to escape.

"You told me you killed her. You admitted you killed Estelle."

He held her down, looking at her strangely, as if he didn't understand. "Fucking crazy bitch," he said. "Of course I killed her."

He punched her hard across the face.

Thomas Crane stared down at Gia's unconscious figure. Right beside her was a photograph of their kid in a broken frame.

"A girl. Fucking figures," he said, standing. He crushed the glass farther under his foot, and then picked Gia up from the floor.

Seven peeled out into the street, pedal to the metal.

What if that's what pushed him to it? All those years of being just that. Perfect Ricky?

Like he hadn't figured that out? Like he didn't know that his brother had boxed himself into a place where he couldn't ask for help? Well, that wasn't good enough. Not nearly.

When he'd read that dossier on Gina Tyrell, Seven couldn't help but recall how totally inept he was at finding the right people to trust. First his wife, then Ricky betrays him. Now Gia. Three strikes, you're out, right?

He could feel that anger building inside him, burning him up. He almost thought of turning around, having another go at it with Gia.

She thought she could read his mind? How about him giving her a piece of it without all that hocus-pocus bullshit.

She'd lied. She'd used him!

Out of nowhere, a ball came bouncing onto the street. He almost didn't see it—or the little girl running after it.

He yanked the steering wheel hard to the left, checking his rearview mirror with a prayer. He just missed hitting an oncoming Volvo as he swerved back to the right side of the street around the little girl grabbing the ball.

He pulled over. The adrenaline had already been on high from is argument with Gia. Now he felt buzzed on it, his hands shaking on the steering wheel. Once the Volvo's driver figured out no one was hurt, the guy took off, in a hurry to get somewhere. But Seven sat there, trying to get his breath back.

When he finally got out of the car, he found the little girl in the arms of her mother. The woman was holding her, crying over and over, "Thank God. Thank God."

Seven kept his distance, letting the mother work it through— the possibility that, just then, she could have lost her baby. She was young and blond. The little girl, maybe around three years old.

Seven knew it was a trick of the mind—the little girl didn't look anything like Gia's daughter. But watching the lady rock her daughter in her arms, suddenly he remembered all those photographs of Stella decorating the walls in Gia's house.

The woman looked up at him, tears flooding her brown eyes. "I only turned my back for a second, I swear."

The realization came to him then, what it must be like never to be able to turn your back, even for a second. To always be wondering if Crane would find them…if he'd hurt them.

Gia would kill to save her daughter.

Seven was a cop. He knew what it meant to keep someone safe. Hell, he wouldn't even hesitate if Nick's life were on the line.

It's what she'd been trying to tell him. Maybe he could never understand why Ricky had killed Scott—he didn't have to. He just had to know that sometimes a person could be pushed to the limit of his conscience, goaded into doing the unthinkable.

"You okay?" he asked the woman. "You want me to call someone?"

She shook her head, still holding her daughter. "I'm okay. I'll take her back inside. I'll get my husband to baby-proof every single door." She looked up at him, shaking her head. "I didn't even know she could reach the knob."

He looked past the woman cradling her child, something choking up in his throat. He nodded. "Okay, then."

He left, knowing the woman wouldn't need a lecture or a warning. God had just handed her a big one.

He sat in the car, looking out the windshield as he turned ove
the engine. There, shining in the bright sky, he could just mak
out the vague image of the moon.

48

'Jesus, Sam," David said. "What the hell is going on? Is this some sort of gang thing, all these killings?"

Sam stared across the table at David Gospel. That was the first thing people brought up whenever something went wrong in Sam's life. *Is this some sort of gang thing?*

He'd asked David to meet him here at the Four Seasons for a light lunch. David had wanted to talk from the moment he'd sat down, but Sam put him off. He'd wanted to see the bastard squirm.

"You look shaken up," Sam said.

"You bet your ass, I'm shaken up. I just got back from meeting with my attorney. They found another one of the beads. This one was lodged in Velvet's stomach. She was my lover, Sam. For fuck's sake, I'm their number one suspect."

He watched David take out his handkerchief and wipe the sweat running down his face. "Apparently, Mimi Tran kept notes on her sessions. Now some asshole supposedly sent the cops what she wrote about me and her attempts to use the Eye, which would include, of course, what the damn thing looked like. Those beads, she described them in exquisite detail."

"Really?" Sam said. "I didn't even know Mimi took notes on her readings."

"Neither did I, believe you me. Now the cops have me linked to all three murders. Lazy bastards. It's fucking clear someone is trying to set me up. But they're going for the obvious."

"Yeah. Go figure. The police trying to make you out as th killer. But then, it's not like they haven't tried to peg you for murder before, right? So why are you so shocked?"

David looked like a prey animal getting a whiff of somethin in the wind.

Sam took a drink of his iced tea, waiting.

"Are you talking about the Long Beach thing?" David askec "Michelle Larson?"

"She was your mistress, wasn't she? Just like Velvet."

Owen had filled Sam in. He'd given him the name Michell Larson. The rest had been easy enough to uncover.

David picked up his water glass and took a nervous sip. "Mi chelle was nothing like Velvet."

"You got that right."

"Look, she was the first psychic I went to about the Eye. Bu Michelle, she didn't have Mimi's gift. The only reason I kept see ing her was because she and I became involved. But it wasn't lik Velvet. Dammit it, Sam. I loved her—you know that!"

"Yeah. Velvet told me about how you were leaving your wif for her and everything."

David looked so startled, Sam actually laughed.

"It's a joke, David," he assured him. "Just a damn joke."

"Listen to me, Sam. Just because I didn't have the balls t leave my wife doesn't mean I killed Velvet."

"Jesus, David, did you think I was accusing you? I'm sorry, mar You know, sometimes I just talk such crap." Sam shook his hea ruefully. But then he nailed his gaze on David. "But I have this ide in my head. Maybe you could help me work it out. Velvet tells yo she's ashamed, you being married and all. She was like that, yo know? She had something you and I lack. A conscience."

He watched David stiffen ever so slightly.

"So she starts to think she should move on," Sam continued his eyes still on his victim. "But that's not what you want. No You want to keep her. You're a collector and Vee, she is a mos exquisite find. You even dangle some stupid-ass job in your com pany—in-house counsel or some shit like that."

How else could David think to keep a woman like Vee? Hadn't
am offered the same?

"At first, she's tempted. It's a good gig, right?" Sam contin-
ed. "But something happens, something she doesn't expect.
he falls in love."

Owen had given him the letter, one of many that Velvet had
vritten to David, according to his son. *She wanted him to leave
y mother,* Owen had said as Sam read the letter, his gut churn-
ng at the thought of Vee's broken heart. *Only she knew Dad
ould never agree.*

Sam reached into his Armani jacket and pulled out Vee's let-
r, the last one she'd written to David, and held it out. David
oked at it as if it were a snake ready to bite him.

"She was leaving you," Sam said, stating the gist of the note.
You couldn't have that, now, could you?"

"I don't know what that is, Sam," he declared, gesturing to
e envelope. "But I swear to you, Velvet never wrote me a damn
tter. Never."

Sam nodded. Of course David would deny it.

He dropped the paper on the table. David grabbed it, making
show of opening it and reading it, acting as if he'd never seen
e thing before.

"Jesus, Sam. How can you be so stupid? It's printed off a com-
uter, for God's sake." He threw the letter back at him. "Anyone
an steal a piece of her stationery and forge her signature."

Sam smiled. "I'll tell you how stupid I am. Mimi Tran came
see me almost a year ago. She told me about your little obses-
on with the Eye. She thought you would be willing to do just
bout anything for another one of the artifacts mentioned in that
tone tablet of yours. I thought, shit. I can use this guy, right? I
ean, who believes in that sort of funky-ass stuff besides a man
eady to be scammed?"

Mimi had told Sam that David was a collector. He'd pur-
hased some kind of clay tablet that referred to magic objects
lling from the sky. The Eye was supposed to be just such an
bject—but there were others. If David thought Sam had con-

nections to finding them, maybe through the heavyweights wit the Chinese triads, he'd be in Sam's back pocket.

Sam took a moment to savor the expression on David's face The disbelief. *Oh, yeah. You've been had. Big time.*

"Remember our first meeting, David? How I dangled all m sources with the triad—how I knew exactly how to get in touc with the right people in the Communist government. It was ju a matter of time before you had more artifacts for your collec tion because I had my finger on an untapped black market."

Sam leaned forward, smiling with great glee. "I made it u David. The whole damn story. That shit about finding the nex object in Vietnam? How the Communists had taken it from som Chinese collection way back when? And my connection high i the government? All bullshit. We've been playing you, David. A of us, Mimi, Velvet and me."

"Holy shit, Sam," he whispered. "Why?"

Sam wouldn't give David the satisfaction of the truth. Tha he'd wanted to be close to him—become the Vietnamese versio of David Gospel.

He picked up the letter and folded it slowly. "I dragged her int it, of course. My sweet, sweet cousin. Brains and beauty? I knev you wouldn't be able to resist. She was supposed to keep an eye o you. Let me know if you were getting impatient or suspicious. Onl she fell for you, you bastard. She fell hard. And suddenly, she's pa of your collection. Just like Michelle Larson." Now, giving Davi a hard stare, he demanded, "Why couldn't you just let her go?"

"I didn't kill Velvet, Sam. I swear it!"

"You killed her, all right. And if you didn't do it personall you made it happen, you *fucking* whack job."

Sam stood. He buttoned his jacket. He couldn't believe he ever respected Gospel. Any man looking for some piece of roc to make him a god was weak.

"I sent the cops Mimi's notes. In fact, I'm working closel with local law enforcement. Go figure."

He leaned over the table pushing his face right up to David' "There isn't a hole dark enough for you to hide in, you piece of shit.

Sam pulled back and rapped his knuckles on the table with a smile.

"Lunch is on me. I hope you choke on it."

Seven stared up at the painting. He could just make out a woman's face. There were black holes where her eyes should have been.

Erika stood next to him. He knew what she was thinking even if she didn't say the words out loud. *Another dead woman with her eyes missing....*

He'd come back to the studio to talk to Gia—to let her know he understood. She was just protecting her kid.

He wanted to help her. She could trust him now. He would never hurt her—never let anyone hurt her or Stella.

When he walked in the door, he hadn't found Gia. What he'd found was a crime scene.

He'd called Erika and she'd sent in the troops, including Agent Barnes, now standing with them. The crime scene techs were going over every inch of the place.

Agent Barnes took in the disheveled room, the front table overturned, the crushed photos.

"No leads on anyone named Rocket," Erika said. "No missing persons report, no body found. Nada."

Barnes nodded her head. "Given the circumstances, this Rocket person will have to wait his turn."

It was clear that whoever had taken Gia, she'd fought with everything she had. They'd found blood on the floor next to her daughter's photograph. The glass in the picture frame looked as if it had been ground under someone's heel.

"You think the answer is in that painting, Detective?" Barnes asked.

Seven kept staring at the canvas. He reached out and pressed the tip of his finger to one corner. The paint was still wet.

He remembered how she always arrived at the precinct with paint under her fingernails.

"She said painting helped her deal with her visions. The paint-

ing of Velvet Tien," he said, nodding toward the other canvas se
up against the studio wall. "It's all there. The hands disappear
ing, the eye in the stomach, the moon on her tongue."

Beside him, Barnes gave him a peculiar look. "So, she's made
a believer out of you."

Seven felt something burn in his gut. He didn't know what he
thought. The newest painting was of a woman with black curl
and missing eyes, obviously dead. She looked like a grown-up
version of Stella.

Even in the best of circumstances, he wouldn't have a clue
what it could possibly mean or how the painting could help them
find Gia.

He turned to Barnes. "You have a better idea?"

The agent seemed to think about it. She picked up her Black
Berry and punched in a number.

"Like you, I do not have the slightest notion what this paint
ing represents, Detective Bushard. But I think I know someone
who might. Lucky for us, the man she's staying with happens to
have a helicopter."

49

David Gospel slammed into his house. He was trapped in a fucking nightmare.

Sam Vi was threatening *him?* That *punk* was telling David to watch his back?

Fuck him. Fuck them all.

And now, even Rocket wasn't answering his phone…when David needed to rally the troops.

He took the steps to his office two at a time. The problem was he'd been too cavalier. He realized that now. Mimi had apparently given Sam some shit on him. The first thing David needed to do was hide the evidence. That meant he needed to get rid of his collection. The only people who'd actually seen him with the Eye were dead, Mimi and Velvet. And wouldn't those notes of Mimi's be considered some kind of hearsay, anyway? It's not like his attorney could cross-examine her about the contents—or was it an authentification issue? Surely there was some rule of law to prevent the cops from using those notes against him.

Dammit, he was David fucking Gospel! He wasn't going down for murder. No way. He wasn't going to say he'd *never* had someone killed, but he wasn't responsible for Mimi or Velvet.

When he reached the landing, he was surprised to find his office door wide open. *Rocket.* He must have come to view the surveillance tapes. David had called Rocket in case he'd missed something. With Jack's help, David had narrowed down the time from when the Eye had been stolen to a ten-hour window. When

Jack claimed there was nothing on the tapes, David had aske
for the pertinent DVDs to be brought here for review.

But why would Rocket still be going over that video? The la
time David had checked in, Rocket hadn't mentioned there wa
anything of interest. Surely, he would have called if the tape
showed something?

David reminded himself that Rocket was a professiona
Trained by Ollie North himself.

He started walking faster, thinking maybe Rocket *had* foun
something, something David missed…something that would te
him who had taken the Eye.

When he walked into the office, Rocket was nowhere in sigh
but he could hear the soft whirr of the DVD still spinning in the driv

David stopped in the middle of the room, catching scent of
strange metallic smell.

The first thing he noticed was his computer screen playing th
surveillance tape. And the door to his private collection, the vau
room behind the mirrored entrance—Rocket had left it open?

He stepped over to the computer first, wondering why Rocke
would be so careless, leaving both doors open like this. Davi
had been desperate enough to give the access code in a messag
on Rocket's cell phone, hoping his man would start the cleanu
process before Sam sent the cops over with a warrant. Shit, an
now it wasn't just the police. Now he had the FBI on his ass. Wit
a warrant, those parasites would have his office inside out withi
the hour.

David sensed that something was very wrong. The compute
seemed to be programmed on some sort of loop, playing the sam
section from the surveillance tape over and over.

Suddenly, he understood why.

He dropped into the leather swivel chair in front of the enor
mous computer screen, his mouth gaping open.

On the thirty-two-inch screen he could clearly see the se
curity men he'd hired. They had just finished installing the ne
cameras and were inspecting the system, making sure they'
covered every inch within the room and vault.

David had watched this tape before. Only now, he noticed something he'd missed.

His wife, Meredith.

She was inside the vault room; the security guys had it open while they were checking out camera angles. He could clearly see her reaching into the velvet-lined drawer, *pocketing* the Eye.

He watched the same three minutes of tape loop over and over. Meredith punching in the code, reaching into the drawer...

He realized Rocket must have seen the same thing. He would have sat here, just like David, wondering how it could be possible. Maybe he'd even programmed the computer to loop over and over—he was great with computers.

Behind him, he heard a woman's voice say, "That which is invisible is always the most dangerous."

He turned around. "Meredith?"

"Very good, David." She started clapping, applauding his revelation. "Little invisible Meredith. Abracadabra, at last you see her."

He couldn't believe it. "You took the Eye?"

He tried to remember how many times he'd watched this very piece of tape. And yet he'd never even noticed her.

Because it was Meredith. Who would give a shit if she was in his vault? Certainly not the security guys setting up the system.

He'd never even thought to discuss her with his security team. *Keep my wife out of my collection....* Meredith was never much of a consideration to David. Jack and his men would just assume she was in the know, hanging around to make sure they did a proper job.

Just as Mimi predicted, Meredith was invisible, to him and anyone who might question her actions.

"What have you done, Meredith?" he asked with growing horror.

She walked toward him. "Rocket called me." She spoke in a strange monotone, sounding as if she were in some sort of trance. "He wanted to show me something."

David remained seated in front of the computer. Meredith pointed to the screen.

"That's what he wanted to show me."

"It's all right, Meredith," he said, trying to stay calm. He had no idea what was going on, but he kept hearing Mimi's warning in his head.

That which is invisible...

To David, there was no one more invisible than his wife.

"I'm not mad, honey," he said, smiling now, trying to sound reassuring. "Really. Just tell me where the Eye is, and we'll forget all about it."

But Meredith was shaking her head. "Too late."

She had her hands buried in the pockets of her enormous dress. Now, she slipped one free.

She was holding a gun. His Beretta. She had the damn thing pointed right at him.

"Meredith? What are you doing!"

"Too late," she repeated.

Suddenly, David realized why the door to the vault was open. He focused there, following the legs encased in black pants inside to his secret vault room. He stood in disbelief.

Inside the chamber, Rocket lay on the floor, his legs peeking out just beyond the door to the office. Next to him was Owen, his arm stretched out over Rocket's chest, as if he'd fallen there.

They were both dead. Shot through the back of the head by the looks of it.

David felt as if his heart would burst in his chest. "Jesu Christ, Meredith."

She kept her eyes on him, the gun pointed at his chest. "I used the Beretta you keep in the nightstand. You showed me how to load and shoot. Remember?"

His head was spinning. Meredith shot Rocket? And Owen? That boy was her heart—her reason for being. No way she could kill Owen. No fucking way!

And still, there they were. Dead.

David hadn't noticed the blood when he'd walked into his office. The room was too big. He wouldn't have seen the blood splatters on the far side on his way to the computer and his desk.

"You never would have noticed me on the tape," she said. She gave a tired shake of her head. "But Rocket, he *saw* me. Always. When you asked him to review the tapes, he couldn't believe I'd taken anything from your collection. He came here to talk to me. He showed me, on the computer. He wanted to help me."

"And so you *killed* him?"

She stared at David as if he'd asked a stupid question. "Of course I did. I had to. I lured Rocket into the vault. I begged him to help me put everything back. He wanted to help me, but I had to kill him. Then Owen arrived. I said to him, 'Look what I've done.' He was standing right over Rocket's body when I shot him in the back of the head."

Suddenly, it clicked. *She's crazy—and she will kill me.* He took a step toward the door.

Meredith followed him with the Beretta.

"Sit down, David."

He dropped back into his chair.

"You killed Owen?"

He regretted the words immediately. He was waving a red flag in front of a bull. If David was obsessed with his collection, Meredith had put her life's energy into their child. She never would have hurt, much less killed, him if she was in her right mind.

She said in a soft, disjointed voice, "There must always be a sacrifice."

He could feel himself hyperventilating. "We'll talk to Rose," he said, trying to get control of the situation. "She can help you." He glanced nervously at the two bodies in the vault. "Meredith, honey. You're obviously not feeling well. Rocket was right. I haven't been attentive." *Jesus!* "But I can be better. Give me a chance to help you, sweetheart. Here, I'll just call Rose."

He reached for the phone…only to have Meredith shoot the damn thing right off the desk.

"He was our child, David. We brought him into this world. We raised him, no one else. We are responsible."

Oh, shit. David Gospel did not like the sound of that.

But the sound of the Beretta going off after she pressed the barrel to his forehead…that sound, he never heard.

Seven watched Stella pace back and forth in front of her mother's painting. Every once in a while, the kid would glance over at him…for reassurance or with suspicion, he couldn't say.

She'd arrived in a squad car with Morgan Tyrell, her famous grandfather. The two of them were brought here from the helicopter pad at the request of Carin Barnes.

But while Tyrell had agreed to bring Stella, he was clearly not on board with Carin's plan to use his granddaughter's "gift." As he'd told Carin and Seven both, Stella wasn't ready for this.

Seven couldn't say he disagreed. If it was the killer who had taken Gia—and they'd found plenty of evidence that he had—if they couldn't find Gia in time, that tragedy would haunt Stella for the rest of her life.

Adding to the drama was Gia's last session with Tyrell, witnessed by Barnes, who had been analyzing the data ever since. Gia had believed all along that Thomas Crane, Stella's father, was behind the killings. She just couldn't prove it. And given the fact that he'd dodged the noose for her mother's murder, she wasn't taking any chances pointing the finger until she had undeniable evidence of his guilt.

"What do you think?" Erika asked.

Seven shook his head. "I'm trying not to. Logic seems to get in the way in this case."

"Maybe you're right." His partner cocked her head, thinking about it. She nodded toward Stella, still pacing in front of the painting.

"Go talk to her."

If only it could be that easy. "What am I supposed to say? I can't fix this."

"Come on, it's just like you were saying…logic doesn't work here. So why not turn logic on its head? Do the *opposite* of what makes sense? Tyrell and Agent Barnes, they're the experts, right? They're saying the kid can't handle this, so hands off. But you know her, right?"

Seven's gaze followed Stella. He couldn't imagine what the kid was thinking or feeling right now.

"I've *met* her, yeah."

"So, do you think she's pacing in front of that painting, waiting for us to tell her what to do? If it were my mother and I thought I could help, no way I'd be waiting for the adults to figure it out, you know?" Erika followed Seven's gaze. "Come on. The kid looks like a pistol to me. But she's only a kid, right? So help her get through this. Go *talk* to her."

He couldn't explain the resistance he felt. He tried to imagine himself as the dispassionate observer, making excuses about how this wasn't his area of expertise. That maybe Tyrell and Barnes were right. Maybe he was just scared. *If it all goes to shit and Gia dies…*

He glanced over at Erika. She mouthed the word, *Go!*

He didn't know much about this sort of thing, just what Gia had told him and what he'd read on the Internet. He didn't even know if he believed in the paranormal. But he knew what he'd seen the night Gia stopped breathing beside him in bed, and he'd seen her paintings and their eerie similarities to the actual crime scenes. If Stella had a touch of what her mother had…

He took a deep breath and walked over to the kid.

"So," he said, falling in step with her as she paced, "how's it going?"

"How's it *going?*" Stella stopped dead, looking up at him. "Are you for real? Some psycho killer just took my mom and you want to know how it's going?"

But behind the bravado, he could see that hint of relief. Someone had engaged her; she wasn't in this alone.

He nodded. "You're right. That was pretty lame. Come on." He tipped his head toward the studio door. "Let's go to the kitchen. You got any soda here?"

She frowned, not making a move. "How *old* are you?"

"Pretty damn old, I'd say. I think you know that I care about your mom. I want to help, okay?"

She kept that stern expression, her arms crossed over her chest. But her hands were shaking. "I'm supposed to figure this thing out," she said. "That's not going to happen drinking a Coke."

"You never know," he said. *Time to turn logic on its head.* "Maybe you need a break."

He headed to the door. When she didn't follow, he stopped and turned around.

"I'm a Pepsi man myself, but Coke will do in a pinch."

She stood there, all four feet eleven inches of her, staring him down. She couldn't weigh more than eighty-five pounds. Everyone else in the room watched, frozen in place.

After a few seconds, she shook her head and walked for the door. She gave him one of those you're-such-a-moron looks only a teenager could pull off, then said, "Suit yourself," and led the way to the kitchen.

Once there, Seven sat down at the small table, acting as if this were no big thing. At the same time, he could feel his heart hammering in the vicinity of his throat, wondering if he was doing the right thing.

Like her mother, Stella was a take-charge sort of girl. She grabbed a Coke and a Dr. Pepper out of the refrigerator. "Glass or can?" she asked.

"Can will do just fine."

She handed him the Coke and popped open her Dr. Pepper. "I've never seen my mom kiss a guy." She took a drink. "But I saw her kiss you."

He knew what she was thinking. He was special...maybe even someone she could trust. *If only I shared your youthful optimism,* he thought.

"Guilty as charged," he said, putting down the Coke. "You know, I'm the one who thought there was a clue in the painting. But I could be wrong."

"No. You're not. She did that a lot, painted to interpret her visions. I was usually pretty good at seeing stuff in her paintings."

Stella looked up, an exact replica of her mother's blue eyes meeting his. "I never told her, but I think she guessed I could see stuff in her art."

"Why didn't you tell her?"

She shrugged. "I don't want to be like her."

"Really?" He took a casual drink from the can. "She seems pretty cool to me."

She frowned. "My mom is a freak. She, like, lives her life obsessed with these dreams and her paintings. Ever since I can remember, people have come here, crying, begging my mom to somehow fix this big hole in their hearts."

"And did she?"

Stella looked away. "Sometimes. Yeah, she could do it. She would make these magic paintings that somehow...healed."

"But her talent didn't help you very much? Is that it?"

"I was okay with it." But she still wasn't looking at him. "I just saw what it did to her. I always sleep with her, you know? She thinks it's because I'm scared. That's what I always told her."

"So if you weren't scared, why do it?"

He could see that she didn't want to tell him. But she didn't have anyone else to trust.

"Sometimes she stops breathing." She took a quick drink of the soda. "But you probably know that already. You stayed here that one night." She glanced up at him. "I know it happened then."

"That's right," he said.

Gia did stop breathing the night they'd slept together. But the door to the guest room had been locked. The last thing Gia wanted was Stella walking in on them.

Which meant Stella knew what happened behind locked doors.

He took a quick gulp of the Coke, trying not to choke on it. "So you have a real connection with your mom."

"Yup."

"Does it piss you off that I like her?" He stumbled over the question, not exactly used to this. "I mean, are you mad that I stayed over that night?"

She shook her head. "I just want my mom to be happy."

He didn't move, didn't breathe. When he thought he could speak without emotion, he looked her straight in the eyes. "That makes two of us, Stella."

He put his hand on her shoulder. He tried with everything he had to convey confidence. Stella just needed to buck up a little, be the brave soldier for her mother. He'd be right there at her side, the guy who kissed her mom.

"You know," he said, "the first time I saw Gia, I thought she was crazy. All that stuff she was saying about demons and her visions. But then, I looked at her again, and it was like *pow!* Honest to God, I didn't know what hit me. I just knew I wanted to be close to her." He gave Stella's shoulder a squeeze and let go. "If you have even a touch of that inside you, I think that if you look at that painting again, and try not to be scared…I think you can help your mom."

She put down her soda. He wasn't sure what she would say or do, but he wanted to give her some space, so he waited. She turned the can on the glass table, round and round. And then, she put the soda can aside and let out a deep sigh.

"Come on," she said.

She grabbed his hand and walked back to the studio.

They were all waiting there, standing almost exactly where they'd left them, like toy soldiers. Seven wondered if Tyrell and Agent Barnes had this all figured out. They knew how to manipulate a little girl into digging deep inside. He was just part of the equation. She'll connect with Detective Bushard….

Stella didn't seem to notice. Still holding his hand, she walked right to the painting.

The girl stared up at the black holes where the eyes should have been. Seven had no idea how much the kid knew about her past, but he squeezed her hand tightly.

"That's my grandmother," she said.

She kept staring at the painting. After a minute, he noticed her eyes blinking rapidly.

"Stella?" he asked.

"Detective," Tyrell warned.

Stella's eyes rolled back in her head; she was clearly having a seizure. Seven grabbed her shoulders, holding on to her, hoping that once again this wasn't some sort of betrayal.

Stella collapsed to the floor.

Seven immediately picked her up, taking her to a chaise lounge set in the far corner. The kid was still breathing, but she was completely limp, like maybe she'd passed out.

Once he put her on the chaise, he knelt down beside her. Both Tyrell and Agent Barnes came to stand over her. Stella's eyes opened.

"One-eight-nine-five-one," she said. "One-eight-nine-five-one."

He looked at Barnes and Tyrell. Agent Barnes immediately had out her BlackBerry. But Tyrell shook his head.

"It could mean anything."

Seven looked back at Stella. She was staring straight up at the ceiling, unblinking, repeating the same set of numbers over and over.

"One-eight-nine-five-one, one-eight-nine-five-one…"

50

Gia woke up inside the trunk of a car, every muscle in her body aching. Especially her shoulders. Thomas had tied her hands together behind her back. Probably with the same duct tape he'd used to seal her mouth.

She could feel that they were on the move. She tried to slow down her breathing. If she hyperventilated—if she passed out again—she would lose whatever advantage she had.

Soon enough, the car came to a stop.

She had seen all this before. She had dreamed this very moment so many times, each and every vision a nightmare. She had tried her best to prepare herself.

But it was all a gamble. And Morgan's revelations earlier, the fact that he no longer believed Thomas had killed Estelle…if Gia was wrong about that, she could be wrong about everything.

The trunk popped open. He stood over her. She could see he was holding a gun.

"Ready, sweetheart?" he asked.

He grabbed her arm and yanked her out of the trunk. They were in an underground garage. He draped a hooded jacket over her shoulders and popped the hood up over her head. He held her tied hands high up her back, making her almost scream with pain.

"Come on," he told her, shoving her forward.

He took her to an apartment on the first floor. With the blinds closed, she couldn't see outside. She could be anywhere.

He pushed her inside and bolted the door. He hooked his arm

hrough hers and dragged her into the room, then shoved her into
. chair and grabbed another chair from the cheap, particle-board
lining room set. He sat just across from her, knee-to-knee, and
troked the side of her cheek with the muzzle of the gun.

Before she knew what he was going to do, he grabbed the edge
f the duct tape and ripped it off her mouth. She bit back a
cream of pain.

He had the gun on his lap. He looked a lot older than Gia re-
nembered. The last twelve years had not been kind. Gia had a
heory, how certain spirits could drain you. That's the kind of
emon Thomas had carried around all these years.

He smiled. "What are you thinking about, witch?"

She didn't reply.

"Come on," he said. "Let's make this a little more fun." He
:aned forward and whispered in her ear. "Beg."

He sat back with a smile, waiting. He started to whistle, as if
e had all the time in the world.

"Not gonna beg for your life, sweetie?" He cocked his head.
Why the hell not? Your mother did."

She hazarded a smile. "Liar—"

He struck her across the mouth with the back of his hand.

"I said, *beg.*"

She licked blood from the corner of her mouth, but stayed
ilent.

"Well, you're not bringing much to the party. *Just get it over
ith and kill me*—is that what you really want?" He shook his
ead. "You look so much like her. When I first saw you in Greece,
ou took my breath away. When I strangled her, I closed my eyes
nd imagined it was you. I pressed my mouth to hers right at the
nd, sucking in that last breath."

"Thomas?" she whispered.

She kept her voice very soft, so that he had to lean forward
 hear her, that horrible smile on his face.

"Yes, darling," he said in total anticipation.

"You were always such an asshole," she told him.

In that moment, she threw her head back, then slammed her

forehead straight into his face like a hammer. The force and
shock of the blow sent him backward, his chair tipping over.

The gun landed on the floor. Immediately, Gia kicked it away
across the linoleum. As Thomas gained his feet, she launched a
roundhouse kick across his chin. He fell to the floor with a groan
of pain.

Gia dropped to the floor. She wiggled her taped wrists out
from behind her back, then slipped her wrists over her heels. Her
hands still taped together, she raced for the gun.

He tackled her from behind. Kicking as she crawled forward
on her elbows, she tried to reach the gun. Thomas threw himself
on her. He flipped her over and straddled her.

"It was no easy thing, killing Estelle," he said, the words coming as if he were out of breath. "I respected her. I even offered
to split the money with her. But I knew she'd never sell the Eye."

Gia tried digging in her heels, hoping to inch back toward the
weapon. But he kept her pinned with his body weight.

"Later, I understood. You see, I held the Eye in my hands. I
felt the warmth of the crystal against my skin. Man, could
spend hours looking into that pale blue. I had it almost two days.
You know, I never would have sold the Eye to Gospel. But by
then, the cops had me and I needed the money." He leaned in
close. "No, I didn't enjoy killing Estelle. But you know what, darling? It's going to be a thing of beauty to snuff the life out of you."

She was still inching back, trying to make some progress toward the gun.

"I left plenty of evidence at your apartment," he continued. "I
can see the headlines now. Serial Killer Takes Out Police Psychic."

Gia closed her eyes and whispered a prayer. She pushed back
with all her strength, finally managing that last inch. She reached
over her head with her tied hands, knowing it would be there. It
had to be.

She grabbed the muzzle of the gun, the only part she could
reach. With the weapon squarely locked between her hands, she
pistol-whipped Thomas across the head.

In that moment, as he let out a guttural cry, she slipped out from under him and jumped to her feet. She fumbled with the gun until she held it by the handle, a finger on the trigger. She pointed the barrel straight at him.

She walked backward toward the door, watching as he stood, rubbing his cheek where she'd struck him.

"Well, you've learned a thing or two over the years."

"I've had time to practice," she said.

"But there's one tiny problem. I don't believe you'll kill me, baby. The father of your child? What are you going to tell Stella? 'Sorry, darling? I killed Daddy?'"

"Maybe I don't have to kill you, Tommy. How about I just hurt you *real* bad?"

He shook his head, still advancing on her. "Not good enough. You'll have to kill me, and you know it. She begged for your life, Estelle did. She didn't care about herself. But her little girl? Oh, you bet she begged."

Gia knew he had waited a long time for this moment. He liked the drama, drawing out the moment. It made the kill more thrilling. He would want to savor every second.

"She knew you were pregnant and in love. But I forgot she was a witch. That damn note she left, pointing the finger straight at me."

Gia kept the gun aimed on Thomas.

"Remember the night you found her note?" he asked. "For two whole days, you let her murderer comfort you. You even agreed to marry me, the father of your child. Your mother's killer."

"Of course I agreed to marry you. I loved you, Tommy." She was almost to the door. "By the way, how are the seizures?"

He looked surprised. But then he chuckled. "I'm betting they're going to get a hell of lot better once you're dead and gone."

"You're wrong, Tommy. If you kill me, you'll only fall faster and deeper into that black hole. That's how the Eye works. It gets inside you. If you don't know how to manage that power, it will kill you."

"Really?" he said in a bemused tone. "Well, as long as you're going first. All these years I've had to hold back, worried that you'd show up one day, another finger pointing at me. But now, finally, I'll be free."

He kept walking toward her. She slowly inched to the door.

He halted, then started to laugh. "It's *locked*, Gina. And your hands are taped together. You'll have to put down the gun to unlock it."

Her back touched the door.

"That's when I'll make my move, see? When you turn for that lock. I have something very special planned for you, my love. It involves an old Vietnamese story. Unfortunately, I will have to cut off those lovely fingers. Maybe I'll do it while you're still alive."

She could feel her breath coming hard, her hands shaking.

"Well, this *is* exciting," he said. "A standoff. I'm almost sorry to put an end to it. So what's it going to be?" He raised his hands in question. "Are you going to shoot me?"

"No," she said very firmly.

He started to laugh. "See? I knew it! I may not be a psychic, but I know character." He walked toward her now, more confident. "You can't kill me."

"You'd be surprised."

She raised the gun and fired into the ceiling. He stopped walking, stunned.

"Catch," she said, throwing the gun at him as she rolled to the floor.

The door burst open.

With Thomas holding the gun, the police had no problem shooting him dead.

51

Seven pulled the blanket over Gia's shoulders. They were standing just outside the apartment building at 18951 Brook St.— which was where, using her BlackBerry, Agent Barnes had found an apartment available for rent in Little Saigon. When she'd called the manager, she'd discovered that it had been taken recently, the renter offering to pay over asking price for immediate occupancy.

Upon hearing gunfire, the police had knocked down the door. It was Seven who had killed Thomas Crane.

"You okay?" he asked Gia.

She watched as staff from the coroner's office wheeled Thomas's body out to the waiting van.

"Estelle told me my father died in a car accident," she said. She kept her gaze on the coroner's van. "Imagine. She knew I had psychic abilities. And still she choked out that lie."

Seven braced himself, seeing that she wouldn't be holding back anymore. She was like one of those soda pop bottles after they were shaken hard. The top was ready to blow.

"My mother had this vision," she continued in a monotone. "She thought that Morgan, my father, was a danger to me. But, you see, she misunderstood. It wasn't Morgan. And it wasn't me."

It all came together then. How, long ago, a younger, pregnant Estelle had a vision: of a father who was a danger to his daughter.

Estelle assumed the danger was to the child she carried…but she was wrong.

"Thomas and Stella," Seven said.

"As I told you, it's not an exact science." Gia shook her head. "I always assumed she lied because he cheated on her. That she was just being stupid, keeping me from my father because he'd broken her heart. I should have known. I *knew* my mother. She wasn't…like that."

He took her hand in his. "How could you possibly have known if she didn't confide in you about her fears?"

She smiled up at him, squeezing his palm. "I was seventeen years old when I discovered Morgan was my father. Morgan Tyrell. Can you imagine? Millionaire philanthropist—parapsychologist to the stars." She shook her head at the memories. "I moved to Boston to live with Morgan. He paid for school, encouraged me to work at the institute right alongside him. I wouldn't even take my mother's calls."

"Hey, you were young. You forgave her, right?"

"I missed her too much—I missed her terribly. And I wanted to understand. I started spending summers at her dig sites whenever I could. And I felt good about it…especially when Estelle and Morgan started up again." She leaned back against Seven, smiling. "I felt as if I was playing Cupid, bringing my parents together. I had no idea."

"And why would you?"

She smiled up at him. "That's nice." She took a breath, closing her eyes—opening them on the exhalation. "I was so naive. I had taken Morgan's name by then, Gina Tyrell. I never told anyone at the site we were related. But we looked so much alike. And she was proud of me. Why wouldn't she confide in Thomas?"

According to the dossier he'd read, Thomas Crane had been a graduate student at Harvard. He'd already accepted a teaching position at Boston University. When Gia showed up at the dig site, he must have known immediately she was Estelle's daughter…and he'd seen an opportunity.

Of course, he'd moved in. But the pregnancy…

"No, I'm not that naive. I used birth control," she said, answering the question Seven would never ask. "Some things are just meant to be."

She would have been in her late twenties, that special time in a woman's life when she would start thinking about beginning a family before thinking about the alternative…he knew that much from his divorce. And there she was, pregnant and in love.

"I was lonely. An all-work-and-no-play kind of girl." She held the blanket tighter. She looked so tired. "Psychic abilities are murder on a love life." She took a moment. "I don't know. I mean, here was this evil, evil man. And yet, he gave me Stella."

Seven had read the dossier; he knew she'd been the one to turn Crane in to the Greek authorities.

"How did you know he killed Estelle?" he asked.

"She left me a note. I found it two days after she'd died. That's when I finally got the courage to go through her things. It was this small piece of paper—but you couldn't miss it, because she'd drawn an image of the Eye in the corner. The note described the vision she'd had so many years ago—the night before she'd found out *she* was pregnant."

"Jesus," he said.

"Even before I discovered who my father was, Estelle came to believe that she was wrong about Morgan. That he wasn't a danger to me—or anyone. In the note, she said if it wasn't Morgan then I should be careful. She said—" she choked on the words "—she said that sometimes it was difficult for her to know where she ends and I begin. That maybe her vision wasn't about Morgan at all, but the father of my child." She shook her head. "She didn't even know I was pregnant. That's why she didn't give me the note."

Seven wanted to hold her tight; he wanted to run away. *Shit.*

"After he killed my mother, Thomas asked me to marry him." Gia looked up at him, her eyes gleaming with emotions. "I didn't know he was her killer. I said yes."

He pushed the hair from her face. He held her close, giving the comfort she needed.

"Ms. Moon?"

They both looked up. A uniformed officer stood next to them, ready to take her home.

She looked back at Seven, almost pleading for this not to be the end.

He sighed. "We'll talk tomorrow."

She gave him a melancholy smile. "Of course. Tomorrow."

52

Tomorrow.

Gia dropped onto the sofa in her front room, exhausted. What a lovely idea, that Seven could forgive her. That he could look into her eyes and never think, *She knew what would happen— she'd seen it all before. She set me up to kill Crane.*

"Not going to happen," she said to herself.

There must always be a sacrifice. That's what she'd said in her trance.

Well, there was no help for it now. She had made her choices—Thomas was dead. And after his horrible confession, she couldn't say she was sorry.

He could never hurt them again.

"Ms. Moon?"

It was a woman's voice, coming from the hall behind her. Every fiber in Gia's being went into high alert.

She turned slowly toward the voice.

Meredith Gospel stepped out from the shadows. Gia recognized her from photographs in the papers. She'd been keeping track of the Gospel family, uncertain as to why her spirit guides had brought her here, until her vision of Mimi Tran's murder.

Meredith stood in the hall leading into the bedrooms. Apparently, she'd been waiting for Gia to come home.

She was holding a gun.

"I came for a reading," Meredith said.

She held the gun almost casually at her side as she glanced around the room as if searching for Tarot cards and a crystal ball.

She settled for the love seat opposite Gia, placing the gun across her lap. "It's my first time so I'm not sure how to proceed."

"I'm sorry, Ms. Gospel," Gia began carefully. "I'm not that kind of psychic. I'm a painter. If you want, you can tell me what's bothering you. I can see if my gift can be of any use."

"Painter?" Meredith shook her head. Her hand tightened on the gun. "I think we'll manage without that, then."

"Can we go into the kitchen?" Gia asked, thinking that in closer quarters, she might have a better chance at disarming Meredith. "The energy there," she said, improvising. "It would be better."

"Oh, I think right here will be just fine. I kill psychics, did you know that? But of course you did. You see the future. How could you not know?"

Gia let the question hang in the air between them, knowing Meredith wasn't looking for her to justify her gift.

"Women like you, Ms. Moon, are evil. You *stalk* the weak minds of those who actually believe in your gifts. You deserve to die."

Gia felt her heart in her throat. She felt blindsided, having seen nothing of this in her visions.

She'd always believed the killer had taken the eyes of his victims because he believed he could use them somehow to tap into psychic powers. But there was also an element of hate. The desire to blind—to disable. She'd thought it was Thomas doing the killing, *his* hate coming through.

"You sound very upset, Mrs. Gospel. I would like to help."

Meredith nodded. "My son, Owen. He is…he is very sick. It's his eyes, you see. A neurological condition. We didn't know his disorder was associated with any sort of…psychological issues. I believe it's quite rare."

Gia had seen photographs of Owen Gospel in the paper, as well. He was always wearing sunglasses, the kind with only a slight tint so that they could be worn indoors.

There's something wrong with his eyes.

That's what she'd told Seven when he'd pressured her for information about the killer. To Gia, it was just more evidence pointing to Thomas. She knew Thomas was experiencing seizures accompanied by rapid eye movement.

"I thought I could help him. I was the Moon Fairy, you see," Meredith said, choking a little on the words. "I would turn Owen into a rabbit and take him to the moon. Rescue him from his father before David could destroy Owen for his potion."

"Potion? I don't understand." Maybe if she could keep her talking, make a connection....

"The Moon Fairy's husband, the king, wishes to become immortal. He must boil all the children of the village, including his own daughter, in moon dew in order for the magician to concoct a potion to make the king live forever. But the Moon Fairy turns her daughter into a rabbit and they escape to the moon together."

Thomas said he'd sold the Eye to David Gospel. Had Gospel believed the object could make him immortal?

"Owen told me that story," Meredith continued. "He told me a lot of things. Strange things that, at first, didn't make sense. He told me David was stealing his *life source*." She said the phrase as if she wasn't quite sure what it meant. "You see, Owen has had several eye surgeries for his condition. Rabbit's eyes, he used to call them. *I have rabbit's eyes, Mommy.* That's what he'd say when he was little."

"Rabbits don't blink," Gia said, thinking desperately how to turn the situation around.

"Owen recently confided that during his surgeries, he believed David would slip into the operating room and steal his life source. Owen talked a lot about life source. That it was in the eyes. I didn't understand, of course. I had no idea his psychosis had become so...profound."

"How could you know?"

"It's a Vietnamese story, the Moon Fairy, a very beautiful fairy tale about a mother's love." She sighed. "I blame David, of course. That stupid collection of his. It was tainted with demons. You can't ask for immortality without paying a price. There must always be a sacrifice, and David sacrificed our son." She stared at Gia. "I couldn't save him. I couldn't be his Moon Fairy."

Gia tried to imagine the forces Gospel had gathered for his collection. Objects of power often had dark entities attached. "Mrs. Gospel, the Eye doesn't have the power to grant immortality."

"I know." She quickly brushed away the tears welling in her eyes. "There were other artifacts David was trying to secure. He had this clay tablet that mentioned objects that came raining to earth from the sky. He did boundless research on the matter. He'd come to believe these were meteorites imbued with special powers. When he heard about your mother and the Eye, he knew it was one of the objects mentioned in the clay tablet. If one existed…"

"So would the others," she finished.

Meredith nodded. "Once he had the Eye, he became obsessed. Hiring women like yourself to get it to work." She sat up stiffly. "He understood it was dangerous, so he let others to do his dirty work. Make the crystal come to life. But we are not meant to see the future. Only God can do that. I'm sorry to say it, Miss Moon, but women like you are an abomination."

Gia could feel her breath coming faster. She forced herself not to look at the gun—tried to make her mind think ahead, imagine some kind of escape.

"When did you first know your son was ill?"

"He started with animals. Of course, I didn't understand the full extent of his disease. That didn't come until much later. We even did an exorcism." She frowned. "I was certain then he had changed, after that. I dedicated myself to God, thanking him every day for giving me my little boy back. The exorcism was unpleasant. Owen began to hide his condition in order that he not be punished."

"But something happened?"

"David sent him away. As always, David was just thinking about himself. If Owen's proclivities became public, the scandal would be monstrous. He sent Owen abroad with Rocket. He was a *very* decent man, Rocket. That was his last name, of course, but we always called him that. He called me Mrs. David. It was rather quaint."

On the love seat across from Gia, Meredith Gospel shook her

head, looking suddenly horrified. "David told me Rocket and Owen were doing missionary work. Imagine. Missionary work."

Gia felt her blood chill. She thought of her session with Morgan, his claim that Thomas hadn't killed her mother. Which didn't make sense. Thomas had *confessed* to her, giving her the chilling details about how he'd killed Estelle.

But now she realized Gospel and his family had to have been there. That David had brought them to Greece to get the Eye from Thomas.

"My son was not performing any sort of charitable work. He was…*honing* his skills like a predator. When he came home, Owen gave me a choice. He wanted to destroy David. He had this elaborate plan. Only, he knew he'd be watched. I had to help. And not only help, but choose the people who should die…or he would kill indiscriminately."

Meredith Gospel gave a deep sigh. She tightened her grip on the gun.

"At first, I wasn't…willing," she continued. "But Owen persisted. He showed me how these women, the ones helping David, were pure evil. How they were trying to cheat innocent people." She met Gia's gaze with a vacant look. "Women like you should die."

She put a plastic Baggie on the table. It contained a set of eyes.

Oh, God, Gia fought the urge to retch.

"I can see that you understand now," Meredith said. "Yes, it was my son, Owen, who took your mother's eyes. He explained to me that the first killer hadn't finished the job. That he'd taken the cold eyes, the stone, leaving the real life source behind, the eyes of a sorceress. I'm sure you don't want David's eyes, but here they are."

Horrified, Gia tried to remain calm. She couldn't even look at the Baggie and its repulsive contents. She tried not to think about her mother or any of the unspeakable acts Meredith described. Gia needed to focus on how to get out of this alive.

"Meredith, I can't read your mind…I can't tell you the future. Please, Meredith, tell me how to help you."

She had a vague, faraway look even as she raised the gun. "I hear Owen's voice *inside* my head. He tells me to do these *horrible* things. When Rocket came and showed me the surveillance tape, that voice told me to kill him, too."

"Your husband's collection, Mrs. Gospel, it may very well have demons, or evil spirits. Demons are attracted to objects of power. They can attach themselves to these objects."

Meredith stared at her. "*You* have power. Do they attach themselves to you?"

"I attract them, yes."

"And me?" She stood, still holding the gun. "Are there dark spirits—demons—attached to me?"

"They cling to you," Gia said in a soft voice. "They weigh you down like chains. They wear the faces of your husband and son and this man you call Rocket," she said, pointing to Meredith's right side, where she saw the dark shapes. "To your left are the spirits of the women you killed," she said, seeing Mimi Tran, Velvet Tien, Xuan Du. "And there are others. The women your son killed. These spirits can be released. Let me help you."

"What do you propose, Miss Moon? Do you want to perform an exorcism, perhaps, like was done to Owen?"

"I can speak with these spirits. I can ask them to move on, help them find peace."

Meredith raised the gun. Gia braced herself.

Only, instead of shooting, Meredith started to cry.

"Rocket wasn't evil like those women I killed. He was a decent man—a complete innocent. Do you know what he asked me right before I shot him? He asked me to take care of his nieces. That dear man loved those girls."

"Give me the gun, Meredith. Give me the gun and it can all stop."

But she shook her head. "I shouldn't have killed Rocket. You're right, Ms. Moon. Those evil things David brought into the house, they've affected us. There's something wrong with all of us. With Owen. With David. And me."

She raised the gun.

Gia screamed, "No, don't!"

But it was too late. Meredith Gospel pulled the trigger, blowing away the side of her own head.

53

Seven stood alongside Gia in her garden. She stood hunched over, her arms wrapped tightly around her stomach. She looked like she was still in shock.

He took her hand and led her to the steps. He sat down and pulled her down beside him placing his arm around her. He knew the exact moment she let go, melting into him.

She was crying.

He held her, thinking about a television show his parents used to watch about a mystery writer who solved real-life murders. Every week, just as the show would start, his dad would say, *If these neighbors were smart, they'd stay away from Jessica. Everybody around Jessica dies.*

They'd found all three bodies back at Gospel's house. The Eye of Athena, the main crystal, had been shoved in David's mouth.

When Seven had first arrived on the scene of Meredith Gospel's suicide, Gia had explained what had happened.

"It's called transference," she said. "Meredith couldn't differentiate between herself and her serial-killer son."

Seven supposed there was a whole psychology about it. And still, it seemed strange, like maybe Gia's other explanation could just as easily describe what had happened to the Gospel family and Thomas. As if anyone who came in contact with the Eye would become possessed by some dark spirit.

When she finally got it all out, the crying, Gia sat back on the steps and took in a deep breath. She looked up at Seven. "Thanks."

"I told you—we're a full service operation."

She smiled. "Go ahead. Ask me."

It still surprised him when she did that, the whole mind-reading thing. He nodded, just going with it. "Did you think it was Thomas killing these women? Or were you just setting him up?"

"Do you really believe that?" she asked.

"I don't know what to believe. Look, Thomas was just standing there, conveniently in front of the door, holding a gun. And there I am, conveniently ready to shoot him. Yeah, I feel set up."

She let out a deep sigh. "Yes, I knew you would be standing on the other side of the door. Everything that happened to Thomas in that apartment I saw in my vision."

Seven sighed in turn. "Why didn't you just tell me?"

But he knew. She couldn't trust the police to believe some crazy psychic. And there was her mother's murder. Crane had gotten away before.

She turned Seven to face her, her touch still able to zing right through him. "I have the power to see the future, but I don't know if I have the power to change it."

"You didn't even try—"

"Of course I tried. And for the record? I always thought it was Thomas who killed my mother, that he was killing these women. But I didn't think the police would believe me. I had to do it the way I saw it happen in my visions. What I didn't know—what I didn't understand—was how it had all gotten mixed up. Everyone under the spell of the Eye just came through in my visions as one voice. I couldn't tell the difference between Owen, Thomas or Meredith."

Gia stopped, as if just figuring something out. She shook her head.

"What?" he asked.

"All this time, I wanted you to believe in my gift." She reached up and caressed his cheek. Despite himself, he leaned toward her. "But now that you do, it's the one thing that will always keep us apart."

"And why's that?"

She pointed to his head. "I made you part of my story, never letting you in on what I was doing. You'll always be wondering what I know next—if I'll use it against you."

At that moment, a limo drove up. The door slammed opened and Stella raced for her mother. Morgan wasn't far behind.

Seven stood and watched the family reunion. It was almost painful to know he couldn't be a part of it. Because she was right—even if he was ready to forgive Gia, he would never forget. No, he wasn't ready to take on Gia and her gift.

Stella was first to break it up. She approached Seven and said simply, "Thank you."

He nodded. "She gives you any trouble," he said, nodding toward Gia, "you give me a call."

Stella smiled, for the first time that face free of its worried intensity. "You bet."

He walked to Gia and kissed her on the forehead. "See you around."

"Where are you going?" she asked.

"Unfinished business," he told her, heading for the car.

Seven waited downstairs at the county jail with the other visitors. The place reminded him of a bus stop. He could hear the flotsam and jetsam of conversations usual for this place.

"He wants me to put up the house for bail, but I told him, 'Baby, you did the crime, now do the time....'"

"I don't know what to do. I just know he's innocent this time...."

"Fucking pigs always picking on her..."

He tried to shut out the noise but still keep an ear open for his name. Erika waited on the bench beside him.

"Thanks for coming with me," he told his partner.

She smiled. "Thanks for asking."

He wasn't going to worry about Erika. She was a big girl. But he did want to—what did Gia call it? Make her a part of his story.

He heard his brother's name called over the intercom. Seven stepped forward with the others making their way to the metal detectors. He flashed his driver's license, not wanting to show his badge as ID as he normally would. At the county jail, he liked to fly under the radar.

He stepped into the elevator, making room for the other bodies crowding in. He waited for his floor, the place where they kept the medicated inmates. His brother was still on suicide watch.

Seven thought of all the things he'd learned the last months. It had been a trial by fire, and now he needed to face that final challenge.

Or maybe it wasn't final at all, he thought, seeing his brother waiting for him behind the glass. Maybe it was just a beginning.

One of Ricky's hands was cuffed to the stool where he sat. He held the phone in the other, looking a bit dazed to see Seven. Probably the drugs they were giving him.

Seven picked up the phone, saying, "Hello, bro. Sorry it took me so long to get here."

"Yes, Terrence, we have the Eye."

Carin Barnes lay back on the hotel bed, cell phone tucked under her chin. On the bedspread beside her was the Eye of Athena, the crystal she'd been searching for ever since she'd met Estelle Fegaris and watched her incredible effect on Markie, her autistic brother.

"Ironically, it's just as you feared," Carin told Terrance on the phone. She picked up the crystal and held it up to her eye. "It's a fake. A beautiful, lovely fake. Professor Murphy confirmed it, although I'm sending it back to you for more testing."

After finishing up her conversation, she hung up the phone and dropped back on the bed. She held the Eye up to the light, the real one—not the fake she planned to hand over to Terrence and the gang back home.

Murphy had tested the Eye, all right, as well as the beads that made up the necklace. The results substantiated Estelle's theory—the twelve beads on the necklace were merely decorative, a precious gem hereto unknown to exist.

The Eye was a different story.

The Eye was a unique crystal. According to what Estelle had told Carin, it worked like a weapon on the brain. Estelle had likened its power to crystals used in the first radios to convert radio waves to sound. The Eye was able to detect and convert brain gamma waves. If used properly, the energy from the Eye would stimulate the part of the brain that, according to Carin's research, was associated with psychic ability.

Mimi Tran's autopsy supported yet another of Estelle's theories: that, if used improperly, the Eye could cause necrosis, or cell death, in the prefrontal lobe area of the brain. The user would experience psychic phenomena, but not because of an increase in gamma wave activity, like that found in the Tibetan monks and the psychic volunteers at Morgan's institute. Rather, the damaged brain then behaved like the brain of someone who suffered from temporal lobe epilepsy. The crystal's user experienced hallucinations. Soon, the crystal would kill more and more cells in the brain, eventually using it up like so much spent fuel.

Carin didn't feel guilty lying to Terrence. If NISA got hold of the crystal, they'd bury it in research, experimenting ad nauseam. Carin was, unfortunately, very familiar with that kind of bureaucracy. And there was the possibility that the crystal might just disappear again—the military, trying to figure out how to use it.

No, Carin didn't trust the government to do the right thing. She could only trust herself and people like her, the ones who believed in Fegaris's vision.

During the hypnosis session in Morgan Tyrell's office, Estelle had given Carin what amounted to a psychic thumbs up, communicating through her daughter. While in a trance, Gia had told Morgan it was Carin who would get the Eye.

But Carin had to be careful. Her boss wasn't necessarily the trusting type. The fake she was handing over was damn good—she, Morgan and Murphy had made sure of it. She'd needed something a collector like Gospel might believe to be the real thing. It wouldn't do to have Terrence suspicious that she'd switched the stones.

Carin poured herself another glass of champagne from the bottle at her bedside. She didn't claim the least psychic ability, but she could swear she could feel Estelle's presence in the room with her.

She toasted the sparkling crystal on the bed next to her.

"To the future."

From the Mary Higgins Clark
Award-winning author of *Dark Angel*

KAREN HARPER

EVIL SPREADS LIKE WILDFIRE...

When bush pilot Lauren Taylor flies a stranger into her isolated hometown of Vermillion, Montana, her actions may be the spark that starts an inferno. Because the mysterious passenger bears an undeniable resemblance to a serial arsonist wanted by the FBI—and he's disappeared into the tinder-dry woods....

FBI agent Brad Hale doesn't have time to fly into picturesque towns based on one woman's vague suspicions, but when Lauren's young son goes missing, he realizes the little boy may hold the key to his investigation. Hot on the stranger's trail, Lauren and Brad will do anything to stop a man bent on destruction...even if that means rushing headlong into the flames.

INFERNO

"Harper has a fantastic flair for creating
and sustaining suspense."
—*Publishers Weekly*

*Available the first week of January 2007
wherever paperbacks are sold.*

MIRA®

www.MIRABooks.com

MKH2404